Pauline Kirk studied at Nottingham, Sheffield and Monash Universities, and spent four years in Australia. She is a member of the Pennine Poets group, a partner in Fighting Cock Press and is on the editorial board of the journal *Aireings*. She has published five collections of poetry and one other novel, *Waters of Time* (1988). In 1995 she received a Yorkshire and Humberside Arts New Beginnings Award. She lives in Leeds.

THE
KEEPERS
PAULINE KIRK

And you never told us what your other life!

Barbara & Ned

A *Virago* Book

Published by Virago Press 1997

First published in Great Britain by Virago Press 1996

Copyright © Pauline Kirk 1996

The moral right of the author has been asserted

A CIP catalogue record for this book is available from the British Library

ISBN 1 86049 337 8

Printed in Great Britain by
Clays Ltd, St Ives plc

Virago
A Division of Little, Brown and Company (UK)
Brettenham House
Lancaster Place
London WC2E 7EN

For Geoff

1

Fear made Esther's mouth dry. Soon her hands would begin to sweat and her pulse rate quicken. The subtlest change in body function would register on the dials. If she was not careful, she would be discovered before the test had properly started.

'Sit down dear,' the nurse said.

Esther sat, feeling high and vulnerable, while the receptionist closed the door. Two rows of buttons and indicators were set into the arms of the chair and a trolley with the usual kidney-shaped dishes and blood pressure gauge stood by the window. The nurse smiled, pulling down the blind with a sharp crack. 'Esther Thomas?' she asked. 'Number 58197/Z/F? You're only here for a routine examination aren't you?'

'Yes,' Esther replied. 'It's a bit unnerving all the same. I can't help but worry about the children too.'

'That's only natural,' the nurse said, tipping the chair backwards. 'The kiddies will be enjoying themselves. There's lots of toys in the crèche. We bought a new stimulator only the other week.'

The chair was soft, like a bed slightly raised, but Esther would not close her eyes and rest, though her head was aching. The cafeteria had been closed, as it always was, a notice apologising for the inconvenience and wishing everyone a nice day. The form-filling had taken hours. Though the waiting room had been comfortable, with the audiovision playing softly and piles of brightly coloured cushions scattered about the floor, time had dragged. Everyone had whispered nervously, without knowing why they were afraid. It was like being choked by an expensive fur coat.

The nurse explained the details of the equipment. Basically it was an adaptation of the stimulators provided for relaxation centres: a series of images would be thrown on the screen (rather like the old movies of the early twenty-first century), and the patient could control their speed and content by pressing the appropriate knobs on the console. The dream machines in provincial clinics were every bit as reliable as those in the capital. Why, a government inspector tested the console every week. If her mind was clean and healthy, the patient need have nothing to fear.

Esther listened, smiling occasionally in agreement, as she had been taught. She must concentrate on anger, instead of fear. If that stupid woman had not quarrelled with her neighbour, there would have been no malicious reports to the local Keeper, no vetting of contacts, and she herself would not have been brought in for reassessment. It was not her error, nor even that of another member of the Movement that had brought her under suspicion. It was the bad temper of a woman she hardly knew. Bad temper was dangerous. It disturbed the carefully created peace.

'Now I'll leave you to it,' the nurse said. 'Remember you must indicate your choice of options. Otherwise, you'll be registed as uncooperative, and we don't want that, do we? If you feel the need to explain anything, just start talking. The machine will record everything you say.'

Gathering her files, she went into the adjoining room.

Esther waited. She knew what to expect. There would be a pause before the image portrayer came on, long enough to increase any patient's nervousness. Since scientific knowledge was reserved for the Keepers, most citizens were already in a state of superstitious fear of anything mechanical. They paid extra taxes because a printout said they were in arrears. They agreed to send their children for voluntary re-education, because a standard letter said they had failed a personality probe.

It was no use telling people the dream machines were just pieces of metal and microchip. The machines offered them beautiful women apparently waiting their pleasure, or trips to Hawaii in their lunch hour. When workers returned home, the audiovision gave a choice of twenty dreams after dinner; while they slept sweet music lulled them. Like all things, however, such pleasures had a darker side. Nightmares were rumoured – nightmares which could reduce even a hardened criminal to screaming terror. Rather than risk such black holes of the mind most people would agree to sign committal forms, and go away quietly with their case packed the night before. Even her brother – poor weak Anron – had signed on the dotted line, and kissed his children goodbye.

To control her nervousness, Esther investigated the machinery about her. It would obviously appeal to every sense through the power of suggestion. There would be a bewildering variety of choices offered her. In that lay the trap.

When the dreams finally started they were surprisingly shabby. The console offered a range of choices: water, fire, childhood, travel, God, love . . . The lights went out too quickly for Esther to read them all and she pressed 'Celebration'. At once the screen around the walls was filled with images of a festival, lights swinging and music blaring. She was shown the various games, voices shouting to her to try her skill. By moving an old-fashioned mouse attachment she could aim a ball or throw a hoop. For some moments Esther played, amused at her increasing success. Then the illusion changed, taking her on a moon roundabout with a group of children. It was as if all the most pleasant memories of her own childhood were being created in and around her.

Suddenly she was in a schoolroom being asked questions about citizenship.

At once Esther was aware of the danger. 'True. False. True. True,' she answered quickly, giving the replies she had been taught.

It was a technique she came to recognise. The patient was lulled by pleasant images, which were abruptly replaced by a string of rapid but vital questions. In a society still terrified by the civil war of 2145, individualism was a threat to stability. A wrong answer could result in an assessment of 'Dissident' being given. The more intelligent one was, the more prone to doubt, and to making a mistake.

The images stopped. Esther stared at the lamp above her, repeating the word 'resist' to herself, until it became a kind of mantra, blocking out all fear.

Then as suddenly as they had ended, the illusions began again. This time Esther was given no choice of topic. Images of childhood appeared in rapid succession. With a sense of shock she recognised her mother, holding her hand at a Keeper's Day rally. Other pictures followed: herself leading a moral education class at school, standing cheering at a youth camp, waiting with Bob outside the Ministry of Family Affairs . . .

Thoroughly frightened now, Esther wanted to tear the bands from her arms and temples. Yet the training had been sufficient. Forcing herself to remain calm, she sat very still. When she was offered a choice between 'Peace' and 'Freedom', she pressed the button for 'Peace'. She pressed it again when 'Knowledge' was offered as another alternative. Immediately she was rewarded by images of a South Sea island. Sweet music played. A few more questions followed, but the examination was coming to an end.

'There now,' the nurse said, as if she were speaking to a well-behaved child. 'That wasn't too bad, was it? You go and collect your little ones, and have a nice cup of tea.' She shuffled her papers. 'If you don't hear from us, you'll know you've been given a clean bill of health.'

The children were quarrelsome after waiting so long, despite the vid booths and reality games made available for them. Trying to reassure them, Esther promised a trip to the park before bed. Tim remained uneasy, however. His nervousness increased Esther's own concern, and she watched everyone warily as they queued for the shuttle back to Moss Edge. Sally of course was her normal self, having blissfully coated herself in body paints all afternoon. Not content unless everyone else enjoyed themselves equally, she shared the remains of a bag of comfits with everyone near her, and smeared Esther's neck with a sticky shade of yellow.

Afterwards Esther looked out over the city, and tried to analyse the examination that afternoon. Who had taken those images of her mother? Was she being watched even then? In those early years Jacki Marshall had not been registered as a Dissident, and her position as a tutor at the State College should have protected her. Yet someone had been making a record of her actions.

In her memory, Esther suddenly heard her mother's voice: 'The Keepers can't last more than another decade. The regime's rotten inside. It must fall soon . . .'

The time-scale had proved unrealistic. Like all the other Dissidents of her generation, Jacki Marshall had under-estimated the power of pleasure to silence opposition. Dying so young, she had no chance to see the Movement grow, and younger women take over the work she had helped to found. She would have loved to see how many others could resist the public dream. Still, at least she had not had time to grow old and bitter like some of her friends. Nor had she had to watch as they joined the vanished ones, or were sent away for treatment . . .

Wearily Esther and her children took the walkway from the shuttle terminus, towards Moor View Dwellings. On the furthermost limits of the city, and outside the dome, Moss Edge was little more than an outsettlement. Within recent years, however, it had been connected to the controlled environment, and a spur added to the shuttle route to Lark Rise now gave access to the central area with its entertainment and administration sectors. As Bob had predicted, property values had risen sharply as a result, and an influx of fourth-strata families like their own had made it quite a desirable place to live, despite the eternal wind that howled off the hills. Before the trees grew, the first settlers had had to put up with even worse winds. According to Mrs Carey you could hardly hear yourself speak twenty years ago, the constant moan around the buildings was so appalling. Mrs Carey always exaggerated though, and a summer gale set her worrying about typhoons.

With a sigh of relief, Esther opened the door of her dwelling. At once, the audiovision greeted her, a babbling compere announcing some all-star prize competition. It was impossible to turn him off since the system was operated by Central Control, but she could change the programme. She wanted to cry but was afraid the sound would be heard next door. Unhappiness was forbidden. Taking a meal from the freezer, she put it in the laserwave, and then transferred it to the holding oven.

It was eighteen hours. The children must be exhausted. Still, she must put their coats back on quickly, ready for the park. Lifting Sally into her buggobile and finding a spinner for Tim, Esther set off.

By the time they arrived at the play area, Number Twenty was sitting on the moon roundabout with her baby on her knee. Coming across casually, she put her older child into the swinger next to Sally. 'I was afraid you'd been picked up,' she whispered.

'I was.' The gears rasped above them. 'For routine examination. I think I did all right, but you've no way of knowing.'

'The group meets at the relaxation centre tomorrow, eight

hours. We have another three members – vetted and cleared. I'll leave you to contact Number One-two-five.'

Helping Sally out of the swinger, Esther ran with her across to the Heroes' Lawn. It was the only expanse of green more than ten metres across in the whole of Moss Edge, and no one was allowed on it, lest the roots of the grass become damaged. Tim was lying in the middle of it, with his hands behind his head. 'Get off there!' Esther ordered. 'This minute!'

'Aw Mum—' he protested, 'I like to smell the growing.'

Smiling despite her annoyance, Esther shook her head. 'You peculiar boy!' she said. 'Come off there, or you'll get us all into trouble. Besides, the nightfog's coming down. If you don't come indoors soon, the acid'll get on your chest.'

She had surived another day. Or had she? In such a cloying, synthetic world it was hard to know reality from illusion. The old woman sitting there so quietly in the shelter, for instance – why was she there so often? She appeared harmless enough, but was that an illusion? One survived only by assuming the apparently real was deception. They must change their meeting place, just in case.

The thrill of the chase returned. Inwardly Esther smiled. To be hunted was at least to be fully alive. Safety was a form of hibernation, a sleeping comfort. Stopping only to put on the children's breathing masks, she walked out of the park.

A few moments later the old woman gathered her knitting. Then she too went through the gate. Perfectly innocently, she followed down Moss Edge Road.

That evening, Esther settled to another evening trying to ignore the audiovision. Her head hummed with exhaustion, and she seemed to be developing a sore throat. If the Keepers could invent a cure for the common cold, she thought wryly, they would give more pleasure than building a hundred showhouses. What she needed was an early night.

It was difficult to sleep before twenty-two hours. The movement of other residents in the dwellings were too easily overheard. Considering how expensive they were, the blocks were flimsily built. They had been intended for retired city officials, not families. True, the estate manager had installed a playing area and refurbished the community room, but the internal walls were as thin as ever. Every voice carried up the escalator wells. A baby's crying could wake four families. When Sally was sick last year she had managed a grand total of ten. Until the audiovision was automatically turned down at twenty-two thirty, a neighbour's *Happy Show* could sound like your own.

Lying half watching her own screen above her bed, Esther also shared the pleasures of Mr and Mrs Harpur's *Game for a Song*. Someone had just won the big prize. Curious despite her scorn, Esther touched the control pad to see what it was. A plump woman in purple trousers was throwing her arms around the compere. 'A holiday in Paris! Five-day travel permit and all expenses paid!' It was a wonderful prize, the jackpot after two weeks of contestant failure. Admittedly it was only the Chunnel, but to have the chance of visiting the Union ... That was everybody's dream – to see what life was really like. Again and again the audience cheered.

Oh yes, it was clever, Esther reminded herself. Such prizes gave the illusion of freedom. Of course one could travel abroad. See, passes were available, given free to lucky contestants. Of course the Union was open to visits, all expenses paid. But it was only open to the lucky few, and then only for five days, just long enough to give a taste of another world that might some day be England, so long as everyone worked together. Five days was not long enough for anyone to get ideas about settling and starting a new life. In any case, who would dare, with family and friends left behind? Still, it was always nice to see someone so happy, Esther admitted, nice to see them famous for five minutes.

At last the programme came to an end. Though an insomniac or shift worker could find a game show at any point of the night, most channels were changing to sleep mode. Choosing an image of clouds drifting above heather, Esther settled back to rest. The light automatically dimmed as her head touched the pillow. Her room filled with a warm comforting glow. Sometimes Esther thought it would be pleasant to have the Outlanders' stark contrast between day and night, but even she would find darkness oppressive after a few hours. Though she had learnt to overcome the city-dweller's fear of the night, it was always alien to her, like a foreign land.

No, Esther reflected as she closed her eyes. It was all very well talking about the honesty of the Outlands, but she would not swap her comfortable dwelling for one of the Sheep People's cold and gloomy habitations, even if Sly did call her soft.

In the middle of the night Esther woke. After that, sleep was impossible. No matter how much she told herself to be calm, her mind would keep going over and over the afternoon's examination. Just as when she was at school, her initial feeling that she had done all right began to seep away. Had she really given the correct answers? Even if she had done so, her pulse rate and sweat flow had probably given her away. Within the next few days the letter would come, cheerfully inviting her to attend for Treatment. If she ignored it, another, sterner one would follow, expressing concern at her failure to take the opportunity being offered her. After that, a medical officer would call in person . . .

Furiously, Esther turned over on her bed. If she was not to lie awake all night, she must control her fear. Sitting up, she put herself into the Ganzfeld position with her hands crossed loosely in her lap. Gradually she shut out the night light above her, and the sound of the audiovision. Time lost all meaning, until she was floating on a formless, nameless sea. For ten minutes, perhaps twenty, she sat there, unmoving, until the hypnagogic images began. Brilliant and dreamlike, they filled her mind with brief snatches of picture, each unrelated to the other: a bridge over a shuttleway, a rat scurrying through thistles, a huge insect buzzing . . . A chair and table followed, and then a beaker full of cordial. There was no sense to what she saw, but each image was brighter than the one before. Suddenly a black cat crossed her vision. 'Tettie!' it whispered, not loud but penetrating. 'We need you.' Then it leapt up on to a ledge and paused, inviting her to follow. When she did not, it miaowed, and disappeared. Abruptly Esther returned to the world around her. She discovered her legs were cramped and the buzzing sound was real. A police surveillance unit was droning in the distance, coming nearer. Getting up stiffly, she went to the window and looked out. The patrol was approaching, its tail lights winking like red stars against the sky. Suddenly, a searchlight beamed from its nose, making a bar of light down to the ground. It looked almost as if someone could walk down it. Turning, the PSU began to hover over the shuttle station, picking out something ahead. Twice it revolved on its axis, before moving off slowly, in the direction of the woods. Just as suddenly as its light was switched on, it was switched off. Whatever – or whoever – the police had been seeking had been passed on to watchers on the ground.

For a full minute Esther stood at the window. Instead of the usual peace that followed meditation, she felt a sense of expectancy, as if she were waiting for someone to call. Normally she could remember little of the images she saw while in Ganzfeld. This time, however, she could clearly recall hearing a voice. 'Tettie!' it had said. 'We need you.' Who had spoken? A cat, that was it. A sleek, black cat. She smiled at her own foolishness. Yet the sensation of waiting would not go away. Obviously, the examination that afternoon had upset her more than she had realised.

Going back to bed, Esther turned up the audiovision slightly so that the music would soothe her, without disturbing her neighbours. But the PSU had woken them already. There was the sound of a sanitary unit being flushed in the dwelling above, and next door a child called out. For a few moments a man's voice answered, settling the boy. In surprise, Esther listened. Last night the dwelling had been empty. Some time during the day, the new neighbours must have arrived.

Mrs Morrison had been full of them all week. They were to have a Patroner living amongst them, she had confided, coming out to share her news as soon as she saw Esther near the recycling unit. No one of so high a rank had moved into Moor View Dwellings before. 'Must have been posted here at short notice,' the woman suggested. 'A Patroner could afford a better place than this. He'll only be renting, of course, until he finds somewhere more suitable.' Mrs Morrison had an ability to read minds few telepaths would have claimed. 'They say he's taking over the new showhouse,' she confided. 'Just imagine! A showhouse director! If we play our cards right we might get free tickets. He's a widower into the bargain, they say. Quite a catch for someone,' she added, managing to wink and nod at the same time.

Smiling at the memory, Esther listened to the audiovision. Mrs Morrison could make a scandal out of a tea beaker. Still, it was unusal to have a Patroner moving in, and if he really was to be the new director at Showhouse Four, he could become quite a celebrity. In the public mind, running a successful showhouse was next to godliness.

The police unit was returning. Even if your conscience was perfectly clear, having one of those things hovering above in the darkness made you feel uneasy. Esther could feel her son's fear as he too lay listening. He would not call to her, regarding that as something only little boys did, but he needed her. Getting up again, she went to his room.

'All right?' Esther whispered.

'That stupid thing woke me up.'

'And me.'

'What are they looking for?'

'Undesirables perhaps, or Outlanders down from the hills.'

'Mr King says all Outlanders should be locked up.'

'Why? They can't help being poor and ignorant.'

'In surprise Tim sat up on his elbow. 'Of course they can,' he insisted. 'Everyone can.'

'Who told you that?'

'Mr King.'

'Then he must be right. He knows far more than me.'

It was so hard to know what to say. If a mother let such lies go unchallenged, her son would never know the truth, but to contradict them ran the risk of getting them both classified as different, if not actually Dissident. At three o'clock in the morning Esther could not cope with such complexities.

'Why do you always defend the Outlanders?' Tim persisted. 'They're all rebels and thieves. They started the civil war in the first place. Mr King's teaching us all about it. The country wouldn't be in the state it's in, but for them.'

'Not all Outlanders fought against the government,' Esther replied. She really could not let that pass. It was not even the official view. 'Many of them were ordinary farmers and tradespeople, who happened to be living outside the towns when the war broke out. You can't blame them for staying there afterwards, or for fighting on the side of the North if that was where they lived.'

'Mr King says they were offered the chance to sign the Allegiance and wouldn't.'

'Many of them did sign it. They're still waiting for the promises to be kept. I'll get you a vidstrip that tells you all about it.'

'Are you saying Mr King's wrong, Mum?'

'No. Just that he's a Southerner. He sees things from a Southern point of view. Maybe he lost his parents in the fighting. He's quite an old man, and the war ended less than sixty years ago. He may even remember it himself. There are a lot of bitter people still.'

Kissing her son's forehead, Esther prepared to return to her bed. 'Don't worry about it now,' she advised.

Tim could be very persistent, and perceptive. 'What did you mean about waiting for the promises to be kept?' he asked.

Esther should not have made that remark. Lack of sleep and anger had made her careless. 'It takes a long time to rebuild a country,' she said more cautiously. 'After the Devastation most of the cities were in ruins. There was no food, no power, no water. Can you imagine what that was like? I can't, even though my grandma and grandad told me about it. The Keepers must have had to make some terrible choices. They decided to rebuild five huge cities on the flattest land, where people could be safe together, and have all the things they needed as quickly as possible. The hillier or wilder places they had to leave until later. Some day there'll be power and transport there too, but in the meantime people have had to go back to basics – grow their own food, rebuild their own houses – they've been given a lot of help. That's why the protectorates were set up. And Mr King is right to some extent. The Outlanders haven't done as much for themselves as they could. They've been too busy fighting their old battles, or stealing from each other. War doesn't bring out the best in people. Now you go to sleep.'

'Mum—'

Pausing at the door, Esther waited.

'How did you know I wanted you to come in?'

'I'm your mum. Of course I know such things. Besides, I was frightened myself. Go to sleep.'

2

The newcomer was talking to Joe, the delivery man, arranging details of payment. Esther smiled towards him in greeting. Quickly she assessed him. At such a distance, it was impossible to sense anything of importance about him – except that he was ill at ease. She had expected a much older man. Patroner Lahr appeared to be only in his early thirties, very young for so high a rank. He was also unexpectedly good looking, fair haired, with deep blue eyes. Like most people nowadays, he was a bit of a mongrel, the name and blond hair suggesting an Eastern Union ancestry, the eyes somewhere warmer. In his case it worked. Yet Esther did not trust him.

Lest she appear over-familiar, she nodded and turned away.

Her new neighbour lingered. 'Excuse me asking,' he began as Joe moved on. 'Is there a message input on this floor? Or do you have to go down to the janitor's room?'

'It's at the end of the corridor,' Esther indicated. 'Just key in your dwelling code and your messages will come up. You can either summarise them manually, or print them all off. When you've finished, key 'Received' and the janitor will clear your entry.'

Two children had appeared in the doorway behind the man, a girl of about ten, with a boy not quite three in her arms. Their youth was also surprising. It was unusual for a man on his own to be allowed to keep such young children. He must have a great deal of influence. Even so, there would be a great deal of pressure on him to remarry. Mrs Morrison might get rid of her daughter yet.

Thanking Esther, Patroner Lahr went back indoors.

It was indeed a fine day, as Joe had said. That was one of the advantages of living outside the city dome. The changing seasons could actually be seen, and provided a constant source of interest. The penalty of course was the endless wind. When Esther returned from taking the children to school her fingers were stiff and blue, and she miskeyed as she called at the message input on her way back to her dwelling. The whole corridor's listing came up, instead of merely her own file.

The Daltons had not yet collected their messages. Nor had the newcomer, Stephan Tomas Lahr. Her error had had the unexpected benefit of letting her know his forenames, and also the names of his children, Imogen and Benn. Smiling, she pressed 'Cancel', and entered her own file.

The first two messages were of interest; one regarding a craft afternoon, and the other requesting her to call her father that night rather than tomorrow. The sun was shining through the window on to the screen, and she had to squint to read the other entries. They were hardly worth the effort, consisting of a couple of useless advertisements, and a reminder to take Sally for her booster inoculation. She could find nothing about yesterday's examination, but then there wouldn't be. Such decisions were not rushed.

As Esther closed down the file, Stephan Lahr himself passed.

'You have a message waiting,' she said politely.

'I'll pick it up when I get back.'

'It's OK, I've finished.' Getting up, Esther glanced back up the corridor. Patroner Lahr was sitting at the console, but staring ahead of him, as if lost in thought. Something about him definitely did not quite ring true. It was hard to say what. Tomorrow, she must try to get closer to him and make a proper assessment.

It was nearly nine hours. If she was to send her usual

Tuesday letter to Bob, she must do so immediately. The personal channel would be closing soon.

Sitting down at the work station Esther keyed in her code. Pausing, she stared out over the woodland, wondering if she should tell her husband about the examination the day before. If anything had gone wrong he ought to have some warning, if only for the children's sake. Finally she began to write.

Dearest,
How are you? We're all doing fine up here. Sally and Tim had a cold last week, and they've given me the statutory snivel. Neither of them wanted to stay off school. They really are very happy here. We did the right thing moving, even if it is difficult you and I being apart.

The words were not those Esther wanted to use. 'Please, my love, I'm frightened and I want you with me,' was what she wanted to say. Such words would have surprised their receiver, and sounded odd if intercepted, a little unstable perhaps. It would be wisest not to tell him of the examination in an open letter, in case something in her tone suggested to the censors that she was afraid of the result. She had better wait until she could see Bob in person – so long as she was allowed to stay free until then . . .

Doubt must not be allowed to gain a hold, Esther told herself firmly. Once more she looked out of the window, to calm herself.

Behind the boundary woods, the hills rose in fold after fold, mysterious and brooding even in spring. Few city-dwellers so much as set foot in them. Without the shelter of the trees, the wind made your nose run and the sun was dangerous on your bare skin. Besides, Outlanders with unpredictable tempers were inclined to appear and tell you you were trespassing. There was always the risk of Marauders too, the dregs of society who made no pretence of obeying the Law, and descended like pirates on unsuspecting outsettlements. No, the hills were not a safe place for a city-dweller to wander.

From Moss Edge, however, one saw only their beauty, touched by the morning sun. There were still patches of snow on the higher slopes. You never saw such views in the central dome, just walkways and dwellings and government buildings.

> I met Polly Smithers last Tuesday. She was saying how pleased she and Fred were that they'd brought the children up North. I hope she doesn't start telling too many of her old chums down in Centopolis, or Nortown will start getting crowded . . .

Before the personal channel closed, Esther managed to fill another three paragraphs with news of the children and plans for the future. Tim was growing a centimetre a day, she swore it, and Sally's speech was coming on wonderfully. The thera- pist said it was nothing to worry about. Now her deafness had been sorted out, she would soon learn. They would come down and visit Bob at Springbreak. Summer wouldn't be far away then, with two whole weeks together in the Holiday Zone. Then one day, only six years off now, he would be allowed to leave his post in Centopolis and take up work in Nortown. Esther's father was trying to line something up for him, but they mustn't bank on that, in case it fell through.

The letter was written, and sent downline, along with the hundred or so other greetings from Moss Edge wives to their Centopolis husbands. As cheerful and hopeful as any censor could wish, it held only half-truths, but at least it told no lies. In any case, Bob would understand a lot of what Esther meant without her saying it. Solid and respectable, a paradigm of the fourth-strata middle-aged male, he had a sensitivity few men possessed. That was what had made Esther finally accept him as her father's choice, that and his impression of a government official with hiccups.

Smiling at the memory, Esther glanced at her timepiece.

She would need to hurry if she was to be at the canyon on time.

Carefully she sorted out the personal things she would need: her travel passes and breathing mask, a file of sunblock and other first-aid needs including a survival bag. Afterwards, she packed the usual volunteer visitor's gifts: a few medicines, a scoop of dehydrated protein in a heat-sealed bag, and some home-baked comfits. Any more would have roused suspicion, though she always felt ashamed to give so little. Even after two years of visits, conditions in the Undesirables' encampment distressed her each time she went. Finally she fetched her scent spray from the bathroom. It was already prepared.

As a matter of course, just before leaving Esther checked the papers in her state certification folder. Her volunteer registration was up to date, as were her vaccination certificates, but the sexually transmitted diseases clearance would need renewing soon. Frowning, she folded the papers back into the folder. She hated making STD applications. All those personal questions about how many sexual partners you had had: in the last month; the last year . . . Esther's answer never changed: 'I only have one partner, my husband, and I don't see a great deal of him.' The nurse would smile, and insist on the tests all the same.

Furiously, Esther flung her wrap around her, and went out of the dwellings.

In the shelter of the woods it was almost warm, the first hint of spring. None of the trees were over forty years old; they had been planted after the great storms when the winds blew across the devastated land, and whipped the soil from the hills, to deposit it as silt in the rivers. Yet already many of the oaks and birch were so tall that the dwellings seemed to be sinking in a sea of brown. At the time people had thought it was madness spending scarce resources on planting trees, but the Keepers had known what they were doing. Every year the winds were a little less strong, the rainfall figures a little higher.

The Keepers had known what they were doing about other things too, Esther admitted ruefully. Though she hated what their regime had become, she had to accept that they had been the saviours of their country. They had kept their knowledge from being lost all through the Troubles and the seven years of civil war that had followed them. It must have been a hard struggle to preserve their skills even before then, when most people scorned learning and science, and cared only for an easy life. Without the Keepers, no one would have known how to rebuild a nation that had been determined to tear itself apart. Yet the woods were an apt symbol for their knowledge. An effective shelter, the trees provided warmth and security, but they were dark and tangled, easy to get lost in if you left the permitted paths.

Closing her wind jacket more tightly around her, Esther walked round the outer edge of the city, towards Fox House settlement. As yet, there was no shuttle link between Moss Edge and other outer suburbs, only into the centre of the city. It was quicker to walk a couple of kilometres into the Outlands and take the old track across the hills, around the city perimeter. The route was under regular surveillance by the city authorities and usually safe enough. A surge of pleasure began to fill Esther's mind. Conscious of her own fitness and the beauty of spring, she walked quickly. The woodland was lovely, but it was stifling compared to the track beyond it. That was an open highway, the route to the top of the world.

As she approached the settlement, Esther began to feel nervous. For the past two weeks her visits had been routine, but there was always the chance that today would break the pattern. She must prepare herself.

Holding her breath for a few seconds as she walked, she fixed her mind on what might lie ahead. By the time she approached Fox House, her expression was bland and sweet, the face of a dedicated volunteer. Behind that sweetness, however, she was acutely alert, in a state of heightened sensitivity.

Fox House settlement was given over entirely to waste – waste products and waste people. It owed its existence solely to the canyon and the refuse dumped there illegally when the city was still a collection of temporary domes. With their usual wisdom, the Keepers had seen that an increasingly unpleasant situation could be used to their advantage. Until disposal machinery could be rebuilt, the new city was in danger of drowning in its own garbage. It was also becoming unwilling host to large numbers of refugees who would not, or could not, work. Used to an easy life before the war, they resented the sacrifices being asked of them by their new rulers, or simply had no useful skills to offer. Decent hard-working citizens were beginning to turn on them. Several residents' groups had already driven whole families from their neighbourhoods.

All right, the authorities suggested. Let such Undesirables be driven out, on to the outer edge of the city. The canyon was a useless gash through the surrounding hills – a weak point in the city's defences and rapidly filling with rubbish. Let the useless and lazy have it as their segment of the city. There they could sort out the city's waste, and keep or sell whatever they found of value. If they did not even have the energy to do that, then they could starve, out of sight of decent folk and without being a drain on the state.

Nowadays of course, there was no need for the hand-sorting of waste, but the Undesirables had been allowed to keep their means of support. Other cities had followed Nortown's example, and all over the Republic, Undesirables acted as final graders and sorters of society's cast-offs. Fox House had its own water supply and regular health inspections. It was even allocated official visitors, to ensure an independent check on conditions. Since it was difficult to justify spending much money, most of those visitors were like Esther, registered volunteers.

The woman at the first gate knew Esther and nodded as she went through. The second guard was new, and insisted on checking her papers.

'Registered volunteer, eh?' he asked suspiciously.

Esther smiled patiently.

'You seriously want to go down there?' Nodding his head, the guard indicated the canyon.

'I volunteered to serve as a visitor,' Esther explained again. 'My duty is to report on conditions, and make any recommendations I think necessary to the city officials.'

The man had only recently been posted up North it seemed, and was rather frightened. She could forgive him a little bullying.

'You wouldn't catch me going down there,' he admitted. 'Unless I was ordered to, of course. The smell makes me feel sick even up here.' He inspected the contents of Esther's sac. 'I see you've brought your own scent spray. We've started providing them now, you know. All you have to do is ask at the security post on your way back. No point in spending your own money if you can help it.' He read the dates on Esther's certificates. 'Your STD is nearly up,' he pointed out.

Esther nodded. 'I shall have to get it renewed next week,' she agreed.

'Don't engage in any sexual activity until you've been reinoculated. Your protection mightn't hold.'

It was the guard's duty to warn Esther, but he did so with a wink which annoyed her intensely.

'I'm a law-abiding fourth-strata mother,' she replied coldly. 'I have no intention of risking my health.' Sensing she was making an enemy of the man, she paused. 'Besides, can you imagine any woman fancying an Undesirable?' Her smile managed to convey that if she had not been a law-abiding mother, she might have considered a nice new guard, and the man was soothed.

'They must fancy each other,' he commented. 'I've never

seen so many children. If the authorities don't watch out, they'll be overrunning the city again.'

There was some justice in his remark. In the central dome children were a rarity, few families achieving their permitted two, but in the Undesirables' settlement they ran everywhere, their voices rising up from the canyon bottom like the cries of young starlings. To Esther's concern a large group of them were waiting for her at the foot of the main path, hoping for some of the comfits she always brought. Last week she had been tugged at and jostled until she felt quite frightened, and had to hold her bag above their heads to get through. She decided to walk along the top edge of the canyon this time, and take the path down the side to Minkin's tent.

Retrieving her papers, she thanked the guard for his advice, and set off.

The relic of some past transport sytem, the canyon was a hundred-kilometre linear desert of thistles and broken concrete, presumably at one time linking the east of the country with the west. The first three kilometres out from Nortown were occupied by Undesirables, their tents and shacks ranged against the canyon walls to gain shelter from sun and wind. In some, the shack was only a kind of front porch, two or three further chambers having been scraped out of the hillside behind it. The longest established had chimneys poking out of the rocks above them. Since each chimney had been shaped from a different piece of metal or discarded food container, the effect was of a crazy children's cartoon. Minkin's was the tallest chimney, but then everything about Minkin had to be biggest and best.

He was waiting for Esther outside his shack. Taking out a very old timepiece, he tapped it meaningfully.

'I'm exactly on time,' Esther responded firmly.

'We wanted you here early,' Minkin grumbled. 'We've got some sick people for you.' Even he had the characteristic whine, the apologetic, 'Don't hit me, I haven't done anything' voice that marked the Undesirable out as soon as he or she spoke. Physically, Minkin was better than most of his kind, however; he had always ensured that if there was any meat going, he got more than his share. He was in fact quite presentable, Esther admitted, and smiled, recalling her conversation with the guard at the gate.

'How many are sick?' she asked.

'Three. There's one we'd particularly like you to see.'

Esther's stomach tightened for a second. Silently she nodded. Though it would be difficult to bug such an encampment, directional listening equipment might pick up their conversation. 'I'll make my inspection first,' she replied.

'Have you brought any goodies for us?' Minkin was deliberately playing up the wheedling tone, also aware of the possibility of listeners.

'Of course. Let me at least sit down while I unpack my bag. It's a long walk round the city.'

Minkin drew back the flap across his doorway, inviting Esther to enter. Her eyes stinging at the smoke from the brazier, Esther sat on the mound of old coats and bedding that served as a settee.

'Medicines, protein and comfits,' she said aloud as she unpacked her gifts. While Minkin made a covering noise opening the three bags, she took out her spray, and unscrewed the bottom. Silently she passed Minkin the roll of money it had contained. He counted it, of course, never trusting anyone, not even his friends.

Taking a scriber from her pocket, Esther wrote a brief message on the discarded wrapper. 'Make this last. They're supplying sprays now. I'll have to find another way of bringing your money in.'

Frowning, Minkin read her message. Few Undesirables could so much as sign their name, but Minkin was clever, and had taught himself how to read and write from discarded papers he had found over the years. His unusual skill had enabled him to become leader of the settlement, and was extremely useful to his allies. Ruefully, he nodded and dropped the wrapper into the brazier near him.

It was time to begin Esther's inspection.

For an hour they visited each dwelling and chatted briefly to the occupants. Afterwards there was the water supply to check, and the sanitary block. 'You seem to have more children than usual,' Esther commented.

'We have some new families,' Minkin admitted. 'Strangers stopping over before moving on to Westover.'

'I'd get them to leave as soon as possible. The guard was remarking on your numbers. If you're not careful, the authorities will find an excuse for a health raid, and round up as many of you as they can.'

Nodding reluctantly, Minkin accepted the truth of her prediction. He was aware of the danger himself, but the families were related to him. He'd see they moved on that night.

They walked towards the sick bay. By now, most Watchers would have become bored and switched off their scanners. In any case, no directional listening device could reach so deep into the side of the canyon. Cut into the rock for coolness and quietness, the sick bay was a perfect place to keep a prisoner under observation, literally under the noses of the guards posted above.

'Who have you got today?' Esther asked softly.

'That's what we want you to tell us. He claims to be a student. Says he can't stomach the system any more and wants out. Mutual friends picked him up trying to make contact with the Sheep People, and ferried him back here. He thinks we're keeping him safe until we can find a route for him.'

'Have you interrogated him?'

'Of course. He did well. We let him think we'd accepted his story.'

'Good. Then he won't be expecting any more questions now. We'll follow the usual procedure.'

Minkin passed Esther her outer robe, and she wrapped it around her to hide her city-dweller's clothes. When she first put such a robe on, her whole body had smelt for days afterwards and almost given her away. Now they kept one sealed inside a protective bag, for her use alone.

Going into the inner chamber, Esther sat on the floor and rocked herself back and forth. For a second she could not bear the pain to come. 'Why me?' her spirit cried. 'Why do I have to keep doing this?' The lamp flickered around the walls of the room, making grotesque shadows on the rock walls. Then gradually Esther's mind quietened, and she waited, still rocking herself, but more gently. She heard footsteps crossing the chamber outside. They were bringing the young man to her. Adopting the Undesirables' typical squatting position, she took up one of the metal rods from the pile near her, and began to straighten it. By the time the young man had put his things on the bedshelf, she had finished a second and was apparently absorbed in her task.

'Who's she?' the young man demanded.

'One of our women,' Minkin replied. 'She's recovering from the plague.' He laughed as the young man stepped back hurriedly. 'Don't be alarmed,' he sneered. 'You're a city-dweller. You won't get our diseases. They're kept specially for us – so that we can die of them.'

Esther merely grunted and continued with her work.

The young man was glad of a change of scene. Esther could feel his relief that at last something was happening. He began unpacking his travelling sac.

Completely without warning, Minkin shouted his first question. 'Why are you here?' he demanded. There was no whine in his voice now.

Startled the young man looked up from his things. 'Because you said I should move rooms,' he said.

'Why are you here?' Minkin repeated. 'Who sent you?'

'Nobody sent me. I was trying to find a way out.'

'A way out to where?'

'To a better life. I've told you before. I thought if I could find one of the sheep routes – '

'What sheep routes?'

'People say there are ways of disappearing, and the Sheep People know them . . .'

'Who told you?'

So it went on, remorselessly. The young man was good, as Minkin had said. He stuck to his story, however much Minkin bullied or cajoled. Every detail of his course and his lecturers was consistent. He could talk about his girlfriend, how his parents would feel when they found he had vanished, what he hated most in the system . . . But he was lying, Esther was sure of it within minutes. As she straightened one rod after another, she could feel his tension growing. He was not just afraid of Minkin's bullying, but of making a mistake in remembering his story. It did not belong to him, however well he had learnt it. Despite his fancy speeches, he did not really feel remorse at leaving his parents alone. He did not really expect them to lose him, not for ever. Nor did he fear leaving civilisation. He was not permanently giving up all comfort and learning, as those who choose the sheep routes must do. When his mission was accomplished, he would get his old life back. Under all his carefully learnt story that hope remained.

Esther began to feel a deep sadness. The young man was so nice in many ways. He was genuinely fond of his girl, and he believed what he was doing was right. The trouble was, if the Undesirables had trusted him as he had hoped, at least one sheep route would have been discovered and a lot of other nice young men and women would have suddenly vanished. Even letting the young man go free but empty-handed wasn't an option. He had learnt that the Undesirables had the means to hide people, and might pass them along some mysterious line into safety . . .

Gathering up the bundle of rods, Esther crawled to her

knees like an old sick woman. Without looking back, she left the room.

'I think he's lying,' she said to Minkin afterwards. 'That's only my opinion. You must act as you think fit.'

'I've never known you wrong yet.'

For a second the sadness was more than Esther could bear. 'Why do you believe me?' she demanded. 'You make me responsible for life and death.'

'Neither of us was born ordinary,' Minkin replied gently. 'We have to live our lives as best we can.'

3

The climb back up the side of the canyon was steep, and Esther was very tired. It was always the same after she had concentrated so hard, and today her mind was as heavy as her body. Minkin had not said what would happen to the young man, but whatever it was, he would not be returning home. The knowledge weighed heavily upon her.

Taking the easier track along the bottom of the canyon, Esther skirted the mounds of half-sorted rubbish: metals in one stack, plastics in the next, wood in another. Everything would be sifted and used if possible, or at least sold as scrap. The stench was worst in the domestic area. There, old clothes were stacked in heaps, smelling of wet and bodies, and discarded vidmats and electronic goods waited for checking. Kitchen refuse was mulching against a huge concrete block, the footing for a bridge that had crossed the canyon in olden times. Shifting her sac on to the other shoulder, Esther walked on. Suddenly a black cat ran in front of her. In surprise, she cried out aloud.

Afterwards, she felt rather foolish. There were feral cats everywhere in the canyon, living off the vermin that bred amongst the rubbish. She was used to them running across her path. Quite why this one should have startled her so she could not think.

The guard examined Esther's sac again as she left the canyon. He was almost apologetic. 'If you can find anything worth stealing amongst that lot, you're better than me,' he joked, nodding towards the mounds of waste. Taking out her scent spray, he checked the lining of her bag.

Esther looked at him directly and stayed calm. Removing Minkin's money would have reduced the weight of the spray. She prayed silently that the guard would not recall how it had felt before, or that if he did, he would merely assume she used a good deal of the scent inside.

'How can you bear being down there all that time?' he asked.

'I'm not usually that long,' Esther admitted. 'I got talking to one of the new families. Apparently they're only staying a night or two, and then moving on. That's why there's so many children at the moment.'

Putting the spray back, the guard nodded. 'That's good news,' he replied. 'May the Keepers' peace be with you.'

As she walked on, past the military quarters and the delivery area, Esther began to feel light-headed with relief. Whatever the poor young man's fate, she had carried out her orders safely.

With a great deal of shunting and shouting, a bulk waste carrier was docking at the bay near her. It spewed its load of metals into the nearest hopper. For several moments the air was full of noise and reflected light. It was hard to imagine foxes had once lived nearby, but according to local legends, that was how the area had got its name. Perhaps there were foxes there still, Esther thought idly. Perhaps they were in hiding among the mounds of refuse, biding their time with the cunning of a thousand generations of survivors. Sly often said cunning was not dishonourable. It was a natural means of survival. Women too could be cunning, carrying their rebellion in their hearts. They too could bide their time . . .

That night, the keep-fit session had already begun when Esther arrived.

'Three, four, clap and swing. One, two and *turn*,' Mrs Martin shouted. Esther stuggled to pick up the routine. Fortunately Mrs Martin had prepared a new set of exercises, and was impatient to begin them. 'Well done, ladies,' she said, clapping her hands. 'Are you all nicely loosened up?'

Politely Mrs Martin's ladies chorused that they were.

'We're going to work on those bottoms tonight. Get them into better shape.'

Half a dozen giggles replied. 'What's wrong with my bottom?' Jilly called out, speaking for them all. She was the clown of the class, and being an architect by profession, appreciated a firm foundation. Slapping her ample backside, she grinned. 'I like a good cushion.'

'You don't get the back view,' Mrs Martin retorted.

Knowing Jilly could take a joke, everyone laughed.

Laying her diagrams on the floor where she could see them, Mrs M. proceeded to perform a series of knots a youth cadet would have envied. 'There,' she said afterwards. 'Now you try.' In her purple leotard and tight little stomach, she reminded Esther of a ripe plum.

After five minutes the women were lying on the floor begging for rest. Mrs M. was merciless. 'Scatter round the room and get into pairs,' she instructed.

The women moved about the hall, bending and stretching. Esther found her way to Jilly's side. Linking hands, they did a few leg stretches together, waiting until the nearest pair had moved further away.

'Who's the woman in red?' Esther asked softly.

'Tammy Nicholson. Number Thirty-Eight – vetted and cleared. Blue headband is yours, I presume?'

Esther smiled. 'It is rather ghastly, isn't it?' she agreed. 'I didn't recruit her for her dress sense. Hattie Coleman – Number Fourteen. She's rather an oddity all round, but clever. Very clever.'

Jilly stretched her other leg. 'Looks a bit incongruous here,' she remarked.

Again Esther could not help smiling. The new recruit was about as comfortable at a keep-fit class as a sonar mast in tights. Still, Hattie Coleman knew about control systems, and could be very useful as a passive, doing analyses of information for Sly perhaps. Whatever work she undertook, a more credible meeting place must be found for her. It was conceivable that she should come along to her local relaxation centre to try a few classes out, but not that she should attend beyond a couple of weeks.

'Heard anything about the examination yet?' Jilly asked.

'Nothing. Still, it's early dys. There's a new bloke moved in next door to me though, a Patroner, name of Stephan Tomas Lahr. It's coincidence no doubt, but I'd be grateful if you'd get him checked. I'm picking up something from him that's not quite right. He's a widower, on his own with two children, Imogen and Benn. That's odd for starters.'

'Stephan Tomas Lahr,' Number Twenty-Four repeated. 'Anything else?'

Standing back to back with their arms linked, the two women bent their knees until they were crouching together above the floor. 'I think Twenty and I were followed last night. The woman with the knitting was there again.'

'That doesn't sound good.'

'Tell Twenty to take the children into town on Thursday – straight after school. I'll meet her at the shuttle. Let's see if our knitter comes for a ride too.'

The music ended, and collapsing in a heap on the floor, the two women pulled apart.

Like the main hall, the sun deck would be a difficult area to oversee. In the hall, the constant music and movement made focusing on any single conversation virtually impossible. In the sun deck, it was the throbbing of the lamps that protected them. Lying head to head, Esther and her new recruit held their first briefing session. Occasionally they punctuated their discussion with louder platitudes, such as two strangers might make to each other while lying semi-naked on rotating beds.

Initially Esther went through the formalities. 'Name?' she asked.

'Harriet Coleman. I've been vetted and cleared. You know that.'

'No, I don't know a Harriet Coleman,' Esther insisted. 'I know a woman called Fourteen. From now onwards, in all dealings with the Movement you'll be known by that number, even by women you meet socially as Hattie. In the end, you'll feel like you're two different people. You'll be able to do things as Fourteen you could never do as Mrs Coleman. I shall always be Forty-Eight to you.'

'What do the numbers stand for?'

'They're given at random, to prevent any impression of seniority.'

'I see.' The woman was nervous. She had dropped the bottle of cleaning fluid as she wiped the bed down, and fidgeted continually with her goggles. Without clothes she looked thinner than ever, her flesh the pale grey colour that comes from spending most of one's life indoors, in a controlled environment. She was a little afraid of Esther. It was a reaction Esther did not discourage. If a new member were picked up before being trained, fear of talking had to be greater than fear of not doing so.

'Tell me about your job,' Esther began.

'I'm a troubleshooter. I work in the Department of National Statistics, analysing figures and records most of the time, but if there's a glitch in a program somewhere, I get sent to sort it out. Sometimes I may have two or three calls a week, sometimes none. There's two of us. We're permanently on call.'

'Do you ever work at night?'

'Sometimes. It's well lit wherever I go.'

'Do you like what you do?'

'I would if I was allowed to be truthful. I get sick of all the lies, though. Sometimes I think I should give up and start a family, but it would be difficult to get back in . . .'

Esther considered the woman's remark. It was hard to imagine her married, much less a mother. If she were at home with children she would have more time to give to the Movement, but her contacts would be lost. 'I'd hang on if I was you,' she advised. 'As you say, it's hard to get back in. Things change, especially in your field I should imagine.'

'The authorities might let me come back sooner. They can make dispenstions for women with special skills.'

'They're tightening up,' Esther warned. 'I'm a fully trained hydropologist – I've worked on Sea Base Alpha Three as well as on land – but when I applied to return, I got a lecture about the importance of child-rearing. I should be satisfied with my honourable role as a mother.'

'I suppose you're right,' the woman agreed reluctantly. 'But sometimes I hate what I've become.'

'Why do you say that?'

'Because of all the lies I have to tell. "Sweetening the answer", my manager calls it. He says it only distresses people to hear bad news. Besides, the bad figures will come good soon, so what's the point in worrying everyone? I doubt if he believes it himself. It comes right down from the top.'

'From the Keepers?'

There was a pause filled by the throbbing of the lamps. Trying to adjust her goggles, Fourteen sat up. Her collarbone made white lines under her skin. She was very frightened. In answer she merely nodded, and then lay down again.

'But why should they want figures altering?' Esther whispered. 'They have our best interests at heart.'

'Like our fathers and mothers.' There was a hint of irony in Fourteen's voice. 'But truth gets lost in the process. The Keepers tell us what they want us to think. Economists, statisticians, professionals like me, we know the country's heading back into trouble. The people the police units chase at night – they're not just a few Undesirables. They're the homeless, the sick, the mentally ill. We have more people undergoing Treatment than at any other time, yet the figures insist how happy people are.'

Dropping her voice even further, the woman looked nervously around the room. Her goggles were too tight, making a red rim round her eyes. 'You can make figures say anything you want,' she continued. 'Quote selectively, compare different periods – six months, say, against two years – change your definitions. Numbers are beautiful things. They're true in themselves. It's a kind of blasphemy to say two plus two equals four point five, or three point seven five, yet that's what I have to say all day. Sometimes I can hardly look at myself in the mirror.'

Esther nodded. The new member was intelligent and well educated. She was also very angry. Her anger would have to be channelled, or it could be dangerous. 'So you joined us to ease your conscience?' she prompted.

'No. I have this idea, you see. If I'm right, I could bring the whole system down.'

'What system?'

'Central Control. The one that manages the lot.'

The room felt very hot and close. Above them the lamps pulsed and throbbed. Lying still, Esther considered her reply. A routine briefing was taking on greater significance than she could possibly have imagined. 'All government systems are protected,' she pointed out. 'Central Control will be the best protected of all.'

'Oh yes, they've got their code words and prohibited entry, virus detectors and disinfectants, as long as your arm. I could still get in.'

'How?'

'Like I said, I'm a troubleshooter.' Sitting up on her arm again, Fourteen whispered urgently. 'Five months ago I was sent to one of the north-west relay stations, to sort a lift program out. There was something funny about the place – too many sensors in the ceiling and too well run. Things are generally pretty sloppy up here. Security's nothing like as tight as it is down South. I got curious, and while I was on my own for a few minutes, called up a few other programs. They were command programs, not just data store and transfer. Do you understand what that means?'

'I think so,' Esther replied.

'The operators at NW7 can change programs as well as receive and convey orders. I haven't been to any other station in the North that has that facility. NW7 is also connected to other stations outside this quadrant – laterally as well as vertically. If someone like me could contaminate one of the programs held there, the virus could be passed right through the network. There are hundreds of programs at any relay station. It should be possible to hide a trojan or a logic-bomb amongst them without anyone detecting it.'

'But how would you get into one of the programs? They'd all be write protected. You wouldn't be able to add anything new.'

Fourteen's voice was unsteady as she replied. 'Oh yes I would,' she insisted. 'National Control sends our top management a memo daily, and a further briefing at the beginning of each week. I never see either, of course, but my line manager is always on about the DU – daily update – and the weekly briefing. They govern our work. It's the same everywhere, from schools to hospitals to police. There's no way anyone can interrupt the DU and WB messages. They contain an override code, to stop someone like me hacking in and tampering with them. The code will be changed weekly, and it will only be in the possession of the Keepers themselves and top administration. If you could get hold of that code, you could ride your virus piggy-back on the Keeper's own orders. You'd need the week's password too, the one that enables the operator to input the orders in the first place. That should be easier. The staff involved will be ordinary people, just banging out what they're told.'

'You've thought about this a lot, haven't you?' Esther asked softly.

'Ever since I went to NW7 and realised what I was looking at. I even have a virus worked out. It's a beautiful, sweet little thing, as neat as you could ask. I've played with it for hours and hours while Donald's been out at night.'

For several seconds, Esther deliberated. 'Have you mentioned this to anyone else?' she asked.

'No.' Despite the heat, Fourteen was shivering slightly. 'I haven't dared.'

'Would you let me share it?'

'If you think it's safe.'

'I shall tell only one person. And I know I can trust them. They'll be able to tell us whether what you're suggesting would work. I can see one major difficulty myself already.'

'Getting the Keepers' code?'

'When we don't even know who our Keepers are, how are we to get close enough to steal something from them?'

'If you believe the rumours, there have been Keepers' women.'

'Have you ever met one?' Esther asked. 'They're either shrewd enough to keep their mouths shut, or they vanish before they can talk. I'm certainly not offering my body to a Keeper for the sake of any code. Besides, I'm not sure plunging the country into chaos is justified, even to overthrow the Keepers. That's what your plan would do, you realise that?'

'Yes,' Fourteen admitted defiantly. 'But truth does matter. Once you sacrifice it, other things go too. My parents were very grateful to the Keepers for getting the country back on its feet, but it's all going wrong – sick, somehow. We're treated like children. Our nice Keepers know what's best for us. So they tell us how to live. How to love, even. It's not good for us, or right. We're like spoilt children, lolling around, wanting to be amused all the time. We don't care that Mummy and Daddy are spending more and more of their income to keep us happy. Nor do we care if other children who won't accept their toys just disappear. Someone has to change things. I hoped the Movement would see what I mean.'

In her desire to make herself understood, the woman had leant forwards, nearer to Esther's bed. She stared at Esther earnestly from behind her goggles.

Esther tried one last question. 'All that's very true,' she agreed. 'I'd be the first to admit it. But when women join us they usually have a personal reason for doing so. What's yours? Jealousy? Thwarted love?'

'Ambition.' Lying down again, the woman analysed her own motives. 'I'm not boasting. I'm stating facts. I'm clever. I'd far rather be good looking or sporty, or able to dance and sing, but I'm clever – brilliant, perhaps. When I was born all the value I have was put in my brain. Donald only married me because he was too busy to notice what he was doing. Yet however clever I am, I have to trot along behind some man. When there's a problem at a relay station, they call Commander Hurst and his assistant. But it's me who sorts the program out. I'm fed up with the whole lousy business. I should get credit for what I do.'

The heater above Esther pinged and went out. Picking up her towel, she sat on the edge of Fourteen's bed so that her whisper was still protected by the second lamp. 'Do you have a dog?' she asked.

Mystified, Fourteen shook her head.

'Then I suggest you get one. No one suspects two women chatting while a dog runs round the woods.'

'You'll have me?'

Smiling, Esther offered her hand. 'Welcome,' she said.

4

When the letter finally arrived, it was pleasantly reassuring. A standard proforma with Esther's name and number filled in by hand, it advised her that the results of her recent reassessment had proved entirely satisfactory. The Director of Mental Hygiene apologised for any inconvenience caused.

Esther's first reaction was to do wheelies on Tim's midicycle. Then she went back to the letter and reread it. So she had been allowed to go. What did that mean? That she was cleared of suspicion? Or more useful left free? The old woman with the knitting had not appeared at the shuttle terminus, but she had been walking in the woods the following day. Esther had been sure it was her, though the knitting was out of sight, presumably in the bag she carried and yet did not seem to own. Old ladies have a special way of carrying a handbag, as if it is a lethal weapon. This one merely held it. Her shoes were wrong too, light and rather down at heel. No self-respecting old lady would have worn such shoes to walk through woodland.

It would be wise to cut down on her activities for a few weeks, Esther decided. Fortunately she would be taking the children to see their father on Tuesday. Until then, she would play the role of mother rather more conscientiously. Besides, the children deserved her undivided attention for a few days. She would start that very evening, by taking them to the rocks after school.

After the confinement of winter, Tim ran like a liberated animal through the woods, and up the track towards Josan's Tower. He had given the rocks that name himself, from a character in one of his favourite story vids. The rocks were his special place, where he could look out over the city, and imagine himself doing noble deeds. Sometimes, to her delight, he would let Sally play. She was the alien princess who must be saved from marauders and then flown back to her kingdom. Usually, however, she was relegated to climbing about on the lower rocks with her mother's help. Her fat little bottom upended, she was inexhaustible, shouting 'There!, There!' and pointing to the topmost crag. Sally was nothing if not optimistic.

But that day the pleasure of anticipation was spoilt. Someone was already sitting on Josan's Tower. To add insult to injury, the invader was female. With long fair hair flying out behind her she leapt a gap that would have made even Tim pause.

The girl seemed to have no fear. 'Imie – ' her father called quickly, 'don't go any higher.' He and Benn were playing ball in the rough grass at the foot of the rocks.

Like Tim, Esther felt thoroughly cross. Josan's Tower was their place, had been ever since she and Bob discovered it a year ago. Until then few others had ventured out from the city so far, and even they had usually walked past. She felt as if a private refuge had been entered by outsiders.

'Oh – it's only Imogen,' Tim said, brightening up a little.

'You've met her already?'

'She's in Mrs Long's class at school. They're moving her up after the holiday though.'

'She must be very clever.'

'Dunno. She uses long words, any rate.' Kicking at a stone, Tim pouted. 'I told her about my tower,' he admitted, 'but I didn't mean her to steal it.'

'The rocks aren't ours alone,' Esther pointed out. 'You'll

have to play on another part. There's plenty of room for you both.'

But Tim could not play his secret games when there were listeners nearby. With sharp disappointment, he began to climb up one of the easier faces. Nodding to her neighbour in greeting, Esther settled down to watch, while Sally scrambled about at the bottom of the slope.

After a few moments Imogen worked her way across the higher rocks, to stand above Tim. 'Hello,' she called. 'Am I on your rocks? I'll go if you want.'

She spoke with old-fashioned politeness, as if she were entertaining guests. It was hard to remain irritated with her. In reply Tim muttered something like 'You can play if you want . . .'

By the time half an hour had passed the two children were scrambling about together. They were being quite sensible, and after an initial fear that they might fall, Esther relaxed. It would be good for Tim to have friends nearer his own age. Most of the children in the dwellings were much younger than him, or five or six years older.

Stephan Lahr was watching too, with an expression of amusement. To all appearances, he was the perfect father, patiently throwing the ball to his son, and then helping him to retrieve it when he failed to catch it. Esther found herself wondering why she had disliked him at first meeting. Vague intuition rather than logic had turned her against him. Like the woman with the knitting, a piece of the ensemble had not quite fitted. It would be wise to try to find out what that piece had been, and whether the man still made her uneasy.

Moving closer to him as if she were merely following Sally's wanderings, Esther smiled. 'Are you settled in?' she asked.

'Thank you, yes.'

'Have you moved far?'

'From Centopolis.'

'My husband's working in the Old City there,' Esther volunteered, careful to mention Bob as soon as possible.

'You live up here alone?'

'We decided I should stay with the children. Tim had a lot of chest trouble where we were before.'

'He looks very well now.'

'Yes. He even plays football for the school sometimes.'

There was a difficult pause. The two older children were scrambling down the rocks to join them. Breathlessly they flopped on the grass. Smiling, Esther sat down beside them. 'Tired?' she asked.

''Course not,' Tim insisted, but he stretched out in the sun.

As Esther had hoped, Stephan Lahr sat down too. 'You've worn me out,' he said to Benn. 'Go and chase a few sheep.'

'Sheep are stupid,' Benn replied. His speech was much better than Sally's, though he was probably only a year or so older. Like his sister, he had fair hair and large brown eyes. The combination was appealing.

'Do you like Moss Edge?' Esther asked.

'It's very pleasant.'

Making conversation with Stephan Lahr was about as easy as lighting a fire with the proverbial two sticks. 'Isn't it?' Esther agreed. 'A lot of the fourth strata are buying second homes here.'

A soft hand touched Esther's ear, startling her. 'You've got lovely long hair,' Imogen said. 'Can I plait it for you?'

The girl's father was embarrassed.

'It's all right,' Esther assured him. Sitting up straighter, she allowed the girl to plait her hair.

'Am I hurting?' Imogen asked.

'No. I like having my hair played with.'

'Why?'

'It turns my toes up.'

A faint smile appeared around the Patroner's mouth. 'Nobody ever plaits mine,' he complained.

'Don't be silly!' his daugher chided him. 'Yours isn't long enough.' Evidently her father was not as serious as he appeared.

'Do you like your new home?' Esther asked her.

'No.' To Esther's concern, the girl's eyes filled with tears.

'You mustn't keep looking back,' her father interrupted. The sharpness of his tone surprised Esther, and it hurt his daughter. Without replying, she got up and walked back to the rocks.

Sighing slightly, Stephan Lahr turned to Esther in explanation. 'We were moved at short notice,' he said. 'She misses her mother too.'

'I'm sorry. I'd heard your wife had died.'

'Such wounds take time to heal.'

Getting up, Tim also drifted back towards the rocks. He hated anyone's feelings to be hurt. The Patroner watched him.

'What was it?' Esther asked gently.

'The usual. You read the statistics, but they don't mean much until it's one of your own.'

The man's words were desperately sad, yet Esther felt no sadness from him. Instead, there was a sort of stillness, a quiet control that hardly varied, whether he was talking of a new home, or his wife's death. Esther had never talked to anyone so calm. The effect was strange, almost uncanny.

'How many years are there between your two?' he asked.

'Nearly seven.' Esther smiled. 'And yours?'

'About the same.' Getting up, the Patroner watched Benn running about on the other side of the field. 'I'd better go and retrieve my offspring,' he remarked, 'before he wears the sheep out too.'

The family left soon afterwards, and Tim could play his private games again. He was no longer in the mood, however, wanting instead to boast about how high he had climbed. 'Do you think we could bring Imogen here with us tomorrow?' he asked. 'She said she'd like to come. Her dad's usually too busy to take them places. He's working ever so hard to get the new showhouse ready.'

'So he is the new director?' Esther asked in surprise.

'Imogen said the last one was dismissed and her dad had to take his place. He came up a month ago. She and Benn stayed with their gran.'

'I gather you like her.'

'She's not bad, not as soppy as most girls. I don't like her dad, though.

'Why do you say that?'

It was curious that Tim should have the same response, but his reply did not help. 'He shouldn't have ticked Imie off,' he said.

All the way back down the track, Esther thought of the family they had just met. In the space of half an hour, the girl had begun to go to her heart. With her large eyes and serious expression, she seemed so vulnerable, yet she was surprisingly mature. Several times Esther had seen her sitting at the message input, noting her father's messages. The little boy was obviously a handful but a pleasant enough child, who would probably grow up into a bright boy. It was the father that was wrong. Talking to him was like talking to a man with no shadow.

Every human being felt some emotion. Even when they were merely holding a polite conversation there was a constant background noise of feeling, a mutter of embarrassment and memory, ambition, hope, fear ... When Esther was a girl, the noise of it had exhausted her and she had sought refuge in solitude, until her father warned her she was in danger of being classified as an isolate as a result. In adulthood she had learnt that her gift – if it was a gift – had its benefits as well as its pain. Like the blind woman who sees only with the aid of an implant, she must accept the constant ache in her mind for the sight it gave her. Twice it had saved her life. Now it was the very absence of warning that was alerting her.

With growing alarm, Esther considered Stephan Lahr. Perhaps he was a religious? Belief in an afterlife would make it easier for a man to cope with his wife's death. Faith should give a kind of warmth, however. Patroner Lahr displayed no feeling, of any sort. It was possible of course that he was a Dissident, like herself. With weapons forbidden to all but the Keepers, many other groups beside the Movement were experimenting with techniques of mind control, and had their telepaths and sympaths. Yet once again, there should have been something there inside him: determination perhaps, a sense of calling or rightness, even anger . . .

A chill passed over Esther's mind. A Seeker could supress emotion. He could also be a good father, so long as that duty did not conflict with his greater duty, to the state. If it did, the emotion would be suffocated, like all other human kindness. The elite of the Keepers' secret police, the Seekers shared much of their masters' knowledge. That was what made them so feared, rather than their ruthlessness, though they were ruthless enough. They could control even their own pain.

Esther was not so conceited as to imagine such a man would be appointed to the directorship of the new showhouse, simply to observe her. A lesser police Watcher would be sufficient. Besides, to dismiss the previous director, and find the new one accommodation within a matter of a week, suggested a much bigger issue was causing the Keepers concern. Unless, of course, by placing a Seeker close to her they hoped to gain access to Sly, or to the Movement as a whole . . .

Her fears were based on no more evidence than a man's peculiar stillness, but Esther had a nasty feeling they were right. It would be wise to warn Sly, and to take extra care herself.

Still, something did not quite fit. Patroner Lahr had one vulnerable point: his love for his daughter. Each time Esther had felt his control weaken, Imogen had been involved. His superiors must surely be aware of his weakness. So why had they allowed him to keep his children after his wife's death? Inevitably such a situation would deepen his love for his daughter rather than lessen it.

As they returned to the dwellings, Esther was still deep in thought, so deep that when Mrs Dalton's cat jumped down from the window-ledge and padded across to her, she started in alarm. Rubbing around her legs the cat miaowed. To her amazement, Esther discovered she was still shaking with surprise, and pushed the cat away. It was black all over, except for a white spot on its tail.

'Hello, Gretchen,' Tim said, and began fussing the animal. It purred and wrapped itself around his feet. Esther could not touch it. Hurriedly she opened the door to their dwelling.

Afterwards, she tried to make sense of her reaction. The cat had frightened her, just like the one in the canyon. That too had been black. She had walked past several other cats without any such silliness. The Vandinskys had a fat tabby, and she had paused on the stairs to stroke it only two minutes ago. So what was special about black cats?

All evening the question tormented her. It was only as she settled into the meditation position before going to bed that the answer came. She had seen an image of a black cat recently, though quite when, Esther could not recall. It had jumped up on to a ledge, asking her to follow it. 'We need you, Tettie,' it had said.

Who the hell was 'we'?

Leaping up in alarm, Esther almost passed out. She had moved too quickly from absolute relaxation to activity, and the blood had drained from her head. Cursing her own foolishness, she went into the kitchen and made herself a drink. Afterwards, she went through the whole routine of exercises the Maestra had taught her. It took two hours, but by the time she finally went to bed her mind was at peace again. There were no images of cats left in it, of any colour.

Mrs Dalton could always be relied on to know the latest rumour. Inviting the woman in for a coffee the following morning, Esther prepared to do a little patient questioning.

According to Mrs Dalton, Patroner Lahr had been at the St Albans showhouse before coming to Nortown. He had built his last house up from almost nothing, to one of the best attended in Centopolis. 'Bit of a magician, they say,' she confided. 'Quite a catch for Nortown, and such a nice man too.'

No, Mrs Dalton did not know where the Patroner had been before St Albans, but she would find out soon. His family aide was a talkative woman, and not averse to talking about her new employer. Why Mrs Dalton should value information so much Esther had never understood. She might of course be an informer – for either side – but it seemed unlikely. Her treasure was made up of romantic inneundo rather than fact. No man should be on his own, according to Mrs Dalton. From the highest official to the lowest domestic, a man needed a woman to hold his hand, and smack it when required. Already she was marrying the newcomer off to half a dozen unattached females in the dwellings. 'Coping with two kiddies!' she gushed. 'Even if he does have a family aide during the day, just think of the nights! I'm surprised he can do his job properly. It's a wonder the authorities allow it.'

Even Mrs Dalton had seen that inexplicable fact. She could only offer one explanation: that the man had established such a good reputation for himself, he could dictate his own terms.

It was not impossible, Esther admitted, as she cleared up after Mrs Dalton's visit. Nortown needed another showhouse. The existing three only seated 20,000 between them, and were becoming out of date. The public demanded an inexhaustible supply of new experiences, and during the past months quite ordinary fourth- and fifth-strata families had shown signs of discontent. To ease the atmosphere, the authorities had made a lot of promises about the new showhouse. As a result, people were looking forward to its opening with increasing excitement. The director who provided the entertainment there would indeed need to be a bit of a magician. Perhaps Stephan Lahr had genuinely been called to replace an inadequate director, and save the day.

On the other hand ... She had never been afraid of cats until he came to the dwellings ...

Sly's report did little to answer Esther's questions. Drawing in her breath as she always did before repeating a message, Number Twenty-Four began:

'Stephan Tomas Lahr, rank of Patroner. Born Centopolis (NE Sector), 2175. Parents Joseph and Marika Lahr, not known. Educated State College of Drama and Entertainment. Graduated 2197. Head technician at Birmingham Entertainment Centre (Midopolis), 2203. Moved to St Albans showhouse in April 2205, where he became technical director. Six weeks ago was appointed director of Nortown Showhouse Four.

Domestic status: Married Althea Staples, known as Thea, 2195. Children Imogen Marika, born May 2198, and Joseph Benn, July 2206. Wife died of leukaemia 8 March 2208.

Appearance: Nordic type: fair hair, blue eyes. Height average to tall. No physical defects or distinguishing marks, though eyes unusual deep blue. Rapid promotion through Image and Media Service. Excellent reputation as director at St Albans, but otherwise character unknown.'

'Sounds a bit of all right,' Twenty-Four remarked afterwards. 'Dunno why you're so worried about having him next door.'

'I'm a respectable married woman,' Esther reminded her.

'But I'm not.'

They laughed together over their tea, but afterwards Esther was quiet, analysing what she had been told.

There were a number of intriguing gaps in Sly's report.

For a start, the man's parents were not known. If they were sixth or seventh strata that would not be surprising, but their son would have to be extremely talented to gain entry to the State School of Drama from such a background. It was not impossible, of course. The Keepers prided themselves on nurturing talent. It was, however, unusual. Then there was the question of his marriage. Unless the date was wrong, Stephan Lahr had still been a student when he married Thea Staples. That hardly fitted the image of a serious, dedicated officer. And where had he been for the first six years of his career?

'Ask for a few more details,' Esther suggested. 'Did the man marry while he was a student? If so, who supported them?'

'What do you mean?'

'Either he had money behind him, which suggests his parents should be known, or his wife worked. If she did, there ought to be information in the employment registers. We might find out more about him through her.'

'Why are you so determined to track him down?' Twenty-Four asked. 'Everyone says what a pleasant man he is.'

'Precisely. How does a pleasant man get to the rank of Patroner? According to Bob, senior officers in Image and Media are all thoroughly nasty, or idiots with influence.'

Twenty-Four smiled. 'You never let up, do you?' she remarked.

'Not when I can feel something's wrong.'

5

Normally, Esther enjoyed speedliner journeys. They were a time of privacy and quiet, despite the noise of conversation around her. Settling back in her seat, she looked out of the window.

Less than two hundred years ago the view outside would have been of an industrial wasteland. Ancient photographs showed coal pits and steel mills, with spoil heaps like mountains, and towns that grew chimneys instead of trees. Now there was nothing but country, an eighty-kilometre barrier as effective as any wall. Few people would attempt crossing such a distance except by the prescribed routes. The woods were too densely planted, the Outlands too inhospitable. It was strange how history went in circles, Esther reflected. Before the industrial period there had been other woods and other wastelands. Mills, coal heaps, streets had come and gone, leaving no sign except a blackness in the earth.

Several other women were travelling down with their children for the holiday period. While their offspring enjoyed the interactive vidmat, the mothers worked, knitting or sewing. One was even stitching a soft toy. Since it was forbidden for a woman with children under fifteen to take paid employment, and the wages of most men below fifth strata were too low for luxuries, there was a thriving black market in homemade goods. Some even risked taking money, but there was trouble if they were found out.

Esther made lace. It was slow and painstaking work, but its intricate patterns intrigued her. Carefully she stitched at a new card, while the speedliner swayed.

The inevitable stop start began as soon as they reached the out-towns. All greenery ended now, except in reserves and walled gardens. Endless crescents and circles of one- and two-bedroomed family dwellings led the way towards the heart of Centopolis, with its quaint Old town, the only part of the original city to be preserved. Each out-town was separated from the next by a border of recreational woodland and nature reserves, but the bands of green grew thinner and thinner. Private transport was still allowed outside the city dome, but the routes were so choked that clearly the dispensation could not last much longer.

As a member of the Image and Media Service, Bob was entitled to a personal transport unit, and since his office was in the Old Town, he was one of the few with a pass into the dome itself. Unfortunately, he had an important meeting that day and could not meet them at the arrival lounge. Rather than delay her journey an extra day, Esther had insisted she and the children would be all right using the people mover. She began to regret her decision as soon as they arrived.

The stairs down to the boarding point were already packed with workers returning from the morning shift. Squeezing herself and the children into the nearest gap, Esther tried to smile encouragingly. As soon as the shuttle arrived everyone surged forwards. By sticking her elbows out firmly, Esther managed to get all three of them on board, though they had to stand. For once it was a relief to take the handsets from the back of the seat in front of them. The nearest one still worked. Sally was fretful and overtired, beyond entertaining, but Tim was willing to be plugged into the first children's channel he could find. Clamping on her own headset, Esther allowed herself to be soothed. At least there were patrols on the shuttle now, preventing the worst excesses of overcrowding. Until they were introduced last year, you never knew whether your jacket would still be intact when you arrived.

It was not just the overcrowding that made a woman feel so vulnerable on the people mover. In Moss Edge, with so many other mothers coping without their men, a woman could almost forget she was a member of the minority sex. In any case, fourth-strata families had been amongst the first to see the dangers of allowing parents to determine the sex of their child at conception. The lower stratas had never been so concerned about the overall health of the nation. Even now, after the practice had been outlawed for over thirty years, many still found ways of ensuring they had male babies in preference to girls. In Centopolis the imbalance was worse than in the other cities, like most problems. On the shuttle that evening men outnumbered women by four to one.

Of course, a woman could trade on her rarity value and have half a dozen men rushing to assist her, Esther reflected. It was also rather nice to know that so long as you did not actually have halitosis and a two-inch moustache, you could always attract a mate. All the same, it was impossible not to feel continually threatened. Merely by virtue of their greater physical presence and louder voices, the men dominated. Everything moved at their pace, or was set at their reach. Though it was against the Keepers' law to harass a woman, with so many men without mates, such laws were difficult to enforce. Few women would travel around the inner area of the dome at night, and even in the out-towns it was wise to have a male companion. No, Esther did not like travelling across the central area without Bob, though she thought nothing of entering places that would have repelled most of the men around her. An Undesirable entering the compartment would have emptied it in seconds.

Bob was full of concern that evening. 'Why didn't you call me?' he demanded.

'You said you couldn't meet us,' Esther reminded him.

'I'd have found a way of sneaking out somehow. You shouldn't have crossed the dome without me. It's not safe.'

To Esther's concern, her husband looked older than when she had last seen him, but then he was working very hard. It was always the same when the new season was beginning.

After the children had gone to bed they settled together on the settee, to fill in the gaps letters could not cover.

'Tell me all your comings and goings,' Bob suggested. 'Who's new in the dwellings?'

Esther smiled. 'There's a woman with a dog called Harry and a husband called Hairy,' she began, 'or maybe it's the other way round. And a family of percussion players.'

'Percussion players?'

'That's what it sounds like. I think they've got one of those home gymnasiums. The weights go thump and the wheels go round. It's quite tuneful. A new bloke's moved in next door too. A bit odd if you ask me, but his children are gorgeous, all eyes and elbows.'

'What happened to the Hendersons?'

'They were moved out very suddenly. None of us heard where.'

'Isn't there a wife?'

Esther smiled again. 'I do believe you're jealous,' she teased. 'The wife died last year, but you needn't worry, I shall keep well away from our Patroner.'

'Why?

'He doesn't seem right to me. He's too nice.'

Bob tapped her nose. 'There are a few nice people left,' he reminded her. 'Like me.'

'You haven't risen to the rank of Patroner. Thank goodness.' Kissing him, Esther paused. There was so much she needed to tell him, it was hard to know where to begin.

Bob considered her expression. 'Your letters sounded unhappy,' he remarked.

'I didn't mean them to.'

'They worried me.'

'Why? What's wrong with the odd grumble? It's impossible for the human mind to be happy all the time.'

'Not everyone would agree with you.'

Sitting up on one elbow, Esther frowned. While they were together as husband and wife they could talk honestly, and there should be no listening devices to fear. Bob checked the dwelling daily. 'Why not?' she persisted. 'The mind's too sensitive a mechanism not to feel pain. If you care about others, you're bound to feel sadness at times, just seeing how their lives get wasted, how they fail to achieve their ambitions. Pain's necessary in any case. When you put your hand into a flame and it hurts you never do it again. Being told not to touch isn't anything like as effective.'

'You think dangerous things.'

'What's dangerous about that? I'm simply saying we're human, not animals. Perhaps most people do desire pleasure and an absence of pain, but surely there are different kinds of pleasure, some higher than others. There are different kinds of pain too, some of them valuable in teaching us things. The Utilitarians went through all the arguments more than three hundred years ago. They had to admit you couldn't solve everything by avoiding all pain and seeking only pleasure.'

Kissing her forehead, Bob drew her to him. 'Listen to Uncle Bob,' he advised. 'Switch your mind off occasionally. You never seem to – well, just enjoy yourself. You're still very beautiful, you know, yet you never spend time on yourself.'

'Are you saying I look scruffy?'

'Of course not. You're always immaculate. But you never do thngs other women do. Like braiding your hair. It looked lovely when you did it over Christmas.'

'I don't like braided hair,' Esther replied. 'It takes ages to do, and then you have to behave yourself to keep it in place. Besides, it makes me look like my grandmother.'

'Why are you ashamed of your ancestry? If I had a Punjabi grandmother I'd boast about her.'

'It doesn't pay to be different.'

'By refusing to follow fashion and braid your hair, you make yourself far more different. You're beginning to stand out in the crowd.'

It was sensible advice. Ever since her father had chosen him for her, Bob had been her wise man, the quiet centre of her whirlpool. 'All right,' Esther agreed. 'I'll do it at the weekends.'

There was a pause between them, while the audiovision flickered. It had already gone into sleep mode, and its soft images made them drowsy.

'Aren't you ever unhappy?' Esther asked.

'I'm usually too busy to notice.'

'Come on. Be honest.'

'I feel low sometimes – missing you and the kids. But I don't go around saying so. It wouldn't do my career any good. Image and Media people are supposed to be positive and outgoing. Having feelings goes with softness, not getting things done. So we suck in our paunches and positively bounce with outgoingness.'

Smiling, Esther leant her face against his neck. It was so good to be with him. 'I was called in for reassessment the other week,' she said, as casually as possible.

'Reassessment?'

Touching his lips with her fingers, Esther silenced his fear. 'Just a matter of routine. One of our neighbours got overexcited and went for the estate manager. Mrs Parker – you know, her of the disapproving hats. All her contacts were brought in for checking, me included. I'll admit I didn't enjoy it, but at least I now have a nice letter saying I'm healthy.' Taking the proforma from her pocket, Esther passed it to him. 'There, you see. I'm a paragon of mental virtue.'

Her teasing only half eased Bob's concern. 'You haven't

been saying things, have you?' he asked. 'Like you were a moment ago?'

When they married they had agreed there would be no secrets between them, but that vow had been broken long ago. Now they told each other only what they felt it was safe to know. 'I've got more sense than my mother,' Esther replied carefully. 'I don't go round making my feelings public. Nor do I criticise our Keepers. I'm a normal, run-of-the-mill fourth-strata mother, a bit dowdy perhaps, but we'll have to alter that. As you say, we don't want me standing out in a crowd.'

Bob did not believe her, as she had known he would not. 'You don't find things any easier?' he asked. 'I hoped when you returned to the North you might.'

'Actually I do,' Esther admitted. 'I can leave our dwelling and find myself with nothing but wind and sky above me. The Keepers haven't learnt to control the wind or the sky yet. Nor have they controlled the Outlanders. Even in Moss Edge there's a sense of the hills being nearby – a sort of restlessness. It isn't voiced. No one would be so foolish, but you feel it. I'm more at home there than here.'

'Is there still talk of revolution?' Bob's voice had dropped to little more than a whisper.

'Not openly, but I don't think the present state of things can last much longer.'

For a while they were silent. 'We shouldn't be talking like this,' Bob warned. 'It isn't safe, even in your own home.'

'Will you report me?'

'I agree with you, deep down. I'm a coward though. I keep my eyes to the ground and hope I can stay safe. And that you and the kids will be safe too. Besides, how can I change things? It's all I can do to keep my job, and pay for all the things we need. Running two homes doesn't come cheap. In any case, I'm a part of what's wrong.'

Gently Esther put her hand on her husband's arm. 'You?' she asked. 'A more decent, kindly man I can't think of—'

'I help peddle the dreams. All of us in the fourth strata do. We make the vidmats, write the scripts, publish the books. We're all part of the system we despise.'

'But if you stopped doing it? All together. Said you wouldn't write another script, make another film?'

'We'd all be sacked, or worse, and our families would drop down to seventh or eighth strata overnight. Tettie, the Keepers know what they're doing. Give your intellectuals privileges and you keep them quiet. We're well paid, but not so well that we can become powerful in our own right. We can have a PTU, buy a second home, choose where we want to spend our lives after fifty. We're the lucky ones. Few of us would risk losing that luck.'

As usual, Bob had identified the problem. 'That's the difference,' Esther agreed. 'Last century the artists and intellectuals led the rebellion, because they were persecuted and had nothing to lose.'

'You need a dispossessed minority for a rebellion,' Bob remarked. 'Like you mothers.'

Surprised, Esther sat up. 'What about us mothers?' she asked.

'Well – I've often thought the Keepers made a mistake forcing women with children to give up work. A lot of you are well educated and you've had a taste of power in your careers. Now you're stuck at home with kids, going potty doing a bit of embroidery.'

'Surely we share our husbands' privileges?'

'But you're not allowed them in your own right. That'd make me mad.'

With his good sense and honesty Bob was as great a threat as any Watcher. The national dream had scarcely touched him. Facts not dreams were what interested Bob. He was also perfectly capable of putting those facts together and coming up with answers.

'You reckon I'm a dispossessed minority?' Esther asked.

Lying back on the settee, she smiled at him. 'Come and make it up to me then.'

The following day, they took a trip on the river. Three ancient pleasure steamers had been renovated and sailed regularly from Heroes' pier. It was fun sitting on wooden seats, while a queer old engine chugged behind them. Tim adored the period uniforms the sailors were wearing, and chattered away to the man at the helm. So long as Sally was amused, fed and warm, she was always fairly good natured. That day she was all three. Strangely, the only discordant note Esther felt was from Bob himself. He was nervous of something. His uneasiness was particularly strong when they were waiting to go on board the boat, yet when Esther asked if anything was wrong, he merely smiled and assured her he was fine.

The second day Bob was more relaxed. He had taken four days' leave so that he could be with them, and the break was clearly doing him good. For Esther it was a reminder of how it felt to be among the privileged, with little sense of being in an overburdened city, with too few resources to offer more than basic living for most of its inhabitants. With a personal transport unit to take them around in comfort, passes to facilitate entry and fuel tokens to spend, life was good. It was possible not to see the crowds waiting for the people mover, the broken escalators, the cramped and boring dwellings. Esther began to wonder why she had ever wanted to move North.

When Bob went back to work, she remembered. A trip to buy food was an endurance test. There was over two hundred people waiting at the fruit counter, the day's allowance having arrived late. The wait was made easy of course, with soothing music and a charming young man walking up and down to explain the reason – something to do with an extra hygiene check 'introduced for your protection' – but it was tiring even so. Afterwards Tim wanted to go to the Fun House, but there had been vandalism at the people mover station. One section of the platform was closed off, so that everyone was pressed closer than ever. It was impossible to see exactly what damage had occurred, but travellers had no alternative other than to believe the notices displayed at the entrance. The culprits had been apprehended, and an attempt would be made to modify their irrational behaviour.

At the Fun House there were problems too. Overnight rain outside the city dome had led to the drains backing up, and there was some minor flooding to the basement regions. Every effort was being made to remove the resultant odour, but members of the public might find it a little uncomfortable. With the honesty of childhood, Tim announced the place stank, but fortunately no one else heard. As they returned home, Esther reflected that not much had changed in the last two years. If anything, Centopolis was even more crowded, more overstretched. For the first time, there was rubbish waiting to be collected in the Old City, not just the poorer sixth- and seventh-strata areas outside the dome. Despite wearing his face mask religiously, Tim had begun to cough again at night, and Esther's own chest felt tight.

No, Esther would not mind returning to the North. She would miss Bob and exhaust herself trying to bring up two children on her own, but she was once again sure that she was doing the right thing. It was necessary to spend a week or so in Centopolis every few months, to remind herself why she had left it.

Bob wished them goodbye in the departure lounge. Normally he came through to the bay with them, but this time he said he preferred a quicker farewell. 'Standing round waiting always makes me feel choked up,' he admitted. 'Stupid, really.'

Feeling near to tears herself, Esther kissed him. There was a wary expression about his eyes she had not seen before. Twice, he glanced at the people near them, as if checking who they were. Despite his good sense, the general paranoia seemed to be affecting him. No one could have need to watch Bob. 'I shall miss you,' Esther said softly.

'And I shall miss you.' Embarrassed in front of others, Bob kissed her briefly, and then picked up both of the children together, making them squeal with delight. 'I shan't be able to do this much longer,' he said, grinning. 'Two tonne weight you are. Be good to your mum, and help her all you can.' Then letting them down, he turned to leave.

'Come and see us off,' Esther pleaded.

'I'd rather not, if you don't mind.'

He seemed to be watching a young man who was checking parcels nearby. In concern, Esther took her husband's hand. 'Take care,' she advised. The young man's face was vaguely familiar. Esther had seen him before, recently.

Drawing her close to him again, Bob dropped his voice to a whisper. 'Remember that I love you,' he said.

All the way to the barriers Esther heard her husband's words. They had a note of valediction that frightened her. Yet when she turned to wave to him, he was waving in return. An ordinary, kindly man, getting a little heavy about the stomach, he was indistinguishable in the crowd.

Working at her lace as the speedliner stop-started its way back through the out-towns, Esther considered the visit. It had been one of the better holidays, when things went right. Yet suddenly there was this unexpected doubt. Where had she seen that young man?

The interminable dwellings were giving way to the first ribbons of woodlands. On the other side of the aisle to Esther, a youth was pointing excitedly out of the window, urging his companion to look too. Both were making their first journey to the North. They were probably joining some rural familiarisation course – one of the schemes dreamt up to correct the over-urbanisation of the population. Like most bright ideas invented by experts, it tended to have the opposite effect, confirming young people in their belief that the countryside was wet and cold, and to be avoided.

If they were indeed going on such a course, the boys opposite would fare badly. Everything about them belonged to the city, from their gaudy face paints to their cropped hair and totally inappropriate boots.

'It must be dead boring living out here,' the first youth suggested. 'Here' was only the outer edges of the city.

'I'd hate it,' his companion agreed. 'No vision palace or theme parks – just a relaxation centre. You might as well be dead.'

When they crossed the Barrier Woods both boys lapsed into silent awe. 'No wonder Northerners are so strange,' the fair one commented at last.

'My dad says they're a danger to the peace.'

'Why?'

'He reckons they're always making trouble.'

Silently Esther passed bobbins back and forth. Sally was asleep. Tim was quietly drawing a picture.

'Commander Adlow says the Outlanders should be forced to come to the city, and do a proper job for a living.'

'Sheep People couldn't do a proper job. We met some once, when we visited my gran. There were two of them sitting at a table, drinking a sort of beer. You couldn't tell a word they were saying, and they didn't half smell. They should have been sprayed all over.'

'Do you reckon we'll meet any Sheep People this week?' The fair one's laugh was distinctly nervous.

'Shouldn't think so. You only find them out in the wilds.'

Gathering up her bobbins, Esther smiled.

It was late by the time they reached Moss Edge. With relief, Esther dumped children and baggage in the hall. Then she went to the living-room door.

The hair across it was broken.

At once panic filled her. There was no possibility of mistake.

Each time Esther went out, she moistened one of her own hairs and pressed it across the door and the frame. Time and again she had done it. Sometimes the door was opened by one of the children before she could check. Sometimes the hair dried and fell off. This time it was definitely broken. One short end remained attached to the frame. The rest was still stuck to the door itself.

For a few seconds Esther stood motionless, wondering if she should grab the children and flee. The outer door had been locked as usual. There were no signs of intrusion. Tim and Sally were wondering why she was keeping them waiting. Carefully Esther stood back as she pressed the control of the kitchen door. There was nothing in there to cause her alarm.

'You two bring your things in here,' she suggested, trying to look bright. 'Sally, let Tim help you.' Her voice sounded strained to her ears.

Turning back to the lounge door, Esther examined the hair. Perhaps it had broken by accident?

No, that was not possible. The draught from the air ducts was not powerful enough to move a fixed sliding door. Her heart thumping, Esther looked into the lounge.

Couch and cushions, plants, audiovision, all the appurtenances of fourth-strata comfort were still in place. Nothing had been moved.

Opening the door fully, Esther went into the room. The cassettes were still neatly arranged on the display unit, the ornaments just as she had left them. Even the kiddyscope she had not had time to put away was still on the floor, exactly where Sally had left it. The hair must have broken as she first placed it on the door.

As she turned to join the children, Esther paused, and looked back again. Something had changed on the display unit.

Since she could be under visual surveillance even then, Esther stopped herself from rushing to the unit. Pretending to clear up after her return, she worked her way across the room. For a year or more she had subtly changed the order of the cassettes each time she went away. This time she had put the *Children's Encyclopedia* upside down. The cassette was now the right way up.

Feeling very sick, Esther put one hand against the unit to steady herself. Someone had been in her dwelling, looking through her things. An out of place cassette and a broken hair was slight evidence, but they were enough. Forcing herself to remain outwardly calm, she walked across to the lace laid out on the board near the window. That too had been disturbed. At least one of the bobbins was out of order.

It was impossible to control her fear any longer. Stuffing her handkerchief into her mouth, Esther ran to the bathroom and was violently sick.

Tim was full of concern. 'Too much travelling, love,' Esther assured him afterwards. Sitting at the kitchen table, she tried to smile. 'I don't think the catering pack agreed with me either.'

'You're not going to be poorly?' Tim asked. He could be very sensible at times of crisis.

'Of course not. I'd be grateful if you'd put the monster to bed, though.'

Then she remembered the bedrooms. As if still feeling weak, Esther got up. 'I'll just go and see if your beds are ready,' she lied.

All three bedrooms were empty. There were no uniformed men waiting in them, nobody sitting on the bed ready to smile as she screamed. Everything appeared perfectly normal.

Once again Esther looked for something out of place. Trying to impose a recallable order on the children's bedrooms would have been like trying to control running water. Her own room though, that was easier. The Watchers had made one slight error. She had left a faint plume of face paint on the dressing table, just as one might after spilling a little from a compact. The powder had gone. Someone had wiped the dresser clean. Presumably it would have shown a finger mark not her own.

After the children had gone to bed, Esther sat working out what to do. Then, pretending to have lost an earring, she searched the dwelling thoroughly. The watchers were experts. They had left almost no trace. She could find no listening device planted by them. There was nothing missing. Nor would Esther have expected there to be. She kept no papers, no lists, nothing to incriminate her or the Movement. All names and places were in her head, or in the lace. That had been examined but not understood. Far more than one bobbin would have been misplaced if the pieces had been moved. Hopefully her invaders had gone away disappointed.

Why had they come? And who had tipped them off? At least half a dozen people had known she would be away: Mrs Dalton and several other neighbours, the janitor, and of course Stephan Lahr. It was impossible to say who might have told the authorities. If she was right about the old woman with the knitting, her movements were in any case being observed. She had no evidence to link the search of her dwelling with the arrival of her new neighbour, but it was an obvious coincidence.

Rest was impossible that night. Bringing her work table into the bedroom where the brighter light would not be seen from outside, Esther began what might be her final report. Meticulously she pricked out the codes on the base material, hour after hour, checking each pin was exactly in place. She recorded everything that might be of assistance to others. Every idea she had thought of but had not yet developed enough to put to the team, she set out briefly. At three o'clock she pricked out the last pattern. If she were taken before she could get the codes to one of her colleagues, her efforts would be wasted. The best she could hope was that the half-finished pieces would be left with her possessions until claimed by Bob.

It was likely that she would be left free a little longer however, particularly as the Watchers had found nothing to establish a case against her.

Only then did the possibility occur to her: perhaps it was not she who was being investigated, but Bob.

Dear, sensible Bob, as mundane a man as you could imagine. And yet. There was definitely that 'and yet.' He had been nervous as he wished them goodbye at the departure lounge, and also at the river. That of course was where Esther had first seen the young man. He had boarded the boat with them. She had noticed him because he was on his own, while the other male passengers were with their families. He must have been tailing Bob on at least those two days, if not the whole week. But why? Bob kept his head down. He said nothing to anger the authorities, did nothing but get on with his job. Or did he? Esther had told him nothing of her own activities, for fear of jeopardising his safety. A wife no longer confided in her husband, the husband no longer trusted his wife. That was the way of the world.

Finally Esther fell asleep, slumped over her table, with her lace clutched in her hand.

6

The following morning Esther was a little calmer. The fact that she was still being allowed to go about her business was a good sign. But she must warn others that she was under observation, lest they incriminate themselves by contacting her. How to do so safely – that was the question. Wherever she went from now on, she would almost certainly be followed. Indeed now she came to think of it, that might be the very reason the Watchers had left slight traces in her rooms; just enough for her to notice and rush to contact her colleagues, but so little she would think them accidental. It was the sort of double pretence you could expect from a well trained agent.

There was only one course of action she could take, Esther decided, though it would need a good deal of willpower. She must stick to her normal routine, and only warn Sly and the others when a suitable occasion arose. Her Watchers must think she had not noticed their presence, and in any case had nothing to hide.

For the first day, Esther walked as normal to and from the school, and then stayed around the dwellings, apparently clearing up after being away. The only change she made was to leave Minkin's money still hidden at the pick-up point. It would be dangerous for her to have it in her possession.

She had no intention of wasting the day, however. All morning Esther had watched for Patroner Lahr, hoping to assess him better. To her annoyance it seemed she had missed him. At twelve hours however, his family aide appeared, taking refuse to the recycling point. Quickly, Esther grabbed her own rubbish container, and joined her.

It was easy enough to get the woman chatting. Mrs Briggs was a chatty sort. Children were her particular delight, whether her own grandchildren or her new charges. According to local gossip, she was very good with them. Imogen and Benn Lahr were fond of her already.

'Beautiful kiddies,' Mrs Briggs confided. 'You can tell they've been brought up proper. No snatching or speaking out of turn. If you ask me, th'lass could do wi being a little less well behaved. It i'nt natural being so grown up. Of course, she misses her mother. She's bound to feel it more than the little one.'

'Mind you, they understand a good deal,' Esther prompted. 'My Sally doesn't miss a trick.'

'Oh aye.' Mrs Briggs gave her rubbish holder a valedictory thwack. 'Benn's sharp as a laser. Like his father, I'll be bound. Now there's a clever man if ever I've met one. You should see the books he's got! Books, not vidmats. Me. I can't abide books, but it teks all sort.'

'What sort of books?' Esther asked.

'Plays, mostly. Stacks of 'em. And history. What's anyone want to read history for? I mean, it's dangerous stuff.'

'Surely his books have been approved?'

Mrs Briggs looked frightened. 'Of course,' she replied. 'They're all proper books. You can see the stamp on 'em. It's just that, well, it seems funny stuff for a decent man to have. I suppose he needs them for his work.' Trying to undo the harm she might have done, the woman put her hand confidingly on Esther's arm. 'And he is a decent man, you know,' she insisted. 'Nothing's too much for him.'

Gathering up her things, Mrs Briggs went back to work.

So Patroner Lahr had a few history books. There was not necessarily any significance in that, Esther reflected. He would need to be familiar with the period in which the plays and pageants for his showhouse were set. History, however, could be a dangerous subject to study, even when carefully sanitised. It could lead the reader to compare the past with the present, and to ask how things had come to be as they were. Patroner Lahr was becoming an interesting subject for study in himself.

Other than that, nothing much happened that first day. Esther almost wondered if her dwelling had not been entered after all.

Still sticking faithfully to her routine, Esther set off the next morning for her official visit to the canyon. As she entered the woods she was certain she was being followed. Yet when she turned round, there was no one nearby. Her mouth setting into a harder line, she walked on. Clearly she had not been imagining things. It was going to be very difficult for her to get a message to Sly, except perhaps along the local line, and that could take days.

All the way through the woodland, Esther was aware of other minds near her, though she could still see no one. Then suddenly, as she crossed the open land beyond the woods, the sensation stopped. Apparently her Watchers could find no way of following her in such barren country without themselves being seen. There would be little need for them to continue anyway. A message could be conveyed to the guard post at the top of the canyon, and her arrival there recorded. So long as she took the usual time between the two points, it could be safely assumed she had kept to the right path. Smiling slightly, Esther walked on, around the city limits.

As she had predicted, the sense of being watched returned near the Undesirables' settlement. Chatting to the guard for a few moments, Esther made certain her arrival was recorded. It was the same guard on duty as last time, and he was pleased to announce that the visiting families had left. Together, they stood looking down into the canyon and discussing the fecklessness of Undesirables generally.

'I shall be a little longer this time,' Esther warned. 'A couple of families have applied for admission to the strata, and I have to help them present their case. I won't by any longer than I can help, I promise you.' She smiled her sweetest smile. 'A couple of hours down there is all I can stand.'

Wishing him a peaceful morning, she went down into the canyon.

Minkin met her as usual and escorted her to his dwelling. As soon as they were inside, Esther wrote on her message pad, 'Sorry, no money. Not safe. My place searched.' Passing both pad and stylus to Minkin, she waited for his answer.

Frowning, Minkin wrote beneath, 'Why?'

Esther shrugged her shoulders in silent answer. 'I suggest we go over to the sick bay straight away,' she said aloud. 'I promised to talk to some of your people about their applications. That'll take an hour or so.'

'There's another problem with the sanitary units,' Minkin complained loudly, as if thoroughly aggrieved. 'You'll have to see that too.'

Clearing the pad quickly, Esther wrote a second message. 'Is Miriam here?'

Minkin nodded.

'Fetch her,' Esther mouthed silently.

They left the dwelling and walked across the settlement. Twice Esther stopped to greet people, making sure she could be seen doing so from the guard post above. Finally they reached the security of the sick bay.

'What's going on?' Minkin demanded.

'I wish I knew,' Esther admitted, 'My dwelling was searched while I was in Centopolis. I've been left alone since I came back, but that could mean anything. Close the escape routes, for the time being at least. Even if I'm left free, you'll be watched, as one of my regular contacts. Obviously, if I'm taken I shall do my utmost not to implicate you in any way, but you have to consider yourself at risk.'

'Who betrayed you?'

Again Esther shrugged her shoulders. 'Maybe no one did. It might not be me the Watchers want,' she admitted. 'My husband was being followed while we were together. I'm sure of it. On the other hand, I was followed part of the way here. There's certainly interest in me.'

'If they've left you alone so long, you're probably safe for another few days,' Minkin suggested. 'They're either using you as bait, or it is your husband they're after.'

'If I'm still around I shall keep coming here, but I won't do anything except my state duties. It wouldn't be wise. Sly will have to find another way of getting the money to you.'

Minkin nodded. 'I'm grateful to you for your warning,' he said more gently. 'You need to consider your own safety too. Wouldn't it be better for you to call it a day? I could open a route for you within hours.'

Esther shook her head. 'I can't run,' she insisted. 'As soon as my disappearance was noticed, all my contacts would be brought in. I couldn't do that to them. And what about my children? Who would look after them?'

'We could arrange passage for them too.'

It was very tempting. Then Esther thought of the sort of life she could be condemning her children to – running round between mounds of rubbish, or trudging across wastelands with a flock of sheep. No, even if she were taken herself, her children would be better remaining in the city. Whatever she had done, they would be well treated. The Keepers did not visit the sins of the parents upon the children, though they might re-educate them.

'Thank you,' Esther replied, 'but I have to see this out. The Watchers can't have found anything in my home. If I behave as if I'm innocent, I may just get away with it.' Aware of Minkin's concern for her, she tried to sound encouraging.

Minkin was about to offer his hand in a gesture of comfort, but he withdrew it, knowing that Esther would have to force herself to take it. No matter how often he washed, his hands and clothes stank of the refuse that surrounded him. Esther felt an unexpected compassion and respect for the man.

'All right,' he agreed. 'But don't underestimate what will happen if the Watchers do pick you up.'

'I shall stay silent, or kill myself,' Esther replied, 'just as you would.'

'I hope you can keep to that, or a lot of us are finished.'

Esther did not need Minkin's reminder. 'I must get word to Sly somehow,' she said, too briskly. 'It can't wait for the normal channels.'

'The Sheep People are back in One Tree Valley. I could ask them to pass the word on.'

Esther considered Minkin's offer. An idea had been forming in her mind ever since she arrived. 'I doubt if you'd be allowed to get near them' she said. 'They'd just keep vanishing ahead of you. It has to be me.'

'But the guards will be watching your every move.'

Her idea finally worked out, Esther laughed. 'Precisely,' she agreed. 'So let's make use of the fact. Miriam's the same height and build as me. If she puts on my clothes and walks around the settlement, our Watchers will think I'm still here. I'll have about an hour to get to One Tree Valley and back. Do you think Miriam will agree?'

'Miriam does what I say,' Minkin boasted. Then, seeing Esther's expression, he laughed too. 'I imagine it would amuse her,' he admitted. Calling softly into the other chamber, he fetched his wife.

As always, Minkin had secured for himself the best that could be had by an Undesirable. Miriam was beautiful, even in cast-off clothes and with her feet bound in rags. She was also intelligent, and had learnt to read and write quickly when Minkin taught her. He had not needed to teach her his hatred of the Keepers. Miriam already possessed that, having childhood memories of her parents vanishing one sunny afternoon.

'Minkin said you wished to see me,' the woman began. Her accent was slow and soft, with a hint of the West Country in it. Minkin had paid a visit to Westover last year, and had returned with her. It occurred to Esther that the families who had stayed last week must be Miriam's relatives. It was easy to forget that an Undesirable could have family just like anyone else.

An expression of quiet devilment came to Miriam's eyes as Esther explained what she wanted. 'But what if one of our own people recognises me?' she asked afterwards.

Esther stood in vexation, realising the weakness of her plan.

Minkin had the answer. 'I'll put the word round we're playing a joke on the new guard,' he suggested. 'Our lot'll like that. They've had enough of his bullying.'

It was a good three kilometres up the canyon and across One Tree Hill. They could not afford to waste time. Going into one of the inner chambers with Miriam, Esther took off her clothes quickly, and swapped them for Miriam's. Miriam was a little slower, unable to resist smoothing the borrowed shirt against her face. 'It feels so good,' she said. 'How I would love something as soft as this!'

Feeling the coarseness of Miriam's jacket against her own skin, Esther was ashamed of her wealth. 'One day you shall have all the soft things you could want,' she promised. 'Everyone will be equal.'

Miriam shook her head sadly. 'I doubt it. My Nikin sees that he never goes without, even if others do, and he's a good man. It's human nature to take what you can for yourself.'

'But there can be a more even distribution,' Esther persisted. 'It's not right that I have so much while you have so little.'

'But I am not so badly off!' Miriam said, beginning to smile. 'You city-dwellers see only one sort of happiness. I have things you don't – freedom to travel and to think as I please, to feel the sun on my face and the wind in my hair. I shall have children too. Here, they come whether we want them or not. There are many of you to rule us now, but without children you will begin to die out. Then we will have the last laugh.'

There was no time for argument. Binding Miriam's rags about her own feet, Esther could see little good in the lot of an Undesirable. Already she felt as if her whole body smelt. Before she attempted to pass the guard, she would have to spray herself thoroughly. 'For the next hour, you're a city-dweller yourself,' she warned Miriam. 'Don't attract attention in any way. Just walk round with Minkin as I would. I've told the guards I'll be talking to people about their applications, so you can spend some of the time indoors, out of sight. You'll find a set of instructions in my folder. You'd better go through them with the families concerned, or they'll be missing the advice they need. I wouldn't want to penalise them.'

Miriam nodded. 'Don't draw attention to yourself either,' she warned. 'Go out the back way, and walk until you're out of sight of the guards. Take care how you walk too. It's always the walk that gives people away.'

For a few seconds Esther's eyes were dazzled by the sun as she stepped out of the sick bay. Pausing, she allowed them to adjust. Children were scrambling amongst the concrete blocks near her, competing with each other to leap the furthest. Once the blocks had made a road looping round above the one that had run along the bottom of the canyon, but it had fallen long ago, crushing the pillars that had supported it. Now the blocks were nothing more than a game for urchins in rags. Esther found herself wondering if one day her own era's walkways and shuttle links would lie broken among thistles. It was a strange thought, as strange as realising that that afternoon might be her last.

Remembering Miriam's advice, Esther resisted the desire to run straight away. Taking the path up the canyon, she walked with her head and shoulders bent, as if expecting someone to strike her at any minute. The rags around her feet and legs protected them from the stones but her skirt caught on the thistles many times. All the while she walked, she kept expecting a shout from behind her, and guards running down the path from the top of the canyon. Nothing happened. The life of the settlement went on around her, uninterrupted. In ten minutes she was out of sight amongst the scrubby trees and bracken that filled the canyon beyond the settlement. Immediately she began to run.

It took her another ten minutes to reach One Tree Valley, for the climb from the canyon was steep and Miriam's thongs kept coming undone, until in exasperation, Esther undid them and ran barefoot. She was of course observed as soon as she began to cross One Tree Hill, but the Sheep People did not show themselves. Once she felt two or three of them behind some rocks right beside her, and the hairs on her neck prickled with alarm. Dropping down into the valley, Esther lowered her hood so that her face could be recognised, and waited for someone to show themselves in return.

'Damn you!' she called at last. 'Stop wasting time! You know me. My number of Forty-Eight. My password is Matrix. Come and speak to me.'

Still no one appeared.

'I have an important message,' Esther called again.

'Who for?' a voice answered. It came from among the rocks just above her, but when Esther looked up there was no sign of human presence. Three sheep were grazing among the rocks. It was very easy to imagine that it was one of them who had spoken. Turning quickly, Esther looked among the rocks on the opposite side of her. As she had anticipated, a face showed for an instant, and then vanished.

'I need to speak to the woman with red hair,' Esther called in reply. 'I will tell her.'

From among the rocks all around her, figures began to appear. Dressed in the grey woollen wraps of the Sheep People, they kept their hoods over their faces so that it was difficult to tell man from woman. Already in a circular pattern, they moved closer to each other and towards Esther, so that she was surrounded. Several carried heavy crooks, while others had stones clutched tight in their hands.

'Don't start playing silly games!' Esther shouted in annoyance. 'I haven't time. I must be back down at Fox House within the hour.'

Still the circle closed, the figures approaching through the rocks in absolute silence. Only the wind whining across the hillside broke the silence. 'If you won't take me to Red, bring her to me,' Esther demanded.

The Sheep People were always unpredictable, and it seemed she had caught them in one of their more unpleasant moods. They resented all city-dwellers to the point of hatred, but usually a working relationship could be established. That day they seemed oblivious of any need but to take vengeance on those who persecuted them. The fact that Esther was an ally made no difference. Inexorably the circle closed around her until she could see some of the faces under the hoods. Several of them were female, but there was no softness in their expression. Esther began to feel alarmed. If she was delayed much longer, she would not be able to get back in time to relieve Miriam before the guard at the top of the canyon began to wonder what was going on. 'Damn you!' she shouted again. 'We're supposed to be friends.'

The figures were only two or three metres from her now. By some unspoken command, they began circling slowly around her. Concern about time began to be replaced in Esther's mind by fear for her own safety. She should have sent word somehow ahead of her. Catching the Sheep People by surprise, and in this kind of mood, had not been wise. As if in some grotesque dance, the movement of the circle began to speed up, so that Esther could not watch any particular figure for more than a few seconds.

Suddenly one of the women lunged at Esther with her

crook, narrowly missing her head. Laughing, she dropped back into the ring. Then another leapt forward, this time only just missing Esther's face. Wheeling round to protect her back, Esther found a third figure darting forward with a crook held like a club. Ducking, she managed to miss the blow. Had it hit her, she would have had a very painful arm for days. The Sheep People were only playing with her. They would not kill her, but they would enjoy hurting her as much as they could.

Trapped in the centre of their circle, Esther could see no way of breaking free. Each time she tried to run between the figures, they closed the gap between them. For an instant, Esther recalled being at children's camp. One day she had been bullied there in a similar way, but by children. They had circled round and round her until she had grabbed one of the boys by the hair and scratched his face horribly before he knocked her to the floor. This time her fury was more controlled, and far more effective. One of the women near her had a sharpened stick which she waved in Esther's face every so often. Waiting until the stick came near her again, Esther lunged forward and grabbed it. Then she twisted it rapidly round.

The sheep woman was heavier than Esther but at that moment her heaviness was her weakness. She yelped in surprise as the twisting stick began to overbalance her. Kicking the woman's feet sharply from under her, Esther yanked the stick in a complete circle. Crashing against her nearest neighbour, the woman fell heavily on to her back. At once Esther had the sharp end poised like a spear, ready to drive it straight into the woman's eye.

'Stop messing about, or I blind your friend,' she shouted. She had never felt so angry in her life.

'I might have known it was you, Forty-Eight,' a voice said, from outside the circle.

Avoiding looking away from the woman on the ground,

Esther called back, 'Then why leave your sheep to play so long?'

'Let her be,' the voice instructed. 'She's on our side.'

One by one the figures dropped back, leaving Esther still standing over the fallen woman.

'You can let her go now,' the voice said.

'Only when you show yourself.'

From behind the rocks just to the left, another figure appeared. Pausing, she let down her hood, exposing a heavy mass of red-coloured hair. In response, Esther removed the stick and the sheep woman got up. Whimpering with relief, she rubbed her back, then suddenly darted up the hillside.

'You have a message for me, I gather,' Red said. 'You'd better come indoors.'

They walked down the hillside, towards a group of habitations sheltering in the valley bottom. Two of the original women were waiting for them already, standing at the door of one of the cottages. Without their woollen wraps, they looked like ordinary Outlanders, in heavy woven skirts and coarse blouses. Their arms were bare and strong, folded with the patience of women who have spent a great deal of their lives waiting. It was difficult to imagine they could be capable of the ferocity of a few moments ago.

Inside the cottage, there was a strong smell of herbs and meat. A side of bacon hung from the ceiling, still retaining the shape of a pig. After so much tension, it made Esther feel slightly sick. Silently Red cut a piece off the bacon side and laid it on a plate. Then she fetched a hunk of bread from the crock on the sideboard.

Normally, Esther would eat meat rather than offend her allies, but that day she declined. 'I haven't time, I'm afraid,' she said honestly, though with relief. 'Thank you all the same. I came to warn you my dwelling was searched the other night, and to ask you to get a warning through to Sly. I've made out a full report which I'll try to get through normal channels, but I might be picked up before I can. I mightn't even get home this afternoon. Who knows?'

'Who knows anything?' the other woman replied. She had the sort of face that was impossible to classify according to any age or strata. No one knew where she had come from, except that she did not speak like a sheep woman, and knew a great deal about healing. When someone was sick and could not be taken to the medical authorities, they were taken to Red. Her cottage garden bloomed prettily, but almost every plant in it had a medical use. That was how Esther had first come to work with her. Knowing so much about plants herself, Esther had been able to advise her on their cultivation. When the chance arose, she had even smuggled cuttings and seeds to her. Yet the relationship between them had never been easy. No one who lived with the Sheep People was easy to get on with.

'I think you owe me an apology,' Esther said. 'Your people frightened me a good deal.'

'You gave as good as you got. It was most amusing to watch.'

'Why did they set about me?'

'You came unannounced. How were they to know you were not tricking us? You're not exactly dressed in your best clothes. Besides, the protectorate officials have been throwing their weight around lately. I imagine it felt rather nice to frighten a city-dweller for a change.'

There was no point in continuing the conversation. Precious time was being wasted. 'You will get my message through?' Esther asked.

'Of course. We'll see Sly is warned.' Softening slightly, Red shook her head. 'I hope you're not picked up on your way home,' she said, 'or at any other time. We've worked well together.'

It was some compensation to receive Red's good wishes. The woman was well respected.

Forcing herself to walk even before she was in sight of the guards, Esther returned to the canyon. She found Minkin anxiously waiting for her at the sick bay. The guards would be asking questions soon, he said sharply. Still gasping for breath after running all the way back down from the valley, Esther was in no mood to apologise. 'How was I to know they'd start playing stupid games?' she snapped. Beginning to take off Miriam's jacket, she ran into the back chamber.

With Miriam's help, she got herself cleaned and dressed. Just before she went out into the open again, Esther hesitated. There was something she ought to say.

Stepping back into the main ward, she waited for Minkin. 'I wanted to say thank you,' she began awkwardly. Unable to continue, she held out her hand in the gesture of friendship. 'Give me your hand,' she asked.

In surprise, Minkin shook his head. 'You don't want to take my hand, lady,' he said.

'Yes I do. I smell too now I've worn Miriam's clothes. What does it matter? I may not have the chance to take your hand again.'

Smiling, Minkin took her hand. 'May peace be with you,' he said.

There was no sign of trouble as Esther walked back around the city perimeter towards Moss Edge. The afternoon was cool and beautiful; so beautiful Esther's eyes stung.

To her amazement, as she entered the boundary woods, Esther heard a wild bird singing. She had only ever heard a wild songbird twice before in her life. Year after year she had walked the woods and heard nothing but the sound of her own feet on the path. Now, suddenly, there was this exquisite music. It reduced her to tears. Her mother had had a recording of bird calls. She used to play it sometimes when Esther was a child, and lament the passing of so much beauty. Yet the beauty had not quite passed. Only twenty or thirty metres away a real living bird was resting among the branches, unseen but heard. If it was an omen, it must surely be a good one.

7

The printer stuttered into life. In pleasure, Esther crossed to read Bob's letter. Then she stopped. The addressee was given as Mrs E. M. Thomas. Bob never used her second initial.

Feeling increasingly uneasy, Esther read the screen. The call sign was definitely Bob's. Yet equally definitely, he had addressed her as Mrs E. M. Thomas. In concern she read his message.

Paradise Publications,
Paradise house

My dearest Esther,

How are you? Is Tim better after his cold? Thanks for sending the stills. I love the one of Sally on the moonrider.

There's not a lot of news to tell you from my end. My mother hasn't been too good again. It seems to have been a combination of rushing about (at her age!), and that nasty chest infection lingering on.

We've been exceptionally busy at work. Paradise was asked to do a big promotion for the authorities, and we've had very little time for anything else. Now things are settling down again, my boss has decided I could do with a couple of weeks' rest. Apparently I've been showing signs of strain. Nothing to worry about I'm assured, but best treated. They're sending me to one of those health farms, all expenses paid, which can't be bad. Unfortunately I havent got the address yet, but as soon as I have it, I'll send it to you. You'll have a new svelte husband by the time you come down again.

Sorry I can't write more, but I'm sending this in my lunch hour.

All my love,
Rob

With a feeling of faintness Esther reread the screen. She had sent no stills of the children recently. And since when had Bob starting signing himself Rob? Or stopped calling her Tettie? The tone was all wrong too. Bob would never use a phrase like 'at her age!' Though possessing a quiet sense of humour, he was never jokey or smart. Everything about the letter rang false. It seemed to be warning her not to believe what she read.

Suddenly understanding, Esther snatched the printout off the roll. Of course Bob did not know his future address. He did not know where he was being taken.

'No!' she shouted. Bending over the table, Esther put her hands to her face. 'Not Bob!' she almost howled.

Half an hour passed before Esther was calm enough to move from the table. Sightlessly she stared into the mirror. 'Why Bob?' her mind kept asking over and over again. Why sensible, ordinary Bob? Bob kept his head down, got on with his job, played games with Sally ... There would be other letters of course, bright chatty descriptions of the health farm, and then of the new office where he had been sent 'for the time being'. She would be able to write back, equally chatty letters about the children and their schools, what the family adviser had said. Perhaps she would even be able to see him again, if he responded well to treatment. But it would not be Bob – not the man she had married.

Grabbing her wrap, Esther went out of the dwelling. Her whole being was filled by a desire to get away from the city. The walls of the dwelling were too thin, the audiovision too insistent. She could not grieve there. Hardly knowing where she was going, she took the walkway towards the boundary woods.

Intense emotion always blocked Esther's sensitivity to other people's feelings. For the first time in years she did not immediately realise that she was being followed. Gradually however she became aware of the characteristic sense of someone being totally on their guard, but enjoying the thrill of the chase. At once she was calm again, and cursing her weakness in letting grief obscure her vision. If the Keepers had indeed taken Bob in for Treatment, she must not show that she feared for his safety, or appear to question her rulers' judgement. Running away to grieve was not a good idea. She would have to suggest some other explanation for her hurried departure from her rooms.

Changing direction, Esther took the walkway along the edge of the woods. For half an hour she crossed and recrossed the settlement, as if taking a stiff walk as part of her fitness programme. Sometimes she speeded up, counting a hundred paces running and then a hundred paces walking. Each time she approached a bridge, she scaled the steps to it in twos, and then ran down the other side. By the time she returned to her dwelling, Esther had the satisfaction of knowing her Watcher was thoroughly cross.

Two hours later, she set off for Moss Edge school. To all appearances she was once again an ordinary fourth-strata mother.

It was difficult to listen to her children's chatter, and smile as if nothing had changed, but Esther managed it. Tim had been picked for the under-eleven soccer team, and was in a state of high excitement. Sally had had a good day too, and was the proud possessor of a length of genetically engineered caterpillar, which she had been told to feed once a mouth appeared.

'Poor caterpillar,' Esther said. 'Trapped in a prison.'

'You like being in here, don't you?' Tim asked, peering inside Sally's jar. 'It's warm inside, and safe.'

That was one way of looking at things, Esther reflected. While he played the Keepers' game – whatever that was – Bob would not be badly treated. Like the caterpillar, he would be fed and kept warm. So long as he could fly at the right time, he mightn't come to any harm. Sly might be able to persuade someone to swear on his behalf. Just occasionally too there was a successful spiriting away. A patient went for a walk around the perimeter of a health farm and vanished. Smiling, Esther tried to imagine Bob living as a shepherd. His flock would look back at him and laugh.

Since her dwelling had been entered, Esther felt slightly sick with fear each time she returned to it. That afternoon her fear was far worse. Letting the front door slide behind her, she stood in the vestibule for a second, gathering courage. Then she checked the lounge door. The hair was unbroken. Going into the kitchen, she made the children a drink. A storm was swelling over the Outlands and the sky was darkening. Though it was only afternoon, they needed the lights on. Automatically the central control came into action, and the strip above Esther flicked into life.

The light! Of course. It was the one place in the kitchen Esther had not checked. If a monitoring device had been left anywhere, it was inside that light.

Tim and Sally had gone into the lounge, to watch the audiovision. For a few moments she joined them. Then, returning to the kitchen, she flicked the booster switch a couple of times, as if the trigger were wearing out. 'Curse it!' she said aloud. 'This strip's going again. I'll have to change it.'

Fetching a pair of steps and a hand-held beam, Esther climbed up to examine the light. Unclipping the case, she felt softly around the inside of the strip. Her fingers touched a small hard object. Smiling slightly, she leant towards it. 'Tim!' she bawled. 'Stop that at once!'

'That should give them a headache,' Esther thought with satisfaction.

Afterwards, she changed what was a perfectly good strip, knocking the monitoring device in the process. It fell upside down into the cover, blinding her Watchers. 'Just look at the dust!' she said. Going back down the steps she fetched the dustsucker.

By then, Tim was coming to see why she had called him, but Esther put her finger to her mouth, indicating that he should not speak. His expression was one of bewilderment, but he had learnt to obey such instructions. Climbing back up the steps, Esther dusted round the shade, sucking up first the metal object and then the lighting strip. Finally she emptied both into the rubbish container.

'Why did you shout at me?' Tim asked.

'I thought you and Sally were up to something,' Esther replied, 'but it was the kids above. Making a terrible row.'

Tim was not convinced, but he asked no more.

Just before the lights dimmed for the night, Esther took the rubbish container along the corridor, and tipped its contents into the shute labelled 'Mixed Waste'. What her Watchers would make of it all she had no idea. They would have experienced several painful crackles already and had their eardrums nearly burst when Esther shouted. It would serve them right. After three days of Tim's football, it might even come as a relief.

For two days, Esther waited for Bob to write again, sending her his address. The longer she waited, the harder it was to hope. Number Twenty was sympathetic, but she was hardly a friend in whom Esther could confide. They shared a common goal, but deliberately maintained an emotional distance between them. Friendship was a weakness exploitable by the enemy.

'Life is short and to be enjoyed,' the ethics tutor had taught at school. 'What people truly desire is pleasure. Pleasure is the absence of pain.' Esther had chanted the principles in class since she was five. In such a philosophy, grief was not profitable. It did not increase the common good. Though she had come to reject such ideas in adulthood, as she ran home from her training session Esther found they were some comfort. Grieving for Bob would not help him, or her. If she was to find a way of getting him safe home, she must have a clear mind. Clarity was necessary for other reasons too. Her full report had still not started on its way to Sly. For four days it had lain on the board in her lounge for any caller to see. Since few people suspected the obvious, it was probably safe a little while longer, there, but she could be picked up tomorrow, or the next day. Until her ideas and knowledge had been passed on safely, she could not rest. Tomorrow, she must find a solution to that problem too.

When Esther returned from her run, she was unusually tired. Though she had intended to go to bed early, she fell asleep in front of the audiovision. When she awoke, it was two hours. Feeling disorientated and cramped, she could not at first think where she was. A peculiar vague fear lingered in her mind, as if she had woken in the middle of an unpleasant dream. For several moments Esther sat on the couch trying to recall what she had been dreaming about. It was something to do with a cat – a black feral cat that had run out of some scrub, and rubbed itself round and around her legs. She had been running along the waterway back from her fitness session, and the animal had given her a dreadful fright.

In annoyance, Esther rubbed her eyes. What on earth was it about black cats that had got into her mind so? She had tried to get rid of the image, and yet here it was, back again. What was so special about it? Had some memory from her childhood returned to haunt her? Or was it something new, being put into her mind? That was a terrifying idea. Yet what would anyone achieve by doing so? She was being absurd even suggesting such a thing to herself. The strain of not knowing what had happened to Bob was affecting her. It was time she went to sleep properly.

Even after she went to bed, however, Esther tossed and turned, waking repeatedly with the same uneasiness. In the morning, instead of blurring into the past, her dream grew more distinct, until she could remember whole sequences from it. All the while she dressed, they echoed in her mind.

She was running along the waterway path. There was a strong smell of cats, and several feral kittens were playing on the grass just ahead of her. She bent to stroke one of them, but remembered that it might be rabid and withdrew her hand. Suddenly a black cat was rubbing itself around her ankles, nearly tripping her over.

Then, just as unpredictably, it vanished, and Esther ran on. Fear began to swell in her mind. Someone was ahead of her, moderating their pace so that she never caught up, nor dropped too far behind. Yet when she stopped, Esther could see no one. To the right of her was darkness. To the left was water. It was safest to stay on the track, but ahead was Falklands Bridge, with its dark pools of shadow, where a man might lie in wait for her. Deciding it would be wise to take the top route over the bridge, she ran up the steps. As she did so, a hand closed over her mouth . . .

Esther smiled at her own stupidity. A psychotherapist would have a good time with a dream like that, she thought wryly. Dark pools of shadow, men lying in wait, water, it had the lot.

Still the dream would not go away. As she got dressed, Esther could not shake off the uneasiness she had felt in the night. It was as real as in the dreams of her childhood. Deciding she might as well recall it all and be done with it, she sat on her bed and tried to think what had happened.

Her attacker had been very quick, and very quiet. She did not even have time to cry out. Within seconds, the breath was stifled in her throat. Someone was coming along one of the walkways, towards the bridge. She tried to call out for help, but could make no sound. Easing his grip on her throat, the man pulled her back into the shadow, and put his arm round her, as if they were lovers. 'Don't so much as move!' he warned. He was a complete stranger to her, yet he kissed her as if he were her chosen one. The voices came nearer along the walkway and a woman wished them goodnight. Then the voices passed by . . .

The recollection faded, and realising she would be late if she sat there much longer, Esther sighed in annoyance. She must set aside some time for meditation. That always cleared her mind.

Yet when she did meditate later that morning, Esther still could not find peace. Like some ancient mariner fixed by an eternal curse, she seemed compelled to go on telling and retelling the story to herself.

What had happened after the people passed by on the walkway?

In vivid detail, the next sequence of her dream began to return to her.

The stranger let her go. He would kill her if she cried out, he warned. 'You must meet someone,' he said. Trying to see his face, Esther found it was oddly flattened and indistinct.

'You almost strangled me,' she protested. Her throat hurt where he had pressed it, and she rubbed at her neck. The man did not reply. 'What do you want from me?' she demanded.

'They're waiting a little ahead.'

'Who are?'

'You'll see when we get there.'

'And if I refuse?'

'You won't refuse. Sly wouldn't want you to . . .'

It was the most vivid nightmare Esther had ever had. Even the dialogue seemed to be burnt into her brain. In bewilderment she gave up trying to meditate and returned to the main room. Perhaps if she wrote her dream down she would drive it from her. When she was a child, she often used to control her fears by writing about them. Even now, drafting her reports always gave her a sense of proportion.

Sitting down at the work station, Esther typed a heading: 'Peculiar Dream. Thursday night.' She smiled at the absurdity of her words.

So what did her dream say she did next? Slowly Esther began to write, putting down her dream as if it were a past event, however illogical. For some reason, it was becoming increasingly important for her to record what she remembered.

Almost of its own will, the first paragraph formed on the screen.

'Why should I come with you?' I asked the man. He had moved a little into the light, and I could see he was wearing running clothes like myself. His face was still indistinct, as if protected by a colourless mask.

'Because our friend cannot come to you,' the man replied.

After that we ran along the waterway towards Whaley Bridge, the young man ahead of me, as if he was pacing me. We approached the Old Moor trading estate. I heard a rat dropping into the water ahead of us, and lights shone from the derelict buildings. I thought we were going into the estate, but when we reached the bridge, the young man went left, towards the water. The moon came out and I saw five steps down to a wharf. A grain barge was moored beside it.

'Down here!' the young man ordered, so I followed him on to the barge and we went down a gangway into the cabin. I could smell grain and something sweet, like flowers. The cabin was in total darkness. Even the portholes were blackened. Turning quickly, I heard the young man go back up the steps and slam the hatch shut behind me. 'Damn you!'

I shouted. 'Let me out of here!' Then an engine started up, and I could feel the barge moving away from its moorings. Stumbling around in the darkness I found a bench seat around the side of the cabin. A dreadful tiredness was coming over me. No matter how hard I fought, I could not stop myself falling asleep. Sliding down on to the bench I passed out.

Pausing, Esther stared ahead of her, trying to recall the rest of her dream. With every moment it became more important that she should do so. Suddenly the detail returned to her, as if another film had been loaded into her mind. Urgently she began typing again. The screen was sprinkled with mistakes, but she could not stop to correct them.

We must have travelled a long way, for when I woke I could hear nothing but water, and the sound of the wind. Someone opened the hatch and came down the steps, their body outlined against the moon. They blocked the opening so that the cabin was dark again. Just before they did, I caught a brief glimpse of stars and clouds, as if we had travelled into the Outlands.

'I'm sorry,' the young man's voice said. 'The moon's too bright for you to land. You'll have to wait here.'

He left me shut in the cabin. There was a slight swell on the water, making the barge bump against the bank. After a while, I heard feet on the deck above me. They walked with a slight limp. As the first man blocked the moonlight, the second passed him and came down the steps. I could not see him, even after he entered the cabin.

'Am I a prisoner?' I demanded.

'Of course not, Tettie,' the newcomer said. His voice was soft and well educated with a slight Scots accent. I felt reassured. He knew my private name, the one only my family use. 'We just needed to make contact with you. You'll be free to go afterwards.'

'What do you want?' I asked. My eyes hurt with the effort of trying to see in the dark.

'A meeting with Sly.'

At once I was terrified. I had thought it was Sly who had sent them. 'I don't know anyone of that name,' I said.

'Yes, you do. He, or she, is your superior. As a trainer and delegate, you're quite senior in the Movement. You have access to Sly.'

The man knew me, yet I did not know him. 'What rank and strata are you?' I persisted.

There was a long silence. I could hear the water lapping against the barge.

'My name is Callum,' the voice said. 'I'm a Keeper of the Third Circle, fourth rank.'

In amazement, Esther stared at what she had written. What on earth was she doing dreaming such things? It was the ultimate female fantasy, the tall dark Keeper who came without being seen, and was gone by the morning ... 'Oh come off it!' she said aloud.

With a mixture of amusement and irritation, Esther shut down the work station, and went to do something more profitable. Cleaning the dwelling was always a good cure for fantasy.

She began in the vestibule. Picking up her training shoes, Esther started to put them away. Then she stared at them in bewilderment. They were covered in yellow mud.

Squatting on the floor beside the shoes, Esther drew in her breath to steady it. There should be no mud on her shoes. The footpath was paved all the way through Moss Edge, right beyond Falklands Bridge. Carefully Esther examined the texture and smell of the mud. It was clay, such as one might find along the unmade stretch near the Old Moor trading estate.

Running into her bedroom, Esther snatched her clothes from the hanger. There were splashes of yellow mud on her trousers too, and a couple of particles of something hard and sharp were caught in the material. Carefully she retrieved one of them. It was a tiny husk of grain.

For a long time Esther sat on the bed with that small speck of evidence in her hand. Then, returning to the work station, she reread what she had written. It was nonsense, madness, but it began to look as if at least some of it was true. A sense of terrible urgency began to afflict her, as if she were being driven by some undeniable force. If she did not write down the rest of her dream, her head would split across the middle. Every detail must be repeated. She could not even abridge her story, nor paraphrase it. It must be recorded exactly as she remembered.

Almost against her will, Esther began to type again.

The young man had told me he was a Keeper. I could not believe him. It was too incredible. 'A Keeper?' I repeated in amazement. My mouth would scarcely form the word.

'You've no need to be afraid,' the voice replied. 'I've no intention of hurting you.'

Standing very still, I tried to see the speaker with my emotions rather than my eyes. He too was afraid. Of me. That's something I've never felt from a man before.

'Why do you wish to meet Sly?' I asked, quite calmly.

The man had moved a little nearer me. I could sense his presence in the darkness, but when I reached out I could not touch him. 'To discuss co-operation between our groups,' he replied. 'I represent a group of like minds, unable to accept what is being done in our name. We wish to join forces with you, and with other Dissidents. Together we may achieve what is impossible separately.'

'You would betray your own side?' I asked.

I felt the man's conflict. He saw himself as a traitor, yet he felt what he was doing was justified. 'The Order is decaying,' he said. 'Our leaders no longer care for the good of others. Some of us have tried to change things from the inside, and have failed. Now we're being picked off, one by one. We have to make one last attempt, quickly, or everyone will lose what little freedom they have left – the Keepers included.'

More than anything in the world, I wanted to see the man

beside me. What he was saying was so unbelievable, I could not take it in quickly enough. 'But to betray your own side,' I repeated.

'If a regime is evil, is it evil to overthrow it?'

I had no idea how to reply. 'Perhaps not,' I said.

The man's conflict was turning to anger, that sort of quiet fury that leads people to do terrible things, or to die as heroes. 'When I was a boy I was taught one basic rule,' he said. 'A Keeper serves his country and its people. What's happening now is not for the good of the country. I am being forced into treason to prevent it.'

Foolish as it sounds, I trusted him. I had no body language to observe, yet I was as sure he was telling the truth as if we were standing in a brightly lit room together. 'I've heard you speak, and I believe you,' I replied. 'But how do I convince Sly?'

'Check the records. Look at how many prominent people have died in the last twelve months. You'll be able to establish the patterns yourselves.'

'And then?' I asked.

'Ask for the meeting between us.'

It occurred to me that I might be able to bargain with him. 'If you really are a Keeper, you have influence,' I said. 'Prove it to me. Find out where my husband is.'

At once I was afraid I might have angered him, but the man asked me for details about when Bob was taken, and his full name. He promised to do what he could. Then he went back up the gangway to the deck. Once again a second figure blocked the moonlight so that I could not see who had been talking to me, but I definitely heard footsteps limp across the boards above me.

My memory of the return journey is confused. I can recall the second man telling me I would be given something to take to Sly in person. It contained the renegades' terms and offer. At first I would be unable to remember what had happened to me. I would think it was only a dream, and give no sign of anything out of the ordinary to those who were watching me. Then gradually I would recall it, and feel no peace until I had done as I was ordered. If anyone tried to take their message from me, other than Sly, I would kill them, or kill myself.

'I'm sorry,' the young man said finally. 'We put a heavy responsibility on you.'

The next thing I remember is waking up in front of the audiovision.

Staring in amazement at what she had written, Esther tried to make sense of it. There was one obvious discrepancy in her account. If she had gone on any mysterious barge trips into the Outlands, she would have been away most of the night. Her babysitter, Amy-Belle, would have been frantic, rung the police at least.

Getting up rather unsteadily, Esther went to the visiphone. Honor Kranz answered.

'It's Mrs Thomas,' Esther began. 'I'm sorry. I've just discovered my timepiece has stopped. I'm not sure what time I got back last night. I do hope I didn't keep Amy-Belle too late.'

'Well – I was getting a bit worried,' Mrs Kranz admitted. 'But it was only the odd hour, and you'd paid Amy the extra so I left it at that. I'd be grateful if it didn't happen again, though. Twenty-two hours is quite late enough for a girl of sixteen.'

'Of course,' Esther assured her. 'You can be sure I won't let it happen again. I don't want to lose a good sitter.'

Shutting down the unit, Esther stared at the dying image. She had been an hour late. She had also paid her sitter for it, though she had no recollection of either now. An hour was not long enough for a trip into the Outlands by barge, but it was time enough for quite a few strange things to happen. If the substance of her dream were correct, rather than the detail, somewhere in her possession there should be a message from the man who had called himself Callum.

Going back into her bedroom, Esther felt in the pockets of

her running suit. There was nothing but the usual chewing-gum wrappers and glucose tablets, and a bit of money. It was just a dream after all. She must have been drinking. For the first time in her life, she had decided to drown her sorrows and got washed out of her mind. Presumably she had lost her way and run further along the waterway than normal, and ended up with mud all over her shoes. Feeling an utter fool, Esther put her running suit back on its hanger.

Suddenly she stopped. Normally she kept her money in the pockets on her shoes, for safety's sake. Returning to the hall, she checked what was in them now. The left one held the customary twenty, folded tight and left there in case of emergencies. The right contained a single coin.

There was nothing to distinguish it from any other coin, but Esther knew at once it contained the message for Sly.

'Oh my God . . .' she said aloud. 'Why me?'

The coin seemed to burn her hand. She could not examine it, or hold it up to the light. She had to get rid of it.

But how? If she could not get her own report to Sly without being observed, how could she possibly get so precious a message through? And in person? Even if her Watchers got bored and let her excape them, it would be dangerous to try to visit Sly unannounced. First she must request an audience. It could be days before she received an answer. In the meantime, she must find somewhere safe to hide Callum's message.

For several minutes Esther considered the problem. Finally she decided the coin was safest where she had first put it: in the pocket of her training shoe. To make it less noticeable, she added two or three other coins of a lower denomination.

An idea was beginning to come to her. Without a full account of the events of the previous night, a request for an audience with Sly would probably be denied. Transferring all she had just typed into lace was out of the question, but put into a simpler code and on to a progfilm, it could be concealed and passed on to Sly. Getting to the normal pick-up point was likely to remain impossible for Esther herself, but Sixty-Seven was not being watched. If Esther arranged a craft afternoon, and ensured that Sixty-Seven attended, she could pass the lace and progfilm to her some time during the meeting. It would be a dreadful risk for them both, but there seemed no other possibility.

A sense of relief was beginning to pass over Esther's mind, as if finding the coin had released her from the compulsion laid upon her. Returning to the work station, she began to correct her account, ready to put into code.

Since then everything seems to have followed the pattern the man who called himself Callum predicted. I woke up feeling as if I was obsessed. I had to recall my dream. Now I am sure most of it was reality. There is mud on my shoes and trousers, the colour of the clay near the Old Moor trading estate. I shall go and check it of course, but I'm certain it is the same. There are also pieces of chaff and grain caught in my clothes. Even more convincing, I have found something I must bring to you in person. Please grant me the favour of an audience so that I may do so.

I also need your counselling and guidance. Whatever happpened to me last night, it has left me feeling very weak of spirit. The initial attack has left no marks on my throat, and I also have a sort of confidence no harm was done to me at any other time. Presumably that was given me to reassure me. All the same, I feel frightened and unclean. My mind has been invaded. Until I see you, I shall have no peace. I have become a tool, against my will. Until now I've never understood why people who have dealings with the Keepers are so afraid of them. Now I understand. Forgive me, Sly. I have let you, and the Movement, down. I thought I could defend myself, yet when the attack happened, I did not even have time to cry out. I would have given any information required of me, done anything I was asked. You have trained me well, and my tutors taught me how to resist pressure, yet I have not developed the strength of will I should have. If you feel I should give up my position, I will do so as soon as I have seen you. What you do with me afterwards is up to you. Perhaps it is time for me to take one of the sheep routes myself. I leave the decision to you.

Staring at what she had just written, Esther tried to think if there was a better way of wording it. She was tired. Yet she dared not leave it as it was on her work station. She must translate it at once into code, put it on to a progfilm, and then wipe not only the disk, but the memory bank too. Rubbing her eyes to clear them, she started on the translation.

8

The women pushed the dining-room tables together and began their afternoon's work. Marsha was making a patchwork quilt and took up most of the far end. Gwendoline made soft toys. Anika preferred marquetry, being more used to a saw than a needle she said. As they worked, the women chatted to each other and swapped tips on household repairs. Only Yasmin had her husband with her. The others were 'Do-it-allers' as Honesty put it, migrants from the South, coping without their men. Their occasional afternoon together was a pleasant way of passing time. It was also profitable. Under Commander Sutton's guidance, every member learnt a new craft within the year, and undertook to pass it on to another woman.

So much help did Yasmin and Esther give each other that the pieces of newly pricked-out lace became confused. By the time the tables were pushed back into place, Yasmin had four of Esther's designs. Only a skilled lacemaker would have noticed, for the two women's work was similar, as one might expect when one was the pupil of the other. Had the Commander spotted the switch however, the result would have been disastrous for both women. Wrapped in one of the pieces was the progstrip Esther had coded two days before.

A burst of laugher gave Esther a chance to whisper, 'Don't undo them in front of anyone. There's something inside.'

Yasmin made no comment, but she went rather pale. After

half an hour she said she had a headache, and apologising, went home early.

Never before had Esther taken such a risk, or asked so much of a colleague. It was not just a matter of passing her reports through to Sly urgently. If that had been all that was involved, she would have waited until she could do so without involving Sixty-Seven. Ever since she had found the coin in her shoe, she had felt as if she were harbouring some living thing, a vile poisonous spider that must be got out of the house before it stung her. She could not even bear to look at it. When she tried to rationalise her aversion, the emotion grew stronger instead of weaker. It was imperative that she seek an audience with Sly. Not tomorrow, or when it was safer, but today. For the rest of the afternoon she felt light-headed with relief.

Commander Sutton was an indulgent tutor. There was always a good deal of banter while the women worked. Olga's latest assignment produced particular hilarity. Olga was on the Family Affairs Consultative Committee, and had been asked to test public opinion regarding a proposed change in the family and marital laws. In view of the continued imbalance between the sexes, it was proposed that the law of Conjugature be extended, so that women over thirty could take a second husband, rather than merely an officially recognised lover, as at present.

'It's really quite sensible,' Olga enthused. 'By the time she's thirty a woman's old enough to know her own mind, and she's probably pretty sick of her first man. It would give a lot more men the chance of marriage.'

'Who'd want two men to look after?' Marsha retorted, hooting with laughter. 'One lot of dirty underpants is quite enough.'

'I don't think many husbands would agree,' Gwendoline remarked more seriously. 'I haven't seen many women taking up the option of a conjugate, have you? It's usually the husband who wants a lover, and if he's lucky enough to find a second woman, his wife has to agree. We may have rarity value, but it's still a man's world.'

'What do you think, Jeddie?' Olga persisted. 'Does your husband mind you having a man up here?'

Everyone turned to Jeddie. Having exercised her right to take a conjugate as soon as she arrived in the North, her experience of such matters was wider than most.

'Occasionally,' Jeddie admitted. 'But most of the time he's fine about it. He'd be awfully angry though if I broke the law and took an unofficial lover, or if I was seeing Mel when he was around. I'm not sure he'd like me marrying him either. He likes to think he's Number One.'

'And you?' Olga continued.

To her surprise Esther realised the other women were waiting for her opinion.

'You always keep yourself very much to yourself,' Olga prompted.

'I suppose it's the way I was brought up,' Esther replied carefully. 'My father was one of the old regime, and never liked the Marital Rule being relaxed. He wouldn't even consider taking another woman after he repudiated my mother. Besides, Bob would feel hurt deep down, whatever he said.' Esther was about to add, 'And I wouldn't want to hurt him at the moment', then thought better of it. It would not be wise to admit her husband had been taken in for Treatment. The wives of men in Treatment were best avoided, lest they too be called in for assessment, and all their friends with them.

The chatter was getting a bit out of hand. 'Would you be allowed to have two children for each man?' Marsha wanted to know. 'Or only one each? I mean, would you have to get a ration book stamped?'

Finally Commander Sutton raised one eyebrow, suggesting her superiors would not approve, and the topic was changed.

It was almost time to go home in any case. The women packed up their materials, and walked across the public open space together.

As Esther had expected, Yasmin met them, returning to the centre for her enhancers she explained. 'So stupid of me to leave them,' she said. 'I'm as blind as a bat without them.'

'I'll go back with you,' Esther offered. 'You still look a bit off colour.'

Immediately they were in the middle of the space, beyond the range of most directional observation posts, Yasmin's manner changed. She was no longer Yasmin Poulter, but Number Sixty-Seven. 'I've passed on your gifts,' she said.

'Already?'

'They looked too valuable to keep. I gather there are others in the family who would like them.'

'Several,' Esther agreed. 'There's no one around at the moment, however.'

Yasmin nodded briefly. 'Then I have some information for you. I've been trying to give it to you since Thursday.'

Closing her eyes for a second, Sixty-Seven concentrated on the exact wording.

'Message from Sly to Forty-Eight,' she began. 'Further information on Stephan Lahr, as requested. 'National records give birthdate 16 August 2175. Not confirmed by other sources, however. No reference to name in internal records of state College of Drama and Entertainment. Student newspapers, awards etc. all checked and negative. Subject known to have been employed as illusionist at Theatre of the Future, Westover, 2199–2201, but no information for period 2201–3. Wife Althea Staples also untraceable until birth of first child 2198. Recommend caution.'

For a second or two Esther could not recall why she had asked for such information. Everything except seeking an audience with Sly had receded from her mind. Then she nodded.

'Is that your neighbour?' Sixty-Seven asked. 'The bloke from the showhouse?'

'Sounds creepy.'

'He does indeed.'

They went back into the leisure centre, finding Sixty-Seven's enhancers on the duct cover, where she had left them. As they walked back into the open, there was time for a few more hurried words.

'I'm sorry I gave you such an unplesant job,' Esther apologised. 'But I had to get that progstrip to Sly somehow. Don't mention it to anyone.'

'Not even Twenty?'

'I don't want to put her at risk too.'

They had reached the junction between two walkways. Taking each other's hands in the gesture of friendship, the women parted.

After that, the hours passed for Esther in a limbo of waiting. Time seemed to be running in heavy boots and getting nowhere. No matter how much she tried to fill her mind with other things, her thoughts returned to the coin in her shoe, and the voice of her dream. It dominated her waking hours and filled her nights. Even her grief for Bob was driven to the back of her mind. Yet she seemed to have unusual energy, as if she was being given strength from outside herself. So long as she did as her dream had instructed, she was able to go about her normal life. If she so much as considered ignoring her instructions and throwing the coin away, her forehead felt as if it was being split in two. The pain was so great it made her sick and she could do nothing for some time afterwards, except lie in a darkened room. Whatever it was that had taken over her mind, it demanded obedience.

Four days later, her summons came. Esther had been granted an audience. She was to go to Hunter's Fold, alone.

Taking her weatherproof suit and boots, Esther packed them inside a reversible sac. Added to the children's usual school sacs it would not be noticed. Then dressed as usual, she took Sally and Tim to school.

A whispered request was enough. If there was any problem, Thirty-Six would take the children back home with her after school. As if merely going for an early morning run before returning home, Esther took the path into the plantation.

She was followed of course, but only by one rather bored Watcher. It was easy enough for Esther to lose him among the dozens of strollers and joggers. She simply stopped at one of the exercise points, spent several moments on the parallel bars, and when her Watcher started looking round him, melted into the passing crowd. In an hour's time, Sixty-Seven would enter the main door of Moor View Dwellings, dressed in the same coloured oversuit as Esther, go up to the seventh floor, and then along the corridor and back down again, minus the oversuit. Such a strategy would not confuse an expert, but Esther's case had clearly been downgraded during the last week or so. Her Watchers were ordinary footsoldiers, happy to believe what they apparently saw, and lead an easy life.

Turning off the path, Esther pushed her way into the trees, until she was out of sight. Quickly she took off her oversuit and shoes and replaced them with the weatherproof cover and boots. The reversible bag became a survival sac. With her hair looped up into a knot and tucked under a hat, she became a passable warden, complete with a warrant and cover story. Though the moors beyond Moss Edge were not often used for sport, this year the Keepers were interested in fresh quarry. All wardens had been asked to report on the possibility of declaring the area closed territory. Since the Keepers' orders on such issues were regularly intercepted by Sly, Esther's story had the added advantage of being true.

The walk across the wasteland was five or six kilometres, and uphill all the way. At eleven hours it started to rain and, sighing, Esther turned up her hood. April had been an unusually wet month, and though it was good to have rain after so many years of dry springs, walking across the valleys was difficult. Even the sandy track along the ridge was sodden.

An hour later the heavy cloud lifted enough for Esther to see the dale opening beneath her. Her eyes stung at its loveliness. A buzzard hung above the rocks, soared upwards and then returned. It was hard to recall the crowds and noise of the city in such a place; almost impossible to imagine a revolution.

Two sheep women were sitting in the warmth of the top barn, waiting for Esther. Sullenly, they escorted her down the slope, towards Hunter's Farm.

Hunter's Farm appeared deserted. There was no movement even when the sheep women opened the back door and led Esther into the kitchen. 'Wait here,' one instructed. It was the first time either of them had spoken, and her tone was unpleasant. Without further explanation, she went out into the yard.

'Eat,' her companion advised more kindly, before she too closed the door.

A meal was waiting on the table – cheese and smoked bacon, homemade bread and cake, country delicacies most city-dwellers would have dreamt of and then found too strong for their taste. With a sense of abiding, inexpressible relief, Esther sat at the table, alone in the silent room. Helping herself to the bread, she began to eat. Sly would come when she was ready.

Half an hour later, the door opened almost soundlessly, but Esther sensed her superior's arrival at once. Getting up, she offered her hand. 'Thank you for letting me come,' she said.

'You have interesting things to tell.'

Immaculate as ever, Sly was the image of country thrift. Her kitchen dresser was full of preserves, a loom stood beside her window. Yet she had been a city-dweller once, and knew Centopolis and its laws. Over twenty years ago she had found it wise to take the Sheep People's route to obscurity. What Sly's name had been before that, no one asked. Nor did they trouble her with questions about her past career. She had fought in the civil war on the side of the North, but in what capacity was never said. Sometimes Sly herself spoke as if she could remember the Troubles almost eighty years ago. It was just possible. The bent shoulders and veined skin were those of a very old woman, even if the mind and voice were young. No one would have been foolish enough to challenge any claim she made. Sly's anger was legendary.

Fear, however, was not what made Sly so respected. The old woman knew every track across the wasteland, and every inhabitant of the dale. No stranger could come within twenty kilometres of Hunter's Farm without being spotted by her, or the Sheep People she employed. No transmission was made on the open channels without being monitored by her. It was said she could enter even the channels known only to the Keepers. Without leaving her silent dale, Sly was the eyes, ears and brains of the Movement in the North.

Sitting at the table, the old woman took some bread. 'Sit beside me,' she invited.

Awkwardly Esther did as she was asked. 'You're not angry with me?' she asked.

'Why should I be?'

'I've let you down.'

'Nonsense, child! You think you have failed because you were overcome. Most men would have been, given as little warning as you had.'

'It's not just the attack. I let someone invade my mind –'

'So would we all, if that someone was a Keeper. Besides, we don't know that you did any of these things. I doubt very much if you were attacked at all – certainly not as violently as you remember. The Keepers don't need violence. It's not their way, or it wasn't until recently. You were more likely persuaded to go, quite gently. They may even have had one of our passwords. That's more frightening than the thought of any violence.'

'Some of it has to be true,' Esther replied in bewilderment. 'There was definitely mud on my shoes, and bits of chaff on my clothes. I've found the steps down to the wharf too, and a mooring ring that had been used recently.'

'Sensible girl. You've tried to cross-check your dream. From what you wrote, I'd judge you were met along the waterway, probably at Falklands Bridge, as you remember. You were then persuaded to run with your guide to Whaley Bridge, and taken down to a barge moored there. After half an hour or so, you were guided back to your home. There was no trip to the Outland. It would be easy enough to fabricate that. Just start the engines and go a little way upstream and then back.'

In silence, Esther looked down at the food on her plate. 'Why should I feel so sure I was attacked?' she asked.

'We are all prey to illusion, my dear, and the Keepers know how to draw on our innermost fears. Most of your dream came from inside you.'

Flushing silently, Esther laughed. 'Then I should be ashamed of myself,' she said.

'Why? You're a young woman, married to a man who's over ten years older than you. You didn't choose him. Your father did.'

'I love Bob—'

'Of course you do, but love doesn't silence every other desire. Nor does it stop the occasional sense of disappointment. Instead, it makes you feel ashamed for not being happy. You have other fears too, deep within you. Ever since you joined us, you've been afraid of letting us down. You think you're not as brave as your mother, nor as disciplined as your father. Those are the sort of thoughts the Keepers can detect and use.'

'I should have resisted them.'

'Your report mentions a sweet smell. That suggests a hypnotic. No one could withstand that.'

In alarm and anger, Esther put down her bread.

Sly shook her head. 'You know very little about our masters, my dear,' she said. 'They have the forbidden knowledge: the drugs, the hypnotics, the ways of making people do what they want. However much we may try to learn such things ourselves, we can never hope to compete with them. Their order has been developing such skills for at least two hundred years. We have only had fifty.'

'That sounds like the counsel of despair,' Esther pointed out.

'We have other skills. Like the vixen, we know how to hide, to run, to set a false trail, whatever is needed. But don't underestimate what we're dealing with. If your contact really is a Keeper, he's a very dangerous man.' Helping herself to some of the cheese, Sly began to eat. 'Come, my dear,' she said. 'We're spoiling your meal talking of such things. I hoped the food would make you feel better.'

'But it has! You prepared me a banquet. I have something to give you though, before I can be completely at ease.'

The coin was in the pocket of her jacket, next to her body. Taking it out, Esther handed it to Sly to see. Without speaking, the old woman turned it several times in her hand, and towards the light. 'Looks ordinary enough,' she commented. 'Have you found anything concealed in it?'

'I've hardly dared touch it. Each time I've tried to examine it, I've felt such panic . . . Clearly, it was intended for you alone.'

'And now you've given it to me, how do you feel?'

'I want to stand on the table and dance.'

'Wouldn't it make rather a mess of the meal?'

Smiling, Esther nodded. 'Take the wretched thing away,' she pleaded. 'And then I can really enjoy myself.'

It was an hour before Sly returned. Esther had eaten more

than her fill. For nearly a week she had hardly been able to face food. Now she was greedy with relief.

'Very interesting,' the old woman said, and smiled a slow, satisfied smile. She sat at the table beside Esther. 'You've brought us gold, not just any old coin. Tell me more about your dream. This man who said he was a Keeper. What was he like? Describe him.'

'I never saw him' Esther admitted. 'All I know is that he called himself Callum, and had a definite Scots accent – probably Glasgow, but refined and well educated. Judging by the position of his voice in the darkness, I'd say he was fairly tall, but he could have been standing on a step I couldn't see. He also walked with a slight limp; not a dot and carry one, more an unevenness of tread.'

'He told you his status?'

'He said he was a Keeper of the Third Circle, fourth rank.'

'There must be more senior people behind him. The Third Circle is nothing special. Were you aware of a hood, or cloak?'

Trying to visualise the darkened cabin again, Esther shook her head. 'A cloak would have made some sound as he moved, but I heard nothing but the voice. A hood or mask would have muffled the words. No, I don't think he was wearing anything unusual.'

'Were the other men wearing anything of note? Black, for instance?'

'The first one was dressed in running clothes, like myself. I didn't see the second one.' Pausing, Esther considered her memories again. 'He could have been in black, though. So could Callum. How else could they have merged so completely into the darkness? There was a moon. It shone in when the hatch door was opened, but I still didn't see their figures. Not even the outline.'

'Good. Now we come to the main question. Why would a Keeper from the middle ranks, dressed in ordinary clothes, but possibly in black, be chosen to give such an important message? And why did he choose you to carry it?'

'He said he knew my position in the Movement, and that I was likely to be close to you.'

'If you've been identified as a Dissident, you may as well go and slit your throat.'

'Or am I known only to him?' Esther persisted. 'But not to the Keepers as a whole? Yes, my dwelling has been searched – you've had my report on that – but I've been allowed to stay free. It's possible I'm being used as bait to catch you, or to implicate the Movement. On the other hand, perhaps the search was only routine. There's also the possibility that it was Bob they were checking, not me. Until I know what's going on, slitting my own throat doesn't seem very helpful.'

The old woman smiled. 'A good answer,' she said. 'Now come and see what you brought.'

In surprise Esther got up. 'May I?' she asked.

'I think we're going to have to trust you. You've become a very important person.'

Crossing the room, Sly indicated that Esther should follow her. Nervously, Esther did so, into a corridor joining the modern Outlanders' dwelling to a much older building. At the end of this corridor an old-fashioned staircase led to a bedroom, from which opened a second, smaller room. By now they were clearly in the original farmhouse. Judging by the panelling and the high leaded windows, it could date from the sixteenth or seventeenth century. Such a historic building could only have survived in so remote a valley. Even in the North, very little property dated from before the Devastation.

Carefully closing the door, Sly stopped. The room smelt of polish and mellow wood. Fascinated, Esther looked about her.

'You're one of the very few I've ever brought here,' Sly said. 'If I weren't absolutely sure you could keep silence, I wouldn't have brought you now. Turn round and look the other way.'

For several seconds Esther waited. When she was allowed to

turn back, a narrow slit had opened in the corner of the room, to the right of the fireplace. It seemed to lead into the chimney. 'This is as old as the house,' Sly said. 'Clever, isn't it? Our forebears weren't as primitive as we think.'

'Is it a sort of hiding place?' Esther asked.

'Nothing's new in the world, my dear. Six centuries ago, if you believed in the wrong religion you could be imprisoned, or even executed. The family who lived here were on the wrong side. They built this secret place for their priest, and kept him hidden here when their version of the Seekers came. Come on in. There's just room for two.'

The priest's room was no bigger than a large cupboard, but even after the door closed behind them, the air inside was sweet. An infra-light was mounted on one wall. In its glow, Esther could see a chair set at a computer console. Long ago, a shelf for a storage space had been cut into the wall. It was filled now with modern dehydrated supplies. Along the other side was a stone bed, made more comfortable by a fillodown mattress.

'If if comes to the worst, I could survive here for several weeks,' Sly said, with satisfaction. 'Go and sit on the bed, while I find what I'm looking for.' Sitting down at the console, she located the file she wanted. Then she called Esther back to her. 'This is the message you brought. It came on a halladot, concealed in the design of the coin itself. Beautiful bit of work. I've copied it, so that we can read it more easily.'

The message came on screen.

Greetings. The bearer will have explained who we are, and that we wish to discuss possible co-operation between our two groups.

Our Ancient Order is being taken over by unscrupulous men, who care nothing for the good of the country. At the beginning of the next session, a bill is to be presented before parliament. This will declare a temporary state of emergency, citing 'internal threats to order and democracy'. 'Seditious

Intent' will be made a capital offence. All meetings of groups such as yourselves will be declared illegal, and your members liable to the death penalty.

We will vote against it, but we will be in the minority. Once the bill is passed, it will not be repealed. You must either disband or, like us, come into the open and fight back. For the past ten years our group has tried on its own to prevent what is happening, from the inside, and we have failed. Now we are being picked off one by one. Co-operation with you could achieve a great deal. The Movement has a national organisation and well-disciplined members. We can offer information and privileged access to services. The various opposition groups in this country have fought each other too long. Now, before it is too late, we must learn to work together.

If you are willing to meet with us, we request the following:
Venue to be arranged by yourselves on neutral ground.
Three representatives from each side to be present.
Guaranteed anonymity at all times, as well as safe passage.
The bearer acts as liaison, and is chosen as one of your three delegates.

An urgent answer is vital. The liaison should take the shuttle from the city centre this Friday evening, returning to the central depot for twenty-one hours. She will recognise her contact.

In fellowship.

'Why me?' Esther asked in a small, tight voice.

'Why indeed? Obviously they feel they can trust you.'

'Do you believe what's here?'

'It has the ring of truth. We've heard rumours of a split amongst the Keepers, and the patterns your contact referred to are clear enough. As for a new bill, I've heard nothing about it myself, but then you'd expect such a measure to be kept secret, to prevent the opposition mounting a campaign before it was passed. Whoever Callum is, he's got sense.' With her fingernail, Sly tapped the screen. 'The opposition has always been split in this country. Instead of fighting the present regime together, we spend our energies making sure other groups don't know what we're doing, so that they can't muscle in. We've betrayed some of the dafter groups ourselves, to stop them bringing the authorities down on us. But co-operation with the Keepers themselves ... That's another matter.'

'Even if they're Dissenters?'

'That sounds like a contradiction in terms.' Pausing, Sly reread the message. 'Still, this warning may have saved a great many of our members' lives, yours and mine included.' Unexpectedly the old woman brought her hand down hard on the table. 'The stupid fools!' she said. 'You can't hold a country down by terror alone.'

There was an awkward silence.

'Not for ever,' Esther agreed. 'There's always the hope a new generation will fight back.'

Equally unexpectedly, Sly smiled. 'A law like this is bound to split the Keepers amongst themselves,' she said. 'Those who uphold the old traditions will be revolted by it. Yes, the more I think about it, the more genuine this message sounds. It also makes sense of a very odd transmission we picked up recently. It referred to an act of sabotage, thought to have been committed by a group known as the Dark Ones. If apprehended they were to be passed straight over to a superior officer, not questioned locally. That intrigued me. So did the description. Apparently these Dark Ones wear black uniforms, and operate at night. To my knowledge no one except the Outlanders can work well at night, and these saboteurs seem to be city-dwellers. Now, lo and behold, we have your Callum, wearing black, and totally at home on a darkened barge.'

'Sabotage sounds too trivial for a group of renegade Keepers.'

'It would depend on what was being sabotaged. Still – ' Sly conceded. 'I doubt if the Dark Ones are Keepers themselves,

but they may well be connected with Callum and his friends.'
Sighing, she shut down the message. 'It's getting virtually
impossible to keep up with all the new resistance groups.
Everyone's shooting off in different directions.'

'Why should they choose me?' Esther repeated.

'Let's try your mother.'

'Are you going to tell me I'm the lost heiress to a Keeper's
fortune?'

Sly smiled. 'No. But your mother had connections in some
very high places.'

A second program came on line. This time, there was file
after file of family groups. All were carefully documented,
with the birthdates of recent children added. 'These are the
people we think are Keepers,' Sly continued. 'We're certain
about a few. They're the ones with an asterisk beside them.
For most, our only evidence is that they've managed to keep
their wealth and lands intact. To do that in such dangerous
times, you need to be either very shrewd or very powerful.'

Returning to the starred entries, she let Esther read each
one in turn.

'They're not the sort of people I would have expected,'
Esther admitted. 'Most of them are businessmen.'

'Businessmen have always ruled this country. The only
difference now is that they do it directly. There's a few of the
old families, like this one – ' touching the screen, Sly brought
up an ancient family title, 'but they've always been outnumbered. Now look at this.' Another file came on line. It was
headed. 'Recent Adult Deaths'. Seventeen of the previous
families reappeared, each with at least two entries. 'Something
rather nasty seems to be going on. Some sort of power
struggle.'

Again there was a pause as Sly called up another file. She
reminded Esther of an ancient spider sitting in her corner,
gathering webs made by others, instead of spinning them
herself. 'The split seems to be between those who still believe

in the old ideals, and a newer breed, which wants power without duties.'

'Which side is winning?'

'The second, of course. It always does.'

'Then heaven help us all.'

'It may already be doing so.' Silently old Sly checked the entries. 'The only Callum I can find is about seventy-three years old.'

'I'd have said he was younger.'

'So would I. Old men don't usually take to revolution. Old women might, but not old men.' There was a distinct twinkle in Sly's eyes. 'Now let's try our theory. Who could have known your mother?'

Esther watched in embarrassment as her mother's name appeared. 'Jacki "Angel" Marshall (née Franklyn), born 2150 . . .' Biographical details followed, place of birth, education, career, marriage to Esther's father, then Captain James Henry Marshall. Her death completed the entry. 'Recommended for destruction, 10 June 2193. Died Euthanasia Chamber between 16 June and 25 June. Committal not recorded.'

The room was very small and very close. With a feeling of tightness in her chest, Esther read the words again. Until then, she had never had confirmation of what she had always suspected. Her mother had not died of pneumonia. She had been executed. That one word summed up so much courage, and so much waste.

Without comment, Sly turned to a second page of entries, headed 'Connections'.

'Jacki's paintings were bought by a number of wealthy families,' she continued. 'We believe at least four of these were Keepers. One of those families may well have followed your progress, out of respect for her. Jacki may even have asked them to do so. After all, she knew she was in danger of being referred for Treatment, and you were still young.'

Lapsing into silence, Sly displayed the families again. None were Scots, or had any male relative called Callum, but she put a 'priority watch' code beside each. Of the supposed Keepers, one was a banker, another owned a transportation company, the third was a newspaper proprietor. Only one had been a politician, and even he was a fish farmer now. 'They look so ordinary, don't they?' she asked. 'Almost boring. That's why they're so powerful. Instead of spending their lives arguing about things in Parliament, this lot rules from behind, from amongst the people they command. They know what the public wants, and most of the time they give it.'

Esther's mind was still reading the entry before: 'Recommended for destruction'. Her eyes stung. Sly would despise her if she showed emotion, and think her a bad risk for lacking control. Closing her hands tightly, Esther remained silent.

'Now I'll show you what some of our suspects look like,' the old woman continued.

A series of photoline images followed, each transferable into profile or full face, as the viewer wished. All were very ordinary second-strata men and women. 'Memorise your mother's contacts,' Sly instructed. 'You may get a glimpse of Callum some day.'

Intently Esther stared at each picture. Her eyes were still blurred by emotion, and she had to blink several times to clear them.

'Some we have no pictures for,' Sly went on. 'All we have for Carl and Simon Miniott are a couple of school photos. Both are way out of date. For the Landers we have even less. This is their youngest son, Philip, but his older brothers Peter and Burgess seem to have kept out of every newspaper and government report we can trace. That's what worries me. We know the senior ranks of the Seekers are Keepers, and any of these men could be working under cover. It's complicated, though. There are a few Keepers who lead fairly normal lives. They're excused routine administrative duties, because they're particularly talented at something, and can serve their country better in other ways. We call them Outsiders. Your Callum may be one of them, but he could also be a Seeker reporting everything back to his hierarchy. Never forget that.'

'I shan't,' Esther replied coldly.

There was silence between them. Sly's manner softened. 'I'm sorry you had to learn of your mother's death this way,' she said. 'Until now I thought it best not to tell you the truth. I was afraid it would embitter you, make you careless perhaps. You've taken it very well; too well.'

'Because I've learnt to control my feelings, it doesn't mean I have none.'

'Quite. Grieve tonight, child, when you're alone.'

Esther shook her head. 'You're never alone in the city,' she replied. 'There's always the audiovision. We have no space to grieve, or to feel joy. The right to feel normal human emotion has been taken from us.'

'You sound very like Jacki,' Sly commented.

'I'm tired of being compared to my mother. I am myself, and no one else.'

'You are indeed.' Smiling, Sly returned to the beginning of the file.

Once again there was a pause. 'Who told you of my mother's death?' Esther asked. The words would hardly form in her mouth.

'An informant within the system itself. Jacki was one of the first to be condemned for crimes against the state, and it was not done legally. Our informant was as shocked as we were.'

Esther considered the reply. 'You've suggested how Callum may have come to know me,' she remarked. 'How does he know you?'

'It has to be the Sheep People.'

'Surely they wouldn't betray you?'

'Not deliberately. I suspect he contacted them too, and won their trust. That's what I'd do if I were a renegade Keeper making a last attempt to save what I believed in – use my privileged access to information, and then contact each of the groups I traced, to see if they'd join me. We may have found the catalyst we've been waiting for. Perhaps we'll get that alliance after all.' Despite her habitual caution, there was hope in the old woman's voice. 'Set up that meeting, my dear.'

'Where should I suggest as a venue?'

'We can use the old church at Stoney Meadows. Let's say twenty-one thirty, a week tomorrow. All their terms will be accepted: three representatives each, with you as one of ours. Guarantees of anonymity and safety for both sides. You know the sort of thing to say.'

'And what if it's a trap?'

'We'll just have to wriggle out of it.'

Closing down the console, Sly began to rise. She was stiff after so long in one position.

'We might get the codes Fourteen wants, after all,' Esther suggested.

A wicked, gnome-like expression came to the old woman's face. 'We might indeed. Think of it! Every transportation signal stuck at red, every audiovision blank. The cities would have no controlled environment, no light, no power. People would panic at the darkness and run screaming into the streets. Then we would strike. I almost feel hopeful.' She shook her head at her own naivety. 'But not quite,' she admitted. 'There's one flaw in it all. However desperate or angry he was, I doubt if a Keeper would approach us – or any other group. Keepers who break their vows don't just end up in psychiatric institutions. They're found dead, with their lips and tongues removed.'

All the way back across the moor, Esther felt the horror of Sly's warning.

9

That night, Esther slept better than since before Bob's letter arrived – better than she had done for over a fortnight. She could not escape the conclusion that the depth of her sleep was a kind of reward, a recompense for the fear and sleeplessness which the meeting with Callum had caused her. Having delivered the message safely, she was now to be allowed peace.

The next night was almost as good, though several times Esther was disturbed by the sound of a child crying. It seemed to be coming from next door, but she was too sleepy to check. On the third night her sleep was more normal, and the child's crying more irritating.

Through the wall Esther could hear Stephan Lahr's voice. He was trying to soothe his son. At first he seemed to have succeeded, but within half an hour, little Benn was calling out for him. Once again Esther heard the father's voice, comforting the boy. Quietness settled on the dwellings briefly. Then the child's wail resumed. So it was for another three hours. If either the boy's father or his sister came, Benn was happy. When he was left alone, he started to fret, and ultimately to howl.

Esther was ready to strangle the child. Unable to sleep, she began to think about Bob. There was no way she could pretend any longer that her husband was too busy, or enjoying himself too much, to send her his address. Paradise Publications had been surprised when she contacted them. They had not heard from him either. Even more worrying, it was not Bob's senior officer who had recommended that he be sent away for a rest period, despite what Bob had said in his letter. Unless she heard from him soon, Esther would have to accept that she would never see her husband again.

As if that was not enough to worry about at three in the morning, she had the business with Callum too. Tomorrow night, some unknown contact – yet one she would recognise – would take her somewhere she did not know, to discuss revolution with people she was surely mad to trust. The more she thought about it, the more Esther felt like grabbing the children and running away from the whole insane business.

Sighing, she turned over on her bed. If she ran away, she would never know why the renegades had chosen her, and she had always hated unsolved mysteries. Besides, the Outlands would not really be any safer for her than the city. Sooner or later, the authorities would make one of their periodic sweeps, picking up everyone without Protectorate licences. To flee successfully, she needed a designated route and help from an experienced group like the Sheep People. Running was not really an option.

Turning over again, Esther muttered imprecations on the child for waking her, and hoped the father was having as bad a night as she was.

The next morning, however, when she saw Stephan Lahr setting off for work, Esther felt almost sorry for him. In the daytime there was apparently no problem. From what she could hear through the wall, little Benn slept long after his father had gone. He woke mid-morning bright and full of chatter, entrancing his adoring Mrs Briggs as usual. Patroner Lahr however, looked exhausted. The opening of the new showhouse was only two weeks away, and the whole of Nortown was looking to its new director to produce a bigger, better, more dramatic event than ever before.

The city authorities were whipping up the excitement, of

course. A civic festival could always be relied on to distract attention from shortages in the shops. All morning, the audiovision carried bright little adverts for the showhouse, and reports on its progress. When Esther went up to the school that afternoon, she found the other mothers' chatter almost totally concerned with the topic. Each had a different story. There would be thousands of virtual reality games; there would be no games, but old-fashioned performances in which everyone could share. The top storey was to be taken up by a hundred private rooms; Showhouse Four was not to be that sort of place at all, but somewhere you could take all the family . . .

The women had conflicting stories about the new director too. One maintained he was from a poor background, proof that everyone did have equal opportunity. Another insisted his father was a third-strata businessman from Centopolis. When Esther unwisely mentioned that Patroner Lahr lived next door to her, she was pestered to tell them all she could.

'Does he really live next door?' Jodie burbled. 'Right next door? He's quite – well, you know. I wouldn't mind having him around to keep me company.'

'I hardly know him,' Esther insisted. 'I take care not to talk to unattached neighbours too much.'

Her denial was received with amused disbelief.

'Your Tim and Imogen are friendly enough,' Mursha pointed out. 'They sit near each other at dinners. I see them when I'm on duty.'

In surprise, Esther looked up. She could hardly forbid Tim to be friends with a neighbour's child, but the idea made her uneasy. She thoroughly mistrusted the father, and would have preferred Tim to have as little contact as possible with the family.

To Esther's relief, the topic changed to Keepers' Day, less than thirty days away now, Mursha reminded them. This year the display would be bigger than ever. She had heard all about it at citizens' class. Malin Lake had been chosen as the venue. It would be ideal. Out there, beyond the city dome, there would be plenty of room not only for the fireworks and lasers that were a traditional feature, but for the huge motorised kites that were already being made in the workshops throughout the city. 'Fifty metres in wingspan,' Mursha confided. 'Each one will take twelve women to lift it on to the launchpads. They'll be all sorts of shapes: dragons, aliens . . .'

Sighing, Esther nodded. In Bob's absence, she would have to buy the children their Keepers' Day presents herself. Maybe he would be back in time to give them to Tim and Sally himself. It was best to try to hope, though she did so with little conviction. Wishing the others a peaceful night, she collected her children and returned home.

Esther had just turned the audiovision down to sleep mode that night when there was a quiet tap at the door. No one ever visited at that hour. Her throat tight with alarm, she checked the visual display. Patroner Lahr stood in the corridor, with his son in his arms.

Pressing 'Speak', she asked what he wanted.

'I'm sorry to trouble you, but I'd be grateful for your advice.'

The reply was so unexpected, Esther slid the door open a few centimetres. 'What about?' she asked.

'I thought you might be able to tell me what to do. Benn keeps crying. You must have heard him. I took him to the doctor today, but she says there's nothing wrong. It's a matter of discipline, she said. So how do I discipline him? If I raise my voice, he cries louder. How can I be sure the doctor's right?'

With a mixture of amusement and suspicion, Esther looked at the man at her door. Unexpectedly, she had the chance to assess him more closely, as she had been hoping to do for some time. She would have to admit him to her dwelling, however, and that might not be wise.

For a few seconds longer Esther hesitated, wondering how to reply. Not to help him would appear strange. Parents were instructed to give each other support, and if Benn was sick after all, she could be accused of being callous. Besides, it was against her nature to ignore a child's unhappiness.

'Would he stay with me for an hour or so?' she asked. 'It might settle him, and I could see if I could find anything the doctor had missed.'

'I don't like to impose on you.'

'It's no trouble. Bring him in. I'd rather not come into your dwelling to see him. That might cause talk.'

'Won't it be as bad if I'm seen coming into your place?'

'Not if you didn't stay long. We're hardly likely to misbehave with a toddler crawling all over us.'

She saw Stephan Lahr smile. 'You're very kind,' he said.

Wondering if she was being foolish, Esther opened the door.

Benn was howling as they went into the kitchen. Taking the struggling child, Esther set him on her lap. After an initial wail of protest, he began to investigate her hair. Within five minutes he had almost forgotten about crying. Though every few seconds he whimpered to remind them of his capabilities, he was a great deal quieter. As she held the child, Esther tried to assess what the father was feeling. He seemed different to their last meeting. The peculiar stillness had gone. This time his manner was just what she would have expected from a man almost worn out by exhaustion and concern.

'There doesn't seem much wrong,' Esther admitted finally. 'I'm afraid your doctor's probably right. The little horror's worked out how to keep you coming at his beck and call. You daren't leave him to cry long, in case people hear, and he's bored with sleep. Sleep's for oldies. Benn wants a bit of life.'

'Unfortunately my life has to be lived during the day.'

Esther smiled. 'He's also afraid of something,' she added. Noticing Stephan Lahr look up, she corrected herself quickly.

'We had a similar period with Tim, and then found he was dreaming about monsters. Which side of the dwelling does Benn sleep on – or rather, not sleep?'

'The front.'

'Would Imogen swap with him? He's probably seeing the shadows from the walkway. It passes close to your rooms.'

Tim had appeared in the doorway, wanting to know what the talking was about. 'Hello Mr Lahr,' he said. His tone surprised Esther; it was one of friendship. 'Is Benn awake again? Imie said she'd push him down the sanitary unit if he cried any more.'

'I'll probably join her. I've brought him for your mum to look at. Do you mind?'

Tim looked at the toddler uncertainly. 'Can I have some earplugs?' he asked.

'Back to bed,' Esther ordered. 'None of us will need earplugs. Will we, Benn?' The boy really was a most appealing child, overtired and tearstained as he was. Like his sister, the dark eyes and fair hair would make him noticeable wherever he went. Even Tim was moved to find him a toy transport, before going back to his room.

As soon as they were alone again, Stephan Lahr got up and walked to the window. Silently he looked out over the square. 'I hope it is just the walkway,' he said. 'If I can't sort this out soon, the authorities will take my children from me. Mrs Dalton's complained already.'

Despite her caution, Esther's sympathy went out to the man. As a girl, she had spent months in children's camps herself, while her father was on a tour of duty. She knew the loneliness of feeling utterly abandoned. For Imogen it would be particularly hard. So solemn and gentle a girl would not mix easily, or be forgiven her strangeness.

Coming to a decision, Esther picked Benn up and took him into her own bedroom. 'Why don't you sleep here tonight?'

she asked him hopefully. 'You can have the bed beside me. See? And these are my pictures and my ornaments.'

She took the child on a guided tour, while his father stood in the doorway. Though he said nothing, Esther could feel the man watching her. Becoming embarrassed, she went back into the kitchen.

'You go now,' she advised. 'Benn'll cry for a few minutes, but he'll soon settle.'

'I couldn't leave him with you all night.'

'Yes you could. The new showhouse is very important to our city. To work well, you need sleep.'

Smiling slightly, Patroner Lahr nodded. 'I do indeed,' he admitted. 'All right. If you really don't mind.'

Esther tried one last question, watching the man's response carefully.

'Excuse me asking,' she began. 'But why were you allowed to bring your children with you? They're very young.'

'I refused to accept the posting if I wasn't.'

'That must have taken a lot of courage.'

Shrugging his shoulders, Stephan Lahr turned to leave. 'I was in a good position to bargain,' he admitted. 'The showhouse was behind schedule, and I have a reputation for working well in a crisis.'

He seemed to be telling the truth.

'That must be a heavy responsibility,' Esther replied.

'A month ago I was afraid I'd been brought in too late. Fortunately I've managed to sort things out since then. As they say, it'll be all right on the night.' Again with that faint suggestion of amusement, Stephan Lahr held out his hand in parting. 'Call me back if you need me,' he said.

Afterwards, Esther sat on the floor of her bedroom, soothing her neighbour's child. So long as she held his hand, he was happy. As soon as she tried to ease her fingers away, he began to stir. He was afraid of the slightest movement in the corridor outside. The sound of the night patrol terrified him.

'Poor little lad,' Esther said softly. 'You don't know what's going on, do you? Except that it's not right, and you're afraid you'll lose your dad as well your mum.' Bending down, she kissed him lightly on the forehead. 'Or is it your dad you're afraid of? I wonder ...' With so young a child, it was difficult to tell. 'Go to sleep now,' she whispered, 'Whatever your trouble, you're safe with me tonight.'

At seven-thirty Imogen Lahr came to collect her brother. 'Naughty, naughty boy,' she scolded, giving him a cuddle.

'Did your father sleep well?' Esther asked.

'He told me to thank you a hundred times.'

'Once will do.'

Sitting on Esther's uncomfortable kitchen stool, the girl swung her legs. In a few years she would be a beauty, though not in the fashionable mould. 'Dad would have come himself,' she explained, 'but he had to leave for the showhouse too early.' The girl's legs were long and thin, the limbs of a young gymnast. 'I made him stay and have some breakfast, or he'd have gone as soon as Auntie Briggs arrived.'

In all Imogen's dealings with her father there was a protectiveness which Esther had until then found amusing. That morning it touched her. 'You look after your father well,' she remarked.

'I'm his secretary. I see to the message input and answer the visiphone, things like that.'

'Doesn't he mind you seeing his messages?'

'Dad knows I won't tell anyone what they say. He doesn't like the message input, you see. He says it stops people writing proper letters.'

It was a view Esther herself had expressed, and she nodded.

'He asked me to give you this.' Climbing off the stool, Imogen found an envelope in her pocket, and put it on the table. Then she scooped up the protesting Benn and took him home.

Afterwards Esther opened the envelope. Inside were three

'privileged guest' tickets for the opening of the new show-house. She could hardly believe what she saw. Most of Nortown would have killed for such a gift, or at least poisoned slowly.

A brief note was attached. 'Thank you. I had forgotten how kind people can be. The enclosed tickets might be some repayment. They'll save you waiting in the queue. Stephan.'

To sit among the privileged ones . . . for just once in her life!

In amazement, Esther showed the tickets to Tim.

'Can we?' he asked, his eyes shining.

'I don't know whether we should,' Esther admitted. 'It mightn't be wise to accept such a gift.'

'Mr Lahr would be offended if we didn't.'

Tim was right of course, as he often was. However pleasant, the man had power. It would be foolish to insult him. Besides, though she was ashamed of her snobbery, for a moment the offer was tempting. When Bob had taken them to the show-houses in Centopolis, they had always had to sit amongst the fourth strata, separated from the lower orders by only a narrow aisle. If she accepted the Patroner's gift, she would be among the privileged. It would be nice for once to be free of patronising officials, to avoid the smell of fifths and sixers with their food and unwashed bodies. The people around her would be city officials, members of the Ministry of Culture, even Keepers' families, though one never knew who they were, of course.

Yet to accept might cause problems too. Even if the gift had not been intended as a bribe, it would make it harder for Esther to treat her neighbour coolly. Already he had signed himself by his Christian name. Whether by chance or design, Stephan Lahr was subtly moving into her life. If he was a Seeker, he was a very clever one. He had identified her love of children as her weakness, and used it to break down her reserve. But to use his own child as the means . . .

Recalling how the Patroner had watched her from the bedroom door, Esther flushed. There was another possible explanation. It was the sort of thing she saw at once where others were concerned, but rarely about herself.

Going into her bedroom, Esther stood looking in the mirror. It was not the first time she had sensed that a man found her attractive, yet it always bewildered her. Bob had said she was still beautiful. If Bob had said so, she must be, but she herself found it hard to see. Though she had taken his advice and used a little paint, she was still too dark and subtle for modern fashion. The beautiful women of the audiovision recalled the reds and yellows of a city bouquet. Compared to them, Esther was like the shade of woodland. Yet some men found her desirable; including, it seemed, Stephan Lahr. The idea made Esther nervous. She would not let him into her home again.

Tim came in to see if she was ready.

'How do you know Mr Lahr so well?' Esther asked him.

'He comes down to the playroom with Benn and Imie sometimes. When he has the afternoon off.'

'You seem to like him. You didn't at first.'

In a matter-of-fact way, Tim nodded. 'He's nicer than I thought. Imie thinks the world of him.'

Hesitating, Esther looked again at the tickets Imogen had brought. Attending the opening of a new showhouse would be a wonderful treat for Tim, the experience of a lifetime. She could not deny him such pleasure, whatever pride or caution advised.

At nineteen hours that evening, Esther took the shuttle across the city, as the renegades' message had directed. To give a motive to her journey, she went to Ridgeway, another fourth-strata suburb, but just inside the dome. There she spent a pleasant hour talking to an old schoolfriend. Just before twenty-one hours, she caught the shuttle back into the city.

Nervously Esther assessed her fellow passengers. There was no one she remotely recognised, or who showed the least interest in her. When she changed shuttles at the central transit hall, she looked even more carefully at those around her, but once again no one made contact with her. Deciding the trip had been wasted, Esther joined the queue waiting to board the Moss Edge shuttle. As she did so, she caught her breath. The old woman with the knitting!

Yes, it was her all right, Esther decided, watching the figure behind her. Could she be the contact?

Boarding the shuttle, Esther deliberately fumbled as she found her tokens. She took just long enough for the woman to have to wait behind her. Straightening up, Esther looked her full in the face. There was no response. With an unsteady hand, Esther pulled her ticket from the machine and sat down. The old woman sat too, at the front. Coolly she took out her knitting.

For six stops the woman knitted rhythmically, then she wrapped the wool round her needles and put the work away. Urgently Esther considered what she should do. Several people got up to leave, including the old woman herself.

Making a quick decision, Esther followed them.

By the time Esther reached the walkway, the woman was well ahead. To all intents and purposes, she was a perfectly ordinary traveller, returning home.

At the junction of the two routes, the walkers divided and thinned. Still Esther followed the woman. The area was becoming dingier, a fifth-strata business locality that had a neglected air. Finally there was just the two of them left walking. Then the woman paused outside a doorway. Pressing the security pad, she waited until she was allowed inside.

Left on her own in the street, Esther considered what she should do. Carefully she noted every detail of the building the woman had entered. It was the end shop in a small parade, with shuttered windows to two sides. The sign above the door announced 'New Age Supplies' but there was no indication what business went on inside. For several minutes Esther hesitated. 'My God, let me do the right thing,' she prayed. Then she pressed the communicator.

A female voice answered.

'Excuse me, I'm lost,' Esther said. 'Can you tell me the way to Whaley Bridge?'

At once the door opened. Stepping inside, Esther found herself entering darkness. For an instant she saw a counter and a display of goods. Silently the door closed behind her, cutting out the light from the street.

She was tired and thoroughly cross. 'Damn you!' she shouted. 'Stop playing games!'

A woman laughed in the darkness. Her voice was young, not that of an elderly traveller. 'Don't be angry, Mrs Thomas,' it said. 'You've done very well. We weren't sure whether you'd even noticed me.'

'Oh I noticed you. Next time you go watching, look to your shoes.'

'My shoes?'

'Little old ladies don't wear light casual shoes, especially to walk in the woods.'

There was silence for several seconds. Herbal coffee and cheeses filled Esther's mind, suggesting that they were in some sort of provisioner's. Reaching out, she established that there was a counter near her, and that the two displays were to her right. Such tangible details were comforting.

'Our friend has a point, Madelaine,' Callum's voice said. Startled, Esther turned to her left. She had not been aware that anyone else was in the room.

'I'm sorry,' the woman said. 'It won't happen again.' She seemed frightened.

'It was a mere detail, but one detail can be enough.' The reprimand was restrained but chilling in its implications. 'You can leave us now.'

There was the sound of a door opening and closing at the far side of the room. Esther's eyes were becoming used to the darkness, and discovering it was not quite complete. Around the shutters, a little light leaked through from the street.

'You found your way here,' Callum said, more gently. 'Well done.'

'You didn't make it easy.'

'We had to be sure you were as good as people said.'

'My group is interested,' Esther replied, ignoring the last remark. 'We agree to a meeting.'

'Where?'

'There's an old church at Stoney Meadows, about fifty kilometres from here. The curator is sympathetic to our aims. She will see we are not disturbed. We suggest next Tuesday, if that's not too soon for you. At twenty-one thirty. Your terms are accepted: three representatives each, myself included, guarantee of safe passage for both sides, and anonymity for both parties. I'm not sure how you'll be able to arrange the last point. I doubt if my colleagues will want to sit in the dark all night. They're not as used to it as you seem to be.'

'Darkness won't be necessary. Just make sure no one sees us arrive or depart.' There was a pause. 'No, I don't suppose I'll be there myself,' the voice added. 'More senior people than myself will wish to be involved. Madelaine will assist you in making arrangements. I'll make her available to you. Give her a bit more training while you're at it. She's very willing, but inclined to cut corners.'

A heavy transport passed outside, its lamps suddenly catching the front of the building. Light flooded through the gaps in the metal shutters and around the edges of the door. Esther heard Callum step back quickly. Then he crossed the room and spoke softly to someone beyond the door. Afterwards, he returned, standing a little further back. His wariness gave Esther an idea. The shutters across the side window were worn, with small gaps in them, letting in more light from the street. If she could force him nearer that window, she might be able to see him.

'You were able to read our message,' Callum remarked.

'Sly compliments you on your technology. Have you any more details on the statute you mention? We haven't been able to trace it so far.'

'It won't be listed until the last minute.'

'Thank you for warning us,' Esther said awkwardly. It was difficult talking to a man she could not see.

'Have you heard from your husband yet?'

'No.'

'You should get a letter tomorrow.'

In relief, Esther caught her breath. 'Is he all right?' she asked.

'He's been cleared of all Dissent. Now it's just a case of waiting for the paperwork to go through.'

Esther did not know how to reply. If she could have seen the man, she might have kissed him impulsively in gratitude, or at least offered him her hand in thanks. 'I'm very grateful to you,' she said lamely.

'I'm glad to be able to give you something in return. Now, unless you have any further questions, I'll wish you goodbye.'

'I'm to be allowed to go?' Esther asked. 'Of my own free will?'

'Of course.'

Turning towards the door, Esther paused. It seemed strange that she should be allowed to leave so easily, able to remember where she had been. 'How did you confuse me so much last time?' she asked, making talk.

'Trade secrets. Don't come here again, by the way. You won't find us.'

Unless she could find a way of seeing the man now, the chance would be gone. 'I was told to confirm our agreement with a handshake,' Esther lied. 'A Keeper's word is his bond, I believe.' Stepping sideways, she offered her hand in the darkness. As she had hoped, Callum moved a little closer to the second window to avoid contact with her. In the faint light from the street she could make out a shape, but no form. Unbelievably, luck was on her side. A second transport passed by. For an instant Esther saw a man outlined against a row of shelves. The features were indistinguishable, but the profile was clear-cut and the hair thick and dark. Then he stepped quickly out of the light.

As the transport rumbled past, Esther heard Callum laugh. 'Neat,' he said. 'Oh yes. You're good. But don't try and see me again. It wouldn't be wise, for either of us.'

The uneven step moved towards the door at the back, and went out. At once the outer door clicked open and Esther was free to leave. There was to be no guide now. She must rely on her memory.

Eighteen hours later, Esther returned, having taken the precaution of borrowing Fourteen's dog. 'New Age Suppliers' had gone. If she had not counted the shops and noted the junction of the roads so carefully, Esther could not have been sure she was even in the right area. The corner shop was now a cheap haberdasher's, the sort of place where you could buy odd balls of wool, and get Granny another crochet hook. Tying the dog up outside, Esther went in and chose a couple of lace bobbins and a pattern book. Shelves, goods, even the smells were different, and with the shutters rolled back for the day, it was impossible to tell if the cracks in them were the same. One detail had not changed, however: a door at the back of the shop, exactly where Esther had expected it to be.

10

Bob's letter did not arrive until the Monday. With shaking hands, Esther tore the printout off the roll. In delight, she found there was actually an address: Sunville Health Centres, Ogden Settlement, West Region 97213.

> My dear Tettie,
>
> Sorry I haven't written much while I've been here, but they really do keep us occupied every minute. I'm feeling a lot better, and have been told I will be allowed back to work as soon as the consultant signs me off.
>
> When I am allowed home, could you and the children come down? I've missed you so much, and it wouldn't hurt for them to have a few days off school.
>
> I finally received a letter from you, yesterday, forwarded from work. Thank you. It meant a lot to me. Am I right in thinking you still haven't got my address? I've written twice, but the personal mail channel here often gets overloaded, so perhaps my messages went astray. I long to hear from you again, and to know how the children are. Do write soon.
>
> With all my love, Bob.

For several moments Esther clutched the paper to her before sending an immediate reply. Since it might be read by others, she worded it very carefully.

My love,

We look forward so much to having you back with us. Of course we will come down to see you. The school will understand.

I'll write more fully as soon as the personal channel opens tomorrow morning. Can you let me know what you want to do about Keepers' Day presents? Shall I get something put by, or do you want to see what you can find in Centopolis?

Hurry up and come home. I miss you very much, Tettie.

With a sense of inexpressible relief, Esther sent the message on its way, and then set off to meet Number Fifty.

There seemed to be no one following her that day, but Esther took no chances. She would have bored a follower to tears, fetching her supplies from the retail centre, renewing her curfew pass, and doing various other items of business. Finally she took the short cut along the waterway, back to the dwellings.

The older woman was already waiting for her, leaning over the rail of Falklands Bridge. They greeted each other like former neighbours meeting again by chance. No one came near them. For a few moments they talked idly of family and friends, making doubly sure they were not being observed. An elderly couple passed beside them and over the bridge, but after that the bridge was deserted. It was safe for talk about more important matters: they were too far from the city buildings for directional surveillance, even with a zoom lens.

'You were five minutes late,' Fifty said.

'I'm sorry, the banking took rather a long time,' Esther replied. She said nothing about losing several minutes while she wrote to Bob. Fifty would have said personal feeling was a distraction, and reprimanded her.

'Try to keep exactly to time,' Fifty insisted. 'I don't like hanging around. Sly got your report. Everything is ready for tomorrow night. I will be joining you as the third representative.'

'And the guards?'

'Eight's seeing to security. We're receiving interesting reports from our sisters in Wales. It looks like the renegades are making a concerted attempt to form alliances. Personally I have no desire to sit at a table with any Keeper – not now, not ever – but if we are to win freedom, we may have to consort with the devil. The difficulty is knowing which devil you can work with, and which will eat you for breakfast.'

Smiling at the other woman's choice of phrase, Esther nodded. 'The girl they call Madelaine contacted me yesterday,' she said. 'The renegades' representatives wish to be allowed to enter the church first, alone. By twenty-one thirty, they'll all be in place.'

A runner was approaching. 'Will you be going to the gala opening?' Fifty asked. 'From what I hear, it should be pretty spectacular.'

'Oh yes,' Esther replied. 'I'm taking Tim and Sally. I think she's old enough now.'

For several moments they chatted about the showhouse until the runner had passed.

'How did Madelaine contact you?' Fifty asked afterwards.

'She was sitting by the children's play area near my dwellings. If I hadn't heard her speak in the shop, I would have thought she was genuinely old. Even her voice was convincing. Whoever Callum is, he has a tight hold on his group.'

'Sly wants exact details of the codes Fourteen needs, just in case we get a chance to ask for them. Can you see Fourteen before tomorrow night?'

'She walks her dog most evenings. I know where to find her.'

Fifty nodded. 'You asked to check Sly's records again,' she remarked. 'What for?'

'I managed to see Callum on Friday. Only briefly, and in very poor light, but I might just recognise him.'

In surprise Fifty turned to her. 'Did you, now?' she asked. 'Good. Very good.'

Praise from a superior officer was rare, and Esther flushed with pleasure. Afterwards, of course, came the sting.

'I hope you're not getting friendly with that neighbour of yours,' Fifty remarked.

Puzzled, Esther replied guardedly, 'I'm getting to know him a bit, inevitably. Our children are becoming friends.'

'Then find a way of putting a stop to it. Your Patroner is a decidedly odd man. His past happens after he's lived it.'

'What do you mean?'

'When Sly reported there were no entries for his school or college days, there weren't. Sly doesn't miss such things. Now we find Stephan Lahr took a leading part in a school play, and won a cup for fencing. He also won a couple of awards at college. Someone's been inventing a past for him. Unfortunately, they were a little bit too slow with their entries. Your first instincts were right, my dear. Don't start ignoring them, however nice the man may seem.'

'Thank you for your warning,' Esther replied. Her throat had gone rather tight.

'I'll arrange for you to visit Sly again,' Fifty said after a pause. 'It might be possible for you to go there after the meeting tomorrow night.'

It was time to part. If they were being watched from a distance, a longer conversation might arouse suspicion. Making the gesture of friendship, the two women went their separate ways.

That evening, Esther left Tim and Sally in the community room, under the care of the children's officer. Apologising that she had not had time to take her daily training run earlier, she promised to be back within the hour. Then she set off through the woods. Taking the main path, she ran through the trees to the wasteland just beyond the city boundary.

Fourteen was sitting on a rock, watching her dog chase delightedly after a rabbit. 'Won't catch the bloomin' thing in a million years,' she said in amused disgust.

Smiling, Esther sat beside her. They did not attempt to conceal their meeting. What could be more natural than two friends from the relaxation centre sitting together on an April evening?

'Is this just a social visit,' Fourteen asked, 'or do you need to see me?' As ever, she was nervous, inclined to clear her throat.

Esther smiled, trying to reassure her. 'There's been a new development,' she began. 'We may be able to get those codes you wanted.'

In amazement, Fourteen turned towards her. 'You must have contacts in high places,' she commented.

Refusing to be drawn, Esther watched the dog trying to worry a large stone. The stone remained remarkably unworried. 'We also need to be certain you've identified Central Control,' she replied. 'How can you be so sure?'

'I went through the expense claims.'

The answer was so simple that Esther could not help laughing.

'Several of our senior staff had put "Base to Control 32 kilometres, return." So I got on my midicycle and rode out from our office for about sixteen kilometres, in as many directions as I could. Malin Lake was exactly the right distance. Then I had a bit of help. One of the claims said, "Base to Control. Diversion via Speedway Two to avoid accident, 38 kilometres." Would you believe it? Our expenses lot insists on so much detail they give a top secret away.'

'But can you confirm that Malin Laboratories is the right building? We need something more concrete.'

'I saw our director standing in the doorway. He wouldn't visit any ordinary control. He's far too well paid.'

Again Esther could not avoid smiling. 'It sounds like you've been taking risks,' she warned.

'There's some scrub above the building. It's easy to hide there. I could do with some more powerful enhancers though.'

'We'll see you get some – only keep them well concealed.' Picking a stalk of grass, Esther chewed at it reflectively. The dog was beginning to stray into the next field, and Fourteen got up to whistle for him to come back. In walking trousers and boots she looked even more awkward than usual. Esther felt a growing respect for her. Harriet Coleman was no beauty, as she herself would be the first to admit. Her eyesight depended on thick lenses and her grace was all in her mind, but already she had served the Movement well.

'Do you need me to find out anything more?' Fourteen asked.

'What about the security system? Will it have changed since you were there?'

'I'm afraid so. I went through the requisitions last month. It looks like they've bought some of those silent, flashing light jobs. You know – the sort that are monitored on a screen in the guardhouse, with a direct link to the heavy brigade if needed. They'll have problems with rats, though.'

'Rats?'

'And foxes. Malin Lake is outside the dome. Every building outside the dome has problems with livestock. If the alarms are set too sensitively, all sorts of animals keep triggering them. We're probably safe in assuming the cellars and perimeters are kept at minimum setting.'

'You're a lovely lady,' Esther commented, laughing.

Acutely embrrassed, Fourteen laughed too. 'Do you really think we can do it?' she asked.

'Perhaps. With a little help from our friends.'

'For nearly a year, I've dreamt someone would believe me.'

'Are you sure your virus will infect other programs?'

'Certain. All the control centres are linked together. How else could the Keepers issue their weekly orders to each government office, precisely at nine hours on a Monday morning?'

Looking back towards the city, Esther smiled. 'How indeed?' she agreed. 'You'd find it much more difficult to disrupt an Eastern Union republic.'

Fourteen grinned. 'Every time you thought you'd got their system worked out, some department wouldn't follow it. Not here though. The Keepers' bureaucracy is immaculate. Their efficiency is their weakest point.'

For a few moments longer the two women sat on the rock together. 'Just in case I get chance to speak to our friends,' Esther said casually, 'tell me again what you need.'

'Just the Keepers' weekly briefing code, and the override code that goes with it. Oh, and the normal access codes, so someone is able to key in my program.'

The word 'just' amused Esther. 'And how is that someone going to be able to get into the building?' she asked.

'I don't know about that bit. Breaking and entering isn't my sort of thing. It shouldn't be too difficult.'

Shaking her head, Esther got up. 'It's not my sort of thing either,' she admitted. 'Nor is working in the dark, with alarms about to go off all round me. Still, Sly has some peculiar contacts. One of them might think it's fun. But could they key in your virus?'

'I'm not sure. I mean, it's child's play to me, but your average burglar probably hasn't much idea.'

As she ran back down the track, Esther considered what Fourteen had said. It was of course the weak point in the whole plan. She had a horrible feeling Fourteen herself would end up having to go in to Mallin Laboratories. The image of Harriet Coleman crawling under a laser bar would have been funny, if it had not been so worrying.

At the time appointed, Esther and Number Fifty were in

position at the front of Stoney Meadows church, with Sly behind it. There was no sign of movement. Only two houses overlooked the churchyard, and they were occupied by the Sheep People. On the other side of an empty paved area, a light showed in a third house. The repeated movement of a figure back and forth against the curtain suggested a mother walking a fractious baby about the room, but there too Eight had placed her guards.

It was very cold, and almost dark. A Protectorate patrol passed overhead, its searchlight making a routine check of the village. Finally it moved on to complete its beat among neighbouring settlements. After its passing, the churchyard seemed even darker. For several moments there was silence until feet approached along the pavement. Two Outlanders came through the wicket gate, and into the cemetery. A woman and a man, they walked with their arms around each other. Pausing beside one of the larger monuments, they began to kiss.

A little amused, Esther watched them. She felt almost envious. Never in her life had she stood in the dusk, kissing a man. Even when Bob was younger, he would have been too proper to behave in such a manner, and she would have been too embarrassed. Laughing softly, the couple turned away from the path and disappeared behind a memorial. There was silence once more.

For some time Esther listened, expecting to hear laughter or soft voices. The cemetery remained completely still. Smiling, she shifted her position. The first two of their guests had arrived.

The next walker was an old man, exercising an even older dog. Carefully Esther watched him pass through the wicket gate. To her disappointment, he continued on down the street, a genuine passer-by. Two minutes later footsteps returned. It was impossible to tell in the deepening night whether it was the same old man or a new arrival.

Even as Esther stared, the man disappeared. How he did it she could not imagine. The third delegate was present.

Crawling forward to Number Fifty, Esther whispered, 'They're here.'

'I saw two of them. When did the third arrive?'

'Just now.'

'They're good,' Fifty commented. 'Follow me in five minutes.' Crouching low, she made her way from gravestone to gravestone, towards the back door of the church.

As she waited, Esther had an uneasy feeling that others had arrived, unseen. The renegades had brought their own guards. They were placed around the cemetery now, armed and waiting.

Running forward carefully, Esther entered the church.

Inside the building there was complete darkness, and the smell of damp plaster. No light or sound betrayed the presence of those who had already entered. Feeling her way down the aisle, Esther went to a low wooden door at the side of the choir. Number Fifty was waiting to let her in.

The vestry was lit by a single minim lamp, which gave a faint red glow. Around it, seated at a table, were the three delegates, with Sly opposite them. Strange as the wait outside had seemed, it had been no preparation for the strangeness of the meeting itself. The people with Sly were little more than shadows. Dressed in black, not the white of the Keepers' hierarchy, they reminded Esther of monks from the olden times, their faces shrouded by hoods. When one of them looked up, she saw that even under the hood there was a mask. Like the one she had seen on the runner beside the waterway, it looked almost natural, yet had the effect of blurring features beyond recognition.

Sly nodded, indicating that the meeting could now begin. It was exactly twenty-one thirty.

The smallest of the hooded figures spoke. The voice was muffled, but it was definitely female.

'Let us agree something straight away,' the woman said. 'Neither of us dares open fire, for fear of attracting attention to ourselves.'

'Agreed,' Sly replied coldly.

'We are therefore safe from each other, and can talk in peace. I shall act as spokeswoman for our side. Who is to be yours?'

The voice was slow and formal, almost courtly in manner. Esther wondered if this was the woman she had seen kissing outside the church, or whether there were other women in the group.

Sly of course was to represent the Movement, but with orders to report to the National Committee before making any commitments.

'I am,' she replied. 'We have read your message, and our agent has reported her meetings with the man called Callum.'

'You understand why we seek co-operation?'

'Not fully. We find it difficult to understand treachery in any form.'

Esther flinched. Sly had opened the bargaining aggressively, perhaps too much so.

The reply was still measured, but cooler. 'We are as loyal to our country as you,' the spokeswoman said. 'Each of us here has vowed to serve the state and its citizens, putting their needs before our own. That is the oath of the Keepers, and therefore of their wives. Now we find we can no longer observe our oath by obeying our own hierarchy. What we are doing is not treason. It is loyalty to a higher cause.'

'Why should we care about your internal conflicts?' Sly demanded.

'Because your own liberty is at stake. As we have warned you, changes in the constitution are being planned, which will give the present Government even greater powers. An offence of seditious intent is to be introduced. It will be punishable by death. To enforce that law, the Watchers will have unlimited access to private property, and full censorship will be introduced. England will become a dictatorship, ruled by a few greedy families.'

'That's what it's been for fifty years.'

One of the other shadows looked up briefly but did not speak.

'No it hasn't,' the woman replied firmly. 'Mrs Marr, you're a sensible woman. You know the Keepers were forced into taking control. No one else could stop the fighting, and the country was tearing itself apart.'

'I'm not arguing about that,' Sly snapped. 'It's the way you've used your power.'

'What would you have done? You're old enough to remember the situation. The cities were in ruins, and the Outlands devastated. The Keepers were the only group with the knowledge to rebuild the country. Our leaders fully intended to step down when their task was complete, but it took longer than anyone imagined. Ten years became twenty, and then fifty. They achieved a great deal. You don't see people starving to death any more.'

'We don't need your propaganda,' Sly retorted. 'We can watch it at home on the audiovision.'

To Esther's surprise, the old woman rose as if to walk out on the discussions. Her anger could be a deliberate pose. She was cunning enough for even such dangerous tactics, but to Esther her emotion seemed real rather than feigned. The renegade delegate had used the name 'Mrs Marr'. If that were indeed Sly's name, whatever she had done in the past must also be known. It would hardly be surprising if for once Sly's famed coolness had deserted her.

'I'm not in favour of propaganda, nor am I proud of everything we've done,' the spokeswoman replied, taking a more concilliatory tone. 'The end cannot justify the means. Nor can leaders assume that everyone who disagrees with them is mad or wicked.'

'You admit that?' Sly asked, pausing.

'Of course. But when civil war is a recent memory, fear of its return makes rulers do unjustifiable things.'

There was silence for several seconds. Slowly Sly sat down again. She looked very old and very tired. 'What are your proposals?' she asked.

Watching the turn of the spokeswoman's head, Esther suspected that the figure on her right was a more senior delegate, to whom she must defer. Though there was no spoken reply, the woman seemed satisfied she could continue.

'Our position is this,' she said. 'Firstly, as Dissidents ourselves, we need to establish links with other well-organised rebel groups. Your Movement interests us particularly. You have a nationwide structure and excellent discipline and training. You're also virtually invisible. Who notices a woman pushing a pram? If you'll join with us, we'll provide you with inside knowledge and financial support—'

'Financial support?'

'We're none of us poor. Our privileges have enabled us to amass personal wealth and maintain it.'

'You're willing to spend your own money?' Sly asked again. That fact, above all, seemed to convince her of the importance of what was being offered.

'What's the point of keeping a fortune to pass on to your sons, if those sons are too corrupt or frightened to benefit? Our money will be useful to buy arms and equipment.'

Fifty could not remain silent any longer. 'You won't fight against your own Order,' she said in derision.

'When a man's leg becomes infected, he goes to the doctor, though he knows the remedy may be amputation. Only the fool pretends nothing is wrong. We are not fools. If our Order must be disbanded for the good of the country, then so be it.'

'What if the rebels turn on you too?' Sly asked quietly.

For the first time the senior delegate spoke. 'Then our fate will be in God's hands,' he said.

'Your friends have declared God is a myth,' Fifty pointed out.

'If the word offends you, let us say we hope luck will be with us. What happens to us is not particularly important. None of us is, in the larger scheme of things. What does matter is that someone is found to take over from us, and prevent the country sinking into civil war again. We need your advice on that. We know the rebel groups. Who should we approach to take over power?'

The question was so innocent that Esther almost smiled.

Sly shook her head. 'It can't be done that way,' she insisted. 'If there's a vacuum, even for a few days, the rebel groups will start fighting amongst themselves. Everyone believes they should rule. There has to be continuity.'

'How are we to be sure you're not tricking us – trying to find out what our plans are?' Fifty asked. 'What guarantees do we have?'

It was becoming obvious to Esther that Fifty disagreed with the way Sly was conducting the negotiations. Her impatience could cause trouble.

'None at all,' the spokeswoman replied. 'Just as you can give us none in return. That's why we've had to perform this charade.' With a gesture of her hand, she included the robes, the darkened church, the whole paraphernalia of secrecy. 'Your strength is that we fear discovery even more than you. The Keepers are harshest on their own.'

'We appreciate the dangers you face,' Sly acknowledged. 'That's why we would like to know why you decided to approach us now. New legislation on its own wouldn't make you willing to risk death, and a particularly painful death for your men. What brought each of you here?'

There was a pause. Sly's question seemed unlikely to receive a reply.

'When a new member joins us, we always seek the personal reason behind their decision,' she persisted. 'Idealism or politics is never enough on its own. There has to be some personal anger or injustice before a sensible, law-abiding citizen will decide to become a rebel. What's yours? Tell us, each in turn, then we may believe your proposals.'

Sly might have lost her control for a few minutes, but she was back on form now. On what the delegates said, and Esther's assessment of their emotions as they spoke, a whole revolution could depend. It was a heavy responsibility. Watching the figures before her very carefully, Esther prepared to judge.

The spokeswoman answered first. 'I have two sons,' she said. 'Three months ago my eldest reached the age of initiation. He has scarcely slept a full night since. He used to be a careless, untidy sort of boy. Now he grows thinner and more silent every day. I can't even ask him what's wrong. We both know he daren't break his vow of silence, and the punishment if he does. His spirit is dying before my eyes, and neither I nor his sister can do anything to help him. One day soon, he will take his own life, just as his cousin did two years ago.' As she spoke, the woman's grief was so real that Esther's own eyes hurt with it. No one else moved. The church was silent and dark, except for the rustle of leaves against the door. 'I don't want to lose my youngest too,' the woman added suddenly. 'I want to get rid of the whole dreadful system before his time comes.'

There was silence for several seconds. 'And your reason?' Sly asked the second figure.

'My reason also has to do with family,' he said. There was a faint clipped accent to his speech which Esther found hard to place. 'Sometimes youth has a clearer vision than experience. It took me until middle age to see what I must do, but my eldest son saw it at the age of fourteen.' There was a long pause, while the man considered how much he should say. 'To understand what courage his stand has involved, you'd have to know him and what he has overcome. He shamed his brother as well as me.'

Again, Esther was aware of family affection and closeness. Whatever the relationship between father and son, it was deep.

Everyone waited for the third figure to speak. Until then, there had been no indication whether it was male or famale.

'And you?' Sly prompted.

'My reasons are – more philosophical, I suppose.' The voice was also male, but younger and drier, the tone of an academic. 'So far I've suffered little personally.' Clearly it was difficult for the man to explain his reasons. 'But I can't accept what's happening to others, or to my country. It's wrong, immoral, even if such a word is out of fashion. I've thought it all through very carefully. I don't particularly want to be a hero, much less a martyr. I'm not the sort. But there is such a thing as honesty.' He reminded Esther very much of Fourteen, with her love of truth.

'Are we lying to you?' the older man asked Esther unexpectedly.

Startled, Esther looked up. 'How should I know?' she asked.

'Because you know what goes on in people's minds.'

'I have never claimed to be able to read people's thoughts.'

'But you can read their emotions. Most of us do it as children. Gradually we find our own pain is enough, and deaden our response. You have kept your ability, like your mother, but in your case it has been heightened and controlled. Tell your colleagues whether you believe us. That's what they'll ask you afterwards, and why we've just had to go through this performance. Have we come to trick you?'

Both sides were waiting for Esther's reply.

'It's impossible to be certain after such a short time,' Esther insisted, flushing slightly. 'I'm not conscious of any threat from you, or of any falsehood. I am conscious of hatred and anger. You hate the most,' she added, turning towards the woman. 'Your colleagues are beginning to despair. They don't really believe this meeting will achieve anything, but they're willing to give it a try. Beyond that, I can't say.'

There was a long pause. Fifty moved her hand in irritation. She was not persuaded by such vague evidence as anecdotes, or sympathy.

'That will do for me,' Sly announced. 'I've never known Forty-Eight wrong on such matters. My report to our National Committee will recommend co-operation.'

In surprise, the spokeswoman turned towards Sly. 'You'll work with us?' she asked. 'You've always been one of our harshest critics.'

'If necessary I'll fight fire with fire – a small dose of the disease to beat the whole infection.'

'And you?'

Fifty sat stubbornly unconvinced. 'Come up with a plan that makes sense, and I'll consider it,' she said. 'But don't expect me to trust you. I've learnt what trusting our Keepers can do.'

'Trust isn't the issue,' the older man replied. 'Help is what we need, and quickly. Whatever action we take, it has to be before the Legislature puts forward the new bill. When it's debated, every male Keeper will have to decide whether or not to accept what's happening. If there's a strong rebellion already established, the waverers will join us. If there isn't, they'll keep their heads down and vote to save their skins.'

'We need a trigger,' the young man added. 'Something that will make the camel kick up its heels and throw its bundle off.'

'I think we can supply that,' Sly replied drily. 'Could you get us the Keepers' weekly briefing and override codes?'

'Why would you want such things?'

'One of our members has had an idea.'

'Really?' The word was drawn into a long reflective pause. 'Yes. It's an obvious weakness. We've identified it ourselves, but we've been unable to find a central control that isn't too heavily protected for us to gain access. Nor do we have an informant with sufficient knowledge to do the actual programming. Except myself, and I'd be recognised. Data processing and maintenance duties are carefully divided, so that no one person ever sees the whole.'

'Someone must run it all,' Esther commented.

'In effect, the system runs itself. Its an ideal situation. You or I might feel bad about sending someone to a psychiatric institution or parting a mother from her children, but a machine doesn't.'

'You mean you don't know who's at the top yourselves?'

The older man shook his head. 'Our meetings are addressed by robed and masked men. We receive our instructions from machines. Even as we rise up the ranks, we only know the segment to which we belong. As an Order, we're so steeped in secrecy, we don't know our own leadership. We would have thrown them out ourselves if we did.'

'Get us those codes, and someone with a knowledge of alarms, and we might bring the whole rotten system down,' Sly promised.

'You know where Northern Control is?'

In answer Esther nodded. She could feel the young man's excitement.

'I think this has been a very successful meeting,' the woman said. 'We will of course have to discuss your proposals amongst ourselves.'

'And we will have to consult our National Committee.'

'Quite.' Rising, the senior delegate extended a gloved hand.

'From now on, I shall take over negotiations,' the spokeswoman said. 'Until the final strike, our menfolk will have to take very little part in proceedings. They run a much greater risk than we women do. For years our fathers and brothers have protected us. Now we must protect them. You have no objection to us using the Sheep People as a channel?'

'None at all,' Sly replied.

The whole meeting rose, preparing for departure in the order that had been agreed.

'Would it be possible for your liaison to stay behind for a few minutes?' the spokeswoman asked unexpectedly. 'One of our agents wishes to speak to her in private.'

In surprise, Esther glanced up. 'Who?' she asked.

'Your original contact. I believe he has some information for you of a private nature.'

'I'm not risking any of my members alone,' Sly insisted.

'I've already had to meet with Callum twice on my own,' Esther reminded her. 'I'm not so afraid of him as I was.' She dropped her voice. 'It may be to do with my husband. Please let me see him. You can make sure one of the guards is near enough to help if I call.'

Reluctantly Sly agreed. 'Any trouble and you run,' she warned.

To Esther's surprise, the spokeswoman lingered as she passed on her way out. 'You have no need to fear Callum,' she whispered. 'He would never hurt a friend. Not deliberately.'

In bewilderment Esther stood in the darkened vestry, watching as the hooded figures left.

For a few minutes those left in the church waited in silence.

'They have us!' Sly whispered hoarsely. 'Tied up in little bows.'

Fifty was inclined to hurt pride. 'Bloody patronising!' she began. 'You'd think the woman was a bleeding royal.'

'She probably is. There's still plenty of the old king's family around.'

'But why tell them so much if you don't trust them?' Esther whispered.

'Because we had no choice. If they know my name, they know what I have been. They know our links with the Sheep People, even that you're a sympath. Unless we co-operate with them, they'll hand us over to their hierarchy. It would be a smart move on their side. Give proof of their loyalty and silence us. Lord! It was subtly done. Just a well placed "Mrs Marr".'

'Does it matter whether we were coerced,' Esther persisted. 'So long as we get what we want?'

At last Sly smiled her knowing smile. 'No, child, it doesn't,' she agreed. 'We need them, and they need us. There must be assurances for the future, though. We don't want to swap one tyranny for another.'

The old woman crossed to the side of the vestry. A brass plaque was set into the wall, reflecting the light. 'Flight Lieutenant John Heptonstall,' Sly read aloud. 'Killed in action, 14 April 1942, aged 23.' Thoughtfully she stood beside the plaque. 'What do you reckon, John?' she asked. 'Which is the better way? You fought your war in the air, boxed up in your ridiculous little planes. We fight in the dark, trading fears with fears. Yours is the noblest, but we've had to survive three times as long.'

Walking briskly back to the table, she waved her hand authoritatively. 'Come on,' she ordered. 'Let's cover our tracks. Forty-Eight, you will be coming back with me for an hour or so. Transport is arranged.'

Through the open door, Esther saw a shadow move in the main part of the church. 'May I go and see what Callum wants?' she asked.

Sighing impatiently, Sly nodded. 'Fifty and I will finish in here, and go out the back way,' she said. 'Join us at the meeting point outside as soon as possible. And take care. Don't start imagining the man is a friend. A Keeper has no friends.'

11

After the minim light, the darkness in the church was so thick Esther felt she could almost hold it in her hand. At first she could not make out where Callum had gone. Then she sensed him sitting on one of the pews towards the front.

Her mouth dry with fear, Esther went towards him. Sly and Fifty came out of the vestry and passed down the side of the choir, and out into the night.

'What have you to tell me?' Esther asked. A feeling of foreboding was beginning to make her skin go cold.

'Sit down. Please.' Once again there was that gentle Scots accent, matched now by a gentleness of tone. 'I won't hurt you. I simply want to talk to you.'

Hesitantly Esther did as the voice asked. She could not see him but his presence was tangible to her, quiet and concerned, almost kind. 'What shall I call you?' he asked. 'It's dangerous for me to use your real name.'

'In the Movement I'm known as Forty-Eight.'

'I don't like calling a person by a number. In my group we use code names. Choose one for me to use for you.'

Esther paused. 'Call me Tess if you like,' she invited. 'It was my mother's name for me when I was little.'

'All right, Tess. When we last met, you asked me to give you my hand, and I refused. Give it to me now.'

The sense of foreboding was increasing. The man had bad

news to give her and did not quite know where to begin. Reluctantly Esther put out her hand, and he took it.

'What is it you have to tell me?' she repeated. 'Is it about Bob?'

'He died last night.'

'But he can't have. I got a letter from him in the morning. You promised me I would, and I did . . .'

'That was written the day before. I'm so sorry.'

In fury Esther got up and tried to leave, but Callum held her hand, keeping her there.

'Sorry?' she demanded, raising her voice. 'Sorry? You killed him. You or your sort!'

'Your husband died of natural causes. His heart failed. You must believe me.'

'Oh yes,' Esther mocked. 'He died naturally. Like my mother did.'

Since the man would not let her go, Esther sat again beside him. It occurred to her that she could cry out, and he would have to release her, but she could not face the questions that would follow. In silence she sat beside him, hard with anger and pain.

'Tess, believe me,' Callum pleaded. 'For once, what you'll be told is true. You'll cause yourself unnecessary pain by thinking anything else. That's why I wanted to tell you myself. So that you wouldn't persecute yourself.'

'How can I believe you?'

'Because I've had the report checked and cross-checked. Your husband had a blockage in the left ventricle of his heart. It must have been there quite a while. He probably felt occasional pain, but didn't like to worry you. They spotted the problem at the medical when he was admitted to the centre, and were making arrangements for surgery. That's why they kept him there for so long. He was cleared of any mental instability within days.'

Now that he had told her, Callum let her hand go. There

was nothing to stop Esther leaving, but she could not move. Pushing her fist against her mouth, she held back the howl that rose in her throat.

'Come here,' Callum said softly. 'Grieve a little. You can't go out in this state.'

It was as if they had known each other for years. Gently Callum put his arm around her shoulder and drew her to him, so that she could cry. For several minutes they sat close. There was nothing improper or threatening in his manner. He held her as a friend would, giving comfort.

Becoming a little calmer, Esther tried to understand what Callum had told her. 'What exactly happened?' she asked. 'If you know, tell me.'

'Your husband collapsed in the refectory yesterday evening. The staff were very upset. There are decent people left in the world still, and Bob was well liked. You've lost a good man, but no one could have prevented it. If there's any blame, it lies with the system that put him under such stress, not with any individual.'

There was nothing appropriate Esther could say. 'Thank you for taking the trouble to explain,' she said inadequately.

'If I could change things I would. I was so pleased with myself. I thought that for once I'd been able to use my influence to help someone.'

'Have you been waiting all night to see me?'

'I was outside, keeping guard.'

The cloth of Callum's jacket was rough against her cheek, and Esther sat up. 'I'll go now,' she said. 'Sly will be waiting for me.'

They both rose from the pew and stood together awkwardly. By now Esther's eyes had become more used to the dark. She could see a man's shape, not cloaked like his colleagues, but in some kind of battlegear, and wearing a loose face mask. 'I don't like you in that uniform,' she said, and realised it was an absurd thing to say.

'I'm not happy in it myself, but needs must.'

Silently Esther looked for her handkerchief. 'I'm grateful to you for warning me,' she said. 'It'll make it easier to cope with the children when the official notice arrives.'

'You mustn't give any sign that you know until you receive it. If you do, you'll arouse suspicion, and do me a lot of harm.'

'Thank you for taking such a risk,' Esther repeated. 'You've been very kind, and I don't for the life of me know why.'

'We're on the same side. I don't need any other reason.'

Turning, Esther walked unsteadily back down the aisle and out of the church.

'What did Callum want?' Sly demanded at once.

'To tell me my husband is dead.'

Suspiciously Sly considered Esther's expression. 'Why should he know about your husband?' she asked.

'Our Keepers know a great deal,' Esther replied guardedly.

She knew Sly was not convinced, suspecting Esther of bringing her personal affairs into her work, but the old woman said no more. As the personal transport unit glided through the darkness, they sat together in silence.

'How did your husband die?' Sly asked at last.

'Of heart failure.'

'Do you believe that?'

'I think Callum was telling me the truth. I felt he was.'

'At least he had the decency to tell you, if decency it was.'

That was the only conversation they had on the matter. Sly expressed no sympathy, and Esther asked none. It was not that she felt no grief. A dull fury was beginning to burn within her. Some day there would be time to mourn for her husband, and her mother, for all those who had died or quietly vanished. Sly was right, however. There was no time for personal emotion now. There was business to be done, and urgent business at that.

The transport took them as near to Hunter's Farm as was safe. After that, they walked. With a skilled guide, the light of early dawn was sufficient for them to find the track. Despite her age, Sly walked strongly, only once pausing for breath as they climbed the ridge. She slipped once or twice as they picked their way down the other side, but then so did Esther. In such poor light, the walking was difficult.

As soon as they reached the farm, Sly took Esther straight upstairs. 'Let's go and see if you can recognise Callum,' she said. 'If we could identify him, we'd stand a good chance of knowing the others. Did you see any more of him tonight?'

'No, only his figure in the darkness, and that he was wearing uniform. He told me himself he was one of the guards outside. That suggests he's an active, possibly a fighter. Look for someone with a military background.'

While Esther sat on the bed the old woman called up her records. A file marked 'JM Con 2' appeared. Carefully Sly went through each of the families suspected of being Keepers who had had connections with Esther's mother. 'Stop me if you see anything interesting,' she instructed.

At the fourth family, Esther hesitated. One photoline image seemed vaguely familiar. 'Mary Lander' she read, 'Born 2147.'

'Stop there,' she asked Sly. 'That woman reminds me of someone.'

'Callum?'

'No. He's much darker. Her face seems familiar, all the same.'

The image dated from 2178, and by now Mary Lander would be sixty-two. She would bear little likeness to the attractive young woman of Sly's records. 'Weren't the Landers among your faceless men?' Esther recalled.

'They were indeed. I've been doing some homework since you came last.'

Sly's new data came on view: 'Burgess Frederik Lander, b. 2175. Parents John and Mary Lander (née ?). Educ. Birmingham College of Technocracy (Midopolis). Employed Sun Electronics 2196. Present whereabouts and emp. not known.'

There was a photoline image now too, though it dated from Lander's days at college.

For a long time Esther stared at Burgess Lander's face. It too seemed vaguely familiar.

'Could he be Callum?' Sly persisted.

'No. The nose isn't straight enough. I know the limp and the accent could be assumed, but I definitely saw Callum's profile outlined against the light. He wasn't expecting me to see him, so he didn't have time to mask himself or cover his hair.'

'I'd be worried if it was one of the Landers making contact with us,' Sly admitted. 'We've been watching the family for a while. Both Burgess and Peter seem to have vanished. Our last sighting of Peter was five years ago. Burgess hasn't been seen for even longer. It's also odd that we know nothing about the mother.'

Continuing on through the four families, Esther found nothing else of interest. None of the images fitted her memory of the man who had called himself Callum.

'Let's look at the others then,' Sly suggested.

Slowly they analysed every suspected Keeper they had on file, the computer extrapolating from the information given to produce profiles from full face, darkened outlines, anything that might assist.

'It's no use,' Esther admitted in disappointment. 'I saw the man so briefly. If you could get more up-to-date images, I'd stand a better chance. Let's go back to the notes you have on my mother's contacts. Something there might help.'

The four families were displayed again: Saunders, Miniott, Jacobsen and Lander.

'The Saunders interest us most,' Sly said, bringing up the detailed file. 'They're clearly on the losing side of something. There have been four deaths in the family within the last five months.'

Fascinated, Esther watched as the old woman brought up

diagrams of the family relationships she had traced. In the Saunders family, the wife had died of leukaemia, a sister had suffered an accident, and two cousins had mysteriously been taken ill, dying within weeks of each other.

'When the renegades wrote of being "picked off one by one" they weren't exaggerating,' Sly remarked. 'Look at the Jacobsens too.'

In that family a father and son had died recently. A chilling pattern was emerging, of an opposition party being ruthlessly eliminated. Not even the children were being spared.

'And my mother's other friends?' Esther asked quietly. 'What about the Miniotts?'

'They seem to have kept out of trouble, like the Landers.'

'What's their connection with my mother?'

'When your father repudiated Jacki, Andrew Miniott commissioned her to paint a portrait of his wife and invited her to stay at his home. But for him, your mother would have had nowhere to live. I've always wondered how much she and Joanna Miniott talked to each other while that picture was being painted. Two women together, both with an interest in art.'

Esther smiled in surprise. 'How do you know Mrs Miniott was interested in art?' she asked.

'It's all recorded in my files. Every detail we obtain is stored here.'

Bringing up a file headed 'JM : AM1', Sly paused. As she did so, Esther could sense a change in the old woman's manner. Sly could keep her emotions hidden even from a sympath, but she could not conceal them completely. Her interest in this particular family was stronger than it had been for the others, and could be of a personal nature.

A whole page of data on Andrew Miniott appeared: biographical details, residence, education. 'This one's a bit of an oddity,' Sly continued. 'The Keepers normally vote through designated mouthpieces. They don't often become members of Parliament themselves. Miniott was never very much in the public eye, but he had a lot of influence. We know he voted against the "Fortress England" legislation, and that he kept money in France, despite the Durham directive. Mind you, he had personal reasons for doing that. His mother was French. He's a fish farmer now. Quite a comedown, though profitable, we gather.'

'What makes you so sure the man's a Keeper?' Esther asked. 'He sounds an independent sort.'

'Precisely. I doubt very much if he would have survived if he weren't a Keeper. Nor would his father. Now there was a nasty piece of work if ever there was one. If Andrew's sons are anything like their grandfather, they're doubly dangerous. Have a look at what we have on them.'

The invitation was purely rhetorical. There was almost no data at all on Simon and Carl Miniott.

For Carl, the entry read, 'B. 2177, Old Town, Centop. Educ. State School of Agricultural Science. Married 2060. Believed farming in NW Protectorate.' His brother's entry contained even less: 'Simon Miniott: b. 2183. Current whereabouts not known. Believed to have quarrelled with father and left home.'

'As faceless as the Landers,' Esther remarked. 'It does sound ominous.'

Pausing, she considered how much she dare question the old woman.

'I remember my father talking about John Miniott. He owned one of the big estates near us. People spoke well of him. He gave a lot of money to projects in the Outlands.'

Sly shut down the Miniott file impatiently. 'John Miniott was a hypocrite of the first order,' she retorted. 'Public benefactor, leading figure in the community . . . and a crawling bit of vermin in his private life.'

'Why do you say that?'

'He found himself a pretty young artist in Paris and stayed with her, safe and sound while the rest of us fought it out here. He had three children by her while he was at it. Then he abandoned the woman and returned to England. Within three years, he'd married a respectable English girl and forcibly adopted the two boys, so that he would have a male heir. That's the sort of power a Keeper has. And they dare to preach the good of the state to the rest of us!'

Snorting derisively, Sly moved on to the Jacobsen entries. 'Did your father ever tell you any of that?' she asked.

'No,' Esther admitted. 'But then, he wouldn't have known.'

They studied the Jacobsen entries together. 'Joseph and Minta Jacobsen are well into their fifties,' Sly remarked. 'From your description, that's too old. Their half-sister Indra is only in her late thirties, though. You're sure this Callum isn't a woman?'

'I wouldn't have thought so.' Pausing, Esther considered the suggestion. 'Though I'm not sure of anything any more,' she added. 'It's an interesting possibility. I'll give it some thought.'

Sly entered a question mark beside the name. She trusted nothing to memory, not because her memory was failing, but in case she was arrested suddenly, or fell ill. Everything she knew or suspected was recorded. No one but Numbers Eight and Fifty were able to access her entries, but to Esther there seemed to be an element of risk in recording anything. It was not her place to query Sly's methods, however; nor would she have dared to do so.

'Now I want to show you something very precious,' Sly continued. A faded vidmat film came on screen. 'This transmission was made twenty-eight years ago, by the daughter of a Keeper who was sympathetic to us. The quality's poor, but it's all we have.'

As Sly had warned, the transmission had clearly been sent by an amateur and in secret, from a height, perhaps from a balcony. The first few seconds were filled by nothing but ceiling. Ornately gilded, it suggested a restored Victorian hall or council chamber. Then the lens panned down to a long table at the far end of the room. Around three of its sides were seated twelve figures, facing towards the front, as if waiting to interview someone. Wearing white cloaks with hoods, they were unrecognisable, yet under their hoods they seemed also to be wearing an opaque mask. While the viewer was aware there was a face behind it, the features were blank.

'How men do love to dress up!' Esther commented.

Sly smiled. 'I couldn't have put it better myself,' she agreed. 'The trouble is, this isn't play. Watch the rest more closely.'

A door to the right opened, and three more figures entered. The central one was without a mask, the hood of his cloak dropped back so that his face and hair were visible. Silently he was brought before the waiting figures.

'Name?' a voice demanded from the table.

The sound quality was even poorer than the picture, and the reply was barely audible. It sounded like 'Paul Hawton' but it could have been Thornton or some similar name.

'Rank?'

'Member of the ancient Order of Keepers, First Circle, second quarter.'

'Charge?'

'That on the night of 17 April 2181, I did breach the vows I made—'

The rest of the reply was lost.

'How do you plead?'

'Guilty.'

Sly enhanced the picture, bringing forward the face of the accused. He was young, scarcely in his twenties, with curly hair that made him look even younger. Though he tried to stand with dignity, he was shivering. Fear stretched the skin across his face. Beads of sweat had formed above his upper lip. It was his eyes that troubled Esther most. They reminded her of the eyes of a cat she had once had to take for destruction. When poor Midge looked from her cage, there had been the same terified pleading in her expression.

'What is the wish of the court? Let each member state his verdict in turn.'

The film came to an abrupt end. With a sense of shock, Esther stared at the blank screen. 'What happened then?' she asked.

'I have no idea.' Sighing, Sly returned the film to zero. 'Our informant had to cease transmitting. We tried to trace the young man, but he simply vanished.'

Again she played the film, in slow motion this time, enhancing each of the seated figures in turn, and then their prisoner. This time Esther could see that there was different-coloured braiding around the edges of the hoods: black for what appeared to be the senior judge, red for the other seated figures, and blue for the two guards. The young man's hood was marked with blue too, though set back off his head. Held in still-frame, his fear was terrible to see.

'Poor young man,' Sly said quietly. 'I've often thought of him. He knew he was about to die. You can see it all over his face. This is what the Keepers do to their own if they step out of line. And this is what Callum and his friends are risking. Now you know why I'm so suspicious of them. A Keeper is never released from his duty of silence. Even on his deathbed he must observe it or bring punishment down on his family. Would you take such a risk – even for liberty?'

'What would you do if you found yourself in their position?'

'Try and change the system from the inside.'

'And if you've tried, and failed? What then?'

Sly shook her head. 'I've asked myself that a hundred times,' she admitted. 'The three we met tonight must never stop asking it. Looked at from one point of view, they're traitors. From another, they're taking the only option left open to them.' Beginning to shut down the program, Sly prepared to leave.

'The young man in the film referred to "The Ancient Order",' Esther remarked. 'It was in Callum's message too. When did the Keepers first appear?'

'Who can say? Some say they're descended from the Templars. Personally I doubt it, though there may be some link. We've found possible references to Keepers in the eighteenth and nineteenth centuries, but even then it's hard to be certain. All we know for sure is that they infiltrated the government during the Troubles, and then fought on the side of the South in the civil war. When the South took over the rest of the country, the Keepers quietly took power over it. Still, you know all that. It's history.'

The young man's face was still held on the screen. In pity, Esther considered his expression again. 'My father believed what the Keepers did was right,' she said thoughtfully. 'At least he did when I was a child. He used to argue that but for them, we'd still be fighting amongst ourselves, scratching a bare existence from the land, without science or medicine, or learning. I usually took my mother's side, but now I can see that Dad had a point.'

'Power corrupts. Absolute power corrupts absolutely,' Sly reminded her. 'It's one of the oldest proverbs there is, but it remains true. The Keepers may have saved the country, but now the country needs saving from them.'

Shutting down the console, Sly got up.

'What happened to the woman who took the film?' Esther asked.

'She worked with us for almost a year. We owe most of our knowledge of the Keepers' rituals and structures to her. Then we had to get her out of the country.' Sighing, Sly paused. 'That's been one of our failures,' she admitted. 'We ought to have been able to get more of their women to join us. Still, when it's your husband and sons – and you have privileges and power through them . . .' The sentence remained unfinished.

12

When the moment came, Esther needed to say nothing. Her son's eyes filled with tears before she spoke, and running to his bedroom, he slammed the door.

For a year or so Esther had suspected Tim had inherited her gift. Now she knew for sure. In some strange way, it had passed down to a third generation. When her mother was young no one believed such abilities existed. Jacki Marshall understood. That was all people said.

Closing her eyes, Esther tried to recall her mother's face. The image that came was an old one, fixed in Esther's childhood: a dark-haired woman, obviously not fully English, nor at home in a respectable marriage to a senior army officer, yet always laughing, always with a game to play. As for her paintings – even as a child Esther had known they were special. Sometimes she used to feel jealous. Then her mother would sense her emotion and put her arm round her. They never needed words. Neither of them ever challenged the fact. If they thought of it at all, they assumed all mothers and daughters were the same.

Now Esther and her son had discovered they did not need words either. Such a gift was a double-edged blessing that cut the holder's peace as well as the pretences of others. Tim would have to be taught now to live with the constant invasion of his soul, the noise of other people's emotions impinging on him. He must also learn how to hide his ability from outside eyes. If it became known that he was a sympath, both Watchers and rebel groups would want to use him in their service. Until he was thirteen or fourteen Esther could train him. Her Maestra's teachings were still vivid in her mind. Ultimately, however, she would have to pass him over to others. The thought brought tears to her eyes.

For the moment, more mundane matters must be considered. With her husband's death, Esther was now the owner of two properties, but unable to afford to maintain both. With very little hesitation, she decided to stay in Nortown. Both children were happy there. She herself did not want to settle back into the mediocrity of fourth-strata Centopolis life.

Nor would she be allowed to do so, Esther realised. As the liaison between the Movement and the renegades, she knew far too much to be allowed to leave Nortown. The South would take her back into its ranks, but that would not be sufficient guarantee for Sly. The old woman mistrusted Southerners still.

She cared even less for the personal feelings of her staff. The renegades' proposals were to have been sent to the National Committee by courier link, but Sly had never been happy with that idea. The fewer people who knew about the renegades' approaches the better, she had argued. As soon as Esther asked to be allowed to go down to Centopolis, Sly smiled in satisfaction. Esther could take the North's report in person.

Knowing Sly too well to argue, Esther had had no choice but to agree, but she felt angry and used. She was not even to be allowed to arrange her husband's committal, without having to carry vital information with her. Yet seen from Sly's point of view, the change of plan was sensible. Who noticed a woman with two children? Even if Esther were stopped for any reason, she would have the best excuse ever. Sly was as shrewd as she was merciless.

As her son slowly fell asleep in her arms, Esther listened to his breathing. Rebellion was a cumbersome vehicle to get moving, but once pushed over an incline, it began to gather momentum of its own accord. She must move the children to a safer place, without arousing suspicion. Bob's mother would have them willingly, but she was getting too old. Perhaps her own father might forget their past bitternesses, for the sake of his grandchildren.

Getting up quietly, Esther pulled on her oversuit. She suddenly wanted to speak to her father, not just for the sake of her children's safety, but out of love for him. Earlier in the evening she had called to tell him the news, but that had been as a duty. Now she wanted to speak to him as a friend.

It took some time for Colonel Marshall to answer. Still dressed in his duty uniform, he had apparently been working late, and had not heard the bleeper. Disciplined as ever, his expression none the less betrayed his surprise that Esther should call again.

'Are you all right, my dear?' he asked. 'Not grieving too much?'

'I just wanted to talk to you.'

'You're very welcome. How are you coping? Have you told Tim yet?'

'I didn't need to tell him.'

Colonel Marshall raised one eyebrow. 'You may have a problem there,' he remarked.

'I think I have.'

They avoided speaking directly, out of habit as much as fear that they were being observed.

'How did you deal with it?' Esther asked.

'I don't know that I ever did. It used to annoy me intensely sometimes. I felt I had no privacy.'

'That's really why I rang. To say I was sorry.'

'What on earth for?'

'For all the quarrels.'

'I doubt if they were all your fault. Army life isn't right for a girl without a mother.'

There was an awkward pause. With a rush of regret Esther watched her father. He was beginning to age, but still sat firm and straight.

'Dad—' she began.

'What?'

'I'm glad you chose Bob.'

'You didn't say that at the time.'

'No, but I came to love him. He was a good man, and you were right about me needing the sort of stability he could give.'

'It's a pity he wasn't younger, but youth and good looks rarely go with stability. When you've finished grieving, go out and find someone of your own choice.'

'I've grown up, Dad. I don't need a man to keep me steady.'

'But you need love. Your temptation now will be to grow too hard.'

Esther smiled. It was infuriating to have a father who was always right.

'Is there anything I can do? Anything you need?' he asked.

'I could do with a break. Could I bring the children down some time?'

'You know you can.'

Esther nodded her thanks. 'We'll fix a date at a more sensible hour,' she said. 'Goodnight for now.'

'Tettie?'

'Yes?'

'I don't know what provoked this call, but I'm glad you made it.'

As the image faded, Esther sat watching the screen. Something good had come out of Bob's death. It had softened her and made her father more ready to be compassionate. Going back to her room, she slipped into bed beside her son.

For a little while longer she considered what to do. Sly's

message could wait another day. That much Esther would insist. However soothed by the Department of Morticians, their father's committal would not be pleasant for two young children. To deny Tim and Sally the gala at the new showhouse would be doubly unfair. She would not travel down to Centopolis until Sunday. Arrangements could be made by visiphone and message transfer until then.

The bereavement counsellor called the next morning. He brought Esther the standard posy of dried flowers and official confirmation of Bob's death. A model of compassionate bureaucracy, the letter was beautifully handwritten, and enclosed Esther's pension statement. Since Bob had been cleared of all seditious activity, her rights would be honoured. The authorities were meticulous in their justice.

A wave of anger passed over Esther's mind and she had to turn away to hide her expression. The counsellor saw her movement. He was patient but firm. Grief was understandable but a dangerous pleasure, he warned. One must recognise that bereavement had its positive side. It reminded the living that they were still able to enjoy life's pleasures. That was why people bought the bereaved gifts, not just in consolation, but in celebration that they had outlived their loved ones.

Politely Esther nodded, and wished the man at the bottom of a very deep pit.

The counsellor coughed discreetly and got out a memo pad. As Esther was aware, he said, the state would be providing gifts for her children, to ensure that they retained happy associations with their father's death day. Esther must name what Tim and Sally most desired, within a given figure of course. (Unfortunately, the budget had been cut slightly this year.)

Having had time to consider the request already, Esther could give a prompt reply: a transmigrator for Sally and a new soccer strip for Tim.

'I'm taking them to the opening of the new showhouse,' she added. 'I thought that would make a nice treat too.'

'Excellent,' the counsellor enthused. 'I'm sure it will be a treat to remember.'

Taking Esther's hand in a limp grasp, he reminded her not to indulge her grief too long, or too deeply, and took his leave.

After he had gone, Esther stood alone in the hallway, with her fists clenched in anger. 'I'll pay them back, my love!' she said aloud. Afterwards, she found her fingernails had made red marks in the palms of her hands.

By early morning on the Saturday, crowds were milling around the new showhouse. All cross-city transport had been discontinued, so that every available people mover could be used to bring the crowds into the centre of the dome, and then back to the suburbs at the end of the performances. Since disappointed crowds were always a risk to public order, the other three showhouses had been ordered to put on special productions, to cater for those unable to get into the new one. But even the best of these could only be second best, and there was a strong police presence to remind everyone of the power of the state, should they allow their disappointment to overmaster their reason.

As Esther walked past the queues snaking round the building, the full worth of Stephan Lahr's gift became apparent. A polite usherette guided her to the door marked 'PRIVILEGED'. As soon as she entered, she was directed to a table, where refreshments and free programme cassettes were available. There was no waiting, and no rude officials. An elderly man with a sober expression and a platoon of chins nodded to Esther, obviously assuming he should know her. Esther nodded back, hoping Sally would not choose that moment to tip her drink all over her.

Esther need not have worried. Both children were entranced. After the austerity of Moss Edge, Showhouse Four was a glimpse of another world. Built to seat 25,000 in tier upon tier of seating, the new showhouse was a triumph of modern architecture. Its suspended canopy created a vast enclosed space without losing a sense of human scale. Though the strata were as usual separated, there was no offensive differentiation between each section, as in most public places. Naturally, the privileged had the best view and the most comfortable seats, but like the courtiers of Elizabethan times, they could be seen by the lower orders, and in a sense formed part of the entertainment.

Nor was the décor of the higher-strata areas noticeably more opulent than the rest. Opulence was the keynote of the whole building. The foyers were designed to produce a gasp of admiration. Their chandeliers and wide stairways echoed eighteenth-century elegance. Nineteenth-century richness was evident in the sofas and red carpets of the landings. Twentieth-century boldness inspired the sweep of the auditorium. The technical equipment was clearly twenty-third century, however: state of the art illusor lights, sonic sound, virtual reality hoods and sensor pads – every device that could delight and beguile. For a few hours, audiences would be able to forget that their lives were confined, their walkways and shuttles overcrowded, their work all-consuming.

Esther had considered herself resistant to such persuasion, yet she felt herself weaken too. For once there was real colour and beauty around her, instead of merely an illusion projected on to a screen. She could forget the problems of the future, even forget her grief.

The theme of the opening event had been announced as 'Our City: Past and Future', a typical Keepers' platitude. The result could have been a standard pageant of historical worthies, with a few artifical spacecraft lowered from the ceiling, and a laser light-show to round it off. Esther had seen similar productions in Centopolis, entertaining but hardly entrancing. That afternoon was sheer magic. Lights, colour, music, movement, all blended in one gorgeous chaotic whole.

From the opening in an eighteenth-century street, Nortown was portrayed at its most vigorous. A rapidly changing kaleido-scope of scenes left the audience breathless. The whole auditorium was taken on a balloon ride over the city. Ten thousand children clenched their hands together as they swung from a dizzying height. They shivered as a storm blew up and drove them off course. Just before they began to feel airsick, their balloon became a magic carpet taking them to seek knowledge in foreign lands. Exotic birds flew past. Dragons flamed. A twenty-foot genie rose from a chemical retort and offered them perfumes and gold from the East. The perfumes were real, wafting about with intoxicating sweetness. So too was the gold – a shower of golden butterflies that flittered from the ceiling. What did it matter if the butterflies were paper? Each one was beautiful, an emblem of renewal settling on to outstretched hands.

At the end of the interval the usual clowns appeared, but they were anything but usual in their antics. Some were lady clowns who trotted pink poodles along the roof of the city dome. Others squeezed through trapdoors in the sky, and chased up and down the clouds. By the time the second half began, Tim was laughing and clapping. Sally was silent with wonder, for the first time old enough to let the sensor pads beguile her.

The finale was a dream of beauty and hope. The future would be a wonderful place, full of light and fine buildings. The same people were shown going about their business as in the first scene, but now they were ungoverned by the limits of time and space. They walked through buildings without doors, and materialised out of emptiness to glide towards the audi-ence. Taking each person by the hand they led them through indoor farms and sea bases twenty times bigger and more wonderful that those of the present. One day, all the work and self-denial would be rewarded. One day England would be rebuilt. Softly, and then with growing power, the Keepers' hymn swelled in the background. Twenty-five thousand voices were united in a glorious upsurge of faith and joy. As the firework display burst around the auditorium, even Esther found her eyes stinging and a lump forming in her throat.

Suddenly normality returned. Screen, clowns, space people, all were gone. All that was left was the smell of perfume and fireworks, and a paper butterfly in Sally's hand.

It took a few seconds for the applause to begin. Everyone was waiting, hoping for further magic. With unnaturally bright eyes Tim turned in his seat. 'Oh Mum!' was all he could say.

They clapped until their hands hurt. 'There's Imogen', Tim said, pointing to the front box. She too was applauding. With her hair braided and coiled about her head, at a distance she looked fourteen or fifteen rather than just eleven. Beside her sat Mrs Briggs and Benn.

His Honour, the City Protector stepped on stage. He had wisely kept his opening speech short, but as the cast made their final bow, His Honour prepared himself for the pleasure of hearing his own voice.

'I think we've all had a cracking good time,' he said to the audience. 'Haven't we?'

In reply 25,000 people roared a single 'Yes'.

Again the cast bowed low.

'How do we show our appreciation?'

At once applause filled the building again, like a storm at sea. When it had almost ended, His Honour raised his hand and the sea was stilled. 'I'd like to introduce you to two people who have made this possible,' he announced. 'First, Commander Beattie Russell of the Northern Entertainments Board.'

A rather large woman in grey stepped from the wings, nodded to the audience and shook hands with the City Protector. 'Please convey our gratitude to your board for organising this afternoon's events,' His Honour enthused. 'And to the Keepers, of course. As always, their generosity is amazing.'

Commander Russell was not to be outdone. 'Three cheers for the Keepers,' she invited. 'Hip, hip—'

The response was wholehearted, if rather out of time.

'And now,' His Honour continued, guiding Commander Russell to one side, 'we must thank the man who made the board's ideas a reality: our new director, Patroner Stephan Lahr.'

Putting his arm round the new director's shoulders, the City Protector propelled him forward. 'We've got a find here, haven't we?' he asked the audience. The ultimate game-show host, he chivvied and cajoled until there was another storm of applause.

Against the City Protector's broad figure, Stephan Lahr looked unexpectedly slight. He stood with dignity, though His Honour's familiar manner must have been irritating. Someone presented a spray of flowers, and he spoke a brief word of thanks. It was traditional for a man to offer such flowers afterwards to a lady of his choice, and for a second Patroner Lahr hesitated. Then, stepping forward, he offered them to his daughter.

Mrs Briggs whispered something, and Imogen got up and came down to the stage. She was as self-possessed as a grown woman, taking the spray politely. Suddenly her control broke, and she threw her arms around her father, almost crushing the flowers. Laughing, he detached himself and made her take a bow. The gesture touched the heart of every woman in the audience. A new people's idol was being created. Next week there would be more than one spray of flowers.

All the way back to Moss Edge, Esther recalled the pleasure of the afternoon. Sally and Tim were tired out but mellow with happiness. They had had a wonderful time, as had all the other children there. Intrigued, Esther began trying to work out how each of the effects had been obtained.

When the house lights dimmed and the music began, a wrap-round vonofilm screen must have been lowered around the walls. On to that had been cast the images that seemed to be the real world. Some of the figures were surely holograms or automata. No showhouse could have afforded so huge a cast. Others were probably manimations. Certainly the dragons and wild animals could not be real. The clowns and acrobats were human though, trained in a long tradition of circus and vaudeville. The fireworks were real too, specially made for setting off in a confined space. Yet to divide such a production into its constituent parts was to deny its magic. That was genuine, and must have come from the mind of the man who had directed the whole production. It was clear now why he had been brought to Nortown so urgently. Rumour had not overstated his talent. Nor had it exaggerated the cost of the showhouse and its gala opening. Truly, the Keepers spared no trouble or expense to give their subjects pleasure.

With her children dozing against her, Esther was at peace. For a while longer she shared the afternoon's dream, the dream that motivated both Keepers and Kept: of benevolent rulers and a happy people. If that dream was not always fulfilled, it was none the less worth dreaming, she told herself. As with any ideal, one should not reject it simply because those who believed in it were mortal. What did it matter if there was more than a hint of the Roman 'bread and circuses' in the Keepers' policies? So long as the bread was ample and the circus as good as that afternoon's, few would wish to overthrow the regime that provided them. Even the rigidly separated strata were acceptable so long as the brightest or most diligent had a chance of rising through them. Bob's parents had been sixth-strata service workers. Through education and his own abilities, he had risen above his family. If the boat is taking most people where they want to go, why risk sinking it?

All through the evening that question went round and round in Esther's mind. The message she was to take down to Centopolis would make rebellion possible. What then? Chaos? A second civil war? What use would that be, even to those who had brought it about?

But when your home is no longer your private place?

That was the sticking point. Something deep within Esther's soul had hardened. Her private possessions had been dirtied by unknown hands, and the husband she had loved had been taken from her. The Keepers had not been directly to blame for Bob's death, but indirectly they had caused it. She could almost have forgiven her mother's execution. Jacki Marshall was an extremist. Extremes were dangerous, particularly in such fragile times. But what kind of benevolence was it that saw nothing wrong in going through a woman's clothes or spying on a good man, holidaying with his family?

No, Esther could not accept such things. Whatever her doubts, she would deliver Sly's report tomorrow.

The journey to Centopolis was uneventful. Though Esther's mouth went dry every time she was spoken to, no one challenged her. As soon as they arrived at Park View Mansions, she unpacked, then took the children straight out again. It was not good for Tim to be in the rooms that had been his father's. Already his chest was troubling him.

First they visited the dwelling agency to discuss the sale of their property. Afterwards, they spent some time in the public amusement area. Tim found some old friends playing there, and was happy to join them. Sally liked nothing better than to be left in the children's enclosure, under the care of the attendant. For a few moments Esther was on her own. Sitting down on one of the public seats, she took out her lace bobbins, and began to work at a collar, as if merely relaxing in the sun.

As she sat, Esther concentrated on the area around her. She concentrated so hard her head began to ache. There was no one within fifty metres. If she was being watched, it was from a considerable distance, too far for even a directional device to detect a careful switch. Dropping her ball of cotton to the floor, she bent to pick it up with her right hand. Right indicated 'safe'; left, 'danger'. She hoped devoutly she had given the correct signal.

A few moments more passed. Casually, a young woman with a baby came and sat on the same bench. 'Do you mind if I join you?' she asked.

'Not at all,' Esther replied.

They began to exchange pleasantries about the baby, and the lace Esther was making. 'What's it going to be?' the stranger asked.

'A collar for my neighbour's little girl.'

'May I see?'

The codes had been exchanged, word for word. Smiling, Esther passed the younger woman the collar, and they discussed the workmanship involved. Still Esther could feel no one watching them. Taking another two pieces of lace from her workbag, she offered them also for examination. Five minutes later, three pieces of lace were returned to her bag, but only two had been made by her. Sly's report was inside the stranger's jacket.

They talked a little longer, then the stranger got up. 'I'd better be going,' she said. 'Nice to meet you.'

After the woman had gone, Esther sat in the sun, steadying her breath. Her hands were shaking as she worked. She had not realised how frightened she had been. Looking up, she saw a second woman approaching the bench.

In alarm, Esther was about to move. Then she recognised the newcomer. In surprise, she waited until her superior joined her.

Sitting down beside her, the principal smiled. 'I believe we know each other,' she said. 'Weren't we neighbours once?'

Mystified, Esther nodded.'Mrs Lacy, isn't it?' she replied.

For the benefit of anyone who might be listening, they talked for a while about Bob's death. Still no one came near them, and the noisy play of the children on the amusements would drown quiet conversation.

'What was the recommendation?' the principal asked.

'That we accept. Your colleague has the full report.' For a second Esther panicked. 'Or shouldn't I have given it to her? Don't say I gave it to the wrong person—'

'Of course not. You've done everything correctly. We'll send our reply back up by special representative. It'll take a couple of days for us to consult everyone.'

Esther wondered why the chief officer of the Southern region should have decided to come, and be sitting now beside her on a park bench. So senior an official rarely made direct contact with anyone, and certainly not with a mere messenger from the North. Curiously, she seemed concerned for Esther's well-being, and a little nervous at meeting in so public a place.

'Have you anything you wish to say to me?' the older woman asked. 'I'm sure you must have.'

Esther considered her reply carefully. 'Would it be possible for me to be told the final decision while I'm down here?' she asked. 'It will be almost a week before I can speak to my own people.'

'Such information is on a "need to know" basis only.'

'You may feel that includes me,' Esther persisted. 'For some reason our new friends have chosen me as their liaison. If your answer is positive, I'm likely to be very much involved.'

To her relief, the principal nodded. 'That's reasonable enough,' she agreed. 'We're not heartless, though we may appear so.' For a second she paused. 'That's why I wanted to see you in person. To know whether you felt angry or used.'

'I did. A little,' Esther admitted.

'It's not surprising. Our Northern aunt is shrewd and effective, but she cares little for the individual. In this instance she's right, however. Events are overtaking us all.'

Silently Esther nodded. It would not be wise to make any further comment.

'Let's see, how can we let you know our decision?' the principal asked reflectively. 'Yes. I think that will do ... At ten-thirty on Tuesday, you will receive a visitor from your husband's employers. She will deliver the standard mourning gift of dried flowers. Dark ones will mean "no". White or yellow, "yes". Be sure you get it right. We will make no other contact.'

'Dark: no,' Esther repeated. 'Light: yes.'

The principal smiled. 'No resentment?'

'Not now.' In gratitude, Esther also smiled. 'As well as our report, I've given your colleague a request for information,' she added. 'The men concerned are Southerners and you may know something of them. Would you be kind enough to check?'

Rising, the principal offered Esther her hand. 'Bereavement is always difficult,' she said more loudly. 'but it can be an enhancing experience.'

'Everyone's being very kind,' Esther replied, mouthing the platitudes a listener would expect to hear.

Exactly as promised, on Tuesday morning a girl appeared at Esther's door. She was holding a box of dried flowers.

'Mrs Hobson said we could give you these,' she said awkwardly. 'We'd like to remember Bob somehow. He was a very nice man. We were all fond of him.'

Taking the box, Esther thanked her. Inside it was a splendid arrangement of dried grasses and flowers, a symphony of yellow and white. The National Committee had agreed to an alliance with the renegade Keepers. Suddenly revolution was a practical proposition.

It was a second or two before Esther could speak.

'We meant them to give you pleasure,' the girl continued earnestly. Her name was Gina, Esther recalled. She worked as a screen operator in Bob's office.

'Oh but they do!' Esther insisted. 'A great deal—' Unable to finish her sentence appropriately, she paused. 'I was just thinking how quickly everything changes.'

'Doesn't it? There's three gone from our department since your Bob was with us; promotion for two, and Treatment for one.' The girl lowered her voice. 'Who'd have thought Mr Beasley would ever need Treatment?'

'Who indeed?'

So that was it, Esther thought sadly. Sol Beasley was a close enough friend for the Watchers to have suspected Bob also. Sol might even have shared some of his feelings with him, and been overheard. He always was a bit careless, losing important progstrips and finding them the next day. He was also very loud. You could always hear Sol talking, wherever he was. A big soft giant of a man, he had never learnt discretion.

It was useless blaming him. Bob might have died in any case.

The girl was still talking.

'May I take some of these to the committal tomorrow?' Esther asked.

'Of course, but only a few. They were meant for you.'

After her visitor had gone, Esther unwrapped the gift. She wondered who had arranged the choice of colour. Mrs Hobson herself? That was an interesting thought. A less likely rebel than the dragon of the computer room could hardly be imagined.

The committal was short and tactfully done. At Esther's insistence, there was even a spray of fresh flowers on the coffin, though the mortician had shaken his head at such extravagance. About twenty people attended, mostly old friends and work colleagues. To Esther's sadness, the two people she most wanted to be there could not come. Bob's mother was unwell, while Esther's own father could not take leave, there being some sort of trouble in his area. Despite his discipline, Esther had heard disappointment in his voice. He had known Bob a long time, first as the younger brother of a room mate at the Military Academy, then as his son-in-law.

After the ceremony, refreshments were provided by the Morticians Department. Each committal group was allowed one hour. For that hour everyone tried to think of something consoling to say to each other, expressions of grief being frowned upon. It was almost a relief when the next group began to arrive.

Embracing everyone again, Esther thanked them, and wished them goodbye. She could not overcome a feeling of being cheated – that Bob had deserved something less perfunctory – but as the mortician had said, why waste precious resources on people who could no longer enjoy them?

That evening, Esther settled the children in front of the audiovision. Sally was not really aware of the occasion, but Tim was listless and withdrawn, learning to retreat into silence rather than be chided for expressing emotion. Giving him a hug, Esther went to make him a drink.

Gina's dried flower arrangement was still standing on the table in the kitchen, and Esther put it back in its box. Even if they were message bringers, the flowers were too expensive to leave uncovered. Unexpectedly, her finger touched something harder than stem or stamen. The centre of one of the daisies was unusually solid.

Looking as it more closely, Esther found a pin pushed deep into it. In alarm she drew the pin out, making sure she did not touch the head. Quietly Esther checked that neither child was watching, then locked the kitchen door. A piece of plastifilm was concealed inside the heel of her shoe; taking it out, she flattened it on the work surface, then pressed the pinhead into it. Faint traces of writing appeared. Taking an enhancer, Esther read what was imprinted on the film:

RED ALERT: BURGESS LANDER. STEPHAN LAHR BELIEVED SAME. MINIOTT HIGH RISK. DETAILS FOLLOWING.

For a few seconds Esther paused, fixing the words in her memory. Whatever the National Committee had discovered, it must be extremely serious for the principal to risk sending an open message.

The wording was necessarily brief, but unfortunately that led to ambiguity. Did 'believed same' mean that Burgess Lander and Stephan Lahr were one and the same man, or merely that there was a red alert coding on both? It made an awful lot of difference. Burgess Lander was one of Sly's faceless men, and probably a Seeker, an officer in the Keepers' secret police – maybe even a Keeper himself. If he and Stephan Lahr were the same, Esther was living next door to someone even more dangerous than she had feared.

That night sleep eluded her. No matter how hard Esther tried to meditate, fear kept her mind churning. Soon she must return to Nortown. Having accepted Stephan Lahr's generosity, it would be impossible to avoid the man without arousing suspicion. Besides, Tim would be playing with Imogen in the community room; Mrs Briggs would be inviting Esther to pop in for a coffee . . . They must move into another dwelling, but that could take months.

Gradually a sense of proportion returned. Even if she had thought Stephan Lahr was a normal neighbour, Esther would have been wary of him. Knowing that he might be a Seeker could not make her more careful, but it could panic her into making a mistake. The principal's warning was welcome, but she must not alter her behaviour towards her neighbour.

Turning over, Esther fell asleep at last.

It was early dawn when she awoke, the lights having just

dimmed in readiness for the day. The hairs on the back of her head prickled with fear. A man was sitting beside her bed, watching as she slept. Seeing her stir, he touched her hand gently to reassure her. 'Come back to us soon,' he said. 'Please, Tettie. Time is running out.'

Though she could not see his face, the voice was unmistakable. Sitting bolt upright, Esther knocked Callum's hand away. The room was empty. There was no one even in the doorway.

Frightened and bewildered, she sat for a full moment trying to steady her breathing. She had been dreaming again.

'Damn the man!' she said aloud.

It was about time she got her mind under control, and put Callum back in his place. He had invaded her mind. Even at such a distance he could call her back.

Leaning back against her headrest, Esther tried to bring some logic to the situation. Keeper or not, Callum ought to be identifiable. Once she knew who he was, she would be better able to fight him.

A few personal details could already be established. The most obvious were the Scots accent and the uneven tread. He knew Nortown well, and probably lived in the city. She had also gained the impression that he was a well-trained and respected leader. Madelaine had definitely been afraid of him, though Callum's manner to her had been patient rather than threatening. Finally, there was the fleeting glimpse she had gained in the shop: of a moderately tall man, with dark hair and a clean-cut profile.

One by one, Esther evaluated each supposed fact in turn and found it unreliable. The accent and limp could be assumed. If she herself wanted to establish a false image without being seen, such details were exactly the sort of thing she would choose. Though Callum knew Nortown well, that did not necessarily mean he lived there now. Madelaine could have been pretending her fear of him. Even the brief glimpse in the shop only established physique and colouring. All

Esther could actually be sure of was that she had sensed his anger during their first meeting and his gentleness during the last.

Pausing, Esther watched the audiovision flicker in front of her. She was missing some important fact, she was sure of it, but for the life of her she could not think what.

A little more was certain about Callum's support group, she decided. Madelaine had been around since March at least, when she first appeared as the woman with the knitting. The male guide knew his way along the waterway. The group as a whole had access to a barge and a shop. They also had the ability to cover their tracks quickly. Such facts suggested a well-established local structure. It was unlikely that everyone involved in it would be a renegade Keeper. So what else might bind them together?

Sly had suggested a link with the Dark Ones, the new group of actives she had traced. That seemed plausible. Callum and his colleague had probably worn black on the barge; the delegates at the church had definitely done so. They had in fact made a rather nice reversal. The Keepers' hierarchy wore white, the symbol of good, and met in the light, yet they were a force of evil. Their opponents wore black, and worked at night, claiming both for the good.

Still there was something eluding her, just out of reach.

Crossing to the window, Esther looked out on the square beneath. The night guard was passing, each sentry carrying a personal lamp to supplement the city lights.

Suddenly Esther realised what had been troubling her. It was so obvious she could not believe she could have missed it for so long. Callum was at ease in the dark. While she had strained every faculty to judge his position, he had known as soon as she moved. That was not normal.

Carefully Esther went over her memory of each of their meetings. When he held her in the church, they had been so close she had felt the line of his collarbone through his jacket, yet she had detected no enhancers or sonic devices, nothing that could explain his unusual ability. Later, when her eyes adjusted to the darkness, she had been able to see his outline. All she had seen was a man in some sort of battle uniform, with a thin cloth mask over his face.

So, if Callum was not using special equipment, what else might enable him to see in the dark?

Night training was an obvious possibility. Since the Outlands lacked the perpetual light of the cities, any official posted there had to learn to cope in darkness. But, however well trained, protectorate officers were never able to move freely, as Callum was. Even the Outlanders only travelled when there was a moon.

What about drugs? The Keepers controlled medicine, along with all other science. Could they have developed some means of enabling the human eye to see in the dark, like a cat's? Even cats need a little light. The barge had been totally, utterly black, as lightless as a cave. Still Callum had known when she moved.

Esther could think of only one other possibility: that the man did not need light, because he had never known it.

Now that would be different, she thought wryly. In the cities, disability of any sort was unusual. Most of the frailties that had dogged the human species could be corrected before birth. An adult who lost his sight would be viewed as a failure, and given little sympathy. It was the duty of all citizens to ensure their good health by a sensible lifestyle. If by carelessness or misfortune an injury should be sustained, it was an equal duty to have it corrected quickly. Despite all their care, people sickened and died, of course, being human. They did so with a sense of surprise, and their families wondered where they had gone wrong.

Yes, Esther admitted, smiling to herself. A blind leader could be very effective. No one would predict any danger from him.

It was a nice idea, but unfortunately it too did not quite fit the facts. A blind man would be unlikely to move his meeting place about, needing to be familiar with his surroundings; nor would he be used to guard a church while discussions took place inside it. No, Esther decided. There was something special about Callum, but she doubted if he was blind. Once she identified exactly what that special quality was, she would probably identify the man.

13

They returned to Nortown the next day. Though Esther had originally intended to stay until all her business affairs were sorted out, Tim was becoming increasingly oppressed by the continual reminders of his father. He said little, but Esther was so aware of his feelings she could not ignore his unhappiness. Besides, though she felt no compulsion to obey Callum's call this time, it was there all the while at the back of her mind. The man had been kind to her. She ought at least to see why he needed her.

When they entered Moor View Dwellings, the old familiar sounds greeted them. Mrs Dalton was watching *Make Your Time,* as she always did on a Thursday. Mr and Mrs Barraclough were settling down for an hour of *Songs from the Shows.* On Channel 20 the Big Match was about to begin. Esther felt relieved, even if the noise was irritating. She was home.

Esther had missed several of her scheduled visits to the Undesirables while she was down in Centopolis. Hopefully, Minkin's money would have reached him by some other means, but he would have no way of knowing whether she had been taken or not. She ought to contact him. The authorities would in any case be expecting her to resume her normal duties as soon as possible. As soon as the children were settled back in school, Esther set off for Fox House settlement.

This time she could detect no one following her. The guard

at the top gate was new, bu he let her through without question. In the canyon children were playing on the blocks of concrete as usual. When they saw Esther coming down the path, they ran towards her and clutched at her hands, begging the comfits she always brought. Everything seemed exactly as it should be.

Minkin came out of his dwelling to greet her. 'We thought you'd stopped coming,' he said guardedly.

'I wouldn't do that,' Esther replied. 'My husband died and I had to see to things.'

Grief still had meaning to the Undesirables, and Minkin's expression was immediately one of sympathy. It would have been good to talk to him of her pain, but even when they were safely inside the sick bay, Esther said little. She had lost the ability to express her feelings in words. Besides, it was time she looked to the future, not the past.

'Have you reopened the escape routes?' she asked.

'Yes, but only with great care. People are still asking questions about you.'

In alarm Esther looked up. 'I thought they'd lost interest,' she said. 'I haven't been followed for a couple of weeks.'

'Two women came last Tuesday. They said they were checking on all registered volunteers. They wanted to know if we were satisfied with your visits.'

'How did you reply?'

'I said you were interested in our welfare, and represented us well.'

'Thank you.'

Minkin shrugged his shoulders. 'I do tell the truth occasionally,' he replied.

'Maybe the women were genuine,' Esther suggested. 'All professionals are monitored, even volunteers.'

'Maybe,' Minkin conceded, 'but there was a man with them too. He stayed at the top talking to the guards. I sent Miriam up to check who he was. She said he had the bearing of a man used to being obeyed.'

In concern, Esther sat down. 'What did he look like?' she persisted.

'Ask Miriam.'

Esther watched Minkin's face carefully, trying to judge whether he was telling her all that he knew. She was beginning to feel uneasy.

Minkin called his wife to them.

'Describe the man you saw at the guard point,' he ordered.

Miriam was used to his self-important manner. 'Thirty or more summers old,' she replied. 'Taller than Nikin by two or three hands. Very blue eyes. He'd be nice for a woman to know, except that he was cold, cold as the water off the moors. A man like that would use a woman and then destroy her.'

'What colour hair did he have?'

'As fair as gold.'

'You're sure he was asking after me?'

'Not directly, but I saw him question the women after they'd been down here.'

The stranger sounded horribly like Stephan Lahr. 'I have a feeling I know who the man is,' Esther admitted.

'I still say you should run while you can,' Minkin said.

'And I still say I can't,' Esther insisted. 'Besides, without a proper route, I'd never survive.'

'If you lived like us you could. The Sheep People aren't going to tell you that, are they? They make a lot of money out of controlling the placements in the villages.'

Esther shook her head. 'I'll run when I have to,' she replied. 'Until then, I intend to stay and fight, from the inside.'

Miriam shook her head. 'I doubt if you'll be allowed to do that much longer,' she warned.

All the while she went about her duties afterwards Esther heard the girl's warning. When one of the old men unexpectedly grabbed her hand, she only just stifled a cry of fear.

'I want your opinion, lady,' he said.

'What about?' Esther asked. The man did not hear her. Arthritic and toothless, he was also very deaf. In the city, the frailty of age was never seen so starkly. When Esther first visited the canyon, the sight of such old people had shocked her even more than the smell and disease.

'What about?' she repeated, more loudly.

'We had these women round last week. They said there was a new ruling. Even the likes of us can apply for the Year of Reward, they said. Dost tha' reckon I should put me name down?'

Appalled, Esther put her hand gently on the old man's shoulder. 'It's not for me to tell you what to do,' she replied. 'Only you can make such a decision. I'd think very carefully before you sign your last years away.'

'I'd have a whole year doing just what I wanted, wouldn't I? As much to eat as I wanted, and any pleasure I asked for. I don't get through so much work nowadays. I don't want to end up being a burden to my family.'

Esther was tempted to warn him that there were ugly rumours. That the state could no longer afford the full year, that some old people had only been given a few months before the nurse brought them their final sleep ... In her dealings with all but Minkin and Miriam, however, she stuck strictly to the official line. 'How old are you?' she asked.

'Ninety summat at least. Happen it's more. I lost count long ago.'

'How long does one year seem?'

The old man did not at first understand her. 'I can never tell one from another,' he admitted. 'They fly past that sudden.'

'Then I'd hang on a bit longer until the years start to fly slowly. Your family are coping quite well. They can spare you a bit of dinner.'

She had given the old man the answer he had wanted, and looking up, he smiled.

As she returned to Minkin's dwelling, the incident troubled Esther. The old man had been willing to make the decision to sign his life to an end, for the sake of his family. She ought to at least consider the possibility of flight.

'If I do have to run suddenly, what would you suggest I do?' she asked Minkin.

'Pretend to be one of us. You can do that easy enough.'

'And what else?'

'If there's a moon, travel at night. If there isn't, set off in the early morning or evening when there are fewer people around. Watch the stream's flow, and you'll find your way through the hills. You already know about what grows in the fields, better than we do. The birds will show you what berries can be eaten. And don't be afraid to steal if you have to. Why should anything belong to just one person? We all have to survive.'

Esther smiled. 'We do indeed,' she replied.

It was time for her to leave. 'Have you heard any rumours about a new group?' she asked casually. 'It may be led by a man who doesn't see too well?'

Minkin's expression betrayed little, but Esther sensed his surprise. 'We're picking up reports of a group of saboteurs,' he remarked. 'They seem to be new. No one knows who leads them, though.'

'What do they call themselves?'

'The Outlanders call them the Dark Ones, but no one's had any contact with them. They appear from nowhere, and vanish afterwards.'

'Interesting,' Esther remarked. Blinking as she went back out into the light, she began to pick her way through the mounds of rubbish, towards the way out of the canyon.

That night, Tim grieved a good deal, but by morning he was calmer, and determined not to let outsiders see his grief.

When Imogen called to ask if he wanted to come out to play, he begged Esther to say yes.

Esther could think of no way of refusing. It was not the time to deny Tim friendship. Besides, the relationship between him and Imogen was a little out of the ordinary. Both of them tall and awkward and out of tune with their surroundings, it was perhaps inevitable that they should turn to each other. It was going to be difficult to end the relationship without making Tim all the more determined to remain friends with the girl.

'Why don't you come in?' Esther invited. After all, it was not the girl's fault her father was probably a Watcher.

Coiling herself around one of the kitchen stools, Imogen talked a little. She was excited, though as usual she could find few words to express her pleasure. While Tim was away, she had been selected for the city's under-thirteen gymnastics team. Apparently she had been in the St Albans local team before they moved, but never in a city-wide one before.

'You've done very well,' Esther said. 'There must have been a lot of competition.' She found herself wishing the mother could have seen her daughter's success. That led to wondering what the mother had been like. A brunette perhaps, judging by the dark eyes of her children. 'I never had a chance to tell your father how good the gala opening was,' she added. 'I imagine he was very relieved when it was over.'

Imogen nodded. 'He even gave Auntie Briggs a kiss,' she said, smiling. 'The authorities sent him a special commendation. It was all done in beautiful letters.'

'Your father must have been very flattered.'

'He just laughed. He said no one expected the building to open on time, and when the show was so good, he was everybody's blue-eyed boy. Dad doesn't think much of success, you see. He says it can go as quickly as it comes.' The girl's maturity was as troubling as it was impressive. 'I'm glad he's doing so well,' she added, 'even if it does mean we'll have to move again.'

Tim looked up in concern. 'Why?' he asked.

'The authorities are finding us a better place than this, something more fitting to Dad's position.'

In relief, Esther nodded. 'When will you leave?' she asked.

'Next week perhaps. We can't refuse.' Imogen's eyes were unnaturally bright. It was hard on her. She had just begun to settle, and once again she was being uprooted.

There was such wistfulness in Tim's expression that Esther put her arm round him. She was glad the friendship was being brought to a natural end, but her son would miss the girl dreadfully.

They spent an hour or so together, feeding and trimming Esther's plants. Imogen was delighted by the feel of the leaves, and the scent of the flowers. She had never seen so many plants in one dwelling. 'Why do you have so many?' she asked.

Embarrassed, Esther smiled. 'I use them to balance the atmosphere,' she explained. 'The controlled environment gets so – flat and uninteresting.'

'Mum was a hydropologist,' Tim announced proudly. 'She worked on a sea base, growing food for the staff to eat. She used to fly backwards and forwards just above the waves.'

'Flapping my arms ever so hard,' Esther agreed, teasing him. 'Yes, I've flown above the sea, and lived under it. It was very beautiful.'

'You mean you were a sort of farmer?' Imogen asked. 'Like the Outlanders?'

'Yes, though I grew food in tanks, or hanging from wires in special houses.'

'Then you must be very clever. Cleverer than my dad, even. He only keeps people happy. You know how to keep them fed.'

The remark struck Esther as unusually profound, and looking up, she smiled. She could understand why Tim liked Imogen's company.

Crossing to the window, Esther looked out to see if it was

still raining. Suddenly she saw Number One-six-six waiting, walking a dog through the deserted play area. The courier could not have come at a more inconvenient time. Imogen might be innocent enough herself, but she was observant, and could well mention something suspicious to her father.

As if casually moving one of the plants, Esther held it up at the window for a few seconds. Then she turned to Tim. 'Keep an eye on Sally while I take the recycling stuff out,' she asked. 'The trailer will be calling soon.'

'I thought you'd never see me,' One-six-six grumbled.

Older than most of the couriers, One-six-six was one of the best, learning what she was told, repeating it as ordered, and then forgetting it straight away afterwards. Like those who provided meeting places, or ran relaxation centres, she was a passive, a member of the Movement who took no part in Dissenting activity – either through age, or infirmity, or sheer good sense – but was sympathetic to its aims.

'I have a priority message for you,' she said. 'Are you listening?'

Nodding, Esther waited. Since One-six-six was known for her memory, what followed was likely to be unusually long and detailed.

'National Committee to Forty-Eight. Information on suspects as requested.

'Miniott, Simon: Quarrel with father questionable. Local enquiries indicate still visits family home; popular with staff. Villagers unwilling to talk. Carl: record of marriage but wife's name not traced. Andrew and Joanna: contacts with Jacki Marshall confirmed. Whole family seem untouched by recent coup. Probably on winning side. Treat with caution.'

'Lander, Burgess: member of Special Investigations Group, senior rank. Nicknamed "The Actor" because of ability to assume different identities. Personal details: believed early thirties; natural hair colour fair, blue eyes but changed as needed. Height medium to tall. Weight about sixty-two kilo.

Responsible for detention of Dissident groups in Centopolis and Birmingham district of Midopolis. Current whereabouts unknown. Extreme risk.

'Lahr, Stephan: Additional details: weight at last medical, sixty kilo; height 193cm. Could be Burgess Lander under new alias. Member of St Albans group reported being questioned by official named in her hearing as Lander. Member subsequently identified this man as Stephan Lahr. Committee unable to confirm identification. Informant since disappeared. Treat as proven until otherwise.'

'Thank you,' Esther said. She felt very cold.

'You're required to attend a meeting on Monday night. Arrangements have been made for Twenty to look after your children.'

'Who's the meeting with?'

'Mutual friends. Report to Number Four at thirteen hours.'

With the recycling in her hand, Esther returned upstairs. Though the day was quite warm, she found she was shivering.

At thirteen hours exactly on Monday, Esther was shown into the kitchen at Hunter's Farm. Sly was sitting waiting beside the fire, already wearing her outdoor wrap. Though it was early summer outside, in that dark stone room it was still winter.

'Our friends can obtain the merchandise we requested,' Sly said.

'You're not as pleased as I would expect,' Esther remarked. 'Why?'

Getting up, the old woman went to the fire and poked the embers. Then she crossed to the window and looked out. Satisfied, she returned to her chair. 'We'll have to play things very carefully,' she warned, 'or we'll find our new friends taking over.'

'I thought that was what you wanted.'

In annoyance Sly looked up. 'You're an uncomfortable woman to be with,' she retorted. 'Yes, in a sense I do. We have to have continuity, and Callum and his friends might provide the focus we need.'

'You'd hand power over to them?'

'It'd stick in my throat, but if I thought it'd lead to a peaceful solution, I would. The people might accept an interim government of good Keepers – as apposed to the evil ones they've just overthrown. They've watched a thousand video novels with a similar plot.'

'The renegades may not want to retain power.'

'They may have to, for the good of the country. It's a question of getting the right balance. Whoever takes over, we must be equal partners. I've had enough of being the little woman working behind the secenes.'

Smiling, Esther nodded. She could not imagine Sly as anyone's little woman. 'Who's to be at this meeting?' she asked.

'The spokeswoman, Callum and Fourteen. They want her to go into Central Control with one of their agents.'

Though it was hardly kind, Esther began to laugh.

'That is indeed the problem,' Sly admitted. 'No one else has the expertise to reprogram the computers. It has to be done on site. Progstrips prepared elsewhere will be rejected. It's Fourteen's program. She knows it off by heart. She'll have to do it, but at present she's refusing to. You'll just have to persuade her.'

Esther's smile faded. The image of Fourteen trying to hold her own against the likes of the spokeswoman was almost absurd. To imagine her breaking into a heavily guarded control building was difinitely so. She had joined the Movement as a passive, and had not even finished her induction into that role yet.

'We'll have to find someone else,' Esther said firmly. 'Fourteen can train them.'

'There isn't time. While you've been away, two of the renegades have been taken. Their enemies are closing in on them. They insist they must get the codes while they can, and Fourteen must set her virus with the shortest practical time limit. Otherwise we'll find ourselves leading a revolution on our own.'

Putting on her outdoor wrap, Sly prepared to leave the farm.

'Can't the renegades find someone themselves?' Esther asked.

'I'm not prepared even to consider that option. We'll lose all control if we do.'

The old woman opened the door, and shading her eyes with her hand, stood for several minutes, checking for anything that would suggest strangers had entered the dale. Apart from the bleating of young lambs and the sigh of the wind through grass, the hillside was silent.

'After fifty years of waiting it seems an ungrateful thing to say,' Sly admitted, 'but things are moving too quickly for my liking. A few weeks ago, you were coming to me with a crazy story about a man in a barge. Now we have money and weapons being salted away, and neatly drawn plans to lay on the table. These people know what they want, and they want it quickly. I'm an old woman. I don't like quick decisions. But then, I don't like this government either. Come on. Let's go and see what Fourteen's decided.'

Below the farm there was a row of ancient cottages, and two barns. Roker's Garth was the furthest cottage, set against the hillside, with a small terraced garden behind it. Access to it could be gained only by a steep path from the lane, itself narrow and winding. A man leant against one of the barns, resting while a dog snuffled around his feet. In the front garden of the cottage two women were working in a vegetable patch. Looking up, they nodded unobtrusively to Sly, and continued digging.

It used to amaze Esther that anyone could choose to grow their food in such dirt and toil. Even if scientific education had been denied them, she used to argue, the Outlanders could discover more modern methods for themselves. Lately, she had learnt to appreciate their love of rhythm, of the changing seasons, even of the contrast between day and night. The squalor of their homes was harder to understand. As soon as she entered Roker's Garth, the smell of meat and human sweat turned her stomach. It was like stepping back into the twentieth century.

At first it was difficult to see who was seated at the table. After the sunlight outside, it took several seconds for Esther's eyes to adjust to the gloom. Fifty had stayed to act as the Movement's representative until her superior returned, and was standing near the door. She was nervous, though only someone who knew her as well as Esther would have realised this. Fourteen was sitting near her, looking frightened. Next to her were two black and masked figures, even more sinister by day than by night. Places at the table had been left either side of them for Esther and Sly to fill.

Fourteen looked up in relief as Esther entered. 'They want me to go into the control room,' she whispered. 'Tell them I can't.'

'I'm sorry to have kept you waiting,' Sly began coolly. 'As our Number Fourteen is only a novitiate, I felt she should have her tutor with her. You have already met.'

The first figure nodded. Whether it was male or famale was impossible to say. Though Esther had been involved in the negotiations from the start, she found it hard not to feel threatened.

'Our position is this,' the figure said. Esther recognised the voice of the spokeswoman. 'We can obtain the codes you want almost immediately. If we leave it any longer, you may not get them at all. It seems we have ourselves been infiltrated. Information known only to us has reached others. We have been trying to persuade your colleague to assist us while we are still at liberty, but she's reluctant to do so.'

'I'm just being realistic,' Fourteen insisted in a small tight voice. 'Can you imagine me climbing through windows?'

'You won't have to climb through any windows,' the second figure said.

Callum had spoken reassuringly, but the muffled voice made Esther's whole being flinch. There was too marked a contrast between the quiet man who had held her in the darkness, and this threatening masked figure.

'All we're asking is for you to pretend to be our agent's assistant,' he said. 'Toby will see you get into the control room. He'll also stand guard while you key in your program. That part shouldn't be difficult, surely? You must know it well enough by now.'

He did not believe what he was saying. Esther could feel his unease, and his misgivings increased her own.

'Why can't one of your own people go?' Fourteen asked. 'I'll supply the program.'

'They've no one with your skills,' Sly cut in quickly.

'I could teach them.'

'There isn't time. Not before Keepers' Day.'

'But Keepers' Day is less than two weeks away,' Fifty pointed out. 'Why does it have to be then?'

'Because that's the one night we stand a chance of getting someone in – and out – of the building unnoticed.' Turning to her, Callum indicated the plan laid out on the table in front of him. 'As you know, this year's celebrations are to be held on Mallin Lake. Here. The control centre is less than two hundred kilometres away. There'll be music, lasers, fireworks, and an awful lot of people. Any noise we make will be drowned out. Even if the alarms do register, the guards are likely to be watching the show rather than their screens.'

Everyone waited for Fourteen to answer. She looked near to tears. 'You've got to tell them,' she pleaded, looking to Esther for support. 'You know me. I trip over my own feet.'

'Describe your plan in detail,' Esther said to Callum. 'Let

me judge if my pupil could cope. How do you propose to enter the building in the first place?'

'Walk through the front door.'

'Walk?'

'A Commander Tate and his assistant, Miss Hughes, will arrive at sixteen hours at the main gate. They'll have been called to sort out a glitch in the lift program. Both will sign in and do some genuine work until seventeen-thirty. Then the Commander will send the normal operatives home to get ready for the Keepers' Day show. He'll promise that he and Miss Hughes will finish what they're doing in a few minutes, and sign out.'

It was so simple it might work. 'And then?' Esther prompted. Getting up, she stood beside him to look at the drawing. Knowing that he too was worried made her less afraid of him.

'At sixteen hours two relief workers will arrive to assist the afternoon domestic shift, show their passes and go inside. They'll come out as soon as possible as Commander Tate and Miss Hughes. Toby and Fourteen will meanwhile have taken refuge here.' Callum indicated a small square not far from the control centre. 'It's a storeroom belonging to the cleaners. At seventeen hours thirty, the domestic teams will leave the building. Then the guards will lock up and switch on the alarms. As soon as everything's quiet inside, our two will make their way to the control room. Your colleague says it will take her about an hour to reprogram the computers – she'll have to work in virtual darkness or the light sensors will go off – and then she and Toby will return to the fire door here, and so out. There's no automatic check on people leaving the building, only entering. The security guards at the main gate will be occupied watching the Keepers' Day show, but to be doubly sure, we've arranged for them to be involved in an argument at about twenty-one hours. Toby and Fourteen will be able to slip through the gates and melt into the crowds.'

It was indeed a good plan, but it left an awful lot unsaid.

'How many guards do you expect?' Fifty asked.

'Only three and a gateman. Mallin Laboratories are intended to look like a normal place of business.'

'And the alarms? Was Fourteen's information correct?'

'As far as we can gather. There's the usual sensors and pressure-sensitive pads. And some rather unpleasant body-heat scanners.'

'Be specific,' Esther insisted.

She could sense Callum's irritation. 'I don't have exact details,' he replied. 'As far as we can tell, multi-scan sensors have been fitted at intervals, to detect any light source or movement. In addition, each door has two pressure-sensitive pads, which indicate if it's opened. The gadgets to watch are the body-heat scanners. Each triggers an automatic soldier with a firing range of about five metres. Set one of them off and you're dead.'

Fourteen had gone very pale. 'Thanks for the encouragement,' Esther said. 'That's just what my pupil needs.'

'I'm just being realistic,' Callum repeated drily. 'It's not as bad as it sounds. We can supply the heat-shield suits.'

'Heat-shield suits?' Sly asked. She was beginning to smile a satisfied smile.

'The reverse of what firefighters or space operatives use. Ours keep body heat in, instead of external heat out. You wouldn't want to stay in one too long, but for a couple of hours it's OK.'

'How do you get through the other alarms?' Esther persisted.

'Toby'll see to those, so long as your colleague gives him a bit of help.'

'Can you really imagine Fourteen managing to defuse an alarm?'

The man might be wearing a uniform designed to intimi-date, but Esther could feel his increasing concern. He found it more difficult to gloss over problems than his companion did. While the spokeswoman was a politician, seeing revolution in terms of theory, Callum was the practical soldier, who understood the reality.

'It's not that difficult,' he insisted. 'You could do it.'

'But I'm not going. My pupil is. What exactly would be required of her?'

'Each alarm has to be disarmed to allow safe passage. Then it must be reset, to prevent a gap showing on the screens. It's fiddly rather than demanding. My people usually work in pairs and practise until they establish a rhythm together. Even if your colleague weren't needed to see to the computer, Toby would have to have someone with him.'

'And the laser bars?' Esther persisted. 'How is Fourteen going to get under them?'

'Limbo dance if necessary,' Callum snapped. 'We'll teach her.'

'We will indeed,' the spokeswoman said, becoming impatient. 'If you make your pupil available to us on Friday, we'll see she gets any training she needs. She'll be returned safely to her home two days before the actual assault, so that she can rest. Obviously we'll have to see she doesn't make contact with anyone during that time.'

'No!' Fourteen cried out, putting her hands over her ears.

'Let me go with her,' Esther said.

'We can't get three in and out of that building,' Callum replied. 'Two's going to be difficult enough.'

'At least let me come to the training with her,' Esther pleaded. 'How would you like to be spirited away somewhere, with no idea where you were going or how you'd be treated?'

'That sounds reasonable enough to me,' the spokeswoman agreed. 'Can you accommodate an extra person, Cal?'

Rolling up the map, Callum paused. 'I don't take passengers,' he warned. 'If Tess comes, she goes through the training the same as everyone else.'

'I wouldn't dream of sitting around watching,' Esther

replied coldly. 'Besides, if you teach me, I might be able to teach my pupil. You haven't exactly gained her confidence.'

'Do we have to?' Fourteen whispered.

Trying to smile encouragingly, Esther nodded. 'It looks like it,' she admitted. 'Don't sound so frightened. It could be fun.' Then she remembered Tim and Sally. 'Sly,' she asked softly, 'can you ask Twenty to look after the children again?'

'Ah yes,' Sly said aloud. 'There are children to consider—'

'We'll see to that,' the spokeswoman interrupted, rising from the table. 'They can go to one of the children's camps for a couple of weeks. No one would find that at all odd. We could say that their mother was suffering from post-bereavement depression and needed a break.'

In concern Esther turned to her. 'Thank you, but we always make our own arrangements,' she said.

'Leaving your children so long with a friend might cause comment, dear. You'd better let us see to things.'

'How do I know you'll return them?' Esther's voice had begun to go dry in her throat.

'You have my word.'

'The word of a Keeper's wife?'

'The word of a colleague.'

Urgently, Esther looked towards Sly for support. The old woman merely gathered up her wrap. 'I'll be going now,' she said. 'Fifty, you can follow me at a suitable interval. The other two will need to stay to discuss arrangements.'

'But what about my job?' Fourteen objected. 'What's my boss going to think if I don't turn up?'

'We'll arrange for you to be seconded somewhere,' the spokeswoman replied. 'Trust us. Everything will be properly organised. And now if we have nothing more to discuss, I'll leave too.'

One by one, Sly, Fifty and the spokeswoman left, allowing a safe interval between each exit. Esther sat beside her pupil, taking her hand in comfort. Callum had crossed to the door, so that he could see his superior leave in safety. For several moments there was silence.

Finally, he closed the door and stood beside the window with his back to them. 'Our leaders are playing politics,' he said. 'It's a stupid game, and it could cost us our lives.'

'Why do you say that?' Esther asked.

Coldly he turned towards them. 'Your friend is totally unsuitable for this job. You know it. I know it. And she's said so herself. I should have been allowed to find one of my own people instead.'

His anger was the final insult. Though she tried hard not to, Fourteen burst into tears.

'That's all we need!' Callum retorted.

Putting her arm round Fourteen's shoulders, Esther comforted her. She could not trust herself to reply and sat in angry silence. At last, Callum relented and sat down beside them. 'I'll do my best to see you're safe,' he promised.

'Is that all you can offer?' Fourteen asked.

'I'm afraid so. In this world it can be as dangerous to have special skills as to have none.'

'Me and my big mouth,' Fourteen said, trying to smile. 'I wish I'd kept my idea to myself. Then I wouldn't be in this mess.'

'I'll be with you most of the time,' Esther reassured her.

Squeezing her hand, Fourteen nodded.

'I'd much sooner you weren't,' Callum admitted honestly. 'You'll be in the way.'

Furiously, Esther got up. 'You think we actually want to come?' she demanded. 'Have you any idea how Fourteen feels? How I feel? Knowing I may never see my children again?'

'I don't see any point in continuing this discussion,' Callum replied, also getting up.

Esther stood facing him. He was a great deal taller than her, but she would not be intimidated. She was tempted to knock his hood off and see who was underneath. 'You stupid, arrogant man,' she said, 'standing there as if you rule the world. Talk some sense into that spokeswoman of yours first, before you take it out on us.'

Callum did not answer, though she felt his surprise. 'Do you know how silly you look in that uniform?' she continued scathingly. 'It's hateful. I much preferred you in the dark.'

To her amazement the man began to laugh. 'I've been told that before,' he said.

'Bloody conceit!' Esther replied, but she too smiled.

The tension between them eased. When Callum had comforted her in the darkened church, a bond had begun to develop between them, and it still held. 'I'm sorry,' she said. 'I suppose it's not your fault either.' Glancing towards Fourteen, she saw that the woman was watching them in amazement, no doubt thinking Esther mad to risk insulting a Keeper. She probably was mad, Esther admitted.

'We have to get on,' she said to Callum more quietly, 'since our superiors have decreed it. I promise not to get in the way, and I know Fourteen will try to do what you ask.'

Nodding, he turned back to the window.

'How will you let us know times and places? Things like that?' Esther asked.

'Madelaine will keep you informed.'

'Is there nothing more to do now?'

'No.'

'Then we'll follow the others,' Esther replied. She sensed that he wished to say something more to her, in private. 'Fourteen, you'd better leave first,' she instructed. 'Go straight home. Don't wait for me.'

For several seconds, Esther stood watching her pupil as she left the cottage. When she closed the door again, Callum was waiting for her at the table.

'What did you want to say?' she asked.

'I'm not sure. Except that I'm sorry. You're right. I was

taking it out on you, but I'm scared, Tess, for myself and for others.'

In surprise Esther nodded. 'So am I,' she said.

'You didn't have to let yourself in for this. You could have kept quiet.'

'Could you have left Fourteen to cope on her own?'

'No.'

There was a pause. 'Next week won't be easy,' Callum warned. 'You'll have to go through everything we do, and some of it's not pleasant. You'll learn a great deal, though, and I shall value your company.'

Esther smiled. 'Thank you,' she said simply. The anger between them had gone, leaving the quietness of friendship. 'Will you make me a promise?' she asked. 'Make sure my children are safe.'

'Of course.'

It was time to leave, yet still they lingered. 'Thank you for warning me about Bob,' Esther added. 'It did help.'

'How are you coping?'

'It isn't easy.' Trying to find the right words, Esther paused. 'But as you say, I'm learning a good deal.' Awkwardly she offered her hand in the gesture of friendship. 'I'll see you on Friday, then.'

'You may not see me straight away, but you'll be well looked after.'

Letting go of her hand, Callum went out into the sunlight. The sheep women looked up as he passed, but said nothing.

As soon as Esther returned to the farm, Sly wanted to know what she and Callum had discussed. 'Are you satisfied with the arrangements?' she asked.

'No. I don't think it'll work. Fourteen isn't the sort.'

'They'll train her. You did well, child, offering to go with her. The Movement will always be grateful to you.'

It began to look as though Esther had been manoeuvred into making her offer. The suspicion made her very angry.

'Callum said you were playing politics,' she remarked coldly. 'Are you?'

'I never play politics. They're far too serious to be a game.'

Within the last few weeks Sly seemed to have aged suddenly. Esther wondered how much her judgement was being affected by the fact – not by senility, but by a desire to see the regime that she hated overthrown before her death.

'The National Committee sent us some more images,' Sly said. 'Come and look at them. See if you recognise our friend Callum from any of these.'

Together they went up into the priest's room, leaving Fifty behind to check that the renegades had safely left the valley. Sly had transferred the photo stills the courier had brought on to her files. Now there were pictures of Burgess Lander, and of Carl and Simon Miniott; though all three were very out of date. A file had also been opened on Stephan Lahr, with a recent picture taken from the *Nortown Gazetteer*. Carefully Esther examined each image, pausing a long time to compare the images of Burgess Lander and Stephan Lahr. There was a definite similarity, though the older picture was of a boy at school rather than a man. Both had fair hair and striking blue eyes. She wished they were not so alike, for Imogen's sake.

'Are they the same man?' Sly asked.

'They could be,' Esther admitted. 'But I couldn't say for sure. We need a more recent picture of Lander.'

'And we're not likely to get that. The man's far too careful, and far too important, it seems. We've been ordered to open a full investigation on him. The National Committee has reason to believe he's in this area. If we can prove your neighbour really is the same man, we have him.'

'What will you do?' Esther asked quietly.

'The committee will issue a command against him.'

Silently Esther nodded. Though the Movement was pledged to non-violence, many of its contacts were not. In a showhouse, with so much equipment around, it would be easy to arrange a man's death.

'Are any of these Callum?' Sly persisted.

'No,' Esther said. 'He's dark. All of these are fair.' Pausing, she considered her own statement. 'That is odd,' she conceded. 'Could the Miniotts and the Landers be related to each other? Or to Stephan Lahr? Try following that one through a bit.'

'I've already started,' Sly said, smiling. 'But I'm glad you saw it as well.'

14

It was still dark when Esther regained consciousness, and the world appeared to be stationary. At first those were the only two sensations she could register. What she was lying on, or where she was, were equally unknown to her. When she opened her eyes, she saw nothing. Pain filled her head, and she turned her face into her pillow.

She tried to recall what had brought her there. All she could remember was taking Sally and Tim to the children's camp.

The emotions of that moment returned to her, and for an instant she was back at the camp. A dreadful sense of foreboding filled her spirit. It was foolish, she told herself. Within minutes, Sally was in the corner ransacking the amusement box. Tim was more dubious, wanting to know what would be expected of him, and sensing Esther's own anxiety. Yet he showed courage. When she came to wish him goodbye, he had been almost calm.

'When will you come for us?' he asked.

'As soon as I can,' Esther assured him, though they had discussed it a dozen times already.

'You will get better, won't you?'

The memory made Esther cry, but her eyes stung so much that she checked her tears immediately. She discovered that so long as she kept her eyes closed, the pain in them was bearable. As soon as she opened them, she felt as if a bright light were being shone straight into them. Cautiously she reached out and began to investigate the world around her. She was lying on some sort of bed roll, directly on the floor. People were talking nearby. It took her several seconds to work out that they were outside her room rather than in it.

Sitting up, Esther tried to think what she should do. Once again she opened her eyes, only to find the pain unbearable. She considered calling out to the voices for help, and then decided it was safer to stay quiet. Taking several deep breaths, she tried to control her terror. Something had happened to her eyes.

Slowly Esther began to count to herself, determined at least to judge the passage of time.

By the time she had counted fifteen times sixty, she dared to risk opening her eyes again. The room was still very dark, but if she ignored the pain and looked ahead of her, she could see a peculiar white glow. Lying down, she counted another fifteen minutes.

When she opened her eyes, the white glow was clearer. It came from a square-shaped area to the front of her. A window. That was what it was.

Unable to bear the light any longer, Esther looked away. Unless she had been unconscious for a long time, the sky outside should be dark, yet when she looked towards the window again, the square it framed was definitely light, a cold yellow, like moonlight.

Footsteps sounded on empty stairs. They crossed a landing, then paused. 'Esther?' a voice whispered.

In relief, Esther sat up. 'Over here,' she called in answer.

Quietly Fourteen came into the room. 'Are you all right?' she asked.

'I'm not sure.'

Crossing the room, the woman knelt beside Esther. 'Can you see yet?'

'No. What have they done to me?'

'Don't you remember? Madelaine put some drops in your eyes. Then you passed out, with the pain I suppose. Whatever made you refuse the anaesthetic?'

Opening her eyes again, Esther tried to focus on the woman beside her, and could see only a blinding white light. 'What sort of drops?' she asked.

'I don't know what they were, but they've had the most amazing effect on me. It's like I can see in the dark. Well – not quite the dark, but so long as I've got a bit of light somewhere. I can see you now quite clearly, yet I know it's dark in here, except for the window. Talk about weird!'

Esther shifted her position. 'How long have I been here?' she asked.

'An hour or so. I wanted to come up to you as soon as I heard, but Jack wouldn't let me. He said, if you chose to control the pain your own way, that was your right. Are you sure you're OK?'

'Just about. How have you been?'

'I slept till this afternoon. The stuff they gave me must have knocked me out.'

'I imagine it did,' Esther agreed drily.

Fourteen giggled nervously. 'Do you reckon I've turned into a cat?'

'Have you grown a tail?'

'Not yet.' Sitting down on the floor, the woman touched Esther's hair with an awkward, gentle gesture. 'I'm so glad you're all right,' she said. 'When I heard you were unconscious, I felt awful, like I was responsible. I mean, you wouldn't be here but for me. Why wouldn't you accept anything from them? Madelaine said you wouldn't even take a drink.'

'I don't take things from people I don't know.'

'But they're supposed to be our friends. That's what an alliance means, isn't it?'

Anxiously, Esther looked again towards the window. Her student was very innocent, and very vulnerable. She needed support, not to be sitting on a floor trying to give her tutor comfort.

'Do you want me to leave you to be quiet?' Fourteen asked.

'No,' Esther replied, trying to smile. 'Talk to me for a few minutes, while we've got the chance. Tell me how you travelled here, and what the place is like. Anything you've noticed.'

'I can't really recall the journey. That's weird too. All I can remember is being taken to Central Wharf, and getting on a water transport. We changed to another boat somewhere upstream, and then I think there was some sort of barge, but after that I honestly don't know.'

'How do you know the second boat was upstream?'

'Because the engines were labouring. If it was downstream you'd hear less noise.'

'Good girl! Did you see anyone?'

'I think the man they call Jack was on the barge. Madelaine must have been too. She started the journey with me.'

The fuzziness was clearing from Esther's mind. 'Who's Jack?' she asked.

'I don't know what he looks like. He wears a mask – they all do, except Madelaine. I'd say he's older than the two we met with Sly. It wouldn't surprise me if he and Madelaine are related.'

Despite her discomfort, Esther's interest was caught. 'Why do you say that?' she asked.

'Because of how close they stand when they talk to each other. You told me to watch that sort of thing.' Fourteen paused. 'I suppose they could be husband and wife,' she conceded. 'Madelaine seems all right, by the way. She was quite worried about you passing out. She said your eyes must be very sensitive, more like an Outlander's than a city-dweller's.'

Fourteen was not as stupid as she sometimes appeared. 'What about Callum?' Esther asked. 'Is he here?'

'Madelaine said he'd be coming soon. That's something else I've noticed. Everyone's waiting for him. Jack appears to be in charge, but I get the impression even he defers to Callum.'

'Madelaine's certainly afraid of him.'

'I'd say it was respect rather than fear. When I asked her about him on the way here, she said he was a good man. How can a Keeper be a good man?'

'How indeed?'

Esther paused, considering what Fourteen had said so far. 'I can't recall how I got here either,' she admitted. In irritation, she rubbed at her eyelids. They felt swollen. 'It's maddening. Twice I've been made to do just what they want, and then to forget it afterwards. I don't even know how it's done.'

'You'd have thought they'd have trusted us by now.'

'They daren't trust us, or anyone else. There's too much at stake. If they're caught, they'll be executed by their own side.'

For several seconds both women were quiet, listening to the sounds from below. 'What sort of place is this?' Esther asked.

'Like an army camp, except that everything's done in darkness. Even when we ate, there was only a minim light. No one's asleep now, for all it's the middle of the night.'

Esther was beginning to feel tired with talking, and her head ached. 'You'd better go back down soon,' she warned. 'We don't want them to think we're plotting something.'

'Hurry up and get better. It's been a bit grim on my own.'

Taking the woman's hand, Esther held it for a second. 'I'll be with you soon,' she promised.

'Please.' Fourteen's voice shook slightly. 'I've never been so frightened in my life as when I first arrived. There were all these people in masks – as if they had no features – and I hadn't the faintest idea where I was, or how I'd got here. Then they insisted on putting some stuff in my eyes, and warned me it was going to hurt terribly. I know you think I shoudn't have accepted the anaesthetic from them, but I don't have your nerve. I'm sorry I let you down.'

'Of course you didn't,' Esther said gently. 'You were probably far saner than me.'

Her feet echoing on the empty boards, Fourteen crossed back to the door.

'Hattie—' Esther whispered.

'Yes?'

'Who brought me up here?'

'Jack.'

'Was he alone with me? You know what I mean.'

The woman turned back in concern. 'I wouldn't think there was anything like that,' she said hurriedly. 'This lot's too serious to think of such things. They're preparing for a war.'

After Fourteen had gone, Esther lay back down on the bed. She tried to recall how she had got there, and could not. She remembered catching the speedliner to Centopolis, as if going to see to her husband's affairs, and then leaving it at Midpoint. A personal transport had awaited her, driven by the standard brisk young man, and she had been brought back to Nortown. Like Fourteen, she had been taken to Central Wharf, and she could recall changing boats somewhere upstream, but she had no memory of a barge. Had she been taken aboard anything resembling one, she would immediately have been on her guard. Instead, once again, a hole had suddenly opened in her mind. However it was done, it was clever, and effective. Neither she nor Fourteen had the remotest chance of recognising their route, or of leading an enemy to the renegades' camp.

Sighing, Esther got up on to her knees, and made her way across to the window. The light from it was still very painful, and she closed her eyes and stood listening. Below her she could hear voices and the sound of feet. The rhythm was that of people running, and then stopping and running again. A gymnasium, she decided, or a training ground. Feeling her way from the window, Esther explored the outer edge of the room. There was an alcove on the far side, where a small lamp glowed, reflecting a blur of light in a mirror. Beside the lamp was a hairbrush and a small pot. When she unscrewed the lid, she found the pot contained a sweet-scented cream. To the left there was also a towel and a bowl of water.

Akwardly Esther splashed some of the water on her face and around her eyelids. The towel fell to the floor as she did so, and cursing, she had to feel around for it. Picking up the brush more carefully, she tried to tidy her hair. Afterwards she smoothed some of the cream on her face and throat. Wherever she was, she could at least keep herself respectable. The fact comforted her a little.

Finally, Esther made her way back into the main room. There she sat against the wall, where it was darkest, shielding her eyes from the glare of the window.

For some time she was alone. Slowly her eyes began to adjust to the light, and to distinguish shapes: first the window-frame, and then the door to the left of it. She recalled sitting on the speedliner after Bob's committal, and trying to think what made Callum so special. Without realising, she had hit on the explanation, and had rejected it as insufficient. It still wasn't sufficient, but it was part of the truth. Callum and his colleagues had indeed discovered a way to see in the dark, and for some reason they had shared it with her.

By the time Madelaine came, Esther could see the girl's outline quite clearly. She was young, with short cropped hair and a straight athletic body. It was hard to imagine she could ever have been mistaken for an old woman.

'I've brought you something to eat,' she said, crossing the room to place a tray beside Esther. 'How are you feeling?'

'Not too bad.'

'Can you see me yet?'

'I can't see your face, but I can tell you're there.'

'Cal would like to speak to you. I'll stay in the corridor outside. You can call me if you want, but I won't eavesdrop.'

'It wouldn't make any difference if you did,' Esther replied coldly. She wondered if Madelaine was genuinely without disguise now. The tone and gestures suggested a third-strata student. There was just the right hint of insecurity underlying the confidence born of power and education. Yet a good actor could adopt such a tone as easily as that of an old woman.

'Will you speak to him?' Madelaine persisted.

'If he wants. I don't suppose I have much choice in the matter.'

In the silence that followed Madelaine's departure, Esther sat trying to place exactly where she was relative to the door, though she doubted if there would be anywhere to run to beyond that. She could hear the muffled sounds of a firing range. In the distance a dog was barking, but no one else seemed to be paying the least attention to the firing. For a training centre to remain so undisturbed, it must be a long way into the Outlands, possibly in rebel-held territory. There had been rumours for some time that whole areas were no longer under the Keepers' control. It began to look as though the rumours were true.

Footsteps sounded on the stairs again, and she recognised Callum's uneven tread. The girl stopped outside the door, while Callum came inside. Not moving, Esther waited for him to approach her.

'How are you?' he asked.

'I'll survive – through no fault of yours.'

'I did warn you.'

'When?'

'At the cottage. I told you things wouldn't be pleasant here.'

'You didn't say how unpleasant.'

'I didn't expect you to refuse the anaesthetic. I ought to have. In your place I would have done the same.'

The reply surprised Esther, and she looked up at him. Her

distorted vision made him appear even more threatening than at Rokers' Garth.

'I'm supposed to be able to withstand pain,' she replied, 'not pass out like a delicate schoolgirl.' Thoroughly cross with herself, Esther looked up at him. 'Oh, do sit down!' she snapped. 'You make me nervous, standing there in that ridiculous uniform.'

To her astonishment, Callum did as she asked, sitting against the wall beside her. 'You haven't touched your meal,' he said. 'You must at least have something to drink. You'll be dehydrating soon.'

'I know what your drinks can do,' Esther retorted. 'My colleague's been asleep for at least a day.'

Taking the beaker, Callum offered it to her. 'Here,' he said. 'There's nothing in this except cordial. It's not even a strong cordial. My granny used to make better.'

'Then you drink it.'

Esther waited. Taking the beaker, he drank. 'Your turn,' he said.

Cautiously Esther took a sip. It was indeed cordial, a light sparkling wine that warmed her and made her realise how thirsty she was. Yet still she returned the beaker to him.

'Now you drink again,' she said. 'Prove there's nothing lurking at the bottom. Some poisons lie heavy.'

He did as she asked. 'Not even a frog,' he said afterwards.

'A frog?'

'When I was a boy I had a cup with a joke frog at the bottom. It used to amuse my guests no end.'

Despite her fear, Esther smiled.

Taking the bread, Callum broke it and ate a piece, before passing her the other half. 'How are your eyes now?' he asked.

'Why should you be concerned?'

'I don't like to think of you being frightened, or in pain. Or that it's partly my fault. I should have explained to you in advance. You're a professional in your own right. I shouldn't have assumed you'd sleep through like your colleague.'

The apology eased Esther's anger a little. 'All right, explain to me now,' she said. 'I can always cope better when I know what's happening.'

'You have been given a drug to help you see. Not in full darkness – the human eye isn't capable of that – but when there's a little light. The pain comes from the effect the medication has on the iris, and on the nerves that translate visual stimuli to the brain. It's always worst the first time. After that, if the dosage is kept up, the eyes begin to tolerate it. Used too long, however, it can cause damage. Someone like me has to have a few months off in each year, but you'll only need the one dose. That will last about four months. With your existing skills, it should make you quite a formidable woman.'

'But why give it to me? I'm only here to help Fourteen.'

'Without the same ability as everyone else, you wouldn't be able to find your way around. We work in darkness, and sleep by day. It's safer. In any case, if your student is to avoid setting the alarms off in the control centre, she has to learn to work without light. If you're to help her learn, you must do the same yourself.'

'Fair enough,' Esther agreed. 'Now tell me something else. I've no memory of how I got here. This is the second time you've done that to me. How?'

'It wasn't me this time.'

'All right. How did Jack do it? You've both invaded my mind. I don't like that. You leave me feeling weak and foolish, and hating you. I can't function properly with hatred in my mind. It blocks out my feeling for other people.'

There was a long silence.

'I can't tell you such things,' Callum said at last.

'At least tell me if I could have resisted it.'

'When a Keeper uses his power, you do as he wishes.'

Callum had spoken softly, but the reply was so menacing that Esther's mouth began to go dry. 'That sounds like a threat,' she pointed out. 'And a very unpleasant one.'

'I don't mean it to. I'm just stating the truth. If a Keeper's any good, he has power over other people's minds. It's a power I hate. It ignores the rights of the other person, and makes normal human relationships impossible. But it's also a very useful defence. I would have given the world not to have had to use it against you, but neither Jack nor I dare risk you knowing where this place is, or who we are.'

'I won't betray you.'

'Not willingly, but if you were taken by our enemies, you could be forced to.'

It was some time before either of them spoke again. 'It's not pleasant knowing you're at someone's mercy,' Esther said.

'And it's not nice saying it. If it's any consolation, you're safer with people like Jack and me than with those we're trying to oust. A Keeper is taught never to use his power for personal gain. It's a rule I've always tried to follow. How could anyone dare risk speaking to me, if I didn't? I'd end up without friendship, or love, everything I need as a human being. I won't pretend I haven't been tempted sometimes, but when I've given in my power's lost me the very thing I've wanted. That's what's happening now, within the Order. Our rulers are ignoring their own principles . . .'

Moving away from her slightly, Callum lapsed again into silence. He had probably said far more than he should.

It was difficult for Esther to frame her reply. 'I'd like to believe you,' she said.

'You'd sense at once if I was lying. A sympath knows such things.'

'Unless you were confusing me again.'

Sighing, Callum looked towards the window. 'That's exactly what I mean,' he replied. 'Because you know what I'm capable of, you'll always assume the worst.'

In bewilderment Esther looked up. Though Callum had tried to conceal his emotion from her, for a few seconds the control had broken. He was beginning to love her. She could not begin to explain such love, or why it seemed rooted in a long-established respect. It had probably begun when he comforted her in the church, and deepened now in concern at her pain. Love for any woman could make him vulnerable. She wanted to warn him of his emotion before he allowed it to develop, but knowing Callum's feeling for her might assist her some day. It would be more sensible to say nothing until then.

'I find it hard not to fear you,' Esther admitted.

'I promise no harm will come to you, Tess, unless you force me to defend myself. You're here under my protection, and I'm honoured to entertain you as my guest. You behaved with dignity just now, even if you did pass out in the end. Jack's convinced you're a Keeper's daughter. That can't do you any harm.'

'Why does he think that?'

'Because we're not allowed to accept anaesthetics ourselves. That's another of our principles.' Getting up, Callum passed her a phial of cream. 'Put this on your eyes after I've gone,' he advised. 'Rub it right into the lids. You'll find it'll help a great deal. Then come down as soon as you're ready. Your colleague needs you.'

'Callum?' Esther asked.

Pausing, he waited.

'Thank you for your kindness.'

After he had gone, Esther sat staring ahead of her. She felt shaky and emotional. For several moments she sat perfectly still, calming herself. Finally she got up and went into the anteroom. Rubbing some of the cream into her eyes, she found it eased the pain immediately. Within minutes, her vision was clearing. For the first time she could see her own reflection in the mirror. The room behind her was still blurred, but she could see her eyes, the pupils dilated and the whites a peculiar yellow colour. Turning, she looked around her. Her clothes had been unpacked and laid carefully over a box. Everything she might need had been put ready. Her quarters were spartan, no more than a bare room in an empty building, but she had been made welcome.

Going back into the main room, Esther went to the window. She could distinguish the shapes of two men walking across a courtyard. Dressed in black, they stood out bold against the moonlight. There seemed to be a fountain or a statue near them. She could see well enough to go and help Fourteen.

Feeling her way down the stairs carefully, Esther came to a small hallway, with doors opening off it. A young man in sports gear was waiting for her. Like the man along the waterway, he appeared to have no face, yet he was not wearing a noticeable mask. 'I'll take you through to your friend,' he offered. 'This way, Ma'am.'

Leading her down several other corridors and across the courtyard, past what was indeed a fountain, he took Esther to the building opposite. They appeared to be in an empty condominium, structurally complete but without lighting or plumbing. The atmosphere was damp, unconnected to a controlled environment system. From the outside the building would have appeared deserted; inside there was movement and purpose. Figures passed Esther continually. It was impossible to tell their identity. Most seemed to be young. All were silent and shadowy, people to be reckoned with, who talked only when it was necessary.

The young man took Esther into a large hall filled with training equipment, even mock-up doors and windows. Fourteen was standing in a doorway, trying to keep one hand at the bottom and the other at the top, while maintaining constant pressure. She looked very like a new yoga student who had not yet got the hang of things. Beside her, a trainer was giving orders she was immediately forgetting. It was all Esther could do not to smile.

'Come and show her how to do it,' the instructor whispered as Esther joined them. 'She says you'll be able to teach her. I certainly can't.'

'You'll have to teach me first,' Esther whispered in return.

'Oh Gawd!'

Fourteen had triggered the alarm. With a gesture of helplessness, the young man switched it off. 'Enery!' he called.

Someone had been sitting in the darkness waiting.

'Allow me to introduce one of our friends,' the trainer continued. 'This is Henry, or Our 'Enery, as he prefers to be called. 'Enery will show you how to break into a building without getting caught. You'll observe that we have a perfectly new condominium here, complete with state of the art technology. 'Enery loves to display his talents.'

A rather large hand shook Esther's vigorously.

'This is Tess,' the young man continued, as if they were meeting at a party.

'I don't know much about alarms,' Esther admitted. She had a strong desire to giggle.

'Got any particular building in mind, Ma'am?'

'A rather nasty one. I'm told we can assume light sensors, body-heat scanners, pressure points, the lot.'

'Laser bars?' 'Enery enquired hopefully.

'I should imagine so.'

'Will the building be in darkness?'

'Definitely.'

'And will you know what you're after?'

'Yes.'

'Righto!' 'Enery's English was as hearty as his handshake, and definitely not Northern. 'Come over here then, lady. Let's give you a feel of things.'

'It's not me who's going,' Esther interrupted. 'I have to pass on your lessons to my pupil. The tall woman over there.'

'Pity.' 'Enery sniffed. 'You look more suited to upending yourself than she does. Still, we'll have to work with what we've got.'

'If it's all right, I'll leave you two together,' the young man said. 'By the way, I'm Dave.'

'Pleased to meet you, Dave,' Esther replied, at last allowing herself to smile. Even revolution had its funny side.

15

When she was not stiff with fear, Fourteen could do a great deal more than she realised, and she was willing to learn from Esther. By the end of the third night, she was competent enough to continue her lessons from Dave direct, and Esther intervened only when needed. For half an hour or more sometimes, she was free to sit quietly against the wall of the training room, watching the comings and goings around her.

Since everyone wore masks, it was difficult to make the usual distinctions between the people around her, but there were voices and gestures to observe, and they told Esther a good deal. Emotions remained the same, whether the physical body was hidden or not. Some of the masks were also not quite complete, ending above the mouth to give greater freedom of speech. They seemed to be worn by the regular staff, suggesting that the full masks were too uncomfortable for constant wear. The shape of a mouth and chin seen in near darkness did not give much away, but it helped. Esther felt she was getting to know certain key figures.

Dave was a thorough professional. He reminded Esther of an army instructor she had met while living with her father. The man known as Jack was definitely older than him, and in command. As Fourteen had suggested, Madelaine could be his daughter or wife, but if she was, he showed her no favouritism. There were occasional tensions amongst the group, as if an existing organisation had been taken over by a more powerful one. The incomers included Jack and Madelaine, and a man known as Mike, who seemed to be the resident doctor. There was also a woman called Tamson who was a more shadowy figure. She served as quartermaster, seeing the trainees were fed and clothed. Callum himself must be an incomer too. He did not reappear for the first three nights, yet his influence was felt even in his absence. Jack might be in charge, but the group was now Callum's. It was not a matter of fear or seniority, but of reputation. Esther suspected it was his idea that had given rise to the group in its present form – and possibly created others elsewhere.

Most of the trainees seemed to be students, intellectuals not yet caught up in the system by the privileges it could bestow. Their voices suggested that women were among their number, enjoying far greater equality than in the world outside. Since all were fully masked however, and wore identical sports clothes or loose black uniforms, it was impossible to be certain how many.

Strangely, five of the staff showed their faces like Madelaine. They dealt with the outside world, Esther decided. After all, someone had to do the shopping and answer the door. Even so, she wondered how they dared risk recognition. If Madelaine was related in some way to Jack, allowing her to be seen would put him at risk too. Intrigued, Esther observed the girl more closely. There was something unnatural about her face. It was too static. As one would expect, there were the odd blemishes, a small mole near her mouth and a rather attractive bend to one eyebrow, but the texture of her skin never altered. She was pretty in an upper-strata way, but there was no life in her prettiness. Reluctantly, Esther was forced to the conclusion that Madelaine's identity too was concealed, but so subtly only a careful and frequent observer would have known.

In such a place of perpetual darkness, night and day blurred. So too did the composition of the trainees living there. Some lived normal lives by day and were brought in at night, to disappear the following morning. Others could spend several nights in succession there. How many in all came and went, Esther could not say; enough to suggest a sizeable fighting force. It would cost a great deal of money to support such an operation. One individual would be unlikely to be able to spend so much without causing comment, but several powerful and wealthy families might be able to.

Their plans were coming to fruition. Thoughout the whole group, Esther could feel a sense of waiting, of working towards a common goal that was now drawing near. The running about in the makeshift gym, the preparation of survival packs – all suggested that an imminent assault was being prepared.

On the fourth night Callum returned, bringing with him a young man he introduced as Toby. Toby was indistinguishable from all the other faceless young men in sporting gear, but he had been chosen to accompany Fourteen into the control centre. From now on he was to train with her, so that they could build up the necessary rhythm, and would be able to co-operate on Keepers' Day itself. Dave was no longer on site, apparently. The first part of this training was to be undertaken by Callum and Esther directly.

All that night, they watched their pupils learning to work together, and assisted whenever there was a problem, which was too often for anyone's liking. Toby had been warned that Fourteen was inexperienced, but not how inexperienced. After the first hour he became annoyed, concerned at the thought of entering a heavily guarded building with so clumsy a partner. Twice, Callum had to speak to him privately, to prevent outright argument. Until then Esther had not realised Callum was a trainer like herself, and not just an emissary. He was a very good one too, patient and clear in his instructions.

By midnight, things began to improve a little. Fourteen got used to the idea of working with a new partner, and Toby realised she was genuinely trying to learn, rather than just being awkward. Esther suggested they all rest a while and, sighing with relief, Fourteen went straight up to her room. She would probably have a good cry and feel better for it; it was wisest to leave her in peace.

Before the hour was over, Callum called Esther into the empty refectory. 'Tell me what I've missed,' he invited, and indicated several diagrams and plans spread across a table. She was surprised that he sought her opinion.

'I don't like the narrow time limit,' Esther admitted. 'Fourteen's still too slow. What happens if she and Toby don't get out of the building before the show ends?'

'They'll have to go back to the cleaners' room and hide there. At five, the morning domestics come on duty. With luck, they'll be able to slip out with them. I've arranged for some overalls to be included with the equipment.'

'And back-up? Who'll be there in case things go wrong?'

'Jack and Madelaine. They'll act as the relief domestics and then sign out as Commander Tate and Miss Hughes. Afterwards, they'll hang around the area. We daren't let anyone else in on the plan. Another of our number was taken yesterday. We definitely have an informer in our midst.'

'Here?' Esther asked in alarm.

'I hope not, but somewhere close to us.'

Together, they looked at the plans again. Mallin Laboratories had been surveyed meticulously since the meeting at the cottage. Now the position of each door and window was marked, and even some of the alarms indicated. Esther did not ask how it had been done. Clearly the renegades still had contacts in very high places.

Finally Callum folded up the plans. 'I have a bad feeling about this operation,' he admitted.

'I've had it from the start,' Esther agreed. 'We'll just have to try and cover every eventuality.'

They returned to the training room. For another two hours Toby and Fourteen continued their practice. They were beginning to get on together a lot better. Callum was no longer to be seen.

The following night, Dave took over again. He was much more serious now, checking for the least carelessness and making Fourteen and Toby practise so repeatedly that even Toby begged for a rest. By the time Callum returned two days later there had been a marked improvement in their performance.

'That's more like it,' Callum said, and Esther sensed his relief. Turning to Fourteen, he nodded. 'You've learnt a lot,' he said. 'It hasn't been easy, I know.'

Fourteen smiled with relief and pleasure.

Madelaine came in, bringing them refreshments. She spoke softly to Callum, surprised that he had come again. 'You must be worn out,' Esther heard her say gently. 'Even a Keeper needs some sleep.'

'I'll sleep when Sunday's over.'

He was sitting on the floor, not far from Esther, resting against the wall. For the first time he was not fully masked, and Esther could see the shape of his mouth. Like most people, if she had dared to imagine a Keeper, she had thought of a man with thin lips and cruel features. The line of Callum's mouth was unexpectedly sensitive, and younger than she had expected. He was also desperately tired.

Madelaine put her hand on his shoulder, and he touched it quickly in acknowledgement. The gesture conveyed long friendship, even love. 'Take care,' Madelaine whispered. 'When people are tired, they make mistakes.'

So Callum was family too, Esther thought, smiling. Now that was an interesting idea.

Afterwards, she went out into the courtyard, the only exercise outdoors any of them were allowed. It was a beautiful night, the wind cool after a hot, unpleasant day. In pleasure, she sat on the edge of the empty fountain.

To her surprise, Callum also came out. 'It's good to be in the fresh air a bit,' he remarked.

'The day's been very close,' Esther agreed.

'You must find it difficult having no controlled environment.'

'I'm used to the Outlands. My father was based in the Protectorate a number of times.'

'Which is why your eyes reacted so badly at the beginning. We should have thought of that. Are you still angry with me?'

'I'm almost enjoying myself,' Esther admitted. 'I like feeling I have something useful to do, and that people round me are all willing to work.' On such a night, it was easy to relax and talk of personal matters. 'Do you feel any happier now?' she asked.

'I ought to. Toby and your Fourteen work well together now.'

'So what's still worrying you? Is it something I can put right?'

'Not unless you can change the way of the world. It's the fact of what we're doing that's worrying me, not the thing itself.'

Not understanding, Esther waited.

'For over ten years now, I've hoped and planned for a revolution. Now it's almost a reality. If your colleague's successful, in two weeks' time there'll be chaos in the cities. The Outlanders will see their chance to turn against their protectors. There'll be civil war. Do I have the right to inflict that on my country?'

'I've asked myself the same question,' Esther replied. 'Many times.'

'Yet if I don't, I'll spend my life knowing I didn't fight an evil I should have fought. What's left of my life, that is. Sooner or later, my enemies will catch up with me.'

'Can't you escape? Get to the Union perhaps?'

'If I was going to run, I'd have run three or four years ago.

It's the choice every political refugee has to make – whether to escape or stay and fight. I chose to stay.'

'Then you have to abide by that decision.'

'Or give myself up, and accept the consequences. At least I'd save other lives that way.'

Running his hand around the bowl of the fountain, Callum lapsed into silence. His despair was so clear that Esther extended her hand to him across the stone.

'What would happen to your family if you confessed?' she asked.

'That's what stops me. But for the thought of them, I'd have gone to my superiors yesterday. There was a suitable moment.'

'You have to finish what you've started, or come up with a better option. My dad taught me that when I was a child. He was very much the soldier; very concerned with duty, and doing what was right.'

'But if what you feel is right conflicts with what you've been taught?'

'The world changes. Maybe what you were taught belongs to another time.'

Nodding, Callum sat looking into the darkness. 'It's always the ordinary people who suffer,' he said quietly. 'The women with children, the old who can't run. They won't have any light, or power, or food. We've planned to preserve supplies, but in a war you can't guarantee anything for anyone. In any case, we may lose. Then everyone's suffering will have been for nothing.'

'We're back where we started,' Esther pointed out. 'All right, suppose you don't fight. What happens to the ordinary people then?'

'They'll still suffer. Not as sharply or as suddenly, but gradually. Tess, you don't know half of what's happening. In another ten years we won't be able to support our population, not without outside help. As a nation, we're spending far too much of our income, keeping people happy. Resources are scarce for the whole of humanity. There's no longer enough cake to go round, and we're getting squeezed out, like the lazy piglet who'd rather sleep than feed himself. How many city-dwellers could cope if their controlled environment collapsed? We've become totally reliant on a technology we can't afford to maintain.'

'You sound like Sly.'

'Such things are obvious to anyone willing to think. The decay begins in the Order itself, and runs right down. Our knowledge enabled us to save the country, but now we sit back and live off the past. That's crazy. To survive, you have to go on learning and inventing, asking questions. There are so many questions that need asking. Every day people in the cities die of leukaemia. Why? Maybe it's the controlled environment itself. That's at least worth looking at, yet nobody dares switch it off. It'd be too unpopular. Look round you and see how many couples have no child, or only one. If you do see more, there's years between them. What causes that? It may be convenient but it isn't natural. At the rate we're going, we'll soon be a nation without children. Do we really want to become extinct?'

'Bob and I used to ask the same question,' Esther admitted. 'I've often wondered if it's the audiovision.' She smiled slightly. 'And I don't mean that the programmes are too good.'

There was a moment's pause. 'You're a very good listener,' Callum said. 'And I've been ranting on. I'm sorry.'

They began to walk round the courtyard together.

'What sort of world do you visualise?' Esther asked. 'In your dreams, I mean.'

'One where I didn't have to wear a silly uniform for a start, or a mask – where no one was afraid.'

'How would you achieve that?'

'By breaking down the distinction between Keeper and Kept. I'd abolish the strata. And end the divide between

Outlanders and city-dwellers. Such divisions may have been necessary when we were fighting for survival, but they waste too much talent now. I'd get rid of most of the other rules too, especially those that invade people's privacy. You can't legislate people into being moral, or happy. Nor can you stop them feeling grief or fear, or any of the emotions that the human species is prone to. There's one thing we must do right now, though: get back into the Union. We can't go on trying to survive in isolation.'

'Would they admit us?'

'If we put our house in order. That means recognising human rights. Yet our stupid hierarchy is determined to make Dissent a capital offence ...' With a gesture of exasperation, Callum turned to her. 'That'll end all chance of us being accepted for thirty years at least. By then, our lower strata will be dying of starvation.'

There was a long silence between them, filled only by the sound of the wind, and their feet on the paving.

'You'll make a very good leader,' Esther commented.

'I don't want to be a leader. When this revolution's over, I shall go home and keep fish.'

Shaking her head, Esther laughed. 'No you won't,' she predicted. 'You're driven by something, like all rebels. Worrying about starvation wouldn't make you risk your life, especially when you could die in such a horrible manner. I wouldn't risk such a death. I find it difficult to imagine how you can.'

Returning to the fountain, Callum sat down on the stone beside her. 'To understand me,' he said, 'you have to understand something that happened to me when I was a boy.'

Esther waited, sensing that he would continue if she gave him time. He needed to talk of it, just as he had needed to share his despair.

'How old were you?' she prompted.

'Eleven.'

'Tell me about it.'

'It's not a nice story.'

'Few stories told by rebels are.'

'I was staying with my grandfather.' Unusually hesitant, Callum paused, wording his reply carefully. 'There was a lake, with an old boathouse. My brother often used to take me there. It was my favourite place. If I sat in the upper room, I could hear the water and the birds around me. One afternoon, my brother left me there while he went to play in the woods. It was almost dusk.' Callum's voice was losing its measured tone, and he paused to steady it. 'I heard a boat come across the water and then voices beneath me. One of them was my grandfather's. Another was that of a young man. He was pleading with my grandfather to forgive him. He kept saying the same words over and over again. "I didn't mean any harm. Sir, I didn't mean any harm ..." Sometimes he cried. In the end, my grandfather stopped him. He said it was out of his hands. There was nothing he could do.'

Turning slightly, Callum sat so that Esther could not see the movement of his mouth. She did not dare to speak. His emotion was increasing, but she found it difficult to read, except as a blurred sense of remembered horror and distress. It affected her, making her afraid too. 'I should have called out,' he admitted; 'let them know I was there, but when I opened my mouth, nothing happened. I heard orders being given. Afterwards most of the men went away.'

Callum paused. Esther could sense that he was very cold, though the night was warm. 'The young man started screaming,' he added. 'He was young and not very brave. They killed him just the same.'

Involuntarily Esther caught her breath.

'Afterwards, they washed the floor. I heard the water splashing on the boards. Finally, the enforcers went away. By the time my brother came for me, the place was deserted.'

Esther wanted to reach out and offer comfort, but she was

afraid to. 'And yet you became a Keeper yourself,' she said gently. 'Were you given no choice?'

'It was my father's wish, and mine. As it happens I could have been excused. There were special reasons, but I would have felt as if I was only half a person. So I told myself I could change things from the inside. God knows, I've tried.'

'Did your parents learn what had happened?'

'I told no one, not even my brother. I'd overheard something so forbidden, I was at risk too. For two years I kept silence, until I almost forgot how to speak. Then I told your mother.'

'How did—' Esther began, and stopped herself urgently. 'No. Don't answer that,' she warned.

Abruptly Callum got up and went indoors.

For a long time Esther sat on her own in the courtyard. Fourteen and Toby crossed between the buildings, returning to continue their work together. Joining them, Esther tried to think about what they were doing, even to joke a little, but all the while she was aware of Callum's presence. He had said too much, and he knew it. She began to feel very afraid.

For the rest of the night, Esther waited. Whenever someone entered the training area she expected them to escort her from it. Every sudden noise made her mouth go dry. Concentrating on one of the mantras her Maestra had taught her, she tried to guard her thoughts. If a Keeper struck, it could be from within the victim's own mind. There were stories of people committing suicide out of fear, or simply growing careless and stepping in front of a shuttle. With so many weapons around, if Callum chose he could destroy her a dozen ways.

Yet nothing happened. She was allowed to go about her normal business unhindered. The waiting was almost as exhausting as the fear.

Callum came into the room but remained at the far end, and for two hours Esther managed to avoid him. Finally the training session ended, and Dave announced he was going to bed. Esther considered suggesting she and Fourteen should share a room that night, but that would put Fourteen at risk too so she let her go. She was alone, apart from Callum.

Crossing the room, he stood beside her.

'You can trace me now, can't you?' he asked. His voice had a deadly quietness that terrified Esther.

'I won't betray you,' she insisted. 'It doesn't matter to me who you are.'

'You caught me when I was tired and low, then drew me on. Oh yes, you're clever.'

'You needed to talk, and I was sympathetic. That's all. Please, Cal—' Gently Esther touched his arm, aware that she was pleading for her life. 'When I arrived here, I was half out of my mind with fear. You told me I could trust you, and I believed you. Now you have to believe me. Unless you threaten my safety, I'll never use what you've told me.'

She was not finding the right words, and it was vital that she should do so, quickly. 'I'm beginning to love you in return,' she said. 'People who love don't betray each other.'

For several seconds Callum watched her in silence. Fear closed Esther's throat. She knew she was very near to death and could do nothing more to save herself.

Unexpectedly Callum turned and left the room.

Trying to steady her breathing, Esther put her hands to her face. She had told Callum that she loved him. Why? To save her skin? That was despicable, but warranted by the circumstances. Or had she really meant what she said? A crazy voice inside her insisted it was the second, though only the first reason made sense.

That afternoon, Callum left the centre. Esther saw him cross the quadrangle below her window. She could scarcely believe she was still unharmed. From Callum's point of view, he had taken a terrible risk in leaving her free, a risk he might well regret bitterly later. Feeling slightly sick with relief, Esther went back to bed. She slept so deeply Fourteen had to wake her for the evening meal.

There was only one more night left of Fourteen's training, which Dave took. Halfway through, Jack came in, to explain that both women would soon be returned to their homes. They would be closely watched of course, and no contact would be permitted with anyone but Sly's designated representative.

'Bloody house arrest,' Fourteen grumbled afterwards. She was quite cheerful, however, infinitely relieved that the week was almost over, and that she had acquitted herself better than anyone had expected.

What would happen to them after Keepers' Day was not mentioned, but Esther could guess. Sly was probably already arranging for them to disappear along one of the Sheep People's routes. Knowledge was a dangerous commodity, and both women possessed too much of it for their own safety, or that of their leaders. The thought that she might not be allowed to collect her children filled Esther with more alarm than having to go into hiding herself. Until then, she had managed to keep Tim and Sally from her mind, telling herself that they were perfectly safe, and probably having a wonderful time. Now she could scarcely stop thinking of them.

Perhaps it was merely her own anxiety that made Esther so uneasy in other respects. Yet as she sat in the refectory with Fourteen, eating their last breakfast before returning to Nortown, her uneasiness seemed to come from outside her, rather than within. There was a discordance she had not sensed before, as if someone had recently arrived who did not belong. All through the meal, the feeling bothered her, increasing rather than declining. She asked Madelaine if anyone new had arrived.

'Half a dozen people,' Madelaine replied airily. As usual, she was very pleasant, but gave away nothing. 'People are always coming and going.'

With everyone masked and dressed identically, it was virtually impossible to tell who might be a newcomer. Yet the longer Esther sat at the table, the more certain she was that one of the people sitting near her was an outsider, someone who did not share the ideals of the rest. They seemed to have something important to do, the thought of which distressed them. Even so, they were sure that it was their duty to complete their task. It was the conflict between those two emotions, duty and regret, that Esther was feeling. In alarm, she looked up, trying to see which of those sitting near her could have felt such distress. There was too much background noise however, with half a dozen people all thinking and feeling simultaneously, being scared of what they were letting themselves in for, or excited, or nervous . . . New trainees at any course gave off a lot of emotion.

Unable to bear the sense of unease any longer, Esther left the rest of her meal and went up to her room. She wished Callum would come back to the centre. Whatever her personal fear of him, she must warn him.

For some time Esther stood looking out on to the courtyard. It seemed incredible that less than a week ago she had been unable even to see the shape of the window. Coming to a decision, she went into the anteroom and stood at the dressing table. There was a microstylus in her bag, and finding it, she laid it beside the minim light. Then, taking the locket from round her neck, she opened the back of it carefully. Inside was a small image of an imaginary husband and children, a distractor in case she was ever taken. Prising it out, she laid it on the table. Attached to the back was a piece of folded message film. For a full minute Esther considered what to write on it. Her memory could often retain images when words or facts vanished. Yet whatever she put must be meaningless to everyone else. Finally she settled for four lines, as if quoting from a poem:

Blind boy sits beside the lake.
What does he hear?
Grandfather Time orders
Birds and men cry in fear.

Refolding the film and putting the image back into the locket, Esther clipped it shut. She was squatting on the floor, packing up the bed roll when she heard Callum's step on the stairs.

'I came to say goodbye,' he said. 'You have no need to be afraid. I'll call Madelaine if you'd rather she was present.'

'No. I need to speak to you alone. I have some information for you.'

Callum closed the door quietly.

'Your informer's here,' Esther warned. 'He – or she – arrived last night.'

'How do you know?'

'I felt their coming. Do you know who's in this latest group?'

'Jack arranges the training sessions. He'd be able to tell me.'

'Can you trust Jack?'

'If I can't we're all finished.'

Awkwardly they stood together in the empty room. 'What do I do?' Callum asked. 'Question all the new arrivals? That would alert our traitor and probably achieve nothing.'

'Leave here,' Esther advised him. 'Don't tell anyone where you're going. The informer knows you, I'm certain of it.'

'I can't just run away,' Callum insisted. 'I have a reponsibility to everyone here. Besides, there's the assault on the control centre. It's the best chance we've had in years.'

'And what if your informer makes sure Fourteen and Toby don't arrive?'

'No one knows the details of the plan except ourselves.'

'Not the details, no, but a lot of people must be aware an assault is being prepared. Toby's known to be your best agent, and Fourteen's obviously clever with figures. A good Watcher might put two and two together.'

Esther could feel Callum's growing alarm. 'I came to persuade you not to betray me,' he admitted. 'I didn't expect you to be warning me of a threat in my own midst. Can I believe you? Or is this just like the other night? Playing on my weakness to save yourself?'

'What from?' Esther demanded. 'You won't hurt me. You don't break promises. You don't even need to. If you can erase the memory of how I got here, you can easily make me forget an embarrassing conversation.'

There was a long silence. 'I had thought of that,' Callum conceded. 'Would you be willing?'

'I'd already assumed you would. I didn't expect you to ask my permission.' Esther was playing dangerously, but she saw no alternative. 'The whole idea scares me stiff,' she added more gently. 'I'd give anything not to have to agree, but I'm safest not knowing who you are. Such knowledge will put me at risk from both sides.'

'Did you really mean what you said the other night?'

'Of course.'

'How can you love me? You've never seen me.'

'I see the man inside.'

'You see my loneliness, I know that. You use it too.' Picking up the hairbrush on the table, Callum turned it over in his hand several times. There was a long silence.

'What do we do about the control centre?' he asked finally. 'The success of that operation is more important than my safety.'

'Brief another two of your people, just in case Toby and Fourteen are stopped. Don't speak to anyone else, not even Jack.'

'There's no one who could take over at such short notice. Except perhaps you and me.'

Chewing her lip, Esther considered Callum's reply.

'Could we do it?' Callum asked, 'if we had to?'

'I don't know.'

'You've learnt everything Fourteen has, and I trained Toby originally. Supposing I managed to get you into the control room, could you key in your colleague's program?'

'If I went over it at home all weekend, I might. I used to do a lot of programming for work. But I'd be slower than Fourteen.'

'And I'll certainly be slower than Toby. The pupil has outdistanced his master. All the same, I suggest we hold ourselves in readiness. We can't let a single informer cost us so good a chance. I'll pack up a duplicate set of everything that's needed. At the last minute, I'll let Jack and Madelaine know the situation.'

Esther's heart had begun to beat quickly. 'We must be mad to consider such a thing,' she pointed out. 'We're both of us trainers, not actives.'

'Have you a better suggestion?'

'No.'

'Then learn that program, just in case. I'll get final arrangements through to you via Sly, not my own people.'

Esther paused, watching him. 'Can we trust you, Cal?' she asked.

'Can I trust you?'

16

Sly's representative was late. To keep herself from watching the time, Esther watered and trimmed her plants. Twice she went back into her bedroom and reread the message she had written. It still made no sense. At the time she wrote it, it must have meant something to her or she would never have gone to the trouble, or the risk, of writing it. Nor would she have been so convinced that as soon as she was home she must look in her locket.

'Blind boy sits beside the lake.' Why on earth had she written down such a silly rhyme? Was it a quotation, or had she suddenly developed an attack of poetry?

The intercom sounded. Expecting Twenty or one of the other local women, Esther answered the door. To her amazement, Sly herself stood there.

In all the time Esther had worked with the old woman, she had never known her come into Nortown. Now she stood dressed like any city-dweller, with a box of comfits in her hand.

'How nice to see you, Auntie,' Esther greeted her. Somewhere nearby, a door opened.

'I was passing through and thought I'd see how you are.' Kissing Esther on both cheeks, Sly offered the box. 'Are you feeling any better, dear?'

'Much better thank you,' Esther replied. 'Come on in.'

The door shut quietly lower down the corridor. Taking Sly's

gift, Esther led her into the dwelling. 'I've been busy cleaning since my return,' she added meaningfully. 'I've finished the kitchen.'

They went into the kitchen together and shut the door behind them.

'What made you come yourself?' Esther asked.

Sly looked round her quickly. 'I daren't send anyone else,' she replied. We too have been infiltrated. The enemy doesn't like alliances being formed.' Sly's sharp glance turned on Esther herself. 'You look – different, child. What's wrong with your eyes?'

'I'm tired, that's all. This last week hasn't been easy.'

'I shall require a full report.'

'Afterwards, when there's time.'

'How's Fourteen?'

'Ready to go on Keepers' Day. She did very well – once she stopped being frightened out of her wits. Has the plan been explained to you?'

'In detail. You and Callum are going as supernumeraries, I gather. That wasn't part of the original agreement.'

'We'd both of us like to see how our pupils get on, and we might come in useful if anything goes wrong.'

'Is anything likely to?'

'I hope not, but as you say, our enemies are getting near.'

Sitting down at the table, Sly recovered her breath. 'I have a message from Central Committee,' she said. 'It was delivered by courier when you were away. I'll repeat it, as soon as I've got my wits back. That wretched journey's scattered them all round my head.'

Esther prepared Sly a drink. 'How did you get here?' she asked.

'Walked. I don't like those shuttle things. Never feel safe on them. Tell me about the training centre. How far is it?'

'I don't know. There's a hole in my memory again.'

In exasperation, Sly put down her drink. 'Can't you stop them by now? You should have been on your guard.'

Standing looking out of the window, Esther tried to recall what had happened to her. 'They took me by surprise on the way there,' she agreed. 'Not on the way back. I agreed to it then.'

'Whatever for?'

'Because I knew too much.'

'What's the technique? Come on, girl. We need to know.'

'It's a sort of telepathy, I think.' Pausing, Esther reconsidered her statement. 'It's as if they've evolved a stage further than most of us. They've learnt how to use abilities we probably all have, but don't recognise.'

To Esther's surprise, Sly did not treat her reply scornfully. She merely nodded and drank her coffee. 'Did you feel anything?' she asked.

'Only that I was at peace, and very safe. This time it was done with—' Esther was going to say 'love' and changed her mind. 'With kindness,' she finished.

'Did you see any of their faces?'

'No. They were all masked.'

'Even amongst themselves?'

'Some of them appeared not to be, but when you looked close, there was a sort of fine skin over their features. Sometimes, when it was hot, people wore a sort of half-mask. The most I ever saw was the mouth and chin.'

'And Callum himself? You must have got to know him a bit. What sort of man is he?'

Staring out of the window, Esther tried to reply. 'I don't know that either,' she admitted finally. For some reason, the silly rhyme she had written returned to her mind, and she tried to think why. There was something at the back of her memory, but it would not come forward.

'You haven't got emotionally involved with him, have you?'

Esther considered the question carefully. Callum had dominated her thoughts since her return, but she could find no love for him in her mind, only repect and friendship. 'I don't think so,' she replied.

'What do you mean, "think"? Surely you know a thing like that?'

'I would have thought so, but there's a sort of emptiness in my mind, as if my emotions have been taken from me, as well as my memory of where I was and how I got back. Other things are quite clear. It's most peculiar.'

'Think carefully, child. Take away their tricks and rituals, and our Keepers are ordinary men, and lonely ones at that. Many a woman has fallen for one, only to find it cost her dearly. Or perhaps you like to feel threatened? Some women do. They're like children peering round the settee.'

'I'm not a child,' Esther replied coldly. 'I'm a widow with two children. How are Tim and Sally by the way, or haven't you bothered to ask?'

Sly smiled. 'Your children are fine. You'll be able to pick them up this Friday morning.'

'Will I still be around to do that?'

'Of course.' Finishing her drink, Sly brushed a hair off her jacket. She was as impeccably neat as ever. 'Now to the information from National Committee,' she said. Staring ahead of her, Sly began to repeat the message. She paused only once, her memory, like her clothes, still immaculate.

'National Committee to Northern Region. Additional information on Lander and Miniott families, as requested by agent Forty-Eight:

'Peter and Burgess Lander: related to Miniotts through mother, Mary (Marie) Lander, illegitimate daughter of John Miniott by French partner, Thérèse Chantall. Cousins of Carl and Simon Miniott. Education paid for by Miniott family. Burgess believed to have been particularly close to Simon in childhood.'

'Hold on, I'm lost,' Esther admitted.

Smiling, Sly settled back in her chair. She enjoyed a good problem. 'The two families are related, dear, just as you suggested. Remember me telling you about John Miniott? The one who found himself a pretty French artist?'

'He forcibly adopted the two sons.'

'That's him. There was also a daughter, who married a man called Lander, it seems. I thought she had been left in France, but it looks now as though the Miniott family took responsibility for her too. They must have brought her over to England after the Civil war. Her husband can't have been very high strata – not high enough to pay for a decent education for her sons anyway, so the Miniotts paid for them to go to State College. Seen from a Keeper's point of view, Burgess has repaid them amply. He's clearly lethal and must be got rid of as quickly as possible. Wait till you hear the rest.'

Staring ahead of her again Sly paused for breath, before continuing with the committee's message.

'Peter Lander currently employed in Outlands Protectorate Agency. Burgess's whereabouts not officially known, but sightings in Nortown.

'Previous aliases Jonathan Carter, Mark Plews and Glyn Honley. Resident in Birmingham area of Midopolis 2203. Confirmed responsible for breaking up local Resistance Units there. Since 2203, biography corresponds to details for Stephen Lahr – St Albans 2205, Nortown sightings this year. Identification of Burgess with Lander considered established. Command to be issued against Lahr/Burgess immediately . . .'

An unwanted sense of sadness made Esther's eyes sting. It would have been easier if she had not grown so fond of Imogen. 'Has the contract been carried out?' she asked.

I couldn't tell you. You know how these things are done. It might take a week or more.'

Esther recalled how her neighbour had stood in the doorway holding his son. Even a member of the Keepers' secret police could love his children, she reminded herself. The evidence against the man was strong. What better place was there to send an agent than a showhouse? People talked carelessly while they were enjoying themselves. They chatted to friends in the bar, arranged meetings over lunch in the refectory. The Northern resistance grew stronger every day. Whole areas of the Outlands were falling to rebel groups. It was only to be expected that Seekers would be sent to the North to identify the ringleaders before they could cause outright rebellion. It would be worth dismissing an uncooperative showhouse director to replace him with a well-trained spy, worth finding the new man accommodation quickly, even allowing him to keep his children if he made that part of his price.

Yet Sly seemed ill at ease over the command, though she had been forced to accept it. 'You're not convinced, are you?' Esther asked.

'The evidence is too circumstantial for my liking. I've seen it happen before. A Seeker attaches himself to an innocent man, and uses him as cover for years. The innocent man is finally eliminated. When the betrayals keep happening, everyone realises they got the wrong one. Do you think Stephan Lahr is our traitor? You live next to him.'

Esther considered her reply very carefully. She wanted to say no but honesty prevented her. 'He may be,' she admitted. 'According to Minkin, a man with blue eyes and fair hair has been to the canyon, asking about me. That sounds like Stephan Lahr. Why would he do that if he's just an ordinary neighbour? I'd much prefer to think the man's innocent but the evidence is against it.'

An expression of relief came to Sly's face. 'I'd hate to think we were wrong,' she admitted, 'but if Minkin says the man's been following you, that's good enough for me. It'll be interesting to see if the renegades are left alone once Lahr's removed, or whether we have a second informer to find.'

Once again, Esther found herself thinking of Imogen and

Benn. She was letting pity for them cloud her judgement. It was time to talk of other things. 'Was there anything more in the National Committee's message?' she asked.

Sly smiled. 'One bit of good news. I think we can discount Simon Miniott.'

'Why?'

'He's categorised VH.'

'Visual handicap? That should have been on our records.'

'We've only just started making enquiries about him. Our sources say he lost his sight in an accident when he was nine. He underwent surgery when he was twenty-two, but it was only partially successful. We've got his birthdate wrong too. He's older than Carl Miniott, not younger; born in 2176.'

Frowning, Esther looked out of the window. 'Blind boy sits beside the lake . . .' Her mind repeated the words. They had something to do with Callum, it insisted, though why she could not remember. Her memories of Callum were blurred or missing, as if they too had been erased. Yet just as a computer in search mode will find alternative routes, so her brain was looking for other ways of recalling what her memory had lost. The silly rhyme she had written had definitely been about Callum. He was the blind boy beside the lake. And Grandfather Time? That was his grandfather. But where was the lake? And what had the boy heard?

Sly was waiting for her reply. Esther decided to tell part of the truth, to cover her silence.

'A memory's going round in my head,' she admitted. 'Callum told me something that happened when he was a boy. Now I can't for the life of me recall what it was. All I know is that it was horrible, and made me respect him a great deal. The spokeswoman hinted dreadful things had happened to her son too. You understand the Keepers' ways. What was she talking about?'

'I assumed she meant the initiation.'

'It sounds as though our Keepers play silly games.'

'The initiation is no game.' Sighing, Sly stared into her cup. She seemed to Esther to be thinking of someone closer to her than the spokeswoman's son, someone she had known a long time ago. 'At the age of fifteen, each Keeper's son is taken to a secret place. He spends five weeks there with the men he will always call his masters. Those masters find his weaknesses and work on them, until he either overcomes them, or breaks. They do it by inflicting extreme pain – mental and physical – randomly, so the poor boy has no way of predicting what will happen next. If he finds it too much, he is invited to commit suicide. That's always been a way we've identified Keeper families: by noting when a boy of fifteen dies. Some survive the initiation, but break later. I'd guess that's what's happening to the spokeswoman's son.'

'How could anyone hurt a fifteen-year-old boy?'

'Survival of the fittest, my dear. Only the strongest, both mentally and physically, become Keepers, generation after generation. There are other benefits too. When you've gone through so much to gain membership of your club, you're less likely to tell others your trade secrets. No boy is excused, except the handicapped or the sick, and they're treated as half a man ever afterwards. That's why I say we can discount Simon Miniott. He won't have undergone initiation, so he won't be allowed near anyone or anything of importance. To lose your sight must be bad enough, but for a Keeper's son it must be doubly tragic.'

Standing very still, Esther looked through the window. 'Blind boy sits beside the lake ...' Her brain kept repeating the words. The idea was impossible. The Miniotts were fair. Callum was dark. Could there be two men, both blind as boys?

Esther began to talk again hurriedly, to keep Sly occupied. 'How long does the training period last?' she asked.

'Six years. The masters teach their boys what it is to rule, and the secret knowledge that will enable them to do so. Less than half of those who start the course are admitted as full members of the Order.'

Sly's knowledge was definitely beyond what a mere listener could obtain, however many transmissions she might intercept. Curiously, Esther tried to determine what the old woman was feeling about the conversation, but she blocked Esther's attempts to read her. They were becoming engaged in a silent duel, each trying to understand the other's feelings, while protecting their own.

'Let me get you something to eat,' Esther offered.

'No thank you dear. I'm quite all right.'

In the silence that followed, Esther went over the words of her rhyme again. Callum had been blind in his youth. The evidence for that conviction had gone from her mind, but the conclusion had not. Something she had heard or seen while she was away had confirmed a suspicion she had already formed. Yet the idea did not make sense. How could a fifteen-year-old boy begin such training, unable even to see the men who inflicted it on him? He would have needed so much courage, and so much endurance. Surely he could have asked to be excused. His family would have been disappointed in him, but they could not have blamed him for doing so.

'I forgot to mention one last bit of information,' Sly added suddenly. Opening her purse, she took from it a small still, such as a woman might carry around to remind her of a loved son or brother. 'This was Burgess Lander seven years ago,' she said.

'Is there nothing more recent?'

'No. The man is very careful. Even this was taken from a playbill.'

Esther examined the image.

'Do you recognise him?' Sly asked.

'It could be Stephan Lehr.'

'But you're not sure?'

'There's too much make-up. I know him, though. If it's not Stephan, I've seen him recently somewhere else.'

'What about Callum?'

'I've told you. Callum's dark—' Appalled, Esther stopped.

'What is it, child?'

'All this time, I've been visualising Callum as dark-haired, because that's how I glimpsed him, once. But supposing I was meant to see him that night? A man like him is far too clever to risk light coming in off the street. He's never showed his face any other time.' Furiously, Esther slammed her cup down. 'Even the colour of his hair and the shape of his nose could have been fabricated. I don't have the faintest idea what he looks like.'

With unexpected gentleness, Sly stayed her hand. 'The Keepers confuse us all,' she said. 'That's half their power. Now think hard. Could Callum be our informer?'

In horror, Esther considered the suggestion. 'But Cal's the renegades' best active,' she pointed out.

'Or is he an even better active, working for the other side?'

For some time Esther stood by the window, trying to recall the order of events. Callum was Simon Miniott. There was no other possible conclusion. The odds against there being two Keepers' sons of a similar age, both blind in their youth, were too high. But was he also the traitor in the renegades' midst? Were Simon Miniott and Burgess Lander one and the same man? Maybe there were not two families at all. The committee's information could be mistaken. Nothing could be taken at face value where the Keepers were concerned.

Her head aching with the effort of concentration, Esther watched the civic guard marching across the square below the window. No, she was certain the informer had entered the refectory before Callum returned. Later, she had felt two separate men, not one. Callum was not a spy, whatever else he might be.

Coming to a decision, Esther turned back to Sly. 'I need to

give you something,' she said. 'It will mean trusting to written record, but I can't think of any other way. Please don't watch what I write, or open it before time. My life may depend on no one knowing what I'm giving you.'

Inclining her head slightly in surprise, Sly turned away.

Esther had replaced the message film in her locket with a clean piece. Taking it out, she flattened it on the table, and wrote on it just three words: 'Callum equals Simon.' As an afterthought, she changed the 'equals' to 'equalled' and added, 'Who now? Try further surgery. French friends?' Finally, she folded it and put it back in place.

'Take the whole locket,' she said to Sly. 'If I ever fail to report in, wait for a full five days, then read what's written here. Don't so much as open it otherwise. This is my insurance policy, but only so long as it remains unknown by anyone except me.'

'And if you do fail to make contact?'

'You will have to decide whether to destroy this or to use it as bargaining power.'

Nodding in understanding, Sly accepted the locket. Then, reaching into her bag, she took out an extra copy of Fourteen's tape. 'You asked for this,' she remarked. 'Why?'

'I want to look through it, in case Fourteen doesn't make it. I might be able to remember the program for another day.'

Sly did not believe her, but she asked no further questions. 'If you can learn that stuff, you're cleverer than me,' she replied. 'You have about nineteen hours to do it in. The tape's set to self-destruct twenty-four hours after I left Hunter's Farm, and I've been travelling for at least five. I don't like you having it in your possession even that long. If I didn't know you so well, I wouldn't give it to you.'

Preparing to leave, she picked up her outdoor wrap, 'We're opening a sheep route for both you and Fourteen, starting time sixteen hours this Friday. You'll be given further details. It's a pity you've got to hang around until then, but we really can't get your children out any earlier than Friday, and I don't suppose you'd want to leave without them.'

Smiling, Esther shook her head.

'If you need help before then, get yourself within sight of Hunter's Farm, but be prepared for trouble. The Sheep People don't like unexpected company.'

'I'll tell Fourteen to go straight to you if there's any problem on Keepers' Day,' Esther agreed. 'You'd better warn them. I'd hate her to come to grief on a pitchfork.'

Sly prepared to leave. Unexpectedly she drew Esther to her and kissed her on the cheek. 'Trust no one,' she advised. 'Not even yourself.'

After the old woman had gone, Esther stayed at the window, working out what to do. She possessed knowledge that could be her own death warrant. If Callum so much as suspected she knew his proper name, he would be crazy not to get rid of her. Meeting him on Keepers' Day as they had arranged was about as sensible as jumping off one of the walkways. She might fall on her feet, but she was equally likely to land on her head. Yet she could not believe the man would harm her. He had tried to remove the memory of his love for her, but it was coming back by a different route, together with her own respect for him.

Wasting no further time, Esther turned from the window. Whatever the risk, she could not fail to keep her promise. Someone would have to enter the control room if Fourteen and Toby had been betrayed. Otherwise, the Movement's best chance of bringing down the Keepers would be lost.

Hurriedly Esther prepared herself a plate of food and a long drink, and sat down at her work station. Somehow she would have to learn Fourteen's program.

A blur of numbers and symbols at first, the sequence gradually revealed its beauty. There were patterns, rhythms as subtle as music. Like a skilfully composed quadrille, it repeated and repeated itself, but never at predictable intervals. If Esther could learn those patterns, she could memorise the program much more easily. Clearly, that was why Fourteen had included them. Fourteen, however, had the advantage of having designed the program in the first place, and knew why every symbol was important. For an outsider the task was much harder; so hard that after an hour Esther's head and eyes ached. She was beginning to realise the enormity of the task she had set herself. Even after the patterns had been understood, there were the link passages to master, and they were lacking in obvious structure. Though the program was comparatively short, designed to be embedded in another longer one, even a skilled courier would have found learning such a complicated message virtually impossible.

Hoping that sleep would refresh her memory, Esther went to bed, but when she awoke she found all she had achieved was to lose another six hours of the nineteen Sly had permitted. She had only seven left.

Urgently Esther began to design herself cue cards, which she could learn more easily than the whole program. To her relief, she found they helped a good deal. By splitting the program into short sections she gradually memorised all but the most random sequences. There seemed no way she could remember those, no matter how hard she tried. After another two hours she gave up the struggle. For the random sections she would have to invent four separate mnemonics, and take them into the centre with her. A single strip of paper taped inside her sleeve would be sufficient, and hopefully meaningless to anyone but herself. Staring into space, Esther tried to think of four silly but appropriate rhymes.

Finally she was satisfied, and wrote out the mnemonics carefully. Then she destroyed the tape and her cue cards, half an hour before time.

There was one final thing to do. Putting on her walking clothes, Esther set off up the track on to the moor. She was followed, but this time by her own side. Among the bogs and rocks, she was able to lose a city Watcher quite easily.

Fourteen was waiting for her at Trodak Cave. Quickly they embraced each other.

'We've put the meeting time off by half an hour,' Esther explained. 'Toby will set off at the original time. If he's followed, or has any reason to suspect the mission is at risk, he'll abort. You are to turn up at the agreed meeting point at fifteen-thirty, instead of fifteen hours, and wait for him no more than fifteen minutes. If he doesn't arrive, leave at once.'

Her eyes wide with nervousness, Fourteen nodded. 'Is someone on to us?' she asked.

'They may be.'

'What do I do if Toby doesn't come?'

'Make your way straight to the barn at the top of Hunter's Farm. Don't go home. Don't pick up anything, or speak to anyone. Just make sure you're not followed.'

'What about my job?'

'Job, possessions, family, everything must be left. Go back home, and you may never be seen again.'

The woman was slient with fear, her mouth trembling.

'It shouldn't come to that,' Esther reassured her. 'But I wouldn't be fair if I didn't warn you we have a traitor in our midst.'

'But this is our best chance ever,' Fourteen protested.

'There'll be another some day,' Esther assured her. 'I'm not risking your life – or anyone else's – if the odds are against us.'

Fourteen nodded. 'Will you be there?' she asked.

'Cal and I will hang around a bit. We'd like to see what happens.'

'You'll clear out if there's trouble?'

'Of course. We're not stupid.'

Taking her pupil's hand in the gesture of kinship, Esther wished her goodbye.

17

Two officials sat in the waiting personal transport, together with a girl cadet. None of them were in the least familiar, but the PTU had arrived at exactly the right place and exactly the right time.

'Good morning, Miss Hughes,' the cadet said. Politely deferential, she was used to the whims of senior staff. The two officials with her were in their late fifties and equally used to being obeyed.

'I'm so glad you could join us,' Callum said. The accent was impeccable: military school, a good university and then officer training, with a tour of duty in the Outlands for good measure. Esther had heard such voices many times with her father. In disbelief, she sat beside him. Grey haired and efficient, he looked the perfect officer, the sort who made speeches at Keepers' Day functions and afterwards presented the awards. Glancing at him, Esther smiled. He was a very good actor, able to catch the mannerisms of a middle-aged man as well as the bearing and tone of voice. With an uncomfortable feeling she recalled that the elusive Burgess Lander was a very good actor too. Promptly she put the thought out of her mind.

The vehicle joined the queue of privileged PTUs making a slow progress towards the lake. Crowds were already gathering around the water's edge, fifth- and sixth-strata families patiently sitting on the grass, with their food packs and mats. On the lake itself officials were busy setting up the last of the firework floats, or motoring purposefully back and forth across the water. In the distance, a motorised kite appeared. Its pilot began circling to assess wind currents and weather conditions. The afternoon was almost perfect for a Keepers' Day display, calm but with just enough breeze to prevent people fainting as they waited. With so little cloud, sun blocks and visors would be needed, but it looked as though most spectators had come prepared. Absurdly, Esther found herself sharing the sense of anticipation, and wishing she could watch the show herself.

Stopping the PTU in a privileged parking bay, Madelaine got out. As chauffeurs are wont to do, she padded round to check her vehicle was in order, and leant in through the window to speak to her passengers. 'Will you be able to see from here?' she asked. She had come on a good deal since she wore the wrong shoes to cross the woods. Despite her nervousness, Esther had a strong desire to giggle. The whole thing was so preposterous: the men's perfect uniform and manners, Madelaine's polite servility . . . everything was absolutely right, and an absolute fraud. They were good at their trade.

Several other officers had secured themselves comfortable viewpoints nearby. The arrival of one more PTU aroused no interest whatsoever. Madelaine rejoined them inside. 'Fourteen and Toby should be meeting by now,' she said softly.

'With this traffic, it'll take them a good ten minutes to reach here,' Jack replied.

The crowds around the lake were deepening, families getting up to claim their vantage points. Many were still arriving. Special shuttle services had been laid on from the dome, and a black blur of people was surging down the hillside from the terminus. Some of the more agile youths at its head ran forward to climb the barriers for a better view, but they were quickly spotted by stewards and turned back. The single kite had been joined by two others. Shaped like monstrous bats, they circled in the distance, above the outer suburbs of the city.

For another fifteen minutes Callum and Jack waited, watching the route down from the city while Madelaine pretended to keep herself busy. Sitting at the back of the vehicle with nothing to do except count the moments, Esther began to feel hot and nervous. Her lips were going dry and she moistened them several times. This wait was not part of the plan, and it was worrying. Her fears began to appear justified.

'The PTU should be in sight by now,' Callum said, scanning the horizon with a pair of enhancers. For the first time, the perfect accent was a little on edge.

'Perhaps they're delayed in the traffic,' Madelaine suggested.

The three kites had been joined by a fourth. Together they began to make a figure of eight above the city, their shadows darkening whole streets. All the firework rafts were in place on the lake, and the lighting rigs secured. Latecomers on the other side of the lake drifted up towards Mallin Laboratories but were turned back by stewards. No one was allowed anywhere near its grounds.

'If Commander Tate doesn't arrive soon, the security staff will lock the centre,' Esther pointed out.

In vexation Jack also scanned the route from the city. 'We could have missed them in this lot,' he said. 'Maybe they're waiting on the other side.'

'No,' Callum replied. 'We agreed to meet here, and Toby does as he's asked. Something's gone wrong.'

'We can afford another ten minutes or so,' Madelaine said, trying to make peace.

'No more than ten,' Jack insisted.

'I say we shouldn't wait at all,' Callum argued. 'Tess was right. Our informer has arranged for them to be intercepted. Either that or they've had to run.'

'So what do we do now?' Esther asked. 'Call the whole thing off, or carry on ourselves?'

'How can we go on without the others?' Madelaine demanded.

Callum answered her. 'Tess and I can go in. We taught our pupils. We know as much as them.'

'It's too great a risk.'

'If we let this chance go, it may be years before we get another.'

'But what if you're taken?' Madelaine pleaded.

'We wont be. We're both pretty level-headed, and we know what to expect.'

'You can't involve an outsider in such a risk,' Jack insisted. 'If necessary, you and I go in.'

'It has to be a man and a woman. That's what's expected at the gate. Two men will be suspected at once. The only other person who could go with me is Madelaine, and she doesn't know the programming. Tess and I have talked this through. If Toby and Fourteen don't arrive soon, it's up to us to choose whether we take over or not.'

'Have you talked about this?' Jack asked, turning to Esther.

'Yes.'

'You're not under any compulsion?'

'No.'

Sighing, Jack returned to scanning the horizon. Five more minutes passed.

'Jack, this is the best chance we've had in years,' Callum persisted. 'We can't let it go. Our forces are ready and waiting. Any further delay and they'll start to drift away. Even if the rest of the Alliance manages to hold together, how much longer do you think our people can last? A month? Two? With an informer in our midst it could be a matter of days.'

'We'll meet that when it happens.'

'You may be prepared to wait around, but I'm not. I have no intention of being executed as a traitor.'

'You have it in your own hands to prevent that. We all have.'

'Jack, merely to look out of the window makes me glad to be alive. I'd keep putting off the decision, hoping I could find a way out of it, until one morning I'd find there wasn't time for me to make decisions any more. I'd rather die fighting than sit around waiting for the knock on my door. In any case, Tess and I might succeed. You haven't even considered that possibility.'

Turning to Esther, Jack looked at her, full in the face. Esther could not have lied if she had wanted. 'What do you feel about this?' he asked.

'I'm scared stiff,' she admitted. 'But if my pupil has been taken, it's my duty to take her place. Besides, I want to bring this whole rotten government down. They killed my mother, because she fought for what she thought was right, and asked awkward questions. When I was a child she was beautiful, always laughing. In a way, they killed my husband as well.' Becoming distressed at her own incoherence, Esther tried to look away and could not. 'I want to fight back, like Callum says. I can't go on living with an audiovision jamming my mind.'

Gently Callum put his hand on hers. 'Tess doesn't need me to persuade her to do anything,' he said quietly. 'I'm making a request, formally to you as my superior. Let us make one last attempt. Tess and I know what we have to do. We've been through it carefully—'

'When?' Madelaine interrupted.

'On the way back from the centre, Friday night. We haven't had a chance to practise as a team, but Tess will be able to sense from my fear when things are going wrong, and if she directs her thoughts clearly to me, I'll know what she needs. We'll work on a different level to most pairs, but it should be effective. I won't put her at any more risk than I can help.'

'Is this really your wish?' Jack asked. He turned towards Esther again.

Esther managed to smile. 'I spent most of the weekend trying to learn Fourteen's bloody program,' she said. 'I'm not wasting all that effort.'

The decision was made. 'Very well,' Jack agreed. 'If Toby and Fourteen don't turn up in another few minutes, you two take their places. But remember, if either of you is caught, we know nothing whatsoever about you.'

A moment more ticked by, very slowly. Eight kites were circling over the suburbs, preparing for the opening fanfare. A huge light display suddenly came on, making the crowds gasp. 'We give thanks to our Keepers,' it said, 'whose generosity is unfailing.' Then the slogan vanished, to be replaced by a second: 'Be patient and wonders will be revealed.' Madelaine let out her breath in a derisory sneer.

The last few moments were even slower. Around the lake loudspeakers boomed into life. 'Ladies and gentlemen, boys and girls,' a man's voice announced. 'Citizens of Nortown. Welcome to our Keepers' Day celebrations which begin in ten minutes' time. There are still good spaces to be had on the south side of the lake, near Mallin Laboratories. Would latecomers please proceed in that direction.'

'Now!' Callum said. 'While everybody's moving.'

Madelaine started the PTU and they joined several others who had decided the south side of the lake might be preferable. 'Take care, Cal,' she said.

'Don't I always?'

'And you,' Madelaine added, including Esther for the first time in her concern. 'We didn't get on too well at first, but you're one of us now.'

As they approached Mallin Laboratories, a second announcement was sounding from the loudspeakers. Showing a pass, Madelaine took them into the visitors' bay. The commissionaire was expecting them, thoroughly disgruntled at their lateness. He had had enough of being asked when someone was going to fix the lift program. His orders were to show Commander Tate and his assistant straight in, but he wasn't going to miss the chance of a good grumble first.

'I've never seen such crowds!' Madelaine complained. 'Couldn't get through them. Just stood there!' She smiled winningly at the commissionaire. 'Is it all right if Major Stokes and I stay outside to watch the show? It'll take the Commander an hour or so to sort the program out, and it does seem a shame to miss the fireworks.'

'That's all you girls think about,' Commander Tate commented testily. 'Pleasure! Shows and more shows. Heads stuffed full of them.'

Esther caught the commissionaire's eye. 'Heaven knows when I'm going to get home tonight,' she whispered.

The commissionaire winked back. He had an eye for pretty women.

A young official showed Commander Tate and Miss Hughes straight to the main computer room. As Fourteen had predicted, security was lax in the North. A Southern control station would have been much harder to enter. The usual operatives were sitting by the windows, wanting to be allowed to go and watch the show. One was even painting a design on her nails. 'Haven't you any work to do?' Commander Tate demanded.

'We're waiting to go home, sir,' the bravest said.

'Why haven't you?'

'We were told to see if you needed anything.'

'You lot look about as much use as a comfit on a hot day.' The Commander was late and cross, and the girls flinched. 'My assistant's perfectly able to cope on her own.'

'Could we go then, sir?' one of the girls ventured. 'We were so hoping to see the show. We wouldn't normally ask—'

'I shall still be here,' an older woman offered.

'Who are you?'

'The divisional officer, sir.'

'All right, clear off,' Commander Tate decided. 'One of you's quite enough.'

Hurriedly the girls began to gather their things and get out while they could. As they left, Esther sat down at the console, and found the lift program on the menu. She was annoyed to find the divisional officer standing looking over her shoulder. If the woman had any computer sense, she would soon recognise Esther was not as experienced as the usual troubleshooter.

Callum understood at once. 'While I'm here, I'll have a look through the expense claims,' he said. 'Miss Hughes can find the fault on her own.'

With an expression of concern, the divisional oficer turned round. 'The expense claims?' she repeated.

'That's what I said. We've been asked to make a spot check at each centre we visit. Matter of routine. What did you say your name was?'

'Miss Dutton, sir.' The DO clearly did not think expense claims were a matter of routine. Her alarm suggested they were in fact in a fine old mess. 'I can let you have the hards, if you really want them, sir,' she said uncertainly.

'That'll do for a start.'

Trying not to smile, Esther settled down to find the malfunction in the lift program. Knowing where Fourteen had suggested it be entered was a considerable help.

The room was sealed from all outside sound, but from the windows lower down the corridor came the music of the opening fanfare. The show had begun. Even the DO began to look toward the sounds wistfully.

'There's metres of them!' Commander Tate grumbled. 'Can't understand why you still use this silly system. Come on, woman! Show me what it all means.'

The DO was not having a good afternoon.

Finally, after half an hour, Commander Tate looked at his timepiece. It was sixteen fifty-five, on a public holiday. Even a

DO should have been allowed home by now. 'We're not going to get through this lot today,' he remarked, almost kindly. 'We'll leave it until later. Go and see the show. Miss Hughes will be finished in a few moments.'

The DO was alarmed. 'But I can't leave you here on your own,' she began.

It was the reaction they had all feared. If the divisional officer could not be persuaded to leave soon, Madelaine and Jack would be signing out at the gate while Commander Tate and his assistant were still stuck in the control room. Someone would spot the discrepancy and the alarm would be raised.

Commander Tate sighed. 'How much longer will you be, Miss Hughes?' he called across.

Esther had in fact found the malfunction ten minutes ago. It was now a question of stretching her work out rather than curtailing it. 'Another half an hour, sir,' she replied. 'This is a fiddly one.'

The DO's face betrayed her disappointment. From along the corridor came the sound of a salvo of rockets.

'Tell you what,' Commander Tate suggested. 'You go and watch the show for a while. If we haven't signed out inside the hour, you can come back in to fetch us.' Still the woman hesitated. 'What is it now? Do you really think I'm going to run off with these?' With a dismissive gesture, the Commander indicated the pile of expense records.

The DO almost smiled. 'They have to be locked away, sir,' she said.

'Very well. Lock 'em away. I've already said I shall have to come another time.'

'When, sir?'

'If I told you, it wouldn't be a surprise check, would it?'

Esther had to look down to hide her amusement.

It was five minutes past seventeen hours before the woman could be persuaded to leave. On any other day of the year she would not have agreed at all, but the pull of a Keepers' Day show was strong.

For another five minutes Esther worked, rapidly closing down the corrected file. She spoke only as Miss Hughes, and Callum continued as Commander Tate, in case they were being monitored. Then they began the walk back down the corridor. At precisely seventeen-fifteen the first of the motorised kites roared over the lake, deadening even the sound of the last rocket salvo.

Immediately Esther and Callum doubled back into the cleaners' room. If the commissionaire had watched his screen he would have seen them, but the kites would have distracted the most zealous guard. A pile of cleaning aids and assorted shelving offered hiding places. Scrambling quickly into position, they waited.

The room was small and windowless, filled to capacity. There was a litle light coming in under the door, enough for Esther to make out the shape of a robotic aid near her. The engines of the kites made the building shake as they passed again directly overhead. Ten minutes went by. If Madelaine and Jack had not managed their part of the plan, all was already lost. In a quarter of an hour or so, security quards would be coming along the corridor to see why Commander Tate and his assistant had not left.

In the darkness Callum took Esther's hand. 'OK?' he wrote on her palm.

'Yes,' she wrote on his in return.

Suddenly there was the sound of doors being opened and closed down the corridor. Security men's voices approached. The building was being locked for the night. Esther's heart beat furiously. It pounded so loudly as the door to the cleaners' room was opened, she was certain it would be heard. A light shone around the cleaning aids beside her, just missing her foot. Then the door was locked.

Other doors were opened and closed all the way along the

corridor. Finally the voices receded towards the main entrance. A faint hum began.

'The alarms are on,' Callum whispered. 'There's none in here. We can talk so long as we're quiet.'

Esther heard a faint snick as he opened the case he had brought. Silently he began to take out the equipment he would need, together with body-heat suits and a small survival pack for each of them. 'Swallow these,' he whispered, passing Esther two capsules. 'They dry your body fluids. The last thing you want is your nose running.' He was very calm, though Esther could feel his fear being held in check. She was afflicted by a sense of unreality. None of this could be happening. Esther Thomas would never have got herself into such a situation. It must be a dream, and a decidedly silly one. 'Now stick this somewhere you can get at it quick.' Callum passed her another capsule, held in a piece of adhesive film.

'How long does it take?' Esther asked, putting it in place inside her wrist. Her own calmness amazed her. She was talking about life and death as if it were merely a recipe for a new food.

'About fifty seconds.'

'Am I really doing this?' she asked.

'No. We'll both wake up in the morning and find we've been dreaming.'

He let them out of the room, from safety into immediate danger. Though the windows of the corridor had been shuttered by the security guards, enough light filtered in for Esther to see clearly. Halfway up the wall the first red light watched. She waited, standing absolutely still, while Callum examined it. His fear was tangible now. So too was his carefulness, and his sense of being suddenly intensely alive. Very, very carefully, he reached around the side of the light. Esther's mouth went dry as she watched. With one quick, clean movement, Callum slid his fingers into the back of the alarm and disarmed it.

If there had been time, they would have practised together for several days, like Toby and Fourteen. Now they had to become a team instantly, or put each other in jeopardy. Trying to judge each other's reactions, they began to move along the corridor. Only afterwards did Esther realise the strangeness of the relationship that developed between them. As Callum had predicted, she could judge from his fear when things were going wrong. At such moments she would stand perfectly still and wait. From the relief that followed, she could also judge when it was safe to move. He in turn could pass on some of his knowledge to her, guiding her at crucial points. Danger made them responsive to each other, but on a level that was above words, and impossible to explain afterwards. Slowly, methodically, they worked their way down the corridor.

The laser bars proved the worst. Set at irregular heights, some were so low that Esther had a good deal of trouble sliding under them. Once her shoulder showed briefly in the light and she froze in fear. For several seconds she waited, expecting to hear a siren sound throughout the building. Nothing happened. In bewilderment she slithered on through, amazed to find herself still alive. Afterwards she remembered that there would have been no sound even if she had triggered an alarm. Everything relied on the observers in the gatehouse monitoring their screens.

That night they were careless, as Callum had predicted. Their system was sending them so many false messages that they ignored the few true ones. They could hardly be blamed. The sudden lights and sounds through the shutters must have set every sensor near the windows bleeping madly.

Twice Callum wrote the time on Esther's hand. They were behind schedule, and losing seconds with each alarm. Her throat and mouth were drying out, while her body inside the suit was wet with sweat. By the time they entered the central control room, she was becoming exhausted. Inside the sealed silence the heat was even greater, and for an appalling instant Esther thought she was going to faint.

The computers were in passive mode, running quietly so that the services they governed continued to function throughout the night. A faint glow came from their displays, each one showing an outline of the operations it controlled. They provided just enough light for Esther to make her way to one of the consoles, but not enough to work by. Callum had brought a tiny minim lamp. Making a shelter over her with a sheet of lightproof material, he switched the lamp on.

Neither of them dared to breathe. If the computers rejected Fourteen's entry codes, not even a Keepers' Day show would distract the guards.

Politely the system came on line. At once Esther called up the lift program she had been correcting earlier in the evening. Then, peeling the mnemonics from her arm, she began to key in Fourteen's program. Every fifth, sixth or seventh entry in the lift control gained a new series of symbols, lost amongst existing entries to all but a most observant operator.

In her makeshift tent, Esther began to lose all sense of time and place. Not even the man standing protecting her from the sensors above was real. All that mattered was that she should recall what she had learnt, and key it in correctly. The gloves on her suit were irritating, despite being the thinnest possible. Several times she miskeyed and had to correct herself. Once Callum had to ask her to put out the lamp so that he could change position. He must have been exhausted standing so long without moving.

Finally, it was done. Replacing the strip on the inside of her sleeve, Esther signalled that she was ready to move. Taking her hand, Callum wrote on it '55'. They were fifty-five minutes behind schedule. The Keepers' Day show would last another hour and a half. If they had been at the door already, it would have been easy to slip into the crowds intently watching the water display, but the front entrance was a very long way off when every alarm or sensor had to be individually disarmed, and then rearmed afterwards.

By the time they reached the cleaners' room they had only thirty minutes left to reach the main entrance. Going back inside, they considered what to do.

'We might make it,' Esther whispered.

Callum shook his head. 'Some of the alarms are new to me. They take longer than I expected.'

'What do you advise?'

'Stay here, and leave when the early morning domestics arrive. If we carry on, we'll run out of time. The guards will start padding around, making up for neglecting their duty, and we'll get caught.'

Esther agreed, looking around her. The room was little more than a cupboard, and they would have to spend over eight hours in it together. 'We might as well make ourselves comfortable,' she suggested.

Risking the minim light for a few moments, they took off the heat suits and folded them away. When the domestics came into the building, the alarms would be switched off, and the best protection would be a suit of overalls. Callum stowed the equipment in the case, and then put that inside a laundry sac he had brought for the purpose. Then they found themselves places to rest against the shelves.

'Sleep a little,' Callum suggested. 'I'll take first watch.'

Nodding, Esther tried to make herself a comfortable space. There were half a dozen sweepers and a robotic aid in the way. For half an hour she dozed, only to feel worse than if she had sat upright all the time. Crossly she rubbed at the back of her shoulders. 'What time is it?' she asked.

'Twenty-two thirty.'

'Is that all?'

'The crowds are leaving. You can hear them if you listen carefully. Pity we didn't make it. No one would have heard us in that row.'

'I never did like the tight time-scale,' Esther said. 'I doubt if Fourteen and Toby would have managed it either.'

'They might have. Toby's faster than me. I'm not really cut out for this sort of thing. Like you, I'm a trainer, not an active.'

Esther smiled. 'No, I can't imagine you doing this often,' she agreed. 'You'd be more at home running a control centre than breaking into it.'

There was a silence between them. Sighing, Callum shifted his position. 'Well, if you won't sleep, I will,' he said. 'Wake me up in two hours. By then you may feel more like resting yourself.'

With a sense of utter disbelief Esther sat against a row of shelves, listening as the man beside her fell asleep.

Suddenly the hum stopped. The alarms had been switched off. At once Callum was awake. 'The guards are coming in,' he whispered.

Esther slipped to the floor beside him. Lying close against each other they waited as the guards approached along the corridor, opening every door.

18

'All clear along here,' a man's voice said, and the lock on the cleaners' room hissed open. There was a click but no light came on.

'Bloody light gone in here,' the voice grumbled. A lamp shone round the shelves, and across the robotic aids. Holding her breath, Esther lay close to Callum, waiting. The light did a second sweep, passing over the laundry sac Callum had brought. It paused, and then went back to the bag, shining on it for several seconds. The guard could not recall having seen a bag there before.

Esther could feel Callum's breath in his chest, held like her own. Silently he eased his hand forward so that the capsule on his wrist would be easier to reach. At last the light moved on, across a bucket.

'This place needs clearing out,' the voice said.

Abruptly the lamp flicked off. Shutting the door, the guard continued down the corridor.

For a long time Callum and Esther lay perfectly still, waiting until the voices passed to the end of the building and then back to the main entrance. At last there was silence. The hum of the alarms began again.

In relief and embarrassment, Esther pulled away. 'I thought we'd had it,' she admitted.

'I was certain of it. We'll have to leave the wretched sac there, in case the same guard comes back.' Sitting up, Callum rubbed his shoulders. 'This is going to be an uncomfortable night,' he predicted. What shall we talk about? I don't suppose either of us will sleep now.'

'Tell me about my mother,' Esther suggested. 'You obviously knew her.'

'Tess, I can't tell such things. If I did, you'd be able to identify me.'

For several seconds Esther considered her response. 'You don't need to guard your words so carefully with me,' she said. 'I know who you are.'

There was a long silence.

'I wish you hadn't said that,' Callum replied. There was an edge to his voice that Esther found frightening.

'Why?' she asked calmly. 'Your interest is best served by keeping me alive. I've written your name down, and given it to Sly. If I go missing for more than five days, she'll read it. If I report in regularly, she won't.'

Again there was silence. 'Shrewd,' Callum conceded. 'But you could be lying.'

'You were born Simon Miniott, son of Andrew and Joanna, elder brother of Carl. Far from being Scots, your family is thoroughly English – apart from your French grandmother that is, and she was never legally a Miniott.'

Esther had expected anger, and felt instead despair, like physical tiredness, draining Callum's strength. 'What else do you know about me?' he asked.

'Your grandfather was John Miniott, a much respected public figure in his time, though he treated your grandmother appallingly. The man I know as Jack is your uncle, and Madelaine is your cousin. You yourself were born in 2176, which makes you thirty-three, the same age as me. When you were nine you lost your sight in an accident. At twenty-two you underwent surgery. It was only partially successful, so you tried again. I don't have details of that. I suspect very few people have.'

Wearily Callum leant against the wall. It was a long time before he replied.

'All right,' he said. 'What do you want from me? You're safe in whatever you ask. I can't kill you. It would arouse suspicion for your body to be found here. And after we leave, you'll be able to hand me in.'

'No,' Esther insisted. 'I shall never use your proper name again. You'll always be Callum to me. All I want is insurance. If I go missing, it'll pay you to find me.'

'If you ever go missing, I'll look for you, Tess. Not to save my own skin, but because I'll be half out of my mind with worry.'

In surprise Esther looked up, trying to judge if he meant what he said. He was telling the truth. 'I'm sorry,' she said more gently. 'I had no right to blackmail you, but I've been taught to trust no one. You could well have tried to get rid of me when this job was over.'

Callum moved further away in the darkness. 'I couldn't get rid of anyone. Not in cold blood. Compassion is my weakness. I learnt that years ago. My masters warned me I'd make a very poor Keeper.'

'In their terms, perhaps. Not in mine.' Esther sat in the darkness, aware that the relationship between them was changing. 'Cal,' she asked. 'How could a good man like you join something so evil?'

'I had very little choice.'

Esther sighed. 'Couldn't you have done anything to avoid it?' she asked.

Turning back to her, Callum touched her hand in the darkness. 'Last Friday I tried to stop you remembering certain things,' he said. 'I knew they'd help you identify me. Now I want you to recall them. I want you to understand why I made the decisions I did – and to forgive me for them.' Gently he took both her hands in his.

Esther felt nothing else, yet as he held her hands the

garbled memories of the previous week began to put themselves into order. It was as if she had fallen asleep, and splashed her face afterwards in cold water. The sensation was bewildering but not unpleasant. Pulling her hands away, she sat in silence, trying to understand what was happening to her. She recalled a conversation beside an empty fountain. Every word and sensation was vivid, even to the smell of the night.

'Do you remember the boathouse?' Callum asked quietly.

'You heard a man being executed there.'

'Slowly and in extreme pain.'

In horror Esther recalled what Callum had told her. 'It was your grandfather who gave the command,' she realised. 'He sentenced one of your own order to death.'

'Can you imagine what such a memory does to you?' Callum asked. 'It haunts me even now.'

'Then how could you become a Keeper? I would rather have died.'

'Which is what I would probably have done, but for your mother. It was partly on her advice that I entered the Order.'

'My mother would never have—' Breaking off, Esther waited in amazement. He was telling her the truth.

'Your mother used to visit us most summers, and I always looked forward to her coming. She was one of the few people I could talk to easily. The memory of what I'd overheard made me silent and withdrawn. My parents thought I couldn't accept losing my sight, but that wasn't the reason. I was afraid I too would be punished, for not admitting I was there, and because I knew who was involved. I despised myself for keeping silence, and yet I dared do nothing else. Your mother understood such feelings, though she didn't know their cause.'

Pausing, Callum put his arm around her shoulder, to make her more comfortable against the shelving. 'When I was almost fifteen, Jacki stayed the whole summer. She was supposedly painting my mother's portrait, but we all knew she had nowhere else to go. Your father had repudiated her. Normally at that age I would have been away from home too, preparing for my initiation, but I'd been excused. Part of me was glad of it. I could stay out of something I loathed. The other part was bitterly disappointed. A Keeper's son has no purpose except to become a Keeper himself.'

Above them the alarms hummed, but Esther was aware only of the man beside her. In the darkness she could forget what he was, and hear the remembered pain in his voice. 'You grew close to her, didn't you?' she remarked gently.

'Your mother used to get up early to work, and I was often awake early too. We'd sit together on the sundeck, her painting, me studying. One morning she passed me some clay. I seemed depressed, she said. Sculpture was a good way of working through one's feelings. So I made a bird, or what I remembered a bird looked like. I can still remember the sense of release I felt. Jacki praised it a good deal. She told me I was clever with my hands, and that I might make a career as a technician, or something like that. She suggested I try to get to college. Before I knew what I was doing, I was breaking down and telling her I was a Keeper's son. I was also telling her why I hated my own race.'

'She must have been very frightened, for both of you.'

'If she was, she didn't show it. She warned me there was no way I could fight the elders on my own. I wanted some grand gesture, she said, like standing up at my initiation and condeming the lot of them. That would achieve nothing, and probably cost me my life. I had only two options: to use my blindness to avoid entry, or to accept my training. The first was the obvious route. No one would expect me to do otherwise, yet I would despise myself. However scared and repelled I was, I wanted to go through the initiation, to please my father, and to prove myself. It was right for me to do so too, she argued. I could try to change things from the inside.

I must always guard myself very carefully though, or I would be corrupted by the evil around me. I've tried to follow her advice, though I haven't always succeeded.'

Shifting his position slightly, Callum lapsed into silence.

As she leant against his shoulder, Esther pictured her mother and a fair-haired boy sitting on a sundeck together, the one painting, the other trying to study. In such a difficult time for both of them, it would have been easy for understanding to grow. 'Would you make the same choice again?' she asked.

'Given the same limited options. We both underestimated what I was entering, but I've gained knowledge I wouldn't have had otherwise. Ironically, I'm very good at some of it too. If the order would only share its secrets the whole of humanity could profit.'

There was a noise further down the corridor, and they stopped talking at once.

'The guard's changing,' Callum whispered. 'That's a transport arriving.'

For some minutes they crouched together, listening for danger. Finally all was quiet again and they settled back against the shelves.

'Did my mother ever speak of me?' Esther asked.

'She told me she had a daughter about my age, and that she missed her a good deal. Perhaps that's why she was so kind to me.' In the darkness, Callum touched Esther's face. 'I tracked you down, you know,' he added. 'Soon after I left college – just to see what you were like.'

'Was I as you had imagined?'

'No. You were as beautiful as I'd hoped, but you seemed too respectable, too much the soldier's daughter. Then I realised you probably had followed your mother, but that you were a great deal more discreet than she had been. That intrigued me. For years I've watched you. I know you a great deal better than you know me.'

Esther smiled. 'I'm glad you were on my side,' she commented. 'I could have been in touble otherwise.'

'So could I. I hadn't realised you were a sympath. It was quite a surprise.

'So was my mother.'

'That explains a good deal.'

Pausing, Esther tried to find words for her next question. It hurt her even to form the sentence. 'How did my mother die?' she asked.

'She simply disappeared. My father was a senior man in the Order, yet even he couldn't trace her. One night he came home, very quiet, and very angry. He'd heard a rumour that she had been executed. "Euthanased" was the word he used. No one had announced the decision, and it had been made without proper authority. All that evening we sat arguing about what to do. It wasn't just a case of grief for a lost friend. Our own safety was threatened. Over the last couple of years we'd distanced ourselves – your mother had become too strident for us to be associated with – but it was well known we'd given her support in the past. Clearly a new regime was taking over, and it was intent on destroying all opposition. We decided to drop out of sight for a while. In a sense, your mother's death was a turning point for us.'

It was some time before Esther could speak. 'Thank you for your kindness to her,' she said.

'She repaid us amply. She never told anyone that we were Keepers, or that we were in opposition to the new Order. I've always respected her.'

Sighing, Esther looked into the darkness. 'It's not easy trying to live up to such a mother,' she admitted.

'One martyr's quite enough. In any case, you underestimate yourself. If what you've done tonight works, you'll be remembered as the woman who started the revolution.'

'Oh Lord! Don't say that!'

He made her rest her head against his shoulder. 'Come on,

sleep for a while,' he advised. 'We're going to need our wits about us in a few hours. I'll take first watch.'

It was four-thirty when Callum woke her. 'Time to get ready,' he whispered. 'The domestics will be here soon.'

Stiff and cramped, Esther stretched out her legs as far as she dare, and then crawled forward on to her knees. Callum had put the minim light on so that they could get ready. She was embarrassed to discover how long she had slept. 'Why didn't you wake me earlier?' she demanded.

'You looked so peaceful. Don't worry, there's time.'

Urgently Esther loosened her hair to make it look unkempt, and then rubbed her hands on the floor to dirty them. As an afterthought she smeared some of the dust on her forehead. Callum passed her the overalls, and she pulled them on over her public service uniform. The correct security badge was attached to the collar, and there were even smudges of cleanser on the cuffs and trouser bottoms. Finally Callum passed her a pair of cheap shoes. 'How do I look?' she asked.

'Fine. Watch how you walk. You've been on your feet for two hours already.'

'And my back's killing me . . .'

Sitting against the shelves, Esther watched while Callum also got ready. Afterwards they put the light out, and waited for the hum of the alarms to stop.

'We'll be safest staying here until the cleaners pass up the corridor,' Callum suggested. 'Then we'll grab a cleaning aid and try to walk out together.'

'What if somebody stops us?'

'You keep walking. I'll stay and talk my way out of things.'

'No!'

'I'm not being heroic, just practical. I stand a much better chance of persuading an overseer to let me out than you do. I'll join you as soon as I can, but if there's any delay, you keep going.'

'I don't like to think of you being taken.'

'It won't come to that.'

The domestics were a litte late. Until then Esther had not noticed quite how small and airless the room was. She longed for a drink.

'Tess—'

'What?'

'I've done a lot of thinking while you were alseep. Would you answer a question—honestly?'

She smiled. 'It depends what it is.'

'Last Friday you said you didn't need to know me. You could love the man inside. Does that still hold?'

'I'm not sure.'

'Try to give me an answer. We mightn't both get out of here alive. I'd rather not die believing a lie.'

Esther tried to think how to reply. 'It was true when I said it,' she began, 'but I imagined a different man then. Now I have to get used to someone called Simon Miniott; from a family Sly so obviously hates. Which is the real man? Until I know that, I can't decide whether I love you or not.'

'All right. That's fair enough. I'll strike a bargain with you. As things are, I can't marry you, but if your colleague's plan works, nothing will remain the same much longer. In two weeks' time, our cities will be in chaos. The Outlanders will see their chance to rebel, and the Resistance will join them. If you and I can survive the fighting that follows, I'll come knocking at your door.'

'As yourself?'

'As myself. If you're disappointed, I'll go away. But if you like what you see, I'll stay around.'

'Will you bring me flowers?'

'Bunches of them.'

'Real flowers? Not just dried ones?'

'The biggest bouquet you've ever seen.'

The hum had suddenly stopped. The guards had switched off the alarms. At once Esther moved urgently towards her hiding place under the shelving. Callum put Esther's fingers to his mouth in a parting kiss, then slid away from her. Silent and still, they waited.

Down the corridors doors started opening. Voices raised in banter approached. Esther found that she was praying the same prayer over and over again: 'Oh Lord, let them not find us. Oh Lord, please let them not find us.' The voices grew nearer. Abruptly the door opened and the light clicked.

'Bloomin' light's gone,' a woman's voice said. 'Lim, fetch a lamp, love, or we won't be able to find our stuff.'

Feet retreated towards the front entrance. Light shone in an arc from the corridor, picking out the cleaning aids stacked near the door. The first woman began helping herself to the things she could see. Breathing as lightly as possible, Esther waited, her face turned into her arm. After a few moments the other woman returned, carrying a lamp. Clambering over the robotic aids beside the door, she hunted for the cleansers and pads she needed. It was all right for some, she complained, sitting around in the front office while others did the work. She'd tell that security man when she saw him. He should have fixed the light last night.

'Too busy watching the Keepers' show,' her companion agreed.

'Did you see much of it?' another woman asked from beyond the door.

'We got a good place this year. Over by the dwellings. Those kites were summat else, weren't they?'

'Our Rosalie didn't half jump when the first one come over. Like a bloody great bat it was. Never seen owt like it.'

'They reckon they were at least forty metres across,' another voice joined in. 'I liked th'gliders best. One of t'pilots nearly didn't mek it our end. Came down ever so heavy. You should have heard th'crowd roar . . .'

So the conversation went on, going over the whole of the Keepers' show in minute detail. The woman in the corridor was called Kelly, it seemed, and had bought her youngest a striker for his Keepers' Day present. With a sense of guilt Esther thought of Sally and Tim receiving their presents at the camp. She wondered if they had liked them.

At last the doms went away to start their work. The door was still open. Getting up, Esther moved softly towards it and waited, trying to sense if there was anyone left nearby. 'Clear,' she whispered.

Taking one of the robotic cleaners, she waited while Callum joined her. Then they walked out of the cleaners' room and down the corricor.

The cleaner made a whirring sound all the way, and proved unexpectedly difficult to control. Callum walked beside it with the laundry sac over his shoulder, as if taking it out to the collection point in the forecourt. Two of the doms passed them going the other way and nodded. They seemed to find nothing strange in meeting two people they had not seen before. As Callum had hoped, the cleaning firm was subcontracting work out, and the workforce changed continually. 'So I says to her,' the nearest woman was explaining, 'what you want a new comforter for? But you know her. If her Martin bought her t'moon, she'd send it back for updating.'

It was still dark outside, but in the lights from the building Esther could see three transports and a trailer parked in the forecourt. If she and Callum could reach those vehicles, they should be able to find some way of hiding on them.

Suddenly a voice called down the corridor. 'Where are you taking that aid? We need it back here.'

'Keep walking,' Callum whispered.

'Oi! Didn't you hear?'

Rapidly Callum passed Esther the sac. It was full of the equipment they had used, and as good as a death sentence if it was found with them. 'Give me the aid,' he said calmly. 'You get this lot outside.'

Then turning back, he guided the machine towards the supervisor.

Esther risked one last look in his direction. She saw an elderly domestic apologising to his superior. Even the servile bend of the shoulders was right. Then she walked on, and through the door.

The commissionaires hardly glanced at her. Guessing that someone had the job of loading the sacs into the trailer, she began to do so, taking care to place her own where she would be able to retrieve it.

'Who told you to start?' a voice called.

Startled, Esther turned round. 'Lim said it were our turn,' she replied, 'and Kelly weren't keen, so I offered.'

'All right. Make sure they don't slip about when we're moving. And keep them separate to the others. We don't want another performance like last week's.'

Breathing unsteadily, Esther carried on loading. She waited until the driver had gone back into the front office, and then climbed into the trailer and buried herself among the sacs. Some contained waste rather than laundry and gave off an unpleasant stench. Her overalls would smell by the time she got out again.

For another half-hour she waited, trying to hear what was going on outside. Callum did not join her. Further sacs were thrown on top and around her. Then suddenly the cover on the trailer was shut, and the transport unit set off.

Esther had no way of knowing where they were going. She hoped it was not back to the depot. It would be more difficult to get out unseen there, and if the trailer was emptied straight into a sorting bay she could have problems.

To her infinite relief, when the transport stopped again, it was clearly at another cleaning job, also outside the city dome. The trailer was left with the cover up, waiting for further sacs to be dumped into it. Even the driver went inside. Security everywhere in the North was slack, as Fourteen had said. As she crouched among the sacs, waiting until it was safe to climb out, Esther thought of Fourteen, and wondered what had happened to her. She wondered too where Callum was. Half hoping he had managed to get into one of the other transports without her knowing, she tried to sense if he was near. There was no one. He had been unable to leave the building in time. Anxiety began to trouble her.

After another five minutes Esther decided it was safe to leave the trailer. Dawn was breaking along the horizon and if she did not move soon she would be seen. Scrambling over the side furthest from the building, she ran quickly towards some tanks near the main gate. Hiding behind them, she waited. No one came out of the building.

By the time the domestics transport left again, Esther was well hidden under one of the tanks, crouched in a shallow depression used for venting fumes. Under the cover of darkness, she had taken off her overalls, and rolling them up tight, put them into the laundry sac to hide the smell. With the sac hidden inside the briefcase Callum had brought as Commander Tate, she was once again a smart public official.

Trying to keep her uniform clean, she waited until the staff started arriving at the building, which seemed to be the main office of a large chemical company. It would be rotten luck if a delivery was made so early in the day, but it was a possibility which kept Esther's nerves stretched. Only when the general public started to arrive did she slide out of her hiding place. Stiff and cold, she made her way along the sides of the tanks until she was able to stand up without being seen. Then she crossed the yard, towards the building. Spotting a side door, she walked firmly towards it. Beyond it was a corridor, which led to other corridors. It took several attempts to find a route to the main entrance, but though she passed several members of staff, no one challenged her. Discovering that she was at last in the main reception area, she walked through it, and out of the front door. The commissionaire looked up. Politely

Esther nodded to him. Then, forcing herself to walk at an even, official-looking pace, she crossed the front yard, and went out through the main gates.

It was absurdly easy. There were helpful little signs all along the main street directing strangers to the nearest shuttle station. Esther did not have the faintest idea where she was, but that did not matter. She simply bought a ticket to the Centre Dome, and waited until the right shuttle appeared. Then she caught another shuttle out to Moss Edge.

For most of the day, Esther slept. She got up each time she woke, and went to the window to see if there was any sign of a message, but the courtyard and windows opposite told her nothing. If Callum had managed to get out of the centre, he should have sent word by now. They had agreed that if either of them was delayed, they would put the other one's mind at rest as soon as they were safe. Esther's anxiety became concern, and then alarm. Callum would not allow himself to be taken alive. She need not fear him telling anyone that she too had been involved. His death would be a serious loss, whether by his own hand or by the guards turning on him. There would be urgent searches and questions. The possibility that the Central Control system had been tampered with would be obvious. Experts would be brought in to find out whether a virus had been introduced.

By morning, it was almost certain Callum was dead, or taken. Keeper or not, he had risked his life so that Esther could walk free. She wished now that she had lied and told him that she loved him, regardless of who he was. It would not have been much of a lie after all. No man had ever interested her so much.

Urgently Esther began to plan what she should do. The equipment they had used was still in her possession and must be got rid of somehow. Even more important, she had to make up her mind whether to stay in the dwelling until it was time to collect the children, or set off at once for the safety of

Hunters' Farm. She could not bear the thought of abandoning her children, yet if she allowed herself to be taken, the safety of others besides herself would be at risk. It was strange that no one had sent her instructions by now.

Suddenly Esther leapt up. An old woman was crossing the courtyard with a heavy bag, pausing every so often to rest. Grabbing Callum's equipment case and shoving it into a food sac, Esther ran to the door.

By the time she reached the courtyard, the old woman was walking through the public play area. Seeing Esther, she went on, towards the waterway. Esther took a different path, watching to see where the old woman joined the main path. At the far side of the open space, Esther turned into the woodland. Then she doubled back quickly, towards the footbridge over the water.

Madelaine was waiting for her at the junction of the two paths. Esther looked carefully around them. They were alone.

'Is he safe?' Esther asked.

'He got back two hours ago.'

'How is he?'

'Dehydrated and very tired, but otherwise all right.'

'When did he get out?'

'This morning, when the cleaners came again. He simply sat down in one of their transports. Everyone assumed he'd got on the wrong one.'

Despite her concern, Esther smiled. 'And what about yesterday?'

'I gather he put in an hour's cleaning, and then hid in a lift shaft.'

Beginning to laugh, Esther handed over the case of equipment. 'You'd better have this,' she said. 'Take care you don't get caught with it.'

'I don't wear the wrong shoes nowadays,' Madelaine replied.

'And Toby? What happened to him and Fourteen?'

'Toby was taken. We know where he is, and we hope to get him out tonight. Your colleague's safe. She watched the meeting place from a safe distance, and when Toby failed to turn up, went straight to Sly. I don't know where she is now, but you don't need to worry. Your warning saved her.'

'Have you identified the traitor yet?' Esther asked.

'No. Everybody we suspect is beyond suspicion.'

'That makes things very difficult,' Esther said. She wondered if she should reveal what the National Committee knew about Burgess Lander, but secrecy was a habit best kept, even with colleagues. 'Look to your family,' she advised. 'They can be more treacherous than friends.'

Madelaine too had brought a bag, ready to take the case. From it she took a small packet. 'Callum asked me to give you this,' she said.

Taking the packet, Esther examined it in surprise. She could feel a protective box inside the wrapping. 'What is it?' she asked.

'A gift.' Madelaine shook her head. 'He asked me to get it on my way here.' She shook her head. 'He can't marry you,' she warned.

'Not as things are.'

'Don't end up a Keeper's woman. They get hurt.'

'I'll do my best to avoid it.'

Putting the packet inside her bag, Esther paused. 'Take care yourself,' she warned. 'In a few weeks' time, things will get nasty. People won't be in the mood to make distinctions. A Keeper will be a Keeper, whether good or bad – and their families will die too.'

'I'm aware of that.' Offering her hand in parting, Madelaine smiled. 'We've gone to ground already,' she said. 'The training centre's empty. Our forces are ready and waiting. We'll have to fight from behind them, but that doesn't mean we won't be fighting.'

Turning abruptly, she walked back along the path.

19

As soon as she was safely back inside her dwelling, Esther opened the packet. Inside was a single, fresh rose. For several seconds she stared at it foolishly, then, very carefully, she took it out of the protective box. It was years since she had touched a real rose, since her father's last tour of duty in the Outlands. The petals felt soft and smooth, and the scent was even sweeter than she had remembered. That single flower must have cost as much as a huge display of dried grasses, yet to most city women it would have seemed a poor gift: just one flower that would die within days. Holding it gently in the palm of her hand, Esther found that she was almost crying.

There was no card with it, nothing to identify the giver, but the choice said more than any words could have done. A white rose for the North, and a real one because she would not settle for less.

Taking the flower into the kitchen, Esther sprinkled water over it. Afterwards she filled the small feeder at the bottom of the protective box. For a full minute more she stood with the rose in the palm of her hand, thinking of a man whose face she had never seen. Then she put the rose carefully back into its box and placed it beside her bed. If anyone came into her room, they would think she had a wealthy admirer and be intrigued, even jealous perhaps, but hopefully that was all.

Returning to the lounge, Esther took out her lace and began making a report for Sly. Frequently she paused, staring ahead of her, trying to decide her future. She was calmer now, able to come to clear decisions. There was no way she could leave Sally and Tim at the camp. Besides, if she fled now, she might draw attention to the Movement, and perhaps jeopardise everything. It was odd that Sly had still not contacted her, but the old woman always had been cautious. By Friday, she would surely send details of the escape route Esther and her children were to follow.

It would be unwise to make any preparations for her departure. Cancelling the milk would be a sure way of alerting the authorities. Still, it would not hurt to go through her things and make sure there was nothing amongst them that could incriminate others after her departure.

Taking a rest from her lace, Esther stretched her back and neck, still stiff after so long hiding in cramped places. Sitting on the floor beside her work station, she looked through the store slots underneath. There were a lot of personal letters in them, and though she had always been careful never to keep – or even receive – anything seditious, she destroyed a number of them. The wording might suggest discontent with the present regime, and even discontent was dangerous. Bob's love letters caused her a great deal of conflict. She could not bear the thought of official eyes reading them, but she did not want to destroy them. Besides, every wife kept her husband's love letters. To have nothing sentimental in the personal slots would look odd. Finally she decided to tie them together and label them 'Letters from Bob'. Hopefully, once the searchers had read the first couple to confirm the description, they would leave the rest alone.

As she worked, something fell to the floor. It was the programme for the gala opening of the showhouse. Printed programmes being rare and likely to increase in value, Esther had kept it. Most productions were accompanied by a slot-in-soundabout, which was merely hired. Smiling, Esther made herself a coffee, and sat in the kitchen to read the programme through, having never had time to do so until then. It all seemed such a long time ago. Tim had not forgotten the afternoon, and Sally still talked of the magic butterflies.

With a sense of shock Esther realised that the man who had created that magic could well be dead by now. Sighing, she wondered what would happen to Imogen. War always hit the children worst. Adults at least had an idea what was happening, but children had no part in such things. They could be left parentless and homeless, with no choice in the matter. Tim and Sally, for instance. What choice had they had in being sent to the children's camp? Or having to flee their home afterwards? What right had she to condemn them to a life in the Outlands, without education or proper medicine? Esther had never felt so guilty in her life.

Glancing round her dwelling, she tried to imagine leaving it for ever. She would miss her books and vidmats most. It would be difficult to spend the rest of her life without the chance to read and learn. Having to eat meat would be a problem, but to refuse to do so would mark her at once as a city-dweller. If there really was a revolution, she might one day be able to return to Nortown, but people had talked of revolution all her life. It was like summer in the Outlands – always looked forward to, and always elusive.

Returning to the programme, Esther turned back to the beginning. There were pictures of the new director and his staff, as well as of the cast and technicians. Carefully she considered the face of Stephan Lahr. It would have been comforting to have found some evidence of cruelty in his eyes, or about his mouth. That was where one could usually see the real man. In honesty she had to admit there was nothing. Caught in a relaxed moment, Patroner Lahr looked less reserved than when she had known him. If she had met him in other circumstances she might well have been attracted to him. Which simply went to show that images did not always tell the truth.

Recalling that she had not been out to collect the day's messages, Esther put down the programme and went along the corridor. There ought to be directions from the children's camp by now. Keying in her code, she began to plod through a list of civic announcements. She had forgotten it was the beginning of the month, and as a dutiful citizen she should have checked the latest health education and legal requirements. The sun was shining through the window beside the screen, making it difficult to read. In annoyance, Esther altered her position.

At last she reached the personal messages. There was an appointment for her to attend a medical on Wednesday. The family support officer wished to check that she had recovered from her depression before she was allowed to take her children home. Feeling slightly nervous, Esther printed out the details. She hated medicals; they could so easily go wrong. A second message told her the time to arrive at the children's camp on Friday, complete with valid medical certificate and identity papers. A third message was from her father, asking how she was. He had tried to phone both her Centopolis and Nortown numbers and was becoming concerned.

The sun from the window had always been a nuisance. Now it was positively painful. Madelaine had warned that the Dark Ones' medication would make her eyes hurt in bright light. Most benefits had disadvantages, she had said, and her new ability would be no exception.

Suddenly Esther recalled a memory. Once before the sun had shone through at the same angle, making reading difficult. After she had taken her own messages, she had looked back along the corridor. Stephan Lahr was sitting at that same message transfer, as if lost in thought . . .

The colour rose to Esther's face. She stopped reading and looked up, straight ahead of her. The idea was impossible.

Or was it?

At the time, Esther had thought Imogen Lahr's self-appointed role of family secretary rather amusing. But supposing, just supposing, Imogen had taken her father's messages because the sunlight on the screen made his eyes hurt? There could be many reasons for that, but one possibility was terrifying. Supposing they hurt for the same reason Esther's eyes were hurting now?

Going back into her room, Esther lay on her bed. The audiovision annoyed her, making clear thought difficult. Twice she turned it down, until the volume control would respond no more. The whole idea was absurd. Central Committee could not possibly make such a mistake.

With a sense of infinite relief, Esther returned to the lounge, to continue sorting her papers.

Yet the idea would not go away. For an hour it niggled, making it hard to concentrate on other matters. Could Stephan Lahr be Callum? Frowning, Esther paused, trying to be logical. She had thought her neighbour cold and unpleasant, but she could be making her usual mistake of accepting appearance as reality. For weeks she had imagined Callum as a Scot with dark hair and a limp, only to learn he was a Southerner with a French grandmother. A good actor will draw on aspects of his own personality to portray even the most unsympathetic character. The silent withdrawn boy Callum had described could well have grown up into an ambitious, uncommunicative man, unable to relate to others. It would not be difficult for him to portray a character like Patroner Lahr.

With increasing urgency, Esther considered the possibility. She had disliked her neighbour because he was not as he appeared, and because she had felt a peculiar emptiness in him. Tim had felt the same. That did not necessarily mean the man was a Seeker. Nor did it mean he was without feeling. Emptying the mind would be a good way of controlling emotion. The man's children clearly did not find him cold. Imogen loved him intensely; little Benn was distraught, sensing that his father was in danger. In the end, Tim too had come to like him. Tim was a sympath, however young and untrained. She ought to have paid more attention to his judgement, not gone on assuming a man was a threat because that was how he had first appeared.

Going back into her bedroom, Esther stood at the window, trying to remain calm. From the first day, she had noticed a peculiar protectiveness in Imogen's manner towards her father. She continually watched him, worried about him, wanted to offer him help, yet felt nervous of offending him by doing so. Supposing his sight had been restored in her lifetime? She would find it difficult to get used to the idea, particularly if there were still odd occasions when he had to call on her, when he was tired perhaps, or the print was small.

'Dear gods!' Esther said aloud, 'what have I done?'

She had assumed it was Stephan Lahr who had been to the canyon checking on her. By repeating her assumption to Sly, she had prevented the old woman from investigating Central Committee's case further. Yet there was only Miriam's description as evidence. Stephan Lahr was fair, but Esther would not have described his hair as being like gold. It could have been another man Miriam saw, someone who looked like Stephan, but was not in fact him.

One final detail recurred to Esther's memory: Callum had not known until recently that she was a sympath. He had told her so himself, while they were at the control centre. If he was indeed Stephan Lahr, that might explain the change in his manner. When they first met, he had not kept his feelings from her, and she had sensed that he was not as he appeared. Later, when he was on his guard against her, she had been unable to find anything strange about him.

It was a small point, a matter of subtle instincts rather than reason, but it convinced Esther more than any of her previous arguments. Going back into the lounge she stood marooned amongst a scattering of papers. Her hand was shaking as she hunted for the showhouse programme again. Hurriedly she opened it to the images at the front. There had to be something she had missed. Scanning through the pages, she tried to find what it was. Suddenly it was in front of her.

At the end of the programme was a section in which the career of each of the main members of staff was described. After outlining Stephan Lahr's progress from technician to director came the passage, 'Patroner Lahr's rapid success is all the more remarkable considering the disadvantages he has had to overcome. Truly he is proof that our Keepers encourage each of us to realise our full potential.'

At the time people had assumed that the new director was from a low strata, an example of the poor boy made good. But what if the writer were alluding to a visual handicap the Patroner disliked having mentioned?

Sitting down on the floor, Esther looked again at the image of Patroner Lahr. Putting a piece of paper across his face so that only the mouth was visible, she half closed her eyes, trying to simulate darkness. Dissatisfied, she got up and shut the blind across the window. Then she tried again. The mouth was sensitive and surprisingly young.

Letting the programme fall to the floor, Esther stared ahead of her. Work was out of the question now. Twice she returned to the programme and went through it again. Twice she found nothing more. She had almost given up when she saw the explanation. On the middle page was a group portrait of the new troupe. Illusionists, actors, props women, they were all there, the sixty or so people needed to keep a populace happy. Stephan Lahr was at the front. Behind him, to the right, was a man who was surprisingly similar in appearance. His hair was fairer than Stephan's, however – as fair as gold.

One of the actors, the caption listed him as Jon More. Hardly able to breathe, Esther retrieved the still of Burgess Lander from its hiding place. She laid the two images side by side. With so small a face in the programme it was hard to be sure, but there seemed to be a definite resemblence. Fetching an enhancer, Esther tried again. Magnified, the likeness was undeniable.

The four names that had tantalised her for days were suddenly in order. Callum had been born Simon Miniott, but was now living under the name of Stephan Lahr. He was not Burgess Lander. That was a different man entirely.

For a moment Esther stood helplessly. Sly had predicted exactly what had happened, but neither of them had been able to sort out the relationships between the two families in time. Even now, Esther was not sure she could prove her case. Snatching up her jotter, she sketched the links urgently.

John Miniott had had three children in France: Andrew, the man Esther knew as Jack, and a daughter. Subsequently he had brought the sons to England. Andrew had married Joanna, whose portrait Esther's mother had painted. Simon Miniott was the eldest son of that marriage. Since his early twenties, however, he had worked under the name of Stephan Lahr. It was small wonder Patroner Lahr had no convincing biography for his youth.

So where did Burgess Lander fit in?

Frowning, Esther sketched the last line of the family tree. John Miniott's daughter had been brought over later than the boys, and had married a man called Lander. Her sons were therefore Simon Miniott's cousins. It was hardly surprising there was a likeness between them.

That likeness could well be Simon Miniott's death sentence. Burgess had become an excellent Keeper, most effective in the fight against rebellion. He must have moved from show-house to showhouse, using his cousin as cover. It was he who should have been accused by the National Committee, but the enforcers had been instructed to kill the wrong man, and Esther had confirmed their verdict.

Desperately Esther tried to think what to do. The National Committee would want more than speculation before they revoked their order, and most of her arguments relied on instinct rather than facts. Yet it would take far too long to find proof. Even the five days she had asked Sly to wait before opening the locket would be too long. In any case, why should Sly connect Simon Miniott with Stephan Lahr? Esther could try to see Sly in person and explain the situation to her, but that might lead the enemy to Hunter's Farm. Someone would have to come to her instead.

Fetching one of Sally's dolls, she placed it in the window, hoping that one of the other women would see it there and relay her distress signal along the lines.

It was Fifty who came. She seemed surprised to see Esther, but did not explain why. She was too angry at Esther using a signal reserved only for emergencies.

'This is an emergency,' Esther insisted. 'We are about to kill one of our best allies. The contract on Stephan Lahr must be revoked immediately.'

'We don't even know who's got it. You know that as well as me.'

'Find out, and call it in.'

'On what grounds?'

'Stephan Lahr's no traitor. He's better known to us as Callum.'

'Callum? That's absurd.'

'It's true, all the same.'

'How do you know that?'

Urgently Esther tried to outline her reasons. As she had feared, they sounded vague and trivial when put into words. 'Just believe me,' she pleaded. 'I'll give you proof later.'

'Why are you so concerned about this man?'

'If he dies at our instigation, the renegades will turn against us. Even if they don't, without his vision the revolution will fail. He's the one who brings people together, who keeps them going . . .'

'You always did overstate things.'

'Do you want to be remembered as the woman who kept this lousy regime in power?'

Fifty stood silently beside the kitchen table. 'I'll speak to Sly,' she promised at last. 'We may not be able to do anything in time even if she believes you. The contract will have been passed down the line. None of us has any idea who will actually carry out the sentence.'

'At least start the process off. Meanwhile I'll try and warn Callum he's in danger.'

'How can you do that?'

'I'll find a way.'

Fifty turned to go. 'Your own feelings are of no importance,' she reminded Esther. 'You know that as well as me. If you've fallen for this man, you must declare it to Sly, and she'll decide what to do with you.'

'If there's any risk to us, I shall let him die. That's hardly the decision of a lovesick woman.'

'I'm sorry.' Fifty paused. 'This whole business has been a right mess, hasn't it?' she remarked. For once her usual firmness was missing.

In surprise, Esther shook her head. 'Not completely,' she replied. 'Fourteen's timebomb is ticking away nicely.'

'I don't understand you. She came to us saying everything had failed.'

'Cal and I did the job instead. Hasn't the spokeswoman told you?'

'We haven't heard from the spokeswoman, or anyone else. The renegades seem to have vanished off the face of the earth.'

Esther smiled. 'They're in hiding, waiting. How could you have so little faith?'

Turning back, Fifty looked at her with large, almost child-like eyes. 'You mean that Central Control really will fall?'

'If I managed to key everything in properly.'

To Esther's amazement the other woman threw her arms

around her neck. 'We nearly missed our own revolution!' she exclaimed in joy. 'I've never seen Sly so low. She said she should have heard from you by now. Oh you silly, foolish woman! To take such a risk yourself!'

'Sly knew I'd have a crack at it. I virtually told her.'

'She didn't think you'd stand a cat's chance of remembering that program – or that Callum would be able to get you into the centre. When we didn't hear from you we assumed you were both dead, or at least taken. We've been covering our tracks ever since. Half our people are in hiding. There's a massive crack-down taking place.'

'Our traitor's been busy.' Carefully Esther ringed Jon More's face with her finger. 'This is the man,' she said. 'Don't wait for contracts to be passed down the line. Remove him at once. If I'm wrong I'll take it on my own conscience.' Tearing the page out, she passed it to Fifty.

Fifty put the page safely inside her jacket. 'When do you collect your children?' she asked.

'Friday.'

'You'd be wise to leave now without them.'

'I can't abandon Tim and Sally.'

'No. I don't suppose I could either. Very well. Make for Dog's Bar as soon as you've got them. You'll be met there.'

'Forgive me if I was hostile at first,' Esther said awkwardly. 'I felt as if I'd been forgotten.'

'We honestly thought you were dead. I'm glad you're not.' Offering her hand in the gesture of kinship, the woman left.

The evening performance was about to begin when Esther reached the showhouse. She had been followed as she had expected, though by which side she could not determine. It had taken her a good hour to lose her Watcher and then she had had to walk several kilometres back to Entertainment Square. To her relief Stephan Lahr was in the building, for she heard an announcer calling for him over the public address system. Joining the queue of people still waiting at the public appreciation counter, she waited.

'I wondered if Mr Lahr would sign this programme,' she said as soon as her turn came. 'It's the gala one. I enjoyed the show so much and there were so many people waiting for autographs I couldn't get it signed then. I thought I'd try again tonight.'

With a patronising smile, the usher took the programme and attached a slip to it, on which he wrote Esther's name and number.

'Mr Lahr used to live near me,' Esther continued, smiling shyly. 'Our children were friends. I've written a little note for him. Is it possible for you to pass it on to him?'

The usher was not sure. It was out of the ordinary.

'Read what I've put if you want,' Esther invited, and passed him the note.

'Forty-Eight, Moor View Dwellings, Moss Edge,' the usher read aloud.

Dear Mr Lahr, I wondered how you were getting on. Tim often asks after Imogen. You said she might have tea with us some time. Could she come next week perhaps? We'd love to see her again.

I'm not sure if you heard that my husband died recently. I'm coping well enough, but inevitably I miss him. Tim and Sally have been very good, but a visit from an old friend would cheer us all up.

By the way, do you remember me mentioning that my aunt was convinced you were someone else? I've worked out who she meant. There's an actor in your troop called Jon More. He is quite like you, now I look at his pictures. I suppose you get used to people confusing you. Tell him he has an admirer in her eighties, who's sure he's the director! Looking forward to seeing Imogen again soon. Benn will be welcome too if you think he'll stay. Best wishes, Esther Thomas (Tess).

'Can't see any harm in that,' the usher admitted. Glancing at the pictures of the cast displayed on the wall near him, he looked intently at the image of Jon More. 'I suppose there is some likeness,' he added. 'Never saw it before.' Then passing Esther's note and programme through a service hatch, he turned to the next person waiting.

Slowly the queue departed, and the foyer emptied. Those who had merely asked for signed programmes received them back promptly through the hatch. Eventually Esther was alone. Even the usher went off to see to business elsewhere.

At last the Patroner came down the stairs. 'Good to see you again,' he said, offering his hand. Esther felt his concern, though he was outwardly calm. 'Thank you for inviting Imie. Would Tuesday do?'

'That'd be fine.'

The usher had reappeared but, satisfied that all was well, he turned away.

'I brought you your programme myself,' Stephan Lahr said, passing Esther the booklet.

As if not quite grasping it firmly enough, Esther let it fall to the floor. They both bent to pick it up.

'Hide, Cal,' Esther whispered. 'Our enforcers have orders to kill you.'

'Tess—'

Straightening up, Esther laughed, as if at the confusion. 'What?' she asked with her lips alone.

'Thank you.'

20

In the silence Esther waited. A sense of someone being near had woken her. Getting up, she put on her night wrap and went into the hall. It was empty and the door was safely shut. In the lounge the lights and audiovision were dimmed to night mode. Shapes and images flickered in the mirror on the far wall, and were reflected back by the polished table. She was not dreaming this time. Callum was sitting on the couch, waiting for her.

'How did you get in?' Esther whispered. For an instant she was very afraid.

'Your note seemed to invite me.'

'To make contact, not to invade my dwelling.'

For several seconds Esther stood watching him, trying to adjust to the idea that the man she had known as Stephan Lahr was indeed Callum. In the soft light of the night mode, he was better-looking than she had remembered. His eyes were very blue, like a boy's. She had feared she would be disappointed, and discovered she was not.

It was possible that there was still a listening device she had not discovered, and everything they said could be heard. As if reading her thoughts, Callum shook his head. 'I've checked the place,' he said. 'It's clean. Just tell me why you accused my cousin, and I'll go.'

Fetching the still image of Burgess Lander, Esther handed it to him. 'This man is a known Seeker,' she said. 'We've been compiling a dossier on him for months. We've traced his progress by the arrests that have followed him – Midopolis, Centopolis, and now Nortown. Each has had its resistance groups broken. Until today we thought you were him. He probably has posed as you.'

Silently Callum took the image.

'A few weeks ago, the mother of one of our members made a formal accusation against you,' Esther continued. 'Our National Committee investigated, and declared the case proven. As Stephan Lahr, you've been sentenced to death, for crimes against the people.'

'I thought the Movement was against violence.'

'Other groups we're associated with aren't.'

'So they do your dirty work?'

'If you like to put it that way. Would you rather we left him to inform on us? He's used you, Cal. He's followed you from showhouse to showhouse, listening in the refectory, watching in the meeting rooms. Our people are on the run already. The arrests are beginning.'

'How can you be sure my cousin is to blame?'

'Was he one of the new recruits that last afternoon?'

Reluctantly Callum nodded. 'I didn't even know he'd joined us,' he admitted. 'One of my deputies recruited him.'

Sitting down beside him, Esther tried to soften what she was saying. 'He may not know you're involved – yet,' she said. 'At first I thought it was you he'd recognised, but I realise now you arrived later than him. It must have been Madelaine he saw. He had a horrible surprise. The authorities had sent him to infiltrate a new group they'd heard of, that was all. He'll work out your involvement soon, and betray you. He'll see it as his duty.'

'In his eyes, we are the betrayers,' Callum reminded her. 'To a loyal Keeper we're madmen trying to return the country to anarchy.'

Again there was a pause. 'What are you going to do about him?' Esther persisted. 'You can act faster than we can.'

'The order is already given. If I'm not back in two hours, my deputies will carry it out.'

A chill passed over Esther's mind. 'What will happen?' she asked.

'My cousin is about to be taken very ill. If he fights he'll survive, but he'll be out of action for at least a month. By then the revolution should have begun. It might even be over. After that, everything will depend on whether he can accept the new Order, or not.'

'You'll forgive him?'

'We shall all have to seek reconciliation, or the country will tear itself apart again.'

'And what of Toby?' Esther asked. 'Will he be able to forgive?'

'Toby's safe. We got him out a few hours ago.' With a gesture of irritation Callum tried the audiovision control. 'If you could only turn this wretched thing off!'

'I've never known silence in my home,' Esther pointed out. 'That privilege belongs to higher strata than mine.'

'It's the one I miss most. To hear wind in the trees . . . Such things are worth more than wealth.'

The time check showed on the screen. It was twenty-three thirty. Callum had been given the information he needed, yet he lingered. Uncertainly Esther watched him. She knew him and yet she did not know him. Stephan Lahr had been an act, just as Commander Tate had been, and the old domestic in the corridor. Now she was meeting the real man who had played those parts. She still thought of him as Callum, because that was how she had first begun to respect him, and because Stephan Lahr had never convinced her. This man was not quite Callum though, but someone far more complex.

'I don't know how to speak to you,' Esther admitted. 'What name do I use?'

'Stick to Callum. It's safest.'

'But which is the real you?'

Smiling slightly, Callum shrugged his shoulders. 'I'm not sure myself,' he admitted. 'The ambitious Patroner who works too hard – he is a part of me. So too is the anger of Callum. Simon was a boy trying to survive, and I lie awake sometimes at night and feel very like that boy again. Pretence can become a habit. Right now, I'm playing at being sincere, but it's still a role of sorts. I can hear myself speaking the lines.'

His honesty impressed her. 'Acting seems to run in your family,' Esther remarked.

'My father was a politician. What do you expect?'

Esther smiled. 'I think I rather like the new man I'm meeting,' she said.

'I don't disappoint you?'

'No, but you disappoint yourself. Why do you judge yourself so harshly? You've given your cousin a fighting chance. That's more than he would have given you.'

Getting up, Callum crossed to the window and looked out of it carefully. 'Wouldn't you feel bad?' he asked.

'I'm not a Keeper.'

'And a Keeper can't feel remorse, or love?' He turned back towards her. 'Tess, I've just given orders that may kill a man. I'm no better than my grandfather.'

'You had no choice.'

'That's never an excuse.'

Esther wanted to offer comfort, but could think of nothing to say. Instead, she went to him and stood beside him. 'You're a very unlikely Keeper,' she remarked. 'How have you survived?'

'By acting my part better than most. Even a boy can act, if his life depends on it. "Nice to meet you, sir." "Of course I'd like to stay with you, Grandad." Callum's tone mimicked a boy's exactly. 'When I was fifteen my masters tried to shape me in their mould, but at the back of my mind I laughed. I couldn't take their rituals seriously. So I pretended again. Now I pretend I don't see too well. "Stephan's all right," they say. "You can forget him. He doesn't know what's going on."

Touching his face tentatively, Esther traced the shape of his chin and mouth. That much of his face she had imagined correctly. 'I think I could love you, ' she admitted, 'if I could only get to know you better.'

'You already see inside me.' Tentatively, Callum touched her hair. 'Tell me what you see tonight?' he asked.

'An idealist, who has had to learn to be a soldier. You slide uneasily between the two roles, yet you play both well.'

Callum smiled. 'Left to myself I would probably have become an artist,' he admitted. 'That runs in our family too.'

'Anyone who can make children laugh is an artist already.'

There was a long silence. Esther could feel his love as clearly as when they had been beside the fountain together. It weakened her resistance.

'Would you let me stay a while?' Callum asked unexpectedly. 'Just to talk and get to know each other. If I go back now, I shall be tempted to change my orders.'

Flushing slightly, Esther hesitated. 'All right,' she agreed. 'I'll make us both a drink.'

When she returned, Callum was sitting on the floor with his back to the couch. It seemed to be his most comfortable position, a habit acquired from years of hard living in training centres or showhouse rehearsal rooms. Smiling, Esther put the refreshments on the table. 'You have to pay for these,' she warned.

'How?'

'By answering my questions. I have two biographies for you, and I'm not sure how they fit together.'

'I thought your records told you everything.'

'They give facts, not reasons.'

'What sort of reasons do you want? So long as my answers won't harm anyone else, I'll try to be honest.'

For several seconds Esther considered what to ask. His eyes were so blue, they disconcerted her. 'Tell me about your wife,' she suggested. 'Did you really marry while you were at college?'

'We grew up together. Love seemed natural between us.'

'You married for love? What did your families say?'

'They thought we were mad, but they supported us. It worked out well. Life's been a lot less interesting since I lost Thea.'

The simplicity of the man's words suggested so much, in so little.

Once again there was reflective silence between them. The real Callum had a lot in common with Stephan Lahr. He found it just as difficult to talk of personal matters. 'Was your wife an outsider, then?' Esther prompted.

'No. Thea was a Keeper's daughter. I couldn't have married her otherwise.'

'I thought perhaps that was why you had to change your name.'

'A Keeper is sometimes allowed to withdraw from the daily running of the Order, so long as he can serve his country better another way. I was able to prove I could. In return, I renounced all privileges my father's rank entitled me to, and took on a new identity. I haven't regretted it. I have far more influence as a Patroner than I would have had as a half-hearted bureaucrat.'

Silently Esther thought what that renunciation must have meant, to the man's family as well as himself. The more she learnt of Callum, the more she respected him. Slipping on to the floor, she sat beside him.

'What more do you want to know?' he asked.

'One crucial date. When did you go to France?'

'What makes you think I went there?'

'Logic. Your family still has money in French banks, despite the Durham directive, and surgery is far better there than here. Let's see, the Dark Ones first appear in transmissions a year ago. You would have needed three or four years before that to be trained yourself, and to make links with other resistance groups. I'd put it at about five years ago.'

'You're a frightening woman. It was four and a half years ago, to be precise. And before you ask, we do have French support. We'd be mad to attempt a revolution without outside aid.'

There was another pause.

'Don't go back to the showhouse,' Esther advised him. 'Collect your children and get to safety.'

'My children are safe. I've arranged to be called away tomorrow night myself, but I shall have to go into work first. If I don't I'll arouse suspicion.'

'Then don't go near any equipment. Don't walk under any gantries, or touch anything with power running through it. Your death will be planned to look like an accident.'

'Do you care what happens to me?'

It was some time before Esther could answer. 'I don't like to think of you being in danger,' she said.

'And I don't like to think of you staying here, waiting for your children.'

Thoughtfully Esther ran her finger round her beaker until it made a ringing sound. 'How do we learn to trust each other?' she asked. 'You fear I'll sell you to save my skin. I know what you're capable of, however gentle you may seem.'

The audiovision played its sweet music, suggesting sleep. 'Read me,' Callum invited, taking her hands in his. 'See if I intend any harm to you.'

For several seconds, Esther sat looking into his face. 'No,' she said at last. 'I can find none. You must answer one more question, though, before I'll feel secure. Did your grandfather deliberately desert your grandmother?'

'Why do you want to know that?'

Embarrassed, Esther looked away. 'I need your side of the story.'

'All I know is what my father recalls, and what my grandmother herself told me.'

'Then tell me that much.'

'It's not particularly remarkable. My grandfather was on business in France. He fell in love with a young French artist, called Thérèse Chantall. He couldn't marry her – she wasn't Keeper's blood – but they lived together. His parents turned a blind eye. There were two older sons in England who could carry on the name. Then one was killed by marauders, and the other died in the riots. Grandfather was called home to take their place.'

'Couldn't he refuse?'

Callum picked up his beaker. 'You don't refuse the enforcers,' he said.

'Sly told me your grandfather stole his sons. She obviously hated him for it, though I don't know why. Was he forced to do that too?'

'He probably thought he was doing his best for them. The Order would also have wanted a male heir and put pressure on him.' For the first time Callum was not telling the whole truth. His reluctance puzzled Esther. 'I don't know quite how it was done,' he added. 'Perhaps my grandmother had signed papers she didn't understand. Or maybe they were forged, as she claims. Either way, it all went through the courts. The children were well cared for. The eldest became my father, the other, the man you know as Jack.'

Putting his arm round her, Callum lifted Esther's chin so that he could see her expression. 'Does that reassure you?' he asked. 'I don't excuse what was done, but I blame the rule more than the man. A Keeper has knowledge and wealth, but not freedom of spirit. Without that freedom, everything else becomes meaningless. By the time I knew my grandfather, he was a cold, empty man. He won nothing in the end.'

Again there was a reflective silence.

'I traced my grandmother while I was in France,' Callum added suddenly.

'How did she receive you?'

'At first she turned me away, but I went again. In the end she welcomed me.'

'You don't take "no" easily, do you?' Esther asked.

'Not if I think something's worth fighting for.' Brushing the hair off her forehead, Callum smiled. 'Don't worry about old wounds,' he advised. 'I won't desert you. That's what all the questions have been about, isn't it? When I stood in your doorway and watched you walking round your room with Benn, I made up my mind that if you were ever free, I wanted you as my wife. Then it was for my children's sake. Now it's for my own.'

The colour rushed to Esther's face. 'I do believe you mean that,' she replied. 'But there'll have to be a lot of changes before you can keep your word. I'd be foolish to rely on it.'

'We'll win, I promise you, Tess. I have more hope now than ever. People are joining forces. The authorities won't be able to hold so many down. The only question is whether I shall manage to see it happen. With both sides against me the odds aren't improving. Please, my love. It's foolish of me to want reassurance from you, but death's a cold companion. I asked you for your promise last time we were together, and you couldn't give it to me. If you can find it in your heart to accept me now, it would make the next few days easier to endure.'

For a long time Esther sat trying to think how to reply. 'I would be afraid of you,' she admitted. 'It would be like marrying someone from a foreign land.'

'But such marriages can succeed. We work well as a team. You know my feelings, and there are times when I can read yours. Our children get on well together. What more could we ask?'

The audiovision announced the time. Still Esther could not

reply. It would soon be midnight, and Callum's orders would be put into effect. She wanted to give him the promise he asked her for, and did not know how to say it.

The controlled environment had clicked to minimum. Even in summer the dwellings were cold at night, their flimsy walls letting in the damp air. The wind off the moor rattled one of the windows.

Awkwardly Esther turned towards Callum. 'One day I'll marry you,' she promised. 'When we're old soldiers boring everyone with our tales.'

In the courtyard below, the night guard patrolled the paths between the dwellings. Their steps echoed off the walls. For a little longer Esther hesitated. The family support officer had often suggested she should take an official lover. It was a matter of civic duty, he had implied: an attractive woman like her, alone in the North. Every time, she had refused. Now she was contemplating inviting Callum to her bed. A relationship without state blessing would bring shame to her if it was discovered. And with such a man ... Even Madelaine had warned her against it.

Getting up, Callum offered her his hand. 'I'll go now,' he said.

'You don't have to leave,' Esther replied.

'And you don't have to invite me to stay.'

Smiling, Esther stood up too. 'You'd be terribly disappointed if I didn't,' she remarked.

'I would indeed. I can see loving a sympath has its advantages. Will you also know when I'm not in the mood?'

'Of course.'

Putting her arms around his neck, Esther began to kiss him. For once in her life she wanted to behave foolishly, to follow her emotions rather than her reason.

'Stay with me,' she invited. 'Please ...'

21

The night lights were dimming when Esther awoke. A cool grey dawn was filtering through the blinds, bleaching the images on the audiovision to a pale yellow. Sitting up on one elbow, she watched Callum. She wanted to touch him, but that would wake him, and there was still a little time before he needed to leave. A sense of dream bewildered her. This man could not be the same as the man she had feared. He certainly could not be a Keeper. When she was a girl, even the title used to make her nervous. The man lying sleeping beside her was not cruel or callous. They had lain and talked of each other and their children, like any normal couple finding happiness together after losing someone else. Unable to resist the temptation, Esther lent forward and kissed his forehead.

'What time is it?' he asked.

'Just after five hours.'

Sighing, Callum opened his eyes. 'I'd better go,' he said. 'Dragging it out will only make things worse.'

'When will you come back to me?'

'The minute the fighting stops. I shall stand at your door like an idiot, with bunches of flowers in both hands.'

Sitting up, he brushed the hair off her face. 'You're very beautiful,' he said. 'All I could wish for, more beautiful even than Thea. I don't want to leave you, but if I stay I'll put us both at risk.'

Esther watched as he dressed. 'Take care,' she warned.

'I always do. I'm no hero, Tess. I plod through life, keeping out of trouble.'

She did not believe him and shook her head.

Reconsidering, Callum sat down again on the bed, beside her. 'I ought to tell you one more thing,' he said. 'It may be important to you.'

A sense of dread filled her. 'Why?' she asked.

'Because the past still lives among us. I didn't quite tell you the truth earlier.'

'I know.'

'When my grandmother realised she wasn't going to get her sons back, she tried to fight for them in the courts. A young woman lawyer represented her. They soon discovered they were fighting more than an ordinary wealthy family. They didn't stand a chance. Finally my grandmother gave up, but her lawyer didn't. She began to gather evidence against the Order, some of it from the inside – from a Keeper's woman, perhaps. Maybe she was one herself. I've often wondered. Whatever her sources, people began to listen to her. The Order was using the Troubles to gain power. It didn't want that sort of attention. A mysterious death would have confirmed people's suspicions, so the lawyer was accused of malpractice and discredited. The last my family heard of her, she'd joined the rebels in the North. We thought she'd died in the civil war.'

Esther's voice seemed to have dried in her throat. 'What was her name?' she asked.

'Catherine Marr.'

'Sly!'

'If she ever learns my family are part of the Alliance, she'll probably pull out of it. She'll also turn on you for loving me.'

'Then I shall just have to make sure she doesn't know. Not even Sly has the right to judge me for these last few hours. My father chose my husband for me. Bob was a good man, but he never once made me feel what I've felt with you.'

Getting up again, Callum bent and kissed her. 'I'll see you after the revolution,' he promised. Then he paused. 'That doesn't sound real, does it? It's like saying "See you after the holidays." Only everything will be changed by then, for good or ill.'

'Will you keep your promises?'

'As surely as I stand here.'

They said no other goodbye. When the morning came, everything was just as it had been the night before. Only Esther was changed. For the first time in her life she had known complete happiness.

For some time she stayed in bed, watching the audiovision. A deep contentment filled her. She wondered what to do with the day. Tomorrow she must attend the medical, and on Friday she could fetch Sally and Tim. There were just three more days to survive.

Unexpectedly the intercom squeaked, startling her. Pulling her wrap round her, Esther went to the speaker. 'Who is it?' she asked.

'Your transport, Ma'am.'

'I'm not expecting any transport.'

'Esther Thomas, Number 58197/Z/F?'

'That's me.'

'We have orders to pick you up to take you for your medical.'

'But that's tomorrow.'

'Eleven hours today it says here.'

In alarm Esther looked about her. 'I'm not dressed,' she said. 'I wasn't expecting you.'

'We'll wait. You've packed your things, I hope?'

'Packed?' Esther asked the unseen voice. Her lips were going dry.

'Of course, Ma'am. You may not be returning. If you don't pass your medical, you'll be kept for assessment.'

Holding her breath, Esther stifled the fear that rose in her chest.

'We haven't all day,' the voice said. 'If you don't let us in, we'll have to report you were uncooperative.'

'Just let me get ready,' Esther said quickly. 'I'll let you in as soon as I'm decent.'

Urgently Esther got dressed, glancing around the room as she did so to see that there was nothing incriminating. The rose was still beside her bed. Snatching it out of its box, she pushed it quickly amongst a dried flower display on her lounge table, and then dropped the box in the waste unit. If the Watchers outside knew there was love in her mind, they would find it and use it against her. Then she went to open the door.

There was a woman in medical uniform and two male escorts, far too many for a normal transport booking. Doors were opening discreetly along the corridor and then closing. Esther could feel the atmosphere. Her neighbours were frightened, both for her and for themselves. It didn't do to have a deviant living nearby. 'Come in while I finish packing,' Esther invited, rather too loudly.

The officials nearly filled her tiny hallway.

As slowly as she dare, Esther packed her things, trying to think as she did so. She must get a message to someone. Callum? Perhaps it was on his orders that she was being taken?

She refused even to consider the idea. No one, not even a Keeper, could have lied to her so completely.

'Is it possible for me to make a few calls?' Esther asked, trying to sound just mildly nervous. 'I have several appointments. I wouldn't want people to worry about me.'

'You can make two,' the orderly replied, following her into the lounge. 'Just say you'll be busy. Don't mention anything about your medical. That might worry your friends.'

The two men waited in the hallway. Finding the number in the local index, Esther rang the showhouse.

A receptionist answered. To Esther's disappointment, the director was elsewhere in the building. 'This is Mrs Esther Thomas,' Esther said. 'Would you tell the Patroner I'm afraid I won't be able to have Imogen after all? I may have another engagement. I'll contact him as soon as I'm free.'

'Ready?' one of the men asked.

'Can't I make the second call?' Esther asked.

'If you're quick.'

Her father was a long time coming to the phone and the female orderly was showing signs of impatience. She kept well out of range of the visiscreen however.

'Hi, Dad,' Esther said brightly. Very carefully she moved her head so that the mirror on the wall would show in the screen. In it should be reflected the two men waiting in the doorway. 'I'm afraid I mightn't be able to bring the children down this Sunday,' she lied. 'Something's turned up.'

For an instant she saw the surprise in her father's eyes, then he had it under control. He was still the disciplined officer, able to hide his emotions.

'That's a shame,' he said. 'I was looking forward to seeing them.' Resolutely he kept his eyes on her, though he must have been able to see the mirror. 'Try and come if you can.'

'I'll give you another ring next week,' Esther promised. 'I must go now. I have to catch a shuttle.'

'Bye, love. Look after yourself.'

The image faded.

'You were being optimistic,' the orderly remarked. 'Planning to take your children away on Sunday.'

'I didn't realise there might be a problem,' Esther replied. 'What about the milk and things? Ought I to cancel them?'

'Everything will be seen to, my dear. You have no need to worry.'

Taking one last look round her dwelling, Esther clenched her fingers hard into a fist. 'Ask them to feed my plants,' she said. 'But don't let them overdo it.' She was beginning to talk too quickly. Picking up her carry-all, she set her face to the door, and walked between the men, down the corridor. All the way along, doors quietly closed.

The transport was waiting at the perimeter of the dwellings. Inside, it had the appearance of an ambulance, though outside it looked no different to a normal public vehicle. The door closed behind Esther with a deadly swish. Everything inside was soft, lacking in form. Pretending to settle her carry-all on the rack, Esther looked round her quickly. There was a narrow line along one wall, just between the roof and the wall panel. Anxiously she tried to see what it was, and remembered she would be being observed. A flask of drink and some refreshments had been put on the service tray for her. It was going to be a long journey, or she would not have been provided with food.

Sitting down in the coach, Esther looked at the line on the opposite wall more carefully. It was definitely a vent, and it appeared to connect with the front cabin, rather than outside.

'We suggest you rest a while,' the orderly's voice said through an intercom. 'It may be a while before we get there.'

'Can I help myself to a drink?' Esther asked.

'Of course, my dear.'

Taking the flask, Esther poured herself some of the liquid. As she had hoped, the transport banked slightly as the journey began. Moving her hand to steady the flask, she knocked it over. Quickly she took out her handkerchief and began dabbing up the spilt drink. Within seconds the cloth was soaked.

'Leave it, Mrs Thomas,' the woman's voice said irritably. 'We'll clean it up when we arrive.'

Putting the sodden handkerchief on the couch near her hand, Esther pretended to be looking outside. The windows were darkened, so that she could see out, but no one could see in.

She heard the sound first, the faint hiss of moving air. As if merely bored and tired, Esther lay down, so that her face was hidden from the camera. Taking several deep breaths of the remaining clean air, she waited while the confuser dropped from the grille, and crept towards her. Then she slid her hand over her handkerchief and brought it to her face. Holding it firmly over her nose and mouth, she waited.

After that, life became a deadly game, with Esther as the only team member on one side, and a continually changing opposition. She was being interred in Psychiatric Hospital Five, Ward B. There were no signs anywhere to tell her so, but she had retained enough consciousness to hear the driver of the transport. An orderly in blue uniform gave her a bed in a little cubicle. Everything would be done to ensure she was comfortable, the woman said. There were toiletries laid out for her use, a personal audiovision with pushbutton control, even beads for her to braid in her hair. Then she gave Esther a lounger suit to wear, and took away the clothes in which she had arrived. The suit was a pretty pink. Esther hated it with every fibre of her being, but she said nothing.

An hour later, they began to question her.

At first it was done quite kindly. A ward sister explained to Esther that she had been diagnosed as suffering from creeping paranoia, a condition that could prove dangerous without treatment. When Esther asked what that meant, she was told the symptoms of her illness were hard to define, since they varied from person to person. Basically she suffered from delusions that the state was against her. Such fantasies must be brought to the surface and removed before she could begin to see life as it really was, and be happy again. It would be wise to share some of her feelings now, so that they could assess which type of treatment she needed. No one would mind what she said. All they wanted was to make her well again.

Though Esther had resisted the confuser, it dulled her

mind and made thought difficult. Smiling nervously, she nodded.

'Be a sensible girl and co-operate with your therapists,' the sister advised. 'Then you'll soon be back home with your children.'

Again, Esther nodded, but inside her mind she could hear a voice warning: 'Don't listen. You must stay silent.' It really was most peculiar, as if she were two people, one dreamily nodding, the other already planning how to resist. Other people's lives depended on her silence. She must never forget that, the voice insisted. If she allowed herself to be persuaded by the smiling jailors who now held her, she would be responsible for the arrests of Sly, and Fifty, and all the other women with whom she had worked. She would also condemn Callum and his family to death. Time and again she had promised him she would not betray him. Now she had to keep that promise.

After the ward sister had finished, medication was brought, a capsule that Esther kept quite easily under her tongue and removed afterwards. Fortunately there were only general scanners in the ward, surveying the room in broad sweeps rather than peering into each cubicle. Shivering on her bed, Esther waited. Her timepiece had been taken from her when she arrived. It would be difficult to keep count of time. In that sealed, comfortable world, there were no clocks on the walls, no personal timepieces. Even the audiovision programmes lacked the usual half-hourly check. Yet to know the passage of the days would be vital, a means of retaining hope. In eleven days' time, the Central Control system should come crashing down. The people who had power over her now would come running out from their wards, wondering what had happened. In the cities, thousands would pour from their dwellings in panic. All traffic controls would stop. On a Monday morning, the effect would be absolute chaos. Then the rebels would strike . . .

Letting down her hair, Esther rebraided it, so that she could add a bead to each strand to signify the passage of each new day.

Finally another orderly came. She was very kind, understanding Esther's bewilderment and inviting her to rest in the health and beauty salon. 'Spend a bit of time on yourself, love,' she advised. 'It'll do you good.'

Compliantly, Esther obeyed. She would be the perfect patient; do everything she was asked, make no trouble, attract no attention. Even a boy can act, Callum had said, if it will save his life. So too could a frightened woman. It would be safer to be mildly ill but co-operative, than sane and worth investigation. She would continue the pretence of suffering from depression after her husband's death. Her alleged paranoia must appear to be a result of that rather than any political views.

Suddenly she was called from the sauna. The orderly would not give her time to dress, and Esther sat in her bathrobe while two men in white uniforms asked her questions. She felt humiliated and vulnerable. She also felt very angry. Her inner fears were being played upon, whilst an impression of absolute propriety was being maintained. The hypocrisy of it all infuriated her, and she almost shouted at the men sitting opposite her.

They wanted to know about her childhood, and what she had thought of her mother. 'I loved her very much,' Esther replied honestly, 'but I also thought she was foolish.'

The remark interested the older man. 'In what way?' he asked.

'My mother was an idealist. Idealists never see things as they are.'

'Such as?'

'Well – it might be nice for each of us to have perfect freedom, but who would get the dinner? In a family, we have to give up some of our freedom so we can live together. The state's no different.'

Her answer seemed to please the older man, but the younger one persisted. 'What do you understand by the state?' he asked.

So it went on, for at least two hours. It was very difficult to concentrate and give only the right answers, and Esther was cold and hungry. Finally she was allowed to go back to her cubicle and get dressed. Lying down in her bed, she tried to control her fury. She found a quiz show on the audiovision; watching other people answering questions would at least occupy her mind.

Most of the other patients in the ward seemed genuinely ill. One talked to unseen presences, sometimes shouting at them in anger. The young girl in the cubicle opposite refused to eat, and would soon be taken away for force-feeding. A third picked at the skin on her fingers until she made them bleed. Two women seemed perfectly sane, however. Their manner was sluggish and resentful, as if they were under sedation. They frightened Esther more than any of the others. In them, she saw her future.

The first night was awful. Esther had spent much of her childhood in the Outlands. Even in Moss Edge there had been the moor just beyond the woodland. Now she was shut inside four blank walls, with the noise of breathing all round her. Sometimes the women shouted out in their sleep. For a dreadful few moments one of them wandered into Esther's cubicle and started picking up her toiletries, until led away by the night nurse. It was impossible to sleep. When Esther did doze for a few moments she dreamt of her children and thought they were calling out to her.

Staring into the night, she tried to focus on Callum. She recalled every detail about him, the way his hair fell across his forehead when he was talking, the texture of his skin, the exact blue of his eyes. Sometimes she even smiled to herself.

There had been no need for words between them. Callum could not, would not, have arranged for her to be sent to such a place. She must not imagine the idea. It was not even a sensible suggestion. More than anyone, Callum needed her silence. In a few days he would find her. Closing her eyes in relief, Esther at last went to sleep.

The next day she was taken to another ward. This was where her treatment would begin, her specialist told her. Individual therapy would of course continue but now there would also be group sessions, during which she could share her feelings with others. They wanted her to be honest. She must not be afraid to say anything. After each session she would also be invited to write down her thoughts. 'Put down everything,' he advised, 'even the things you're ashamed of. We're beyond being shocked here. Perhaps your sense of being under attack has led you to join some foolish group or society. It happens quite often. Confession will make you feel so much better. Everything you say will be treated in absolute confidence.'

'Oh yes?' Esther thought, but she joined the group, and sat talking in nervous little spurts, inventing a new personality for herself, based on Esther Thomas, but not the real Esther . . .

All that day and the next, the real Esther was watching, trying to fix facts in her mind: the names of her fellow patients, what they said and where they came from; the numbers on the orderlies' sleeves, anything that would give shape to a formless world. Even such facts were difficult to establish. More patients arrived at Psychiatric Hospital Five than ever left. There ought to have been a growing number within the buildings, yet there was not. Somehow patients just disappeared. They were moved on to other wards, one of the other women whispered. For a few days you saw them exercising in other gardens or resting on other sundecks, then you didn't see them again. There were rumours of a Ward A, where uncooperative patients were treated, but no one knew in which block Ward A was situated. They suspected it wasn't a nice place, but didn't like to ask.

Esther had never known such silent, creeping fear. It filled her mouth, and dried her tongue. Sometimes her medication was given her in liquid form, and the orderly stood over her while she drank it. For hours afterwards she felt dreamy and remote, happy just to watch the audiovision or lie on the sun deck. The effect seemed to be cumulative, for even if she managed to avoid taking the next dose, her mind did not quite return to its original sharpness. She found it increasingly difficult to guard what she said in the group sessions, and she dreaded the sudden order for individual therapy. It always came when she was least prepared and at her most vulnerable. Soon, in a day or two perhaps, she would be telling the consultants everything they wanted, and thanking them for their kindness. She must find some way out, while she still had the wit to do so.

An overheard conversation hardened Esther's resolve into desperation.

The orderlies' room was next to Esther's cubicle. As she lay on her bed watching the audiovision she could often hear them talking to each other. If she concentrated very hard she could catch what they said. That evening a new staff nurse had been assigned to the ward, and was asking questions about what would be expected of her.

'Watch old Silko,' an older voice advised. 'She's a stickler.'

'And bad-tempered with it,' another voice agreed. 'Mind you, if you'd spent a year on Ward A, you'd end up funny.'

The other patients were taking their evening exercise, but Esther had stayed inside, pleading a headache. The orderlies did not know she was there.

'What's so special about Ward A?' the new voice asked.

'Final Treatment. It's where they send the recalcitrants. Some of them are quite violent – criminals, politicos – the worst of the lot. Most are sent direct by the courts, but there's always a few others who make a nuisance of themselves in other wards.'

'We've got a politico in here now,' the first voice confided. 'You can tell them the minute they walk in.'

'Which one's that?'

'The dark one. Gives me the creeps, always watching you.'

With a start Esther realised the orderly meant her.

'She's not taking her medication,' a fourth voice said. 'She'd sleep better if she was. They'll be moving her to Ward A before the week's up.'

'What if Final Treatment doesn't work?' the newcomer persisted. She sounded a little upset.

'We don't ask that.'

'No one asks. They're called for, that's all. Then their things are bundled up and sent home.'

The conversation could have been deliberately staged, but its meaning was the same, whether overheard by accident or design. Esther must bend somehow, or she would follow her mother into Ward A and beyond.

Getting up, Esther walked to the office at the end of the room. 'I need to talk to someone,' she said. She had begun to shiver uncontrollably.

For three hours they questioned her. She gave them truths, but only safe truths. Sly would have left Hunter's Farm by now. That had always been agreed. The renegades' training centre was empty. Madelaine had said so. It would be known already that there were renegades amongst the Keepers, joining with other groups like the Sheep People. Giving that information could do no more harm than the man called Lander had already done.

Playing one last role for her life, Esther sat at a table, opposite a changing sequence of questioners. She gave each what she sensed he wanted. Yes, she had been a member of the Movement. Yes she had become quite senior in it, a trainer and delegate. Now she regretted her folly in becoming involved. There were a few dangerous rebels, but in the main the Movement was made up of misguided or maladjusted women. The fools not only encouraged treason against the state and its generous keepers, but even denied nature. 'They say women are as strong as men,' she scoffed. 'That they are their equals. When a woman's expecting a child, how can she be as strong as a man? It was my mother who led me into such stupid ideas. I thought she was so beautiful, so clever ... Now I see she was wilful and dangerous. She used to say revolution was necessary, even if it meant a return to the Devastation. How can anyone be free when they have nothing to eat and nowhere to live?'

In the end they let Esther go, only to call her back again in the middle of the night and begin again. She was exhausted and beginning to lose all hold on reality. If they had questioned her any harder, she would have broken and revealed more than half-truths, but her persecutors were so pleased with what she did give them that they simply let her talk. Everything she said was taken down. They checked facts and names, and then cross-checked them. They even asked for map references for the training centre. Esther genuinely could not remember if she had ever known them. 'My mind's all confused,' she said, pretending to cry. 'Let me sleep. Please let me sleep.'

For four hours they left her alone, then she was awoken abruptly and the questioning began again. Esther replied in a dream, repeating her lines. Only willpower kept her upright in her chair. For much of the final session, she was useless to them.

She had never really believed it would work. When she was taken to another ward, she knew it was Ward A, and despaired. Lying down on her bed, she fell into an exhausted sleep.

All the following morning Esther watched as people came and went around her. The women near her were sitting knitting or sewing. It seemed such a strange thing to do. An orderly brought her a drink. 'How do you feel, my dear?' she asked, quite kindly.

'What are you going to do with me?' Esther asked.

'Do, dear? Don't you remember? You were admitted yesterday. Poor love, you were in a proper state. Therapy often has that effect. Coming to terms with your own mistakes is never easy.'

Still Esther did not understand her. 'What will happen to me?' she repeated.

'That depends on you. If you take your medication and listen carefully at the re-education classes, you'll soon be on the mend. One day you might be allowed to go home for a visit. You'd like that, wouldn't you?'

Smiling, Esther nodded. She could not focus on what was being said. A terrible vagueness was beginning to overtake her mind. It was as if she was being smothered in soft, warm blankets. If she slept again she might feel better. Lying down, she let the dream close around her. Somewhere, far away at the back of her mind, a voice was crying, but she could not recognise it. A name was printed on a card at the foot of her bed, but she did not recognise that either. Her proper name was Patient 12, Ward B1 . . .

Esther had saved Callum and her colleagues in the Movement, only to lose herself. She drifted to the sun deck or sauna, sat politely listening to the re-education sessions, did everything that was asked of her, and understood none of it. All sounds and sensations were muffled. Nothing had form or meaning for her. It was not unpleasant. She felt quite contented, in fact, as if she were lying on a soft couch watching the dream channel on the audiovision. Such awareness came to her only occasionally, however. Most of the time she simply was, a dreamlike being floating beyond thought or place.

After some days – months, perhaps, she could not say – Esther awoke to find a man in white standing beside her bed.

'You have friends in high places,' he said. 'They're not satisfied with the way you're being treated.'

Esther looked up at him in bewilderment. 'I have no complaints, sir,' she replied. His face was blurred.

'The decision is not yours. You are to be moved to another hospital.'

'Thank you, sir,' Esther said politely. 'When do I leave?'

'Now.'

Still dazed with sleep, Esther got up, and tried to find her things. Then she recalled that she had none.

When the transport came there was a little group of patients standing watching on the sun deck to see it go. They were not wishing her goodbye, just attracted by the unusual fact of someone leaving. 'Lucky sod!' Esther heard one of the orderlies say.

'You don't know,' her companion warned. 'There's worse places than this.'

The words echoed in Esther's mind.

She was asleep when the transport came to a sudden halt, throwing her on to the floor. There was shouting outside, and the engine was thrown hurriedly into reverse. This time something hard hit the side of the vehicle, so that it slewed at a peculiar angle. The doors at the back were being forced open, a laser cutter breaking through the seal. In terror Esther crouched on the floor.

Two men forced their way into the vehicle. They were masked and black, like creatures out of a nightmare. One of them put something near Esther's face, making her gasp and begin to cough. 'Run, Tess,' a voice said. Hands grabbed hers and pulled her towards the open doors. Then she was on a bank, above an old stone bridge. Stumbling and falling, Esther began to run down the grass.

The shouting continued. Splashing through the water, Esther ran under the bridge. Beyond it she could see a culvert. There was a peculiar roaring behind her. Someone was calling to her, but she could not understand what they were saying. Dark shapes were running away from the transport. 'Get clear!' she heard someone shout.

Plunging into the culvert, Esther hid. Weapons were being fired. Hidden by the bridge a battle was being fought. The transport burnt fiercely, turning the water red with its light. Then the weapons were silent.

Crouched in the water running through the culvert, Esther waited. She could see the river and the opposite bank, framed by the shape of an old brick outflow. The flames of the fire still lit the water. Two figures appeared in the distance, running down a track that led from a farm settlement about a kilometre away. They climbed over a fence on to the riverbank and ran on towards the burning transport. A few minutes later they returned, walking.

'Won't get much out of that,' a man's voice said, carrying clearly across the river.

'Might get a few metals,' a woman replied.

'What you reckon it were all about?'

'Let 'em kill each other if they want. It i'nt no skin off our faces.'

The couple turned back up the track, and there was silence again.

Splashing her hands and face in the culvert, Esther tried to remember what had brought her there. She discovered she was wearing a sort of hospital suit, in a pastel green. The colour surprised her; for some reason she had expected it to be pink. There was a peculiar mark on her wrist, a set of numbers. They would not rub off, no matter how much she tried, and she grew quite distressed by their persistence. She had no memory of such a mark ever having been made. Her hair was also elaborately braided, though she could not recall why.

For a long time Esther huddled in her culvert, shivering with cold. Whoever had attacked the transport had vanished before the two Outlanders arrived. The river was deserted, except for a couple of ducks further down it swimming in the shallows. There was no sound other than wind and water. She was in a valley, cutting through wild country. All around her were stony hills and fast-moving streams. Instinct warned she must put as much distance as possible between herself and the burnt-out transport. Confirming her fear, a police PTU appeared in the sky, coming down towards the valley. As soon as the men inside it had investigated the scene of the crash, she must move on. Until then, it would be wise to crawl further up the culvert.

For an hour the police searched the area, two separate groups splashing around in the river under the bridge. If they had actually entered the culvert they would have found Esther, for the outflow became a narrow pipe and she could not crawl any further.

'Must have been engine failure,' she heard one of them say. The suggestion surprised her. Was there no sign of the battle she had heard? Finally the police went away.

It was early afternoon, and the sun was pleasant on the river. Crawling out of her hiding place, Esther sat warming herself on a rock, hidden under an overhanging tree. Painfully, she tried to recall who she was. Her name was Esther Thomas, but it was also Esther Marshall. That didn't make sense. The numbers on her wrist were her identity code, with some extra symbols she could not understand. What had her mother and father been called? Were they Marshall or Thomas?

Slowly Esther recalled a few shreds of identity. There had been a man called Bob. That was why her name had changed. Her parents had been called Marshall, but she had taken Bob's name. There had been another man too, but she could not remember his real name. Like her, he seemed to have had more than one – Simon, Callum, Stephan . . . Which was the right one? She remembered that he had been tall and fair and gentle. The names Tim and Sally also kept coming to her mind, but she could not place them.

As night fell Esther set off walking upstream, through the water's edge, so that she would leave no scent. She must make for higher ground, avoiding all cities and habitations. People were dangerous.

Within an hour she was hungry. In such a stony valley there was no food to find, except a few bilberries that stained her hands and mouth. Once she used to know about berries, and fungi, and how people grew things to eat. She must try to recall what she had known.

All night Esther walked. There was a good moon. A wind-swept garden at the foot of a stream provided her with some pea pods and beans. Spotting washing on a line at the back of another habitation, she took a man's shirt and trousers from it. They were coarse and far too big, but less conspicuous than the horrible green suit she was wearing. At dawn, she settled down behind a wall and slept.

For most of the day Esther rested, startled at times by people passing along a track at the top of the hill. Occasionally sheep came and investigated her. By evening her mind was beginning to clear. She was Esther Thomas, born Esther Marshall, daughter of Colonel and Jacki Marshall. The man called Bob had been her husband. For the past ten days she had been in a hateful place that called itself a hospital. She knew it was ten days, because there were ten beads below the green marker on each strand of her hair. How there could be as many as ten Esther could not imagine. Nor could she imagine why it had been so important to mark each day. Since braided hair would immediately show she was a city-dweller, Esther took out the beads and buried them under some stones. Her hair fell unkempt about her face, making her look like an Undesirable.

At once Esther remembered a man called Minkin, and a settlement of tents along a concrete canyon. There had been a girl too, beautiful despite her foul-smelling clothes. 'Pretend to be one of us,' Minkin had advised. Why should she pretend to be an Undesirable?

Because everyone would be against her, she recalled. The police would be looking for her. Even if she had been presumed dead, the Protectorate officials would not let her travel without proper papers. The Sheep People would not help her. They did not like city-dwellers escaping without paying for their assistance. Only Undesirables could come and go as they pleased, because they were too dirty and low to matter, and because they knew how to live off the land.

A small stream trickled down the hillside near where Esther was resting. Sheep and cattle had churned up its bank, seeking water. Crouching low amongst the bracken, Esther ran towards it. She rubbed the wet peat on her face and hands. Finding some splashes of cow dung, she smeared her clothes with it until they smelt. 'Follow the water,' Minkin had said too. Of course. The stream bed would provide an easy route through the bracken.

The day was almost over. Following the stream, Esther scrambled up the hillside towards a rocky ridge. There, she stood using the setting sun to regain her sense of direction. A valley plunged away to the south. In it there was a glimpse of water, a considerable lake. Another glinted to the west, much further away. Beyond, a wide plain opened out from the hills. Esther could just make out the line of the sea to the far west. On the horizon to the south there was the silver outline of a city dome. All around the plain near it, the metal and glass of moving transports flashed in the sun.

A few years ago, Esther had flown across just such a pattern of lakes and coast. The city on the horizon must be Connurb. Her children were waiting for her in Nortown. She must walk across the hills, always heading east, until she reached them.

As the sun gradually dropped, Esther was surprised to find she could still see enough to walk safely. The moon was pale and partially obscured by cloud, but it gave her enough light. She decided to walk on as long as she could see to do so. Hunger forced her to drop down into a valley, to help herself to some turnips and raspberries she saw growing in a small enclosure. To her delight, she found a jacket hanging on a hook in an outhouse. In so high an area, the night air was bitingly cold. As she walked on afterwards, gnawing at a turnip, she discovered she was very happy. She was free. She could remember her own past. Callum had loved her enough to trace her, and then secure her freedom. He had kept his promise.

22

For two nights Esther walked, sleeping in the day. Whenever anyone challenged her, her story was the same. She was a poor Undesirable, making her way from Connurb to Nortown, where she had heard the pickings were better. Once a farmer set his dogs on her and she had to climb a gate hurriedly, but mostly the Outlanders let her pass without harm.

By the third morning, Esther was crossing an area of barren uplands still showing the effects of the Devastation. There were few fungi and berries to be found, and she was sick with hunger. Finding a warm place in a barn, she curled up behind a hay bale.

For several hours Esther lay awake, her mind clearer than it had been for nearly two weeks. She wondered if it had been Callum who had pulled her from the transport. Finally she decided the figure had not been tall enough. It was definitely Dave's voice that had shouted to her. What had he been trying to tell her? Perhaps she should have waited where she was, and not set off walking on her own. Cursing her own stupidity, Esther fell asleep.

She awoke with a start. 'What's tha doing here?' a voice demanded.

Startled, Esther sat up, to find a stream of cattle passing either side of the barn, and a man and young boy staring at her. In the past, she would have heard them a kilometre away, and it galled her to realise how vague she still was. 'I were just passing through,' she pleaded. 'I weren't doin' no harm.'

'Tha don't look fit to do harm,' the man said, almost kindly.

Esther spotted the water bottle he carried. She was desperately thirsty. 'Would you give a poor woman a drink?' she begged.

'Nay lass, tha looks in need o' more than water.' Passing her the stone jar, the man waited while Esther drank. Then he gave her a piece of bread. It was hard and dry, but to Esther absolutely declicious. As she ate, she was aware that the man was watching her. She had spread the jacket over her like a blanket while she slept, and the sleeves of her borrowed shirt were torn. Embarrassed, she picked up her jacket. Suddenly the man stepped forward and seized her arm, making her cry out in fear. 'What's this on thy wrist?' he demanded.

'It's nowt that matters,' Esther replied. 'Just a bit o' tattoo I had done when I were a girl.'

'Give us here.' Turning Esther's arm, the man examined it. 'This i'nt no tattoo. Where were this done?'

'It's nowt,' Esther insisted. 'Just me number. I couldn't remember it, so I had it put on me arm to remind me.'

'Lye, go and fetch thy mother,' the man whispered, 'and not a word to anyone.'

Still holding Esther's wrist firmly, the man read the numbers, and the symbols after them. They seemed to mean something to him. 'Where are you from?' he asked.

'Connurb.'

'Nay, lass. Where were thou interred?'

A woman appeared in the doorway. She too examined Esther's arm. 'P.H. Five!' she said, her voice was barely above a whisper. 'How did she escape?'

'They let me go home,' Esther lied.

'That they did not! No one comes home with their mark still on. It's took off first. Category Bs don't get home at all, not until they're grinning idiots, fit for nowt but knitting. How did you get out?'

'I had friends,' Esther admitted.

'Where are they now?'

'I don't know. I think I was meant to wait for them, but I was too stupid and confused to understand.'

'We'd best bring her indoors,' the man whispered to his wife. 'We've got someone out o'ordinary here.'

Offering his hand, he helped Esther to get up. 'You're at Lambton Farm, with friends,' she said. 'Our names are Shem and Molly Burton. We'd be honoured if you'd rest with us.'

That morning Esther bathed in a tank at the back of the house, and then ate as much as she wished. Afterwards she slept in a soft bed. When she woke there were clean clothes for her to wear. She felt as if she had slid into Heaven. When she asked her hosts why they were so kind to a stranger, the Burtons looked at each other and smiled.

'You've been in a place we all fear, and have come out to tell the tale,' Molly Burton replied. 'You'll be a very precious possession to those who can appreciate you.'

All that evening people came quietly to the house, to be shown into the room where Esther rested. They took her by the hand, and wished her well. Afterwards they stood in the kitchen talking softly. Esther could hear their voices beneath her. It was as if she were a celebrity or a precious exhibit to be displayed. When she asked Molly Burton why she was so important to them, the woman shook her head sadly. 'Nay, lass, tha's not thysen yet,' she said, 'or tha'd know why we value you. One day you'll be a key witness.'

'Who for?'

'The prosecution.'

Esther's last visitor was an elderly man who had brought a young girl with him to act as his scribe. He questioned Esther about what she remembered of the Psychiatric Hospital, while his companion wrote everything down. Though Esther tried to remain calm, she became distressed several times, and had to stop. The old man was very patient. He wanted everything she could remember, even the merest detail, names of patients, methods of treatment . . .

Slowly Esther drew them from her memory. She discovered part of her had been noting such things very carefully, at least for the first four days. She could give exact descriptions, colour of hair, even numbers on uniforms. By the time she had finished, two hours had passed. The old man got up, an expression of triumph on his face.

'Well done, my dear,' he said. 'Very well done.'

'I didn't think I'd noticed so much, ' Esther admitted.

'My daughter went into such a place,' the old man replied, and his lips set into a hard line. 'She came home ten weeks later. Now she does nothing but watch the cows and smile. There's no harm in her, but there's no soul neither.'

Passing Esther her statement to sign, the young girl nodded. 'When the revolution comes, we'll bring these people to justice,' she promised.

After they had gone, Esther settled back against her pillow and laughed in relief.

Less than thirty-six hours after the Burtons had taken her in, Esther continued on her way. Her children needed her, she insisted. Molly Burton understood her anxiety, but shook her head at Esther's blistered feet. 'I'd feel th'same meself,' she agreed, 'but it wouldn't hurt for you to stay a while longer.'

Esther did not add that the Central Control system would come crashing down soon. After that, she would have very little chance of finding her children, or any of her family. She did not really believe the system would fail. Fourteen could have been wrong. She herself was bound to have made a mistake. The authorities could have discovered the virus. No action of hers was likely to have such earth-shattering results.

Still, the possibility was there, and she must reach Nortown as soon as possible.

The Burtons gave her food and a little money – as much as they could spare. Esther hid both carefully, for Marauders sheltered in the higher hills and sometimes attacked travellers on the routes below them. Kissing Molly and Shem in gratitude, Esther set off in the late afternoon sun. She would keep in touch, she promised. One day perhaps the Keepers would be brought to justice and she would give her statement in person.

In the cool air of the hills the last traces of the confusers left her mind. She thought a great deal of Tim and Sally and of Bob. Callum returned to her mind too. She wished she knew if he had survived. The rose he had given her would be shrivelled by now. She wondered if it was still amongst the dried grasses where she had hidden it. Presumably her dwelling had been searched since she was taken. Was there anything else in it that could have incriminated him? Or the Movement?

The question troubled Esther. Finally she dicided that there was nothing except the showhouse programme. Fortunately the page she had torn out of it included images of everyone on the staff and could not lead the Seekers to any one person.

With a start, Esther realised she was not sure how long ago that had been. For ten days she had been kept in P.H. Five, and then she had walked for – how long? Three days. After that she had stayed with the Burtons for the best part of another two. That made two weeks. The Central Control system would be coming down that very night.

Suddenly Esther saw her error, and almost wept aloud. She had not been arrested until Tuesday, three days after she and Callum entered the centre. It was at least eighteen days since she entered the Control Centre with Callum. The system should have fallen already.

Esther had never known such despair. It was worse than

anything she had felt in P.H. Five. For the rest of her life she would wander the hills as an Undesirable, without children, home or love.

Climbing on to some rocks, Esther looked towards Connurb, far to the west now. The last rays of the sun reflected off its dome and caught the craft scurrying in and out of the portals. As the sun dropped behind a bank of clouds, the lights of the city came on all at once, perfectly controlled as ever. Dusk settled over the plain. Slithering down the rocks, Esther began to walk on, aimlessly, her spirit at its lowest ebb.

Two or three hours later, she heard voices ahead of her. Several figures were standing on a ridge to her right, looking down across the plain. From somewhere far away came a strange moaning sound, like a distant wail. Other figures were running along the track towards her. They too looked in bewilderment towards the sound. Hardly daring to breathe, Esther joined them.

'What's going on?' a man called from a dwelling below them. His voice was blown back by the wind and almost lost.

'T'city's all in darkness. Look!'

Scrambling on to the top of the rocks, Esther looked down. Below her there was nothing. With only the moon to give light, the plain was like a dark, formless sea.

'Listen!'

Everyone listened. It was as if they were hearing a distant scream, a frantic howl of fear and surprise. Gripping her hands tight, Esther tried not to cry out herself. The Central Control system had come down after all. It had taken four days longer than Fourteen had predicted, or maybe she herself had keyed in too long a wait.

'T'power must've gone,' one of the figures near her suggested.

'Eh – them city types won't like that. They can't cope wi'darkness. It frightens them.'

The howl came and went with the wind. Sometimes there

was the crash of metal on metal. Esther never dreamt what it would sound like: the wail of ten million panic-stricken people. The lifts would be stuck, the traffic controls jammed. Even doors would be refusing to open. Within minutes, air inside rooms would go stale. A great city was dying in front of them.

A few lights flickered back on as emergency generators were started in hospitals and police headquarters. One went straight out again, as if snuffed by unseen hands. Already there was the sound of sporadic firing from one of the out-towns. Rebel groups had begun to seize the chance to settle local scores.

'Did you ever see anything like it?' a man's voice asked.

'It's the beginning of th'end,' another answered.

'Nay, it's just summat broke down. Th'Keepers'll have it sorted in minutes.'

Others were appearing on the rocks, running up from the nearest settlement. 'Th'Protectorate office's in darkness,' one of them shouted. 'They're running round in circles trying to put t'lights back on.'

A kind of angry growl began to develop amongst the crowd. 'Why should they have lights at all?' a woman shouted. 'We have to mek do wi' tallow. Let's keep 'em dark a bit longer.'

'I say we should put more than their lights out!'

Turning on his heel, one of the men strode purposefully down the track. Two or three others followed him, and then another four. Within seconds the whole crowd was heading down the hill.

There would be no reaching Nortown now, or her children, at least until the rebellion was over. Silently Esther stepped into the darkness. There was only one place she could think of to seek shelter. As soon as she was out of sight, she began to run back to Lambton Farm.

Molly Burton was slow opening the door. 'Let me in!' Esther shouted. 'I have news!'

Within hours of the Central Control system coming down,

the Outlanders began their insurrection. Shem and his eldest son were amongst the first to answer the call. Ripping up the boards in an outhouse, they revealed twenty or so picks and shovels, old iron bars and other things that could crush or maim. Urgently they began passing them up to Esther while Molly quietened the two younger children. Then grabbing a handful of weapons each, Shem and his eldest son ran down to the settlement square. Bringing what was left, Esther followed, leaving Molly to guard the farm. Already an ominously silent crowd was gathering around the water trough.

Other weapons were being handed out. There was a sackful of torches too, though each was given out with the instruction that it was not to be lit until the order was given. Fifty years ago the Outlanders had been divided into quarrelsome bands of unarmed rebels. This time they were prepared.

Moving together in silent groups, the villagers advanced on the offices of the Outland Protectorate. Without power or orders, the officials inside were packing up to seek support from their headquarters. They did not hear the advancing crowd until it was too late. Esther could not stay to watch.

Running back up to Lambton Farm, she found Molly standing purposefully in her kitchen, the other children dressed and ready to flee.

'Has it begun?' she asked.

Esther could only nod in reply.

Molly had already prepared them a hiding place. Locking up the house, she led Esther and the children to the cold store just behind the farm. Supplies of food and bedding were spread on the rock floor. 'We've waited so long for this,' she said, hushing the baby. 'So very long. A whole lifetime.'

Gently Esther held the other child to her. 'We'll have the Keepers out in days,' she promised.

'But it's come at such an awkward time, with the harvest to get in and the little ones so young. I won't be able to see to the livestock without Shem and Gareth.'

'Revolution's never convenient,' Esther pointed out. 'I'll help you.'

'But why should you help? You hardly know me.'

'Because you were kind. And because I need somewhere to hide.'

The toddler was falling asleep in Esther's arms.

'The Alliance man told us there must be as little killing as possible,' Molly said. 'But it'll depend who keeps control. Some of th'hotheads want revenge. They say they'll tek no prisoners.'

'Who was this Alliance man?'

'I don't know. He just appeared a few months ago. All over the hills there's been strangers turning up, offering to train us and provide arms.'

There were a few moments' silence, filled by intermittent firing in the distance. The Protectorate was beginning to defend itself. Suddenly a dull red glow lit up the skyline. In its light a dozen men and women were outlined against the hillside. They were heading down to the valley, to join the crowd already attacking the Protectorate offices.

Just before dawn there was a lull in the fighting. Molly seized the opportunity to check if her livestock were still safe, while Esther took the children back into the warmth of the farmhouse.

'They're all right, but the milkers won't give us much,' Molly said as she returned. 'Poor things, they're as frightened as we are. We'd better tek them to the top pasture. They'll be safer up there.'

Taking a pair of kitchen scissors, Esther cut off her hair, close to her head, like a man's.

'You shouldn't have done that!' Molly cried out. 'Your hair was lovely.'

'It would have got in the way,' Esther insisted. 'Besides, I feel better without it. The nurses made me sit in front of a mirror for hours, putting silly beads in it. I don't want to be reminded of those days.'

Finding a pair of the eldest boy's boots, Esther put them on. They were too big, but they would do. She looped one of Molly's shawls round her to make a carrier and strapped the baby in it. Molly took charge of the toddler. Then they both went out into the yard.

There was a great deal to be done, as fast as possible. As Molly had said, the cows must be taken to the top field where they would be better hidden from Marauders. Hay must be got in, before the storms of autumn, and hidden. The pig must be killed, to provide meat for the coming weeks. Since the fowl could forage for themselves and be enticed back with Molly's special call, most were let loose. The last two Molly grabbed, expertly wringing their necks afterwards. The Burtons had been prepared for such a situation for years, but two babies had arrived since they first joined the Resistance. Molly Burton had less time and energy now. Without help she would have had a hard task to survive.

Esther had been a farmer too, though in a very different time and place. For hours she had stood at laboratory tables cloning generations of bigger and better plants. In comparison, Molly Burton's farming was crude and laborious, but it would keep them alive. After the confinement of P.H. Five, even hard labour was pleasurable.

For the first two days, the fighting hardly touched Lambton Farm. In so out of the way a place, there was little passing traffic. At night, the sky was lit up by burning buildings, but only in the distance. A tracery of fire sometimes burst across the valley, but it was directed at others. On the third day, however, army transports began to come up into the hills. With their vastly superior force, they would have crushed the Outlanders' rebellion, had not other strangers appeared, men and women in vehicles with the insignia of the Keepers painted out and "ALLIANCE" superimposed. The newcomers fought alongside the rebels, keeping the insurrection going. Then they passed on, to assist others.

By the fourth day, refugees from the cities began to find their way into the hills. They brought stories of much worse down south. 'It's out-and-out war,' one declared. They were given homemade ale and bread in return, for news was a precious commodity. Once refreshed, they were warned to continue their journey: so harsh a land could not support more than the few already existing off it.

On the sixth day there was an increased sense of urgency. The firing that lit the sky had a new ferocity. Until then the rebels had been acting as separate groups. Now they began to join together as one. No one knew who the leaders were, but it was rumoured they included Keepers themselves, who were using the rebellion to bring down their own hierarchy. Whoever they were, they surely had the support of some of the army. No rebel force could have mustered such weaponry. The insurrection had become civil war.

All through the next three days the sky was filled with fire and movement. The settlements in the Outlands were deserted. Together Molly and Esther took the children to an ancient mine shaft on the outer edge of the farm. Leaving the cattle to fend for themselves, they sheltered there. With cooked chicken and salted pork, they would not starve, and they were safe from anything but a direct hit. The shaft was sodden after the previous night's rains, and the children fretted a lot, but as Molly said, comfort was relative. They were living like royals compared to the poor souls trapped in the cities.

Esther thought a good deal about her role in bringing about such suffering. A month ago, if she had visualised what her action would lead to, she would have refused to enter the control centre. Now her time in P.H. Five had hardened her. If innocent citizens suffered, so be it. It was better to act quickly and firmly than let an inhumane regime continue.

Later she would regret her anger, but it gave her strength throughout those long days and nights sheltering in a dripping hole.

Shem and Gareth visited them once, dresseed in a makeshift battledress. The two little ones were noisy with delight, and had to be quietened urgently.

'Nortown's fallen,' Shem said, tearing at a chicken leg. 'Connurb should be ours in another day or so.' Washing the chicken down with water, he leant back against the wall with a ferocious satisfaction. 'The Keepers can't hold out much longer. They're split among themselves.'

'Then there are renegades in the Alliance?' Molly asked.

'Aye. They gathered it together in't first place, and provided a lot of t'money and arms. Don't mek sense to me. Why fight against your own?'

'To try to change things,' Esther suggested.

'A rat don't lose its teeth because it's fur's gone white,' Gareth retorted. 'Th'only good Keeper's a dead one. I'd string em all up.' He was fifteen, and inclined to talk big.

'How are things doing down south?' Molly asked.

'It'll be a longer struggle down there,' Shem admitted. 'The Southerners always were more for th' regime. You wouldn't expect them to bite th'hand that fed them. Midopolis is a battlefield, they say, but the Welsh Protectorate is definitely taken. The Irish and Scots republics are sending aid, and there's talk of the Union favouring our side too.'

Throwing back her head, Molly laughed in delight. 'Remember when we used to sit on the hillside and plan all this?' she asked her husband.

'Aye, lass. We've had to wait a while, but it's been worth th'wait.'

Along the shaft, water dripped relentlessly. 'You said your father were down south,' Molly remembered. 'You must be worried about him.'

Esther sighed. 'My father's in the army,' she replied. 'He'll have been ordered to fight against the rebels, whether he likes it or not.'

'Some of th'officers have joined the Alliance,' Shem said. 'They've been giving advice. A couple have even brought their units wi'em.'

'Do you know which ones?'

Shem shook his head.

'Would you really like to string the renegades up?' Esther asked Gareth. 'They're in the same position as my dad.'

For several seconds the boy considered his answer. 'Happen not,' he conceded. 'If what Alliance man says is true, th'revolution wouldn't have begun but for them.'

'Revolution don't mek no distinctions though,' Shem warned. 'There's a big house near here, burnt to th'ground. People said the family who lived there were Keepers, because they were wealthy and held high positions. Every one of 'em died in the fire. They was always straight wi' us; paid good rates on their farms. I almost felt sorry when I saw it.'

After Shem had gone, the two women tried to settle the children back to sleep. 'You're very quiet,' Molly remarked.

'The two men I love were both born on the wrong side,' Esther replied. 'I'm likely to lose them both.'

Silently Molly took her hand in the darkness.

On the sixth day, Shem came again on his own. 'I reckon tha can come out o' hiding now,' he said.

Together they walked back to the farmhouse, to find the building still standing, but everything of value in it gone. Still, they had a roof left, as Molly said. That was more than Esther might find when she returned to Nortown.

There was a great deal of excitement in the valley below them. Leaving Molly and Shem to reclaim their home, Esther went down the track to see what was happening. Alliance vehicles were standing in the square and a screen was being set up against one wall of a derelict building. She asked one of the Alliance officers what was happening, and was told that there would be a broadcast to the nation that evening. It would be shown not only in the cities, but in every settlement of any size throughout the Outlands. Esther's heart lifted in joy. The very fact that the Outlanders had been included marked the change that was beginning.

For the rest of the day word spread throughout the area. By sixteen hours there was a crowd waiting in the settlement. The smell of human bodies was awful. To make the stench worse, a pigsty drained across one corner of Lambton Square. For the young Alliance officers who had just arrived, the contrast with the privileges they enjoyed must have been frightening. Two of them fetched a stack of large sealed trays from their vehicle and laid them on tables placed across the square. Suspecting there was food inside the trays, the crowd pressed forward dangerously.

The Alliance officials were firm, but determined. Order must be preserved, even in a rebellion. As Esther watched, her head throbbed with the clamour of other people's emotions. She felt as she used to do as a girl, before she learnt to cope with her sensitivity. Yet though she longed to walk away into the solitude of the hills, she stayed. Her distress was a kind of expiation, an atonement for her part in bringing about the suffering that surrounded her.

After the food was distributed everyone was asked to go back to the far side of the square, where they could see the screen. They were asked rather than ordered. Several people remarked on the fact.

'Looks like we're going to have some entertainment,' one of the city refugees said to Esther. 'About time too. I'm fed up wi' sitting around doing nowt.'

The complaint struck Esther as peculiar and she looked up. Shifting her position, the woman turned to Esther confidentially. 'I hope they get the audiovision on again, don't you?' she asked. 'It should be *Friend to Friend* now. Sixteen-fifteen every Friday. I watch it regular.' After nearly three weeks of civil war, the woman still knew it was Friday and time for her favourite programme.

'You like watching *Friend to Friend?*' Esther asked.

'I love to see people's faces when their friend comes in. Haven't seen each other for years, and there they are, standing in the same living room. Mind you, I'm not sure I'd want some of my old friends walking through my door. A right lot they were.' The woman laughed. Then she burst into tears. 'I haven't got a door any more,' she remembered.

Unexpectedly, the square filled with music. It was the sort of uplifting theme that had always heralded public announcements, and people sat obediently down where they were standing. A few even found some food and began eating, as if they were at a showhouse.

The Alliance's first national broadcast was wonderfully directed and produced. Whoever had been given charge of making the transmission knew the public taste and how to persuade. Dry arguments would not win a civil war, nor would force. Anyone wishing to rule had to stir the emotions of a people sated by spectacle in the cities, and brutalised in the Outlands. Reality must be established in place of illusion.

First there was the heading, 'Why Revolution?' with exciting pictures of the fighting during the last three weeks. Immediately afterwards came the common people, just like those watching in the square. Dressed in ordinary clothes and speaking in ordinary voices, they talked of their experiences of repression under the old regime. Some were relatives of the vanished ones. With poignant family portraits behind them, they spoke of missing sons and daughters, husbands, wives. Afterwards came the statistics, visually displayed so that the Outlanders could understand them. The graphs became images, of real people with names and occupations. 'So many people,' the voice said. 'Where did they all go?'

Answers were suggested in a few chilling pictures. That suburb had its unnamed building, this its court with no jury, only judges. Two crematoria had been found, but there were no records of the dead. 'This is England,' the voiceover said. 'Not some American dictatorship or Eastern theocracy. This is the country we struggled to rebuild after the Devastation. All of us must share the blame. We did not intend such things, but we allowed them to happen. We should have stood together and said "Enough". But each of us was afraid. We feared that if we spoke out, we too might disappear or be found mentally infirm. So we told ourselves the stories were untrue, that things would get better soon.'

All the while the voice spoke, the sad little images continued. The nation was taken inside a psychiatric hospital ward, with its listless patients sitting in their cubicles, and attending a re-education class afterwards. The transmission was of poor quality, evidently made in secret, but Esther found it too painful to watch. A silence had begun to settle on the crowd. Those who had been eating stopped. 'We were right to be afraid,' the voice stated. 'This is how the authorities silenced those who did speak out. Perhaps you've met some of the cured ones – a shadow of their former selves, interested in nothing but food and sleep. Ask yourself, "Could I have withstood such persuasion?".'

Understanding that an audience could sympathise for only a short while, the director changed the scene abruptly. Now a group of people stood in the foyer of a showhouse, as if posing for a family photograph. 'You have heard of the Alliance,' the voiceover continued. 'This is what we look like. Each of us has decided the time has come to stand and be counted, to fight against the evil that has overtaken this land. We're not particularly brave; no different to you. We represent many different organisations. Some have opposed the regime for years, but dared do so only in secret. A few were Keepers themselves, who became sickened by what was being done in their name. You may call them mad, or traitors, but who are the real madmen and traitors? Those who oppose evil, or those who perpetuate it?'

As the question was asked, the camera focused on the members of the Alliance, giving the name of each and the group they represented. None was actually named as a Keeper. The public response was still too unpredictable.

With a start Esther realised the commentary was being spoken by a figure at the front of the group. A tall greying man, he was addressing the nation with the eloquence of a politician and the presence of an actor. The voice was faintly familiar, though no longer muffled by a mask and black hood. Closing her eyes, Esther visualised a darkened church and three figures seated at a table. One had spoken with that same slightly too careful English, the faint hint of a foreign childhood. She did not need the subtitle to know he was Andrew Miniott.

Behind him was an old woman, erect despite her age, with eyes that even in a group image were striking in their determination. Sly had survived. She had decided to work alongside Andrew Miniott. What it had cost her, Esther could only imagine. Minkin and Miriam were present too, though hardly recognisable in decent clothes. The captions named them as Undesirables, however, Minkin representing the North, Miriam the West. For fifty years the title had been an insult. Now it was listed with pride. To their left was a fair-haired man, very like Andrew Miniott about the eyes and mouth. The caption recorded that he was Carl Miniott, representing the Welsh Protectorate. Urgently Esther looked for his brother, and found him standing on the other side of the group. His face was thinner, but he was alive. 'Simon Miniott, the Dark Ones,' the voiceover announced.

Esther hardly heard the rest of the sequence. 'The battle is not yet over,' Andrew Miniott was saying. 'Each of us must return to continue the fight in our own towns, among our own people. We do not fight as separate factions. We fight as one, an Alliance of the people for the people. The chaos that followed the last civil war must not be allowed to return. As soon as the old regime admits defeat, the day-to-day business of running the country must be re-established. An interim cabinet will be chosen from the people you see here, drawing on their special skills and interests. We promise today, before the whole country, that free elections will be established as soon as it is safe to do so.'

The final section was a tribute to those who had fought the regime in the past and had died or been imprisoned for their resistance. It was a kind of roll of honour, and also a reminder of the ruthlessness of the regime that the Alliance had been formed to overthrow. With a tightness in her throat Esther saw her own mother's image. She looked very beautiful, as Esther remembered her from the days when they were still a family together. 'Jackie Marshall, known as "Angel", the heading recorded. 'One of the founder members of the Women's Movement; executed without trial or jury.' It was good to see her being honoured at last.

The music swelled. 'Join us, and those who have gone before,' the voiceover urged. 'The battle is nearly won. Nortown and Connurb are ours: Midopolis will be so soon. Centopolis cannot hold out much longer. Let us fight together to overthrow the last remnants of the cruellest regime in English history. And afterwards, when we have won, work with us to bring about an honourable and fair peace. That will be the hardest battle of all. Without such a peace, there will be another Devastation, another civil war; if not straight away, then within our lifetimes. This time we must heal the wounds properly. North must not be oppressed by South, Outlander must have the same rights as city-dweller. There must be no strata that are too low to be treated as human beings, no strata too high to obey the law. Education and technology must be available to all. Privileges must be earned, not controlled by a powerful few.'

It was a clever speech, which touched the heart as well as the reason, and drew on the grievances of city-dweller and Outlander alike. By the time the transmission ended, even the surliest onlooker in the square was nodding and saying, 'About bloody time . . .' The cause of the Alliance was furthered more in that forty minutes than by forty days of fighting.

As the music faded, Esther turned to Molly. 'I need to go back to Nortown,' she said.

'But it's not safe for you to travel yet. Besides, you don't know what you'll find at th'other end.'

'I must give it a try. My children won't know if I'm alive or dead, and there are friends I must rejoin.'

'Was he on the screen tonight? I wouldn't ask, only I saw your expression.'

Esther smiled. 'He'll be a very important man now,' she admitted. 'He may not be able to keep his promises, but I have to give him the chance.'

Molly squeezed her hand. 'Thank you for helping me,' she said simply.

With an escort of three of Shem's group, Esther set off the next day, dressed as an Outlander, with a wide-brimmed hat against the heat and baggy clothes to protect her skin from the sun. At night they slept rough; by day they took the high tracks, avoiding other groups. It was still too difficult to say who was friend and who was enemy. Even from the hills, the devastation in Connurb could be seen. The dome had been shattered and most of the buildings in the central area destroyed. In the suburbs, refugee settlements showed as lines of white-extruded polymer bubbles, each providing a family with temporary shelter. Before winter came on, more permanent buildings must be constructed, or the children would die of cold. It was a terrible sight: a great city almost destroyed by its own people.

At the border between the north-east and north-west quadrants, Esther was to be handed over to another escort. For three days she walked well, hardened by her wanderings and by her time on Lambton Farm. It never occurred to her that she could not make the distance. On the fourth night, however, she woke suddenly, sweating with pain. There was a peculiar burning sensation in her chest. Breathing deeply, Esther lay watching the stars, wondering what was wrong with her. By dawn the pain had eased a little, but she still felt dizzy and sick.

For three hours more Esther walked, bewildered by what was happening to her. Sometimes she felt fine. There was no pain, nothing. Then she would feel so tired she could scarcely move one foot in front of the other.

Shem had seen that she was in difficulties. 'Do you want to rest? he asked.

'I shall have to. I'm sorry. It's not like me at all.'

Her own words gave Esther the answer. It was not her own pain she was feeling, but someone else's, someone close to her in emotion if not in distance. Her father, or Tim perhaps – or Callum . . .

There was a new Alliance checkpoint below them. She would have to risk seeking their help. With Shem's guidance, Esther made her way down the steep path into the valley. As soon as she had stated her name, the officer got up and offered her his hand. 'Welcome,' he said.

'You know me?' Esther asked in surprise.

'You're a much-wanted woman. Before the war, there was a DIPR order against you. A month ago I would have had to arrest you. Things change. Now my orders are to offer you hospitality, and anything else you may need.'

'What's a DIPR order?' Esther asked.

'Detain and Isolate, Pending Removal.'

There was an old-fashioned mirror on the wall of the room. In it Esther saw an Outlander woman, unkempt and dusty, with cropped hair and a bruise on one cheek. 'I'd like a bath,' she said, 'if that's possible.'

'We can fit a screen up for you,' the sergeant offered. 'We could probably find you clean clothes too. There are several women officers here.'

'Would you also find out if my father's alive? His name is Marshall. Colonel James Marshall of the Fifth Brigade.'

'Colonel Marshall joined the Alliance on the second day. He brought not only his own battalion, but two others.'

Sitting down at the officer's desk, Esther cried in relief.

23

Trying to walk with dignity, Esther crossed the room to her father, only to spoil everything by running the last few paces and throwing her arms around him. The junior clerk retired tactfully.

For a long time Esther and her father held each other. 'You changed sides,' was all Esther could say.

Still he held her, rocking her as he used to do when she was a child. 'I thought I'd lost you,' he said, several times. Stepping back he looked at her. 'Your hair,' he said. 'You had such beautiful hair. What did they do to you?'

'They made me into a beautiful object, until I wasn't a woman any more. So I cut it all off. Now I look a mess, but at least I'm real.'

When they were quieter they walked out into the yard. 'What made you come over to us?' Esther asked.

'It was the look in your eyes on that last call. I was back ten years, imagining your mother being taken away. I could see the men in the mirror in their white coats, and I thought I would never find you again. No one should ever feel so helpless.'

'Do you know where the children are?'

'Safe. I can take you to them if you wish. The war can spare me another few hours.'

Throwing her arms around him again, Esther kissed him in sheer joy. Then, letting him go again, she rummaged for her handkerchief. She could not find one and he offered her his. 'How did you find them?' she asked.

'I didn't. It was your friend.'

'Cal?'

'He arranged for them to be collected from the camp, in my name. Then he hid them in readiness for the war.'

'He contacted you? An officer in the army? You could have had him arrested.'

Smiling, Colonel Marshall nodded. 'He nearly frightened the life out of me,' he admitted. 'I came back to my quarters one night, and found him and two other men waiting. He said he wanted to talk to me about my grandchildren. I didn't know whether to listen or holler for help, so I listened. It seemed safer.'

Esther smiled. 'It's all bluff,' she assured him.

'A convincing one.'

The junior clerk came out to see if they needed anything. Clearly Colonel Marshall was also an honoured guest. After the clerk had gone, Esther and her father sat on an upturned wagon in the yard. They talked softly, trusting no one but themselves even now.

Hesitantly Esther looked at her father's face, trying to assess what he felt. 'Did Cal tell you anything about himself?' she asked.

'No. That's always been part of the understanding. I think I've worked it out, though. How did you manage to keep silence, Little One? What you knew could have bought you your freedom overnight. That must have been a terrible temptation.'

'But it would have cost me my soul.'

'And killed the man you love. When I told you to find yourself a man of your own choice, I didn't expect you to settle for a Keeper. If I hadn't seen how Tim worshipped him, I would have wondered how you could even speak to such a man.'

'You don't think I'm mad then?'

'I'd say you were unwise, but when a war's brewing, wisdom goes out of the door.'

'Does Tim really worship Cal?'

'Not as a father. No one'll ever replace Bob in his mind – but as a friend, a man he can look up to. He's grown very close to Callum's daughter too. Parting from her would grieve him almost as much as losing Cal.'

Dropping her voice almost to a whisper, Esther turned to her father. 'Could you accept Cal?' she asked, 'knowing what he is?'

Colonel Marshall sighed. 'We have many peculiar people working together at present,' he said. 'A renegade Keeper is little different to a turncoat Colonel. Take care, though. You're not dealing with an ordinary man, however much he wishes to become one. Besides, the people are taking their revenge. No Keeper is safe yet.'

Awkwardly Esther paused. She felt as if she were sixteen again, trying to talk to her father about her first love. It was hard to break the pattern of years; grudging respect on her side, distant affection on his. 'I need your advice, Dad,' she said.

'You've never taken it in the past.' The criticism was made with love, not in judgement.

'You've never said what I wanted to hear.' Smiling, Esther kissed his cheek. 'This is deadly serious though, and I'll listen to what you suggest. I'm afraid Cal's been hurt. Badly.'

'We visited the children together a couple of days ago. He was all right then.'

'Could something have happened since then? I can feel someone else's pain. It comes and goes, as if they're trying to control it. Could it be Cal's, or am I still half crazy?'

Silently Colonel Marshall looked towards the ruined farm buildings beyond the yard. 'Let's go and see Imogen,' he advised. 'She's even closer to her father than you are. She may know more.'

'But how could I feel someone else's pain, and at such a distance?'

'I don't know, but I learnt never to ignore your mother's instincts. It may be that you've developed her ability a stage further. Besides, the man you love is a Keeper. Who can say what a Keeper can or can't do?'

They travelled alone from the checkpoint, though the young officer tried to insist they take an escort. A tracery of fire across the sky reminded them that travel was still not safe, and Esther's father took a great deal of care, using the lie of the land to hide them. Turning towards the north-east, their PTU headed across open moorland, coming ultimately to the remains of a small settlement in a tree-filled hollow. The habitations had been burnt to the ground.

'We have to walk from here,' Colonel Marshall said, indicating a track across the side of the hill. It led to another settlement, which had also been burnt, though a square of stone buildings survived. The yard between them was scattered with charred equipment and upturned carts. Everywhere there was the stench of war. Despite the silence, Esther was aware that they were being watched.

'Where are Sally and Tim?' she asked. Her voice sounded small and frightened.

'Where no one could think of looking for them: in a place of defeat.'

An old man came out of the cattle byre, startling them both. Colonel Marshall greeted him. 'I came to see my grandchildren,' he said.

'Aye,' the old man agreed. 'They're up top farm now.'

In relief, Esther smiled. 'I'm their mother,' she said, offering her hand.

'Aye,' the old man agreed.

It was difficult to know what to say to him. 'Thank you for all you've done,' she replied.

'We've been well paid.'

'And the other two children? Are they well too?'

'Aye.'

Curiously Esther looked around. 'What happened here?' she asked.

'Th'soldiers come up three weeks since. They took everything they could, and burnt t'rest. To set an example, they said.'

'Were many killed?'

'Nay. Callum sent us warning. We just slapped t'cows round their backsides and drove t'sheep up 'tops. We're trying to round 'em up now.'

Colonel Marshall smiled. 'Have you heard from Callum lately?' he asked.

'We hear rumours.'

A chill passed over Esther's mind. 'What sort of rumours?' she asked.

'A man from th'Alliance passed through yesterday. He said th'Dark Ones had been attacked. It were a last kick, he said, like a dying horse, lashing out.' With the resignation born of decades of misfortune, the old man shrugged his shoulders. 'Callum were one o' them Dark Ones, weren't he?' he asked.

'I've heard so,' Esther's father replied, noncommittally. He took a handful of barter tokens from his pocket. 'If he should be delayed, keep his children till he comes,' he asked. 'It's not a lot, but it's all I have on me.'

The old man took the tokens. 'Every bit helps,' he acknowledged. 'This'll buy us some seed corn, once t'fighting's over.'

'I have nothing to give you,' Esther apologised. 'At the moment I'm as poor as you.'

For the first time the old man's manner softened. 'Tha's no need to worry about payment,' he said. 'Th'big uns have been earning their keep. Workers is what we need now, more than money. I'll tek you up to find 'em.'

Together they walked up the hill, towards a group of rough buildings standing stark against the sky. A figure came from one of them. Esther could just make out that it was a girl. The old man called to her. In reply, the girl turned towards the hill above her, and putting her fingers to her mouth, gave a single piercing whistle. A moment later a boy appeared, running down the track, with a dog bounding ahead of him. Waiting until he was level with her, the girl also began to run.

Esther recognised Tim first. Even at such a distance he looked taller and stronger, his skin browned by the sun, his hair a whole shade lighter. The girl he was chasing was Imogen.

Throwing himself at her, Tim hugged Esther until she could hardly breathe. 'I knew you'd be all right,' he boasted. Then he burst into tears. Too full of emotion to speak, Esther held him to her. Recalling Imogen standing beside them, she held out her hand to include her too. Silently, Esther's father watched, his normally severe expression softened.

Afterwards, the four of them sat down on the hillside and tried to be sensible.

'You'll be wanting to see Sally,' Imogen suggested. 'I'll go and fetch her.' Though her clothes were those of an Outlander, she had not lost her old-fashioned politeness. It went to Esther's heart.

'Stay with us a bit,' Esther pleaded.

'You and Tim should talk first,' Imogen replied. 'You don't need me around.'

'I'll come with you,' Colonel Marshall offered. To Esther's surprise, he put his arm round the girl's shoulder, and together they set off back up the hill.

Gently Tim touched the bruise on Esther's face. 'You look so thin,' he said, 'and your hair's different.'

'I've been helping a friend on her farm,' Esther replied.

'There was only the two of us to do everything, so it was hard work.'

'Where was that?'

'I'll tell you some time. I'd rather hear your story first. How did you get away from the camp?'

'A lady collected us. She said she came from Grandad, but she took us to a house in some woods. Imie and Benn were already there. I've lost count how many places we've stayed at since.'

'Who was the lady?'

'Someone Callum sent.'

In surprise Esther paused. 'Who told you to call Mr Lahr Callum?' she asked.

'He did. He said Lahr wasn't his real name, and it wasn't safe for us to use it any more. He's a soldier, you know. We thought he was just a Patroner, but he's been a soldier for years, in secret. He told me about it, and that I was never to say anything to anyone about him, or who he was. Don't worry. I won't give him away.'

Esther nodded. Another boy might have let such a secret slip after any number of warnings, but Tim could sense the fear of adults and try to understand it. Callum had been right to take him into his confidence. 'Has he looked after you all the time?' she asked.

'He couldn't stay with us himself – he was off fighting – so he found people to have us instead. It's been quite fun really, except when the fighting got really bad. We had to hide in a cave then, with some other children. That bit was horrible.' Remembered distress made the boy's voice unsteady.

'You must have been very frightened.'

'Even the grown-ups were. Poor Sally and Benn cried a lot.'

'And Imogen?'

'She's been fine. You'd hardly notice she was a girl. She's only cried once and that was the night before last. She woke up in a terrible fright and said something had happened to her father. Has it?'

Looking away, Esther chewed at the skin on her lip. 'I don't know,' she admitted. 'It may have.'

'Funny, i'nt it?' Tim asked. 'I knew it had. Just like I can tell you're worried now, even without looking at you. Imie says I'm weird.'

'You are weird. You get it from me.' Esther ruffled his hair. 'I'll explain sometime,' she promised. 'But Imie's a bit weird too, in her own way. That's probably why you get on so well.'

The others were halfway down the hill, Sally falling headlong on her face in her haste to be first. Imogen helped her up. Holding Sally's hand she ran on with her, jolting Benn in her other arm. Esther's father made a more sedate pace down the track. As she watched them, Esther smiled. She felt happier than she could ever remember feeling, except perhaps for when she was with Callum.

Imogen and the little ones reached the bottom of the track.

'Mummy!' Sally cried out triumphantly. 'Mummy back!'

'Whose mummy?' Imogen asked.

'Mine! My mummy been long way.'

In delight Esther snatched up her daughter. Colonel Marshall smiled. 'Now she's started talking, she hardly stops,' he warned.

'Thank you,' Esther said, turning to Imogen.

'All I did was keep saying things.'

Esther smiled, trying to break down the girl's shyness. 'I need your advice,' she said. 'Tim tells me you had a nightmare about your father. What was your dream? Let's see if it's the same as mine.'

At once Imogen's eyes filled with tears. Yet she stood firm, a Keeper's daughter. 'My father's been hurt,' she said simply.

'Do you know where he is?'

'Beside some water.'

'Where.'

'I saw some trees nearby and birds flying about. They made a sort of cawing sound.'

Urgently Esther took her hand. 'Did you see any people?' she asked.

'Lots of them, wearing funny clothes. I tried to tell Mrs Rothwell, but she said I'd just had a nightmare. It wasn't a nightmare. Dad's taught me things . . .'

'What sort of things?'

'Secret things. He said he didn't see why he had to wait until he had a son, when he had a perfectly sensible daughter already.' Becoming distressed, Imogen let go of Esther's hand and moved away sharply. 'He'll die if we don't do something soon,' she insisted. 'The pain makes him so hot and yet he's cold too. I can't explain.'

Esther glanced towards her father for permission. Silently he nodded. 'Come back with us to Nortown,' she said. 'We'll ask people to look for your father. You can show them where the trees are.'

'Shall I come too?' Tim asked.

'You'd better stay and look after the little ones,' Colonel Marshall suggested. 'We'll come back and fetch you as soon as we can.'

Tim nodded in acceptance. The gesture reminded Esther very much of her father.

The sky had begun to take on an ominous leaden colour as the PTU set off again for Nortown. Soon the winter gales would begin, making travel in the Outlands impossible. Already, it looked as though the first autumn storm was brewing. The PTU was not intended to carry three, and it was too lightly built to withstand buffeting against rock and woodland. They must keep to the lowland as much as possible, though the route across the open waste would have been far shorter. All three of them were very quiet, aware of danger, and the passage of time. Only once did Imogen seek reassurance, and then it was not for her own safety.

'Why do you care if my father's hurt?' she asked unexpectedly.

The directness of the question took Esther by surprise. 'Because I love him,' she answered honestly.

'Aren't you afraid of him?'

'Are you?'

'Of course not. I know him.'

'Well then, you've answered your own question.' Smiling, Esther put her arm around the girl's shoulder. 'He'll be all right. You'll see,' she promised.

'And if he isn't? Where will Benn and I go?'

'You could stay with me,' Esther offered.

'Could we? I'd like that. But what would we live on?'

'I'll have to find a job somehow. When the war's over, there'll be a lot of work to be done.'

Molly Burton had warned there might not be a roof over Esther's head when she returned to Nortown. Not even Molly had visualised the ferocity of the authorities' anger against the city. Nortown had led the rebellion. Now even the suburbs were devastated. The dome was shattered, and every route out of the centre blocked. There was no way Esther could go to the dwelling in Moss Edge, even if it still existed. Reluctantly Colonel Marshall had to leave her and Imogen at the central Alliance base. He had already been away from his post too long, and must return at once before the impending storm made travel too dangerous.

Standing on the arrival deck, Esther considered what to do next. They could appeal to the senior officer at the desk, and ask him to organise a search party. She did not trust him, however. It was hard to define why she had formed the impression that he was insincere, but it was strong enough to serve as a warning. In any case, the man would be unlikely to believe them, and they would waste time trying to convince him. Showhouse Four was still standing. It would be safer to see if they could find one of Callum's friends there.

It seemed incredible that the Entertainment Sector should have survived almost intact, when whole blocks of dwellings were nothing but scars in the ground. But the showhouses had been built to last, of old-fashioned materials in keeping with their individual periods, and neither side in the battle had wished to be seen as deliberately destroying the people's main pleasure. Now the showhouses stood amongst the rubble, symbols of an age that was ending and a new one that was beginning.

Each had become a refugee centre. The music that used to cheer and invite from the entrances was stilled. No slogans and exhortations boomed across the square. Instead, queues of bedraggled families waited passively for registration. There was a peculiar quietness, despite the numbers. People talked softly of the things they had seen, or waited apathetically, too bewildered to speak except when spoken to by an official. The local battle had been won, but the fear remained. It began to press on Esther's spirit. Later she would sympathise, but there was no time now. If she was to think clearly, she must close her mind against the emotions of those around her.

Above the entrance to Showhouse Four, the hoardings still urged: VISIT THE NEWEST, GREATEST SHOW IN NORTOWN, but the words had been burnt in several places, and the lights hung drunkenly, unlit. At first Esther could think of no way of entering the building, without waiting in the queue that snaked from it. To try to go ahead of other refugees would cause trouble, and they had no passes to grant them entry by any other door.

'Go round the back,' Imogen advised. 'I know my way round. If Billy's in his room, I can attract his attention.'

Attracting Billy's attention involved climbing on to a window-ledge and peering in through the window, both of which Imogen did expertly. Within minutes they were standing inside the assistant director's office. A man wearing the insignia of the Alliance stood up quickly, and offered his hand in the gesture of kinship. Esther did not know him, but as soon as he spoke his voice was familiar. He had been at the training centre; then she had known him as Dave. In delight, she took his hand.

'It's so good to see you,' Dave said, several times. 'Welcome home!' Esther felt him looking at her curiously, but he was too tactful to make any remark. In borrowed combat uniform, she must have looked decidedly odd as she entered the room. 'We thought you were dead,' he told her. 'Why didn't you wait for us? We would have brought you safely back here.'

'I was too stupid to hear what you were saying.'

'Of course you weren't stupid! We should never had expected you to understand, not after what you'd been through. How on earth did you survive in the Outlands on your own, without food or help?'

'I managed. There's food if you know where to find it. And kindness.'

Turning to Imogen, Dave shook his head in mock disapproval. 'And what have you been doing?' he asked. 'You look quite grown up.'

'I've looked after sheep and cows.' Smiling, Imogen sat on the edge of the desk near him. She was obviously fond of her father's friend, and happy to find him there. 'It's been almost an adventure, only I was so worried about what was going to happen.'

'It's almost over,' Dave assured her.

'Are all our friends safe?' Esther asked. The question could no longer be avoided.

Dave glanced warningly towards Imogen.

'You don't have to pretend,' the girl replied. 'I know Dad's been hurt.'

Dave sighed. 'I'm sorry, Imie,' he said. 'I wish I didn't have to be the one to tell you.'

Esther's mouth had gone very dry. Silently she watched Dave, trying to assess what he was feeling. Grief, uncertainty, anger – a whole confusion of emotion. He had been very close to Callum for a long time; since they were at college together, perhaps.

'Is my father dead?' Imogen demanded.

Getting up, Dave stood awkwardly beside his friend's daughter, not knowing how to comfort her. 'Your father was a very brave man,' he said. 'He died saving others.'

'Tell me what he did,' Imogen insisted. 'I'm not going to cry.'

Glancing towards Esther, Dave sought her advice. She nodded.

'It happened the night before last,' he continued gently. 'Your father and I were at one of the training centres when it was attacked. There were only a few of us, and the recruits were all young and untried. Before we knew what was happening, the building was ablaze and we were trapped.' As Dave paused, Imogen watched him with large frightened eyes. 'Cal ordered me to take the recruits to a window, and warn them to be ready to run for it. If we could get to some trees beyond the yard, we'd stand a chance. Meanwhile, he'd try to create a diversion.'

Still Imogen waited. Her silence was harder for an adult to cope with than tears would have been.

'I couldn't stop him, Imie. I didn't even understand what he meant to do. He walked out of the building, straight towards the enemy's fire. By then he'd taken his mask and hood off, so our attackers could see who he was. The firing just stopped. It was like everyone was frozen with surprise. It was long enough for us to make a break for it.'

'And afterwards?' Esther asked. Her eyes stung.

'By the time I looked back, Cal was being taken towards a PTU, with an armed guard round him. Suddenly he ran for it. Perhaps he hoped to make it to us. I don't know. He didn't stand a chance. One of the soldiers shot him, and he fell. Then a guard walked up to him as he lay, and fired at him, point blank. It wasn't an act of war, it was an execution.' Unable to continue, Dave rubbed his eyes. 'After that, we opened fire ourselves, and fought it out. Most of us got away, but Cal just lay there.'

There was a long silence. Looking up at Esther, Dave shook his head in bewilderment. 'I can't even begin to think of Cal as a traitor. He was a good man, who died as bravely as he lived.'

'He's not dead yet,' Imogen insisted.

Uncertainly Dave paused. 'If it helps to go on hoping, you hope.'

'Imie's not just hoping,' Esther said, walking across to the window. 'I feel it too. Cal's alive, however daft that sounds.'

'How can he be? I saw him fall. I saw the execution too.'

'Did you actually see him buried?'

'No. When we returned the next morning, his body had gone.'

In relief, Esther let out her breath. 'Could someone have taken it?' she asked.

'It looked like Marauders had been down overnight. Maybe they thought there was money to be had from his family. Tess, I'd like to believe Cal's alive as much as you, but he couldn't have survived such wounds.'

'A Keeper's harder to kill than an ordinary man,' Imogen said quietly. In surprise, they looked towards her.

'Stasis,' Esther recalled suddenly.

Dave frowned. 'What on earth's that?' he asked.

'One of my tutors told me about it, years ago.'

She could sense from Imogen's reaction that she was getting near the truth. The girl would not break her vow of silence, but she wanted to save her father too.

'It's a kind of self-induced coma,' Esther continued, watching Imogen carefully. 'It protects the body against shock, and allows the tissue time to heal. If Cal survived the first shot, he might have anticipated the second. He'd have to be very good at such things, though.'

'He's good,' Dave agreed. 'He frightened the life out of me once, when we were climbing together. He missed his footing and fell. By the time I reached him there was no sign of breathing. I thought he was dead, yet he came round a couple of hours later. All he'd done was break his leg and suffer concussion. When I told him I hadn't been able to find a pulse, he just laughed and said I'd never make a doctor.'

Crossing to a map on the wall, Dave stood looking at it.

'You saw people in strange clothes,' Esther reminded Imogen. 'Could they have been wearing bits and pieces stolen from others?'

The girl nodded. Hope made her eyes even larger.

Esther also looked at the map. 'Supposing, just supposing, Cal is alive,' she said, 'where would we start to look?'

'Find us a lake,' Imogen said, 'with trees beside it.'

Dave caught his breath. 'How far would you say Marauders could travel in a night?' he asked.

'To hear of a battle, come down and then return? If they had horses, they could cover twenty kilometres easily. Look for a lake about ten kilometres from your training centre.'

'There's a small tarn eleven kilometres to the north. It has some trees along the western shore.'

At once Imogen was leaping up. 'We have to go there,' she insisted.

'I'll see if I can get us a transport,' Dave agreed. Anxiously he looked out of the window. 'There's a storm brewing. We'll have to set off at once, in whatever I can get.'

'We'll need gold,' Esther called as he crossed to the door.

'Gold?'

'Marauders understand gold, not money. If they have got Cal, they'll demand a ransom.'

'There's a chain of mine in the safe,' Imogen remembered.

'It was my mother's. Dad put it there when we had to leave the dwelling. He said it wouldn't be safe for me to wear it.'

Dave found her the key. 'Have my ring too,' he said taking it off his finger.

Since even an Undesirable would wear earrings if she could find them, Esther had kept her gold studs. Quickly she took them out, and added her wedding band to the collection on the desk. 'Beg anything else you can get,' she advised Dave. 'The Marauders are bound to have realised Cal's important. They'll want a lot for him.'

'Dad said there was a letter in here for you,' Imogen said, standing at the safe. 'He kept leaving them for you, in case you came back.'

24

How Dave managed to obtain the cargo carrier he never explained. It was grindingly slow and heavy to handle in flight, but at least it was already fuelled and would withstand all but the fiercest weather. With two of Dave's recruits as guards they set off into a leaden sky. Imogen sat close to Esther against the wall of the hold, with Dave and his companions opposite. Apart from introducing the recruits as Melton and Burns, Dave said little. He was worried about the approaching storm and bewildered by the strangeness of the events in which he was taking part. A sensible, practical man, he was out of his depth.

As they travelled, Esther read Callum's letter. The envelope was marked CONFIDENTIAL and sealed with the Alliance seal. Inside was a single sheet of paper, dated the 25th, the same day as the attack on the training centre.

Tess,

I'd like to write a love letter to you, but I haven't time. In any case, I've written half a dozen already, and when I've read them through, they've sounded so foolish I've torn them up afterwards. How are you? If you're reading this, you're at least alive. I've been half out of my mind with worry ever since you disappeared.

My love, what you must have endured, and at the hands of my own people. How did you keep silence? I kept expecting to hear that my family had been taken, and nothing happened. How can I ever thank you?

Your children are safe with mine. If you contact your father he'll take you to them. He joined us on the second day, bringing his own and another two battalions. Our admin will have his latest address. Tim has grown so much you'll hardly recognise him. Life in the Outlands suits him. Sally's fine too. Imie's got her talking. You and I will have to keep our promises to each other, if only so that we don't have to separate our children.

Now to business. How do you fancy working with me when the fighting ends? My father is determined I should be gainfully employed. There isn't going to be much call for showhouse directors until more important things are provided, like food and housing. I doubt if the sort of entertainment the old regime favoured will be needed in any case. Dad suggested I become interim cabinet minister for the arts and I'm afraid I burst out laughing. Now he's saying I could co-ordinate the reconstruction of the North. That's not such a bad idea, but I would need help. My eyes wouldn't cope with all the reports and message transfers – the gumph that goes with any business. I could employ a secretary to breathe fire at my door, but you'd be better company. Your credentials are impressive. I'm a Southerner and tainted with money and privilege. You have two generations of Northern Dissent behind you. Between us, we represent so many different factions and could heal so many divisions.

Could you let my father know your decision if I'm not around? He's trying to sort things out in readiness for the victory.

The war's almost over, my love, and the Alliance is winning. Some day soon we'll sit and share our adventures. Until then, take care.

Cal.

Several times Esther rubbed her eyes to clear them. There were no windows in the hold, and she had nowhere to look except straight ahead. Imogen was falling asleep against her, exhausted by fear and the day's experiences.

'Dave,' Esther whispered.

'What?'

'Could you come over here? There's something in Cal's letter I don't understand.'

Moving closer to her, Dave smiled.

'Cal speaks of his father sorting things out, in readiness for the victory. What does he mean?'

'Andrew Miniott was elected interim president last week. When the Alliance takes over, he'll be leading the new government.'

Appalled, Esther sat with the letter loose in her hand. 'You mean Cal's likely to be son of a president?'

'He has a healthy disregard for the whole business. According to him, his father would be wise to give up power as soon as it's safe to do so.'

'Maybe, but a president's son has to do what the politicians say.'

'If Cal sets his mind on something, they'll find it difficult to stop him. He's a war hero now, and popular with the troops.'

'A war hero will be just as difficult to know.'

The old cargo ship lurched suddenly in a gust of wind. With their backs to the wall of the hold and nothing to sit on except rolls of blankets, they felt every movement. Dave put his arm round Esther to steady them both. 'What's the matter?' he asked gently. 'Are you afraid Cal will forget you?'

'I'll be an embarrassment.'

'Why? You'll be important in your own right. You brought the Central Control system down. As soon as you give witness against those who held you, people will hear about you. I imagine Andrew Miniott would find a marriage between his son and a heroine of the Resistance quite convenient.'

Esther smiled. 'You're as cynical as Cal,' she retorted.

'I wouldn't call Cal cynical. Just realistic.' Dave paused.

'Funny, isn't it?' he asked. 'You can get to know a man well; have a drink together, rag each other about women, and never get inside his mind. I don't know when I first realised Cal was a Keeper. I could never quite believe it. He was too nice a bloke. What would a Keeper be doing living like the rest of us? And Thea – she'd have to be a Keeper's daughter herself, yet she'd be sitting on the floor after a show laughing like the rest of us.'

Safe from all eavesdroppers, they could talk of dangerous things.

'Didn't you wonder when Cal changed his name?' Esther asked.

'Why should I? It was hard for him to get work. When he got some of his sight back, it made sense for him to make a new start. Get rid of the stigma, if you see what I mean. Once he'd got that start he did well, and remembered his friends. I've climbed up the ladder with him. Quite a few of us have. And working together in one job has made it easier to work together in other ways.'

'You think a great deal of him, don't you?'

Sighing, Dave nodded. 'We've known each other since we were at state college. You don't often get a blind student, and rarely one so gifted. Cal had the sort of talent you usually find in an artist, only with him it was mechanical things. He seemed to see with his hands. People made fun of him, said he was only half a citizen, yet he was determined to use his talent for good. He worked and worked, until he was the equal of us all.'

'And now? Were the Dark Ones his idea?'

'Cal knew what darkness was like, and how much ordinary people feared it. He was also willing to bang a few heads together until the Resistance groups stopped arguing amongst themselves.'

They paused, both of them aware that they had been assuming Callum was alive.

'Whatever you do,' Esther advised, 'if Cal is being held by Marauders, don't tell them who he is. They'll haggle over the ransom for days, while their prisoner dies in front of them. They might even sell him to the enemy for a higher price.'

The outsettlements were almost deserted, controlled by Alliance forces, and serving as front-line bases for a final assault against the enemy. Since even the old-fashioned weapons of the Marauders could bring down a slow-moving cargo carrier, the rescue party landed some distance from the tarn, and prepared to continue on foot. Dave persuaded Imogen to stay behind with the craft. Though she was a good walker, better indeed at finding her way across wasteland than the two new recruits, she would be a liability if there was trouble. Marauders were fond of taking hostages, and a young girl would be an obvious target.

'If we do find your father, he'll need you on the journey back,' Dave said to her gently.

Imogen was too sensible to argue. 'When you see Dad, don't speak too suddenly,' she advised. 'Give him time to know you're there.'

All the while she walked across the moor, Esther wondered what the girl had meant.

If the tarn had been empty of all signs of life, Esther would not have been surprised, though she would have been bitterly disappointed. As they climbed the last ridge and looked down towards the water, she caught her breath. In the shelter of a clump of trees, just beyond the water's edge, was a Marauder settlement. A crazy confusion of abject poverty and stolen wealth, it appeared almost deserted. Most of the habitations looked as though they had been made from rubbish picked up after troops had passed, or traded with Undesirables from the cities. There were even parts from an army transport in one of the roofs. Two women sat outside a tent made from bits of coloured cloth.

Leaving Burns posted on the rocks above the settlement,

the other three walked down to the tarn. The pain in Esther's chest had begun again. Though it made her very tired, it gave her hope. An old man came out of one of the habitations and stood waiting for them. The party had clearly been expected; word must have been passed from settlement to settlement ahead of it.

'We've heard you're holding a prisoner,' Dave said.

'Tha's quick,' the old man replied. 'We only sent word yesterday.'

For a second Esther felt very dizzy, and had to clench her hands tight. Dave managed to stay calm. 'The Alliance believes in acting quickly,' he bluffed. 'Who are you?'

'Jaboth, leader of the Freed Ones of Darley.' Despite his age, the man spoke with the arrogance of a powerful Marauder. Judging by the amount of gold about his person, he was indeed successful amongst his kind. 'Who might you be?'

'Officers of the new Alliance. Take us to see this man. If he's the one we seek, you shall have your reward.'

'How do I know tha's not come to kill him?' the old man asked. 'A man like him must have many enemies.'

Glancing quickly at Dave for his agreement, Esther tried to look confident, 'I'm his wife,' she lied.

Jaboth's manner changed immediately. 'Tha can go, Your Highness,' he replied. 'It i'nt often we have a Princess round these parts. The rest stays here.'

It was all Esther could do not to laugh. Clearly Callum had been talking himself out of trouble. The old Royals were wealthy still, and even a minor Prince could be worth keeping alive. 'Where is my husband?' she asked, adopting what she hoped was a regal tone.

'Tha'll find him by t'water. Mind tha don't go near him, nor speak to him. Just walk to end of t'promontory there, and look. We'll be here watching and talking terms. A prince's folk can pay a fine ransom, I'll be bound?' The old man's voice was oily with cunning.

Esther set off towards the water's edge uneasily. When she looked back, Dave and Melton were talking to the leader of the Freed Ones of Darley. She had the strong impression other eyes were watching her besides theirs.

Callum was sitting on the bank of the tarn, looking across the water. A rough piece of cloth protected his shoulders from the wind, but otherwise he was still in the uniform he had worn on the night of the attack. The jacket had been cut away so that strips of torn material could be used as bandages around his chest and left arm, but a dark stain had soaked through. He must have been very cold sitting in so exposed a place. The wind across the water was already carrying a fine mist of rain, but he did not seem to see it. Esther could feel his pain, but it was distant, as if kept under control. She recalled Imogen's warning: if she spoke to him unexpectedly, his control would inevitably be broken. The shock might be enough to kill him.

Silently Esther watched him. Above the trees, crows circled and cawed relentlessly, but the injured man did not move. She had never respected him so much. The image of a boy sitting beside his grandfather's lake returned. The strength of will she saw now must have had its origins then. It was not just a result of initiation and training. It was part of the man himself.

Going back to the others, Esther nodded. 'What are your terms?' she asked.

The old man smiled, showing three sharp teeth. 'What tha's brought'll do,' he said. 'If we hang on, we'll end up wi' nowt. Th'young man can't last much longer. Come inside and drink to it.'

To have refused the invitation would have been dangerous. Leaving Melton outside to watch his companion on the rocks for any warning signal, Esther and Dave followed the old man.

The habitation he took them into was the strongest and largest of the settlement but still little more than a shack. It stank of meat and smoke from an old metal drum serving as a cooking pot on an open fire. In it a stew was simmering. Some farmer had lost his prize lamb recently. For an instant the smell turned Esther's stomach.

A table filled most of the central area. Far too ornate for such a setting, it too had presumably been stolen during the recent fighting. On it a young girl set coarse bread and a pitcher of potato whisky. An antique clock ticked the time away remorselessly. As she began to eat, the bread stuck in Esther's throat.

'We got ourselves a fine prize,' Jaboth boasted.

'Where did you find him?' Esther asked.

The old man tapped his nose, suggesting sagacity. 'There's good pickings after your lot has been killing each other. We find all sorts of things.'

'We'd thought our friend was dead,' Dave admitted.

'So did we.' Jaboth laughed loudly. 'When a corpse threatens to strangle you, you get a bit of a surprise. One of our lads is still shekking.'

Dave smiled. 'That's Cal,' he agreed. 'How did you know he was one of the old royals?'

'He said so hisself.'

Looking down into her drink, Esther just about kept her face straight.

'He i'nt no royal,' a voice said.

In surprise Esther turned round, to find a woman had entered. Though her clothes were made up of patches of different materials, there was a dignity in her manner that contrasted with the old man's arrogant cunning. She wore a necklace of stained wood and berries and her hair was intricately plaited. In city clothes, she could have passed for the wife of a fourth-strata official.

'This is Morpah, the healer,' Jaboth said, with evident pride.

'There i'nt no finer this side o'moor. Your friend would have had a hard time but for her.' The old man spat into the fire. 'Our weapons kill, but they do it quick. Yours go on burning the flesh for days afterwards. And they call you the civilised ones!'

'Thank you,' Dave said, getting up and offering the healer his hand. 'It sounds so inadequate, but that's all I can think of to say.'

'Your friend survived on his own,' Morpah replied. 'All I've done is clean his wounds and give him strength.'

'We'll see you're repaid.'

'I want no payment. I refuse no one, rich or poor. All I ask is to have some questions answered. What manner of man is your friend? He's no royal. The royals are soft, used to easy living. This man fights. I've nursed many folk, but I've never come across his like.'

'He has a great deal of courage,' Esther agreed.

'He has more than courage. No human being can keep his heart beating just by thinking of it.'

It was difficult to know how to answer her.

'The religious can do peculiar things,' Dave parried.

'Aye, the religious can turn themselves into ghosts and back again, or so people say. Personally I doubt it. It's true your friend lives in th'spirit, but he's no ghost. He's flesh and bone. He feels pain, yet he never cries out. He won't sleep, even at night. Sometimes he'll lie down but most o' th'time he just sits there, willing himself to stay alive. I want to understand his wisdom, and share it.'

'You must ask him when he's recovered,' Esther advised her.

Morpah nodded. 'It would be good for him and me to share our knowledge,' she agreed. 'We are two of th'same, though we come from different starting points. Take him back to your medicine. Your doctors can repair tissue. We can't.' Turning abruptly, the healer walked out of the habitation.

Running after her, Esther caught Morpah's arm. 'There must be something we can do to repay you,' she insisted. 'You need so much up here.'

'Very well. Get us medicine for our little ones. We lose them to th'water sickness. I can save some, but not enough.'

'When the war's over, you shall have clean water,' Esther promised. 'Then your babies won't sicken in the first place.'

The woman shook her head. 'We've heard many promises.'

'But this time they'll be kept.'

Morpah looked towards the figure sitting beside the tarn. 'Happen they will,' she agreed. 'Let me wish your husband goodbye. I'll give him something so that he can stand the journey.'

'He'll accept your medicines?'

'My medicines don't dull the mind.'

The rain was no longer a fine mist, but blowing across the hills, the foretaste of worse to come. Anxiously Esther glanced towards the sky.

'Aye. You must get him to lower ground,' Morpah remarked. 'We lose our own sick when the storms begin.' Smiling, she considered Esther's face. 'Do you really know what that man is?' she asked. 'Or are you not quite human yourself?'

Esther did not reply.

The healer nodded. 'All right, my dear,' she conceded. 'Keep his secrets. I wish you good fortune, one woman to another.'

When Esther returned, everything had been agreed. The leader of the Freed Ones of Darley offered them his hand. 'Your friend can go,' he instructed. 'The horses will be saddled while you fetch him.'

Having never really believed that Callum would be alive, neither Dave nor Esther had planned how they would get him back to the carrier. 'You'll trust us with your horses?' Esther asked in relief. A horse was a Marauder's most precious possession.

'Tha shall have one for th'prisoner, and one for th'lad who guides him. I didn't bring a man all th'way here to have him die walking home.'

Since the old Marauder had already been paid, his concern for his former hostage was hardly logical. Despite his bravado, he was capable of kindness.

Together Dave and Esther set off towards the promontory. It was raining hard now, and very cold. 'You go ahead,' Dave said. 'You'll want a few moments together.'

Gratefully Esther walked on.

Callum was sitting waiting, still watching the water but aware that someone was approaching. Turning towards her, he managed to smile. 'Afternoon,' he said.

Unable to find words, Esther stood foolishly. 'You gave us such a fright,' she said.

'Not half as much as I gave myself.' Though he spoke lightly, Callum's breathing was shallow and his voice strained. 'What happened to Fourteen's time-scale? Did she get the date wrong, or did you?'

'It was probably me,' Esther admitted. 'I never could get my sums right.'

'You kept us all guessing nicely. When the system finally came down, we'd gone home for tea.'

Sitting beside him, Esther took his right hand and put it to her mouth.

'You've had your hair cut,' Callum remarked.

'If you say you don't like it, I'll push you in the tarn,' Esther threatened. Though she joked, she was near to tears. 'How have you survived? You were hit twice, the second time point blank.'

'For what it's worth, I was only hit once.'

'But Dave saw you.'

'I had this bright idea I could pretend to be wounded and

play dead on the ground. In my scheme of things, the enemy was fooled and walked away. When I heard the enforcer walk towards me, I knew I'd got it wrong.'

'My love,' Esther said inadequately.

'I remember feeling quite calm, almost relieved. At least they wouldn't take me alive. Then I got very angry. They should let me give my side of things, not shoot me outright. It wasn't justice. I wanted to survive, so I could fight back.'

'And when you came out of the stasis? What happened?'

Callum glanced towards her quickly, then looked back over the water. 'A Marauder was trying to pull the ring off my finger. His breath smelt and he was determined to break my knuckle. It wasn't a good moment. I started talking very fast.'

Despite her concern, Esther smiled. 'It's the first time in my life anyone's called me "Your Highness",' she commented. Unable to control her emotion any longer, she put her face against his shoulder and burst into tears.

'No,' Callum said, stroking her hair. 'Don't cry. We've come through. We're the lucky ones.'

Dave had reached them, and was standing at a distance, waiting until it was tactful to join them. Seeing him, Callum nodded in greeting. 'You took your time,' he complained, smiling.

'I was busy writing your obituary.'

'Was it a good one?'

'Glowing.'

'Then you'd better save it. It'd be a pity to waste your work.'

Awkwardly the two men paused, their silence saying more than their words.

'Your father's been frantic,' Dave nodded.

'Really?' Callum's tone conveyed surprise.

'Why should you doubt it?'

'Dunno.'

'He values you now.'

Again there was an awkward pause. The wind was growing

stronger, and all three of them were getting wet. 'We need to move,' Dave reminded them. 'There's a cargo carrier coming as close as it can for us, but it can't get right up here. There's nowhere flat for it to land. The Marauders are saddling up two horses. Can you walk back to the settlement?'

'If you point me in the right direction.'

The journey back to Nortown was terrible. As long as Esther lived, she would remember it. All the way down from the tarn the rain lashed into their faces, soaking them through. The cold numbed their hands and stiffened their lips. Callum had learnt to ride as a boy, but he needed every reserve of skill and determination to stay mounted. If the lad riding beside him had not held the rein so firmly, the horse would have bolted. The rest of the party walked, cursing the weather and growing increasingly anxious as the wind strengthened. Even a solid old cargo carrier would find flight difficult in an Outland storm.

Esther walked beside Callum. Most of the time they were silent, Callum concentrating so intently on the journey that he seemed to be almost asleep. Once, however, on an easier stretch of track, he turned to her. 'Did you read my letter?' he asked.

Esther nodded.

'What did you think of my proposition? Could you work with me?'

'I think so.'

'You'll have to teach me to lead an ordinary life again. My days have been pretty disorganised lately.'

'You'll never lead an ordinary life,' Esther warned him, 'however much you may want to.' The noise of the wind and the horses' hooves drowned all but shouted remarks, or she would never have risked such a reply.

For several seconds Callum said nothing. 'No,' he agreed. 'It's a rather frightening feeling, realising you're not just different in the way you see things, but in the way you're made.'

'Morpah says you're not quite human.'

'I begin to fear she's right. What do you think I am, Tess?'

'I don't know, but it'll be interesting finding out.'

As she touched Callum's hand she found it very cold, but the fingers were closed around the reins. 'Would you mind if Dave swapped places with you for a bit?' he asked. 'I have something to discuss with him. Send Burns over in a few minutes as well. I shall need a second witness.'

The request puzzled Esther but she did as he asked.

By the time they reached the cargo carrier, they were exhausted and shivering with cold. A bed had been prepared for Callum in the hold, but he would not lie down. 'If I sleep, I've had it,' he insisted. 'Just get me home. I'll rest there.'

Sitting against the wall of the hold, with his daughter beside him, Callum closed his eyes. He spoke to Imogen softly, as if explaining something. Esther watched the girl's response. Though she was frightened, she agreed, with the carefulness of an adult making a difficult decision. Closing her eyes also, Imogen sat silently beside her father. When the craft took off, neither of them moved or spoke. In some peculiar way, the daughter was giving the father strength.

The full force of the storm hit them within minutes of take-off. The old cargo ship juddered in the wind, dropping unexpectedly into an air pocket, and then struggled back up again. With no windows to look out of, the effect was doubly sickening. Esther prayed silently that the battered frame would hold together. A journey that should have taken no more than twenty minutes began to lengthen frighteningly. Twice the craft was blown off course to the south-east and had to arc back towards Nortown. Once it slewed sharply to port as if about to hit the ground. Imogen was finding it hard not to cry, and her father put his arm round her to comfort her. He was deathly white, for the first time gasping in pain as the craft dropped again. Esther could feel Imogen's growing anxiety. Silently, with his arm still around his daughter, Callum slid into unconsciousness.

When the voice crackled over the intercom to warn them they were landing, even Dave swore in relief. 'Bloody hell,' he said. 'That wasn't my idea of fun.'

'My father's dying,' Imogen said. Her voice was so calm it might have been an adult speaking.

'Get Cal out first,' Dave called, 'as soon as we land.'

To their surprise, there was a medical team already waiting.

'Got your message,' one of the orderlies said. 'We'll have him at the hospital in no time.'

Another two orderlies lifted Callum urgently on to a stretcher. The storm howled around them, whipping up pieces of debris and flinging them against the side of the cargo ship. A sudden sense of alarm made Esther run forward. These were no ordinary orderlies, she was sure of it. 'Don't let them take him, Dave!' she screamed.

At first Dave could not understand her panic. 'Cal needs help,' he said. 'As fast as possible.'

Imogen caught Esther's alarm. 'Where are you taking my father?' she shouted. 'I want to come too.'

The team was already bundling Callum into a transport unit. One of the female orderlies turned back to the girl. 'Your father must come with us,' she replied. 'You know that.'

At once Imogen was quiet, though she put her hands to her face.

'What the hell's going on?' Dave demanded, his voice almost lost on the wind. He was unarmed, having decided the sight of a weapon might inflame the Marauders, but was ready to fight with his bare hands if necessary.

The woman merely shook her head. 'Your friend will be given good care,' she said. 'Thank you for all you have done for him. If he lives, we will return him to you.'

Callum was already inside the transport unit. There was

nothing more either Dave or Esther could do. They had brought him back to safety, only to have him claimed by his own people. The medical team was well armed and had the advantage of surprise. Even if Burns and Melton had been able to get from the cargo ship in time, there would only have been four adults and a child to oppose them. The engines of the ambulance were throbbing. Helplessly Esther watched as the doors were secured. 'Cal!' she called. Her cry was drowned by the roar of full thrust being engaged. With the wind howling around it, the ambulance slewed round and headed south into the storm.

Imogen stood watching it depart until there was nothing more to see. They left her alone, respecting her grief.

'What was the old saying about frying pans and fire?' Dave asked, his voice thick with emotion.

'I sincerely hope that lot were his friends,' Esther replied.

'Imie seemed to think so.'

Hearing her name, Imogen turned to them. She had been crying, but she pretended calmness now. 'A Keeper has to die with his own people,' she said. Fortunately Melton and Burns were out of hearing.

'And if he is not ready to die?'

'Then he will have better surgery with them. They should have let me go with him. He'll need a support.' She was saying more than she should, and stopped abruptly.

'Your father asked me to see you stayed here,' Dave replied gently. 'He appointed Mrs Thomas as your official guardian.'

In surprise Esther glanced towards him, though she nodded her agreement.

They made their way towards the flight deck. After an unscheduled mission there were a great many forms to fill in. Exhausted, Imogen rested on one of the couches in the waiting room.

'What's this about me being Imie's official guardian?' Esther asked Dave. 'I'm very happy to be, but Cal's family will probably have other ideas.'

'He's named you as his Conjugate.'

'What?' In amazement, Esther stared at him.

'Since Cal's wife is dead, you're entitled to his pension and to have care of his children, so long as they express a willingness to stay with you. Imie has already done so in my hearing.' Dave raised one eyebrow. 'I hadn't realised you and Cal were so close,' he admitted.

'We weren't. There was never anything official between us. Why did he say there was? I would have looked after his children out of love. I didn't need to be forced. Are you sure he knew what he was saying?'

'Cal made the declaration when we were coming down from the tarn. Burns was a witness. In the event of his death, he wished you to have his effects, and to be treated as his wife.'

'I don't merit recompense. I don't even want it.'

'Then I have no idea what he intended.'

Esther was becoming increasingly angry. 'To force his parents into a corner,' she retorted. 'You said yourself Cal is becoming a hero. Everybody has stories of how the Dark Ones appeared out of nowhere to help the local Resistance. If his family try to stop him marrying me, people will want to know why. How do his parents answer them without admitting they're of Keepers' blood?'

Dave shook his head. 'Don't judge Cal too harshly,' he advised. 'A dying man doesn't think too straight.'

After Dave and Imogen had gone, Esther stood alone on the flight deck, trying to calm her emotion. In the lowlands the storm raged less fiercely but with an unpredictable vindictiveness, catching up the debris of battle and throwing it back down again. Most of the refugees had been found shelter. A few huddled in the lee of the ruined control tower. At that moment she would have changed places with any one of them if it would have brought Callum back.

'Come on, Your Highness,' a voice said behind her. 'I've found you and Imie somewhere to sleep.'

Turning round, she found Dave had returned. Silently she put her head against his shoulder, and let him comfort her.

'Where?' she asked.

'Lily's Saloon. I'll bet it's the first time you've slept in a saloon.'

Showhouse Four was full, but the Wild West Bar Trail still had room. The whole complex had been refurbished just before the war broke out, to compete with the newest addition to Entertainment Square. Now a five-metre-tall Red Indian stood implacably in the foyer, watching over a queue of refugees as they registered. The sign above him announced, HO DOWN TONITE and LILY'S SALOON AND BAR. There was no power, and the words merely hung there instead of flashing in red and green. Lily herself should have been announcing the times of the next show, but the automaton was strangely still, seen for the first time to be a mechanical toy. Esther was shown her bed, a strip of extruded foam that was to be laid out each night and rolled up in the day to make space for her to sit. Until the war was properly ended, that would be her home. Imogen was already asleep.

Her head throbbing with tiredness and relief, Esther lay down. Tier upon tier of balconies rose above her. There was a full-sized stuffed horse on one level, complete with white-hatted rider. Bar room, chorus girls, blackjack tables, even a shootout at the OK Corral featured on others. Without animations or holograms, all were still. Though the sensor pads had stopped working as soon as the lights went out, a scent of straw and beer still pervaded the atmosphere. It was being rapidly overlaid by the smell of wet clothing and human bodies.

The woman at the desk had lent Esther a stylus and a reply

pad. Sitting up on one elbow, Esther took them out and began to construct a letter to Andrew Miniott.

"Sir," she wrote, deciding directness was the best approach.

   I believe your son has told you about me. My name is Esther Thomas. I am the daughter of Jacki Marshall, former leader of the Women's Movement, and Colonel James Marshall, who is currently fighting for the Alliance in the Fifth Division. Your son is known to me through our work together in the North. To me he is Callum, and I loved him before I knew he had any connection with your family.

   Before his disappearance, he left a letter inviting me to assist him in co-ordinating the reconstruction of the North, a post which he explained you had offered him. I would be willing to take on such a role as a representative of the North, and as a recompense for my own part in bringing about so much suffering. As I hope you know by now, Callum has been traced. He had been badly wounded, and may not survive. I would rather undertake the work with him, but if I must do so alone, then I will, so long as you think me acceptable.

   Since I am a widow with two children to support, I would need payment and a proper contract of employment. Imogen has also expressed a wish to stay with me, at least until her father recovers. If I can find accommodation, I would like to keep all four children together, as they have grown used to each other, but I shall of course accept your wishes in this matter. As the children's grandparents, you and your wife may wish to come and collect Imogen and Benn from me.

   I enclose a curriculum vitae for your information.

   Yours sincerely,
      Esther Thomas (Mrs)

Reading the letter through again, Esther sighed. It was not as she had hoped, but it would have to do. She was too tired to write another. Settling down again, she put the reply pad and stylus safely under her pillow. In the spaces near her, children squabbled and ran around, while their parents talked, or ate. Above the balconies and silent automata of Lily's Saloon, the storm still raged. Closing her eyes, she slept.

Dawn was filtering through the roof lights when the pain began again in Esther's side, waking her. Sitting up, she breathed deeply in an effort to control it. Suddenly Imogen cried out, waking the family near her.

'Nightmares,' Esther explained, satisfying them. On her hands and knees, she moved to Imogen's side. The girl was lying with wide, terrified eyes. There was such agony in her expression that Esther lifted her up and held her, trying to attract as little attention as possible.

How long the worst intensity lasted Esther could not afterwards say. It was probably no more than five minutes, but the pain nearly broke them both. At last, as sharply as it had begun, it ended. Letting Imogen slip back on to the bed, Esther lay down exhausted beside her. Within seconds they were both asleep.

Eight hours had been called when Esther awoke, and people were talking all round her. Imogen was lying staring at the decks above her. She was very pale. Gently Esther touched her hair. 'Are you feeling better?' she whispered.

Imogen nodded.

'Do you have any idea how your father is?' Esther asked. 'Can you tell?'

Her eyes filling with tears, Imogen shook her head. 'I can feel nothing now,' she replied. 'He's either dead or asleep.'

There was no rational explanation Esther could offer for what had happened in the night, but it had been no dream. For a little longer she lay wondering what to do. Though she would never have sought favours for herself, for Imogen's sake she must do so. The girl needed safer lodgings. She was not just a Keeper's daughter; she was granddaughter of Andrew Miniott. Her value as a hostage would be enormous, even now. More than safety, though, she needed quiet. The girl's concern for her father was leading her into regions which would bewilder minds older than hers, and she had no masters to guide her. Her father must have predicted such a possibility. If he could not trust his own people to care for his daughter, a sympath had the best chance of understanding what she was feeling.

Getting up on to her knees, Esther kissed Imogen's forehead. 'I'll find somewhere better for us to sleep tonight,' she promised. 'Then we can fetch the others.'

'That'd be nice,' Imogen agreed.

'We'll see if we can find Mrs Briggs too. I have a job to do. With four of you in tow, I'm going to need help.'

Rather to her amusement, Esther discovered she had become an important person. The exact reasons for her importance had not been explained, but she was given immediate respect when she approached the officials at the front desk. One of the private suites on the top storey could be made available for her. At present it was being used as a storeroom, but the boxes could be moved.

Smiling grimly, Esther looked around the suite before fetching Imogen. Intended for privileged officials and their pretty companions, the rooms were an odd place to bring children. Their red and gold décor contrasted with the piles of foodstuffs waiting for distribution. But the suite was warm and safe, and a distinct improvement on a bed strip laid across a floor.

That afternoon, by good fortune and a great deal of scanning of refugee entries, Esther traced Mrs Briggs. The old woman was happy to return to her two little loves, and to accept another two, with the promise of payment some day and a comfortable settee now. Taking one look at the suite as the official opened the door, she tutted in disapproval. 'There's been some fine goings on in here, I'll be bound,' she remarked. 'Look at all them mirrors!' When she saw the red chairs and beds her disapproval was complete. Rolling up her sleeves, she began to give everywhere a good scrub down. 'To mek it feel cleaner, if you see what I mean.'

It was two days before Mrs Briggs declared herself satisfied that the suite was fit for decent folk, and the children could be fetched from the Outlands. As she watched Benn and Sally exploring their new home, Esther felt a sardonic pleasure. With their sticky fingers and disregard for privilege, they were celebrating the end of a regime.

She was assisting some of the new arrivals in the main dormitory when a young official picked his way between the beds. 'You have someone to see you, Ma'am,' he said. 'Two ladies. Wouldn't say who they were, just that you would know them. Would you like me to stand guard?'

'It might be an idea,' Esther agreed. 'There's still a few idiots around bearing grudges.' With the officer accompanying her, she went back to the main office.

As soon as they entered, a woman got up to greet her. The second visitor was younger, not much more than eighteen, and was standing near the window.

'I hope we haven't called at an inconvenient time,' the first began.

At once Esther recognised the voice. 'I know this woman,' she said to the officer. 'It's all right.'

As soon as he had gone, Esther offered her hand. 'You survived,' she said with pleasure. 'I'm so glad.'

'It's good to see you safe too,' the spokeswoman replied. 'We were worried about you.'

The older woman's manner was too formal for closeness, but Esther sensed that she wished to be friends. Her stiffness was a matter of habit and upbringing rather than choice. 'You have an advantage over me,' Esther admitted. 'I don't know what to call you. "Spokeswoman" doesn't sound right now.'

'My name is Glade. The Honourable Margaret Glade, daughter of the Young Pretender to the Throne. Such titles seem absurd now. I prefer to be known simply as Mrs Glade. Acting President Miniott asked me to bring you various papers, and to offer you his thanks.' Placing a packet on the desk in front of them, Margaret Glade turned towards the girl beside the window. 'Forgive my rudeness,' she apologised. 'I should have introduced my companion.'

The younger woman came forward. 'I'm Jessica,' she said. 'Jessica Miniott, Simon's cousin.'

In surprise, Esther paused. Though the face was not as pretty as she had imagined, the height and voice were right. 'Madelaine?' she asked.

Awkwardly the girl held out her hand. 'That's how you've known me,' she agreed. 'You once told me off for wearing the wrong shoes.'

With genuine pleasure, Esther embraced her. There was nothing formal about Madelaine's response. Laughing with relief, she kissed Esther's cheek. 'We've been so lucky,' she said. 'All of us have come through.'

'Even Cal?' Esther could scarcely speak for joy.

'You'll have to get used to calling him Simon soon,' Mrs Glade reminded her. 'The rebel you knew has become a president's son.'

'I'm more interested in knowing how Cal is than in his rank. Is he all right?'

'You haven't changed.' Mrs Glade's smile belied the sharpness of her reply. 'For a man who has been so near to death, Mr Miniott is remarkably well. Our surgeons have been able to repair the tissue damage.'

Esther tried to find words for her relief. She discovered she was shivering, and had to sit down.

Madelaine put her hand on her shoulder, understanding. 'If you hadn't found Cal when you did, he would have died,' she said. 'As it was, we nearly lost him. For hours I sat beside him, willing him to live. I never realised until then how much I would miss him.'

Taking out several packets, Margaret Glade passed them across the desk. 'President Miniott asked me to give you these gifts for the children,' she said. 'You'll find your own two are included. I believe their names are Sally and Tim.'

'I'll see they have them tonight,' Esther promised. 'Could you tell Cal we're staying in one of the suites on the top floor here? I've traced Mrs Briggs, and for the time being, she's helping me. When he has accommodation himself, she'll be happy to take up her old post again.' Wondering what the Miniotts thought of her relationship with Callum, Esther paused.

'You'll find all you need to enable you to take up your position,' Mrs Glade continued. 'There are also some suggestions from Simon as to how you might work on your own until he can join you. It would be best to start as soon as possible.'

'I've already begun. If children aren't occupied, they run wild. It's been quite easy to set up classes in the showhouses, with so many mothers who used to be teachers. We've had to sort out hygiene arrangements too. I'm afraid conditions were getting a bit unsavoury.'

Margaret Glade nodded. 'Simon chose well,' she said.

'Where is he now?'

'At home, being fussed over by his mother. It will do them both good.'

Unexpectedly Mrs Glade offered Esther her hand. 'In the old world we would never have met,' she said. 'Yet we have worked together and ended a hateful system. If that is the meaning of Alliance, I'm glad to be a part of it.' Turning abruptly, she went out.

Madelaine's farewell was warmer. 'Welcome to the family,' she said.

'You mean that?' Esther asked in delight.

'Of course. If Cal wants you, that's good enough for me. Besides, I've found a nice young officer. I could eat him whole.'

'And if Callum married outside, you might be allowed to do so?'

'Fair's fair!'

After they had gone, Esther sat at her desk and looked through the contract that Acting President Miniott had given her. She would be able to keep the children fed for at least three years. In relief she sat staring ahead of her, trying to plan her future.

Seeking some guidance, Esther scanned through the notes Callum had sent. Written in a hand she did not recognise, they had presumably been dictated to a secretary, or to his mother. It was odd to think of him with a mother fussing over him. The very idea made Esther smile.

Though she did not have time to read the pages in detail, the final paragraphs caught Esther's attention. They were a kind of creed, which could guide the recovery.

Sitting beside the tarn, and then in hospital afterwards, I've had plenty of time to think. We must reach out to the people the old regime forgot, or we will have more trouble; if not in this decade, in the next. To my way of thinking, everyone in our society has an equal right to education, medicine and food. They also have a right to privacy of the spirit, to decide who to love and what god to worship, without being watched by some self-appointed Keeper. Such rights must not of course threaten the rights of others. How you achieve that balance I'm not sure, but I'm certain it must be sought. What justification can there be for letting an accident of birth determine whether a child grows up healthy and powerful? Or dies in poverty, from water sickness and hunger?

If he had chosen to go into political life Callum would have written fine speeches. By deciding not to do so, he would probably keep his ideals longer.

Do something to help the Marauders, please, Tess, for my sake. Their very existence condemns us. I would steal if I were reduced to their level. They can also teach us a great deal about survival on limited resources. I would have liked to return to talk to Morpah straight away, but I doubt if I could survive an Outland winter just yet . . .

Callum had identified the same priorities as herself: to begin with the children and then build on their contacts with the outcasts of society, the Marauders and Undesirables.

Putting the papers away, Esther examined the children's gifts. There was an extra box, she discovered, addressed to her. Curiously she opened it. Inside was a pair of gold ear studs. A message was attached: "A small repayment for what you gave my son. I would have missed Cal sadly. Tell him so, please, for me. We have lost the art of talking to each other about anything but war." The wording was so unexpected, it moved Esther almost to tears.

There was a second, longer paragraph: "Cal will return the wedding band himself. You must decide how to receive it, in memory of the past, or for the future. If it helps you make up your mind, we did not need to be forced into accepting you. My wife and I value you through your mother, and in your own right. There are also other good reasons why a union between our families would be welcome. The old ways are not quite dead, however, and Cal's fears usually have good grounds. He may be right to urge a quick marriage to forestall opposition. Let your decision be of your own free will, even so. Love has rushed many a woman into worlds she did not understand, or like."

Crossing to the mirror, Esther put the studs in place. Her hair had grown, making a softer line round her face, and peace had taken the dark shadows from under her eyes. For the first time in months she felt she was beautiful.

25

The day of the Armistice was extremely busy. Esther had a great deal to see to in the refugee settlements. Another twelve families were moving out to dwellings which had been declared safe to reoccupy. Though there was no definite news that the war was over, rumours flew around the dormitories like butterflies. There was a sense of relief in the air. The children felt it first, running about and refusing to be quietened. A couple of Outlanders began one of the old dances in the middle of Entertainment Square, and everyone stopped to look. A few embarrassed souls joined in, to find their feet in knots. Everyone was waiting for the news that must surely come.

It was late afternoon before Esther had time to herself. Without the lighted dome above, dusk was settling in the square. At exactly eighteen hours, the power was switched back on for a measured three hours, and the refugees in the showhouses began sorting themselves out for the night. There was a lot to do, cooking the evening meal, laying down bed strips, finding children.

Pausing uneasily, Esther looked around her. She had a peculiar sense that Callum was near. Intently she watched the movements around her, only to look away in disappointment. There were no newcomers; every one of the refugees was known to her by sight.

Still the feeling remained. Going into one of the other

dormitories, Esther looked for him there. Once again, she found only the usual occupants. By the time she had walked through the whole ground floor, and then the ones above, she was thoroughly irritated. Clearly Callum was not in the building. The general excitement was affecting her. Either that, or love was teaching her senses to play tricks. Finally she crossed to Dave's office to make a final check. If Callum had indeed returned, Dave would know. The room was empty.

Suddenly Esther knew where Callum wanted her to go. The request was as clear in her mind as if she had heard him speak aloud. Furiously she went upstairs, to the very top of the building. A door marked ROOF AREA ONLY. Trying it, she found it open as she had expected. Beyond was a small landing and three steps leading to another door. Callum was sitting on the bottom step, waiting for her. His arm was protected by a healer sleeve, but his eyes were laughing.

'How dare you fetch me here?' Esther demanded.

'I needed to talk to you.'

'You promised never to use your power for your own good.'

'I'm here on business, as well as love.'

Her anger checked, Esther stood watching him. 'Couldn't you have put a call out for me?' she asked.

'And announce my presence? I'm not supposed to be here.'

Relenting, Esther sat on the step beside him. 'Are you really alive?' she asked.

'I feel as if I am.'

She touched his face gently, anger and relief still conflicting within her. 'You shouldn't have returned so soon,' she chided. 'You still look pale. You should be tucked up in bed.'

'There's an answer to that, but I don't think I'm up to it yet.'

Smiling slightly, Esther tried to assess Callum's mood. There was a new quietness about him. It was not the emptiness she had felt when they first met, but a kind of peace, the peace of a man who had been on a long journey and returned with tales too strange to tell. There was so much she wanted to say to him, but even as she drew closer to him she heard the sound of footsteps coming up the stairs.

'Later,' Callum whispered. 'We have business to attend to first.'

Wondering who could be approaching, Esther got up and went to the door. To her surprise, it was opened by Fourteen.

'Forty-Eight!' Almost throwing herself at Esther, Fourteen hugged her. In delight they embraced each other, then laughed in embarrassment. Fourteen looked well, the pallor of city life replaced by an Outland tan and brighter eyes.

'Fancy me finding you here!' she said. 'I was just doing a bit of exploring.'

'How odd!' Esther replied drily.

'Isn't it? I'm so glad to see you're alive! When we heard you'd been taken, I thought I'd never see you again.'

'What happened to you? Where have you been?'

'It'd fill a vidmat!'

A more serious note entered Fourteen's voice. 'I've done a lot of things I'd never have dreamt possible,' she explained. 'If I'd known what my bright idea would lead to I wouldn't even have told you of it.'

'What's done is done,' Esther insisted. 'Now we must rebuild. They say the Armistice will be signed tonight.'

Callum was still sitting on the steps. Seeing him for the first time, Fourteen drew back. 'Isn't that Patroner Lahr?' she whispered. 'Were you and – ?' She giggled. 'Have I disturbed something?'

Getting up, Callum offered his hand in greeting. 'You know me better in black,' he said quietly.

'Callum!' Fourteen's teasing turned to fear. 'And I thought I was doing a bit of exploring!' she retorted. 'What do you want this time?' Though her voice shook, she resolutely ignored his outstretched hand.

'There's a job that needs doing, and I don't know anyone else who could do it so well.'

'I'm not helping you. I've seen where it leads me.'

Still Callum held out his hand, and still Fourteen ignored it. 'Please,' he asked. 'Let us at least be friends. I fought on the same side as you.'

'What happened to the Scots accent?'

'It went the same way as the limp.'

Fourteen almost smiled. 'You look as though you've been wounded,' she commented.

'My own people caught up with me.'

'I never imagined a Keeper could be hurt like the rest of us.'

'We bleed just the same. Give me your hand. We're allies now.'

'All right. For old times' sake, that's all.'

Awkwardly Fourteen accepted Callum's greeting, though her suspicion did not diminish.

Again footsteps sounded on the stairs. 'Cal?' Dave's voice asked.

'Here.'

The two men nodded to each other; they needed no other greeting. Mystified, Esther looked towards Dave. He smiled reassuringly. Evidently he knew Callum's intention.

'Now we're all here, we'd better make a start,' Callum said. 'It will be dark soon. I'm sorry I brought you here as I did, but I needed you to witness something. Dave, would you try that door? I'd like you to confirm what I have found.'

Crossing the room, Dave mounted the steps towards the roof. As soon as he touched the door, a security warning sounded. "Maintenance staff only beyond this point," the computerised voice announced. "All passes must be shown."

Ignoring the warning, Dave tried the door. It was locked. Callum passed him a key pad, and for several moments Dave stood keying in various combinations. The door remained solidly shut.

'Remember, I was director here,' Callum said quietly. 'Why should a director be forbidden to admire the view from his own roof? Dave, let us through, please.'

Fourteen glanced towards Esther for explanation, but Esther could only shrug her shoulders. Taking out a small electronic reader, Dave passed it over the lock several times. Finally he was able to release the security lock.

The door led to yet another flight of stairs, on to the roof. Without the protection of the dome, the controlled environment outlets screamed in the wind. Sheltering in the doorway, Esther looked about her. She could see the rebuilding work in the central area of the city already well under way. Checkpoints and troop encampments looked like old-fashioned children's toys.

'That must be it,' Dave said, indicating a structure a few metres across the roof. It appeared to be a workmen's rest point.

Keeping to the lee of the outlets, Dave made his way to the cabin. With the wind tearing at his uniform, he crouched down to work at the lock. Finally he had the door open. The others ran across to join him.

As soon as she stepped inside the room, Esther caught her breath. Bank upon bank of screens flickered in front of her. Every one showed a different part of the building to eyes that no longer watched. On one, the refugees in the main auditorium talked; on another people walked across a foyer. Even the dormitories were on screen, a woman making her bed for the night.

Stepping forward, Dave tried a control panel, and a new set of images came on view. To her horror Esther recognised Sally and Benn. On the screen beside them was her own bed, a quilt laid across it ready for her to retire. Again Dave touched a number, and other private rooms appeared, filled with boxes of food. He brought the sound on line. Perfectly clearly, they could hear a woman and a man discussing whether to return to their dwelling. On the centre bank of screens, their every expression showed. It was like being God, watching the mortals beneath.

'How long have you known about this place?' Dave asked. He sounded rather shaken.

'I worked it out a few months ago. There was too much electronic activity. Besides, when workmen keep coming and going from a roof area, you get curious.' As he watched the images flickering before him, the line of Callum's mouth hardened. 'It was the last straw. I felt like my art was being stolen from me. My shows brought people into the building to enjoy themselves, and they were spied on while they were here. Even the private rooms were being peered into. I hated having those rooms at all, but the people who used them had a right to privacy.'

'I never realised how bad it had got,' Dave admitted. 'Do all the showhouses have surveillance like this?'

'I imagine Showhouse Two does. That was recently refurbished. I doubt if the older ones have anything so sophisticated. All the while I was sitting at home yesterday I kept thinking that somewhere in this building the spy screens were still flickering, watching the refugees.'

'What a hateful system!' Fourteen too was visibly upset. 'Now I've seen this, I feel better about what I did.'

'I hoped you might.' Crossing to her, Callum put his hand on the woman's shoulder. 'You understand this sort of stuff,' he said. 'Show me how to disable it.'

'I can't think of anything I'd rather do.'

Sitting down at one of the consoles, Fourteen keyed in various commands. She waited to see the response. Suddenly the screens went blank. The words ON HOLD. CARE NECESSARY appeared. 'That will do for a start,' she said with satisfaction. 'Now let's find the main power switch.'

For ten minutes or more Fourteen examined each piece of equipment. Finally she tried a single command. The screens died.

All three onlookers breathed a sigh of relief.

'Shall I tell anyone about this?' Fourteen asked.

'Of course. Everyone must know the ways of the old regime. If you're willing, that could be your role. You served the Alliance well in war, but we could use your skills in peace too.'

'What would you want me to do?' The woman was both frightened and flattered.

'See how many other places like this you can find. Don't let a single spy camera or recorder survive. They'll be a temptation to us if they do. Before you disarm it, record each centre as you find it. Take pictures, notes, anything that can be used in evidence for the courts. If you can show that senior people were involved – at government level – it will exonerate the Seekers a little. I have personal reasons for wanting that. Justice must be seen to be done, however, for everyone, Keeper and Kept.'

Esther glanced towards Callum, and he nodded. His cousin had survived.

'What about expenses?' Esther asked.

Callum smiled. 'Businesslike as ever,' he remarked. 'Everything will be arranged. Until your colleague has her own staff, Dave has agreed to help.'

In amazement Fourteen stared at him. 'You're offering such a job to me?' she asked.

'You'll do it well.'

There was a new confidence in the way Callum spoke. Even Dave was aware of it.

'Who are you?' Fourteen asked. 'How come you have so much power?'

An expression of understanding came to her face. 'Of course! You were on the Alliance broadcast. You're one of the

Miniotts . . .' In bewilderment she stopped. 'But that doesn't make sense. You're a Keeper!'

'Betray that fact and you could still do my family a lot of harm.'

Fourteen stared at him in disbelief, and then fury. 'What did we fight for?' she demanded. 'Nothing's changed. Maybe you lot aren't as bad as the last, but you're the same race – the same dictators by another name. You hijacked our revolution.'

'I hope not. My father intends to step down as soon as possible. He only took the position after much persuasion – to prevent another Devastation.'

Still white with anger, Fourteen looked towards Esther. 'Did you know?' she demanded.

'I guessed.'

Crossing to Fourteen, Callum stood beside her. 'Tess has protected me with her silence,' he said gently. 'Now I'm asking you to protect me too. I had hoped that when the Keepers' rule was broken those of us who were left could come into the open. It isn't going to be that simple. People fear what they don't understand. They want to destroy it. If you go out that door and repeat what you know of me, I won't last more than an hour. Even the children will want me dead. Surely there's been enough killing?'

Fourteen did not want to soften. Anger still struggled against reason. But ambition was an equally strong force. Grudgingly, she hesitated. 'I've never been one to turn down a good job,' she admitted, 'and I'd like to pull the plug on places like this.'

The danger was past. Fourteen would keep silence too.

Dave was indicating that it was time to leave. In relief, Esther joined him at the door. Then she stopped. She was convinced they were still being watched. Looking round her, she tried to explain the sensation: there was nothing to be seen. Yet the uneasiness remained. Mechanical eyes were observing them from above.

'We haven't found every viewer,' she warned.

Looking anxiously at Dave, Callum paused. Fourteen returned to the console, and stared intently ahead of her. She seemed to be listening, though to what was not clear. Outside, the wind howled across the roof and the aerials screamed, but in the cabin there was silence. 'Yes,' she agreed. 'There's some sort of back-up surveillance, even when the main power's off. It's recording us now. Look for another power source.'

'Store cells!' Urgently Dave began to look around the room. 'Whoever installed this equipment expected us. Either that, or they wanted to watch their own Watchers. Lord, what a state of mind''

It was Callum who found the panel. Behind it were three sealed units.

'Take care,' Dave warned. 'They're live.'

'So how do we switch them off? I came to silence this place. I'm not leaving until I do.'

'There aren't any switches. Once installed, this stuff runs itself. It absorbs energy every time the main power is on, and then chunters along when it's off. It's the same principle as a beta alarm, though I've never seen it used like this before.'

'Alarms can be disabled,' Callum insisted.

'A store unit is much more powerful than an alarm.'

'Then we'll just have to be more careful.'

As if he were approaching a nest of snakes, Callum slid his hand inside the cover. Esther had gone very cold. Slowly Callum closed his fingers over the back of one of the units. Holding his breath for a second, he steadied himself. Then he snatched at the unit, jerking it clear. There was a flash of light which stunned them all. A smell of burning filled the room.

For several seconds none of them spoke. Even Dave had gone white.

Fourteen broke the silence. 'That was a terrible risk,' she said. 'Why on earth did you take it?'

Shrugging his shoulders, Callum dropped the unit on to the floor. 'Because I needed to,' he replied.

In fury Esther turned on him. 'I walked half way across the Outlands looking for you,' she snapped, 'and now you risk your life again. Don't you want to live?'

Putting his arm around her, Callum appealed to her. 'I have to clear my soul, Tess. Otherwise I shall remain part of the evil I hate. You of all people should understand such things.'

Fourteen was watching them. In embarrassment, Esther moved away. 'It's nearly dark,' she pointed out. 'We'd better get back across the roof.'

Glancing towards Callum, Dave smiled. 'You two go first,' he suggested. 'We'll take pictures of this place before anyone tampers with it.'

As Esther turned to follow Callum outside, Fourteen caught her hand. 'You must be mad,' she whispered. 'How can you love a Keeper?'

'I saw the man inside.' Esther could not resist teasing her colleague a little. 'Tell you what though, the stories are true.'

Fourteen laughed. 'I wish you luck,' she replied.

In the warmth of the stairwell Callum and Esther held each other briefly. Even there they could not be alone: children were running up and down the staircases below them.

'Come with me,' Callum invited. 'I know somewhere quieter.'

'More secret places?'

'This building is full of them. I must leave soon. I'd like to be with you for a while first.'

Taking her hand, he led her back down the stairs, along several corridors, to a room marked TECHNICIANS ONLY. As they entered, Esther looked round her in surprise. The room was glass fronted, looking down on to the stage of the main auditorium, fifty metres below. Equipment and control panels lined the other walls, still left as they had been after Show-house Four's final performance.

'Welcome to my other home,' Callum said. 'This is where I spun my webs and wove my spells.' Below them the refugees were walking about or talking to each other. 'This isn't the show I would have wished to present, but it's improving. When people sit chatting, things are returning to normal.'

'Can they see us?'

'All they see is a balcony in front of us.' Callum brought her nearer to him. 'I've dreamt a lot about this moment. All the time I sat by that tarn I kept feeling so – cheated. I wanted the chance to get to know you, and to explain my feelings to you.'

For a long time they kissed, standing amongst the silent equipment. Finally Esther pulled away. 'Why did you lie about our relationship?' she asked. 'You didn't need to force me into a corner, or your parents.'

'My love, I wasn't thinking of the future. I didn't believe I had one. All I wanted was to provide for you, and make sure Imie could stay with you if she wanted.'

Watching Callum's face, Esther tried to assess whether he was telling the truth. 'Whether it was deliberate or not, you've trapped me into marrying you,' she pointed out. 'According to the law, a widow must marry her Conjugate as soon as possible.'

'Such laws belong to the past. The state has no power now to determine people's private lives. If you don't want to marry me, say so. People will talk for a while, and then forget it. If you marry me, let it be of your own free will.'

It was hard to accept how much things had changed in a few brief weeks. Before the revolution, her life would have been governed at every stage. Now she was free to make her own decisions. Such freedom was an awful responsibility. 'I was angry,' Esther admitted. 'I thought you had deliberately trapped me.' Moving nearer to Callum again, she laid her head on his shoulder. 'When will you come back?' she asked.

'I should be fit enough by the weekend, but there's something I'd like to do before returning. Could you cope for another week?'

'I imagine so. Why?'

'That's one of the things I wanted to talk to you about. I need your advice. I had a couple of visitors last Sunday.'

'What did they want?'

'They invited me to train as a master.'

Incredulously Esther stared at him.

'Yes, I laughed myself,' Callum agreed. 'But they said I was skilled in the secret things, that I had outfaced death and proved myself a leader – a great many flattering remarks.'

'What was your reply?' Esther's voice sounded strained in her ears.

'That I wanted nothing to do with an organisation that could torture a fifteen-year-old boy.'

In relief, Esther nodded. 'I thought the Order was finished,' she said.

'The Order has survived hundreds of years. It will take more than a revolution to finish it.'

'Have we won nothing?'

'A breathing space. Time for a new start, perhaps. That's what I wanted to talk to you about. Ever since my visitors left, I've been thinking. If the Order is killed off, the knowledge it has guarded for centuries will die with it. That would be a great loss. Yet leave just a few discontented survivors and it will go underground and grow stronger with every generation. We will have checked the infection, not cured it. What we need is a new Order, dedicated to sharing the secret things, not to concealing them. Do you see what I mean?'

'Knowledge is power,' Esther agreed. 'Share that knowledge and you share power —'

' – and prevent trouble in the future.'

Callum's voice was taking on the same urgency as Esther had heard when he talked of the coming revolution. He was the thinker still, the idealist who came up with the ideas, and then made them work. Smiling, Esther nodded. 'Go on,' she invited.

'We could set up a sort of Academy of the Mind, open to all who could understand. No member would be under any sort of compulsion, though you might have something like the old Hippocratic oath: to use any skills gained for the saving of life, never for the ending of it. Initially there would still have to be secrecy, to protect those who are of Keepers' blood from attack, but the need should pass. What do you think? Does it make sense to you?'

'Where would you fit into all this?' Esther asked.

'At the back, as usual. If I could belong to such an organisation, I might be of some use, rather than a sort of shadow, neither Keeper nor ordinary man.'

Esther considered Callum's expression. He was genuinely seeking her advice, on matters that were far beyond her. 'Have you discussed this with anyone else?' she asked.

'Just my father, and a few of the elders. Before I talk to anyone else I need to know how you feel. Could you still love me if I remained a Keeper – even if of a different sort?'

In surprise, Esther paused. 'I never expected you to be anything else,' she replied. 'You've always belonged to a land I know nothing about, and you will have moved deeper into it now.'

'Then come into that land with me.'

'How can I?'

'My love, you're further along my route than you realise. Think back to your first night here. Tell me what you felt.'

Esther did not reply.

Callum answered for her. 'At five hours that morning I watched the dawn through the blinds, and cried out with pain. If you and Imie hadn't shared it with me I couldn't have borne it. I didn't call you. I would never have inflicted such suffering on either of you. Madelaine was my support, and I didn't even want her to go through with it. You shared with me because you wished to do so.'

Esther could not deny what he said, however much it frightened her. 'I don't understand,' she admitted. 'I don't know what I did, or how I did it.'

Callum held her to him, reassuring her. 'Then let me teach you.'

'You'd teach an outsider? And a woman at that?'

'You would be a good student.'

'Maybe,' Esther agreed. 'It would certainly be interesting finding out. I would be afraid, though.'

'No! Not you! Not my Tess.'

Pausing, Callum reached in his pocket. 'I'd forgotten about this,' he recalled. He passed her a wedding band, wrapped in sealant. 'It's only cheap. There aren't many shops open during a civil war. I'll get you a better one some day.'

Esther unwrapped the sealant. 'Which wrist do I wear it on?' she asked.

'That's up to you. Right for the past, left for the future.'

For several moments Esther stood considering her answer. As Fourteen said, she must be mad. The prospect of living with such a man was so strange as to be almost terrifying. Yet if she refused Callum she would wonder all her life what she had missed.

Undoing the seal Esther put the band on her left arm. Emotion made her clumsy and the catch was difficult to close. Smiling, Callum reached out to help her. As he did so, his fingers touched the numbers on her skin. 'As soon as the trials are over we'll take these wretched marks off,' he promised.

'I'm used to them now.'

'I'm not. Every time I see them they'll be a judgement on me.' Putting her wrist to his mouth, Callum kissed it.

There was a tenderness between them they had not found until then. The refugees in the auditorium below were settling their children to sleep. High above them, Callum and Esther held each other close.

'I'd better go and see Imie,' Callum said at last.' 'She'll know I'm here.'

'Go now,' Esther advised, 'before she gets jealous. If the others are awake, they'd like to see you too.'

'I can't stay long. I have a transport coming at twenty-two hours.'

There was wistfulness in Callum's manner as he looked round. 'I used to dream of having equipment like this,' he admitted. 'If things had gone differently I might have stayed here for years, putting on my shows and listening to the audience laugh. For me that's happiness. That and being with the people I love.'

'There'll be shows again,' Esther promised.

'But serving a better purpose, I hope.'

'Give me the key to this room and I'll lock up,' Esther offered. 'I could do with a quiet place while you're away.'

'Make whatever arrangements you wish over the next week. A marriage between the son of a president and the lady of the showhouses could be quite an event. It might be wise to keep it quiet.'

Esther burst out laughing. 'The lady of the showhouses?' she repeated.

'That's what people are beginning to call you.'

Smiling, Callum kissed her forehead. Then he went out, closing the door quietly behind him.

For an hour or more, Esther remained in the technicians' room, looking down on the refugees. She felt a deep abiding peace, such as she had not felt for years.

When the final warning sounded over the Tannoy, she started in surprise, recalled to her duties. In a few moments the power would be switched off. Getting up, she went for a last walk around the building.

'That's the one,' she heard a woman whisper as she passed.

'One of the old royals, they say. Big house and everything. Gave it all up for love.'

Trying not to laugh, Esther walked on.

'Mrs Thomas?' a voice called.

'Yes?'

'There's a delivery for you. Will you accept it?'

'It depends what it is.'

'Flowers, Ma'am. We've checked them. They seem all right.' The young officer lowered her voice. 'Real flowers, Ma'am.'

'Real flowers?'

'Yes, Ma'am. You wouldn't think any would have survived this last few weeks. Would you come and look? They're in the foyer.'

Shaking her head, Esther followed the young officer downstairs. Dave was standing holding a bouquet of Outland flowers.

'I've done some daft things for Cal in my life,' he grumbled, 'but this is the daftest. For goodness' sake take them, Tess. I feel a right idiot.'

'I think I'll leave you standing there,' Esther replied. 'You look cute with a chrysanthemum in your ear.'

Taking the flowers, she looked at the gift tag. 'It's not the season for roses,' it said. 'Will these do instead?'

THE LEFT HAND OF DARKNESS

Ursula LeGuin

'From the first page you find yourself totally immersed in it, and at the last page you come out with a start and a shiver' – *Damon Knight*

This outstanding science fiction classic is the story of Winter, a cold planet where the inhabitants are all of the same sex. They know nothing of space travel or life beyond their own. So when a strange envoy arrives from space inviting Winter to join a vast coalition of planets, he is met with fear, mistrust and disbelief.

SNOW STORMS IN A HOT CLIMATE

Sarah Dunant

'Dunant ekes out the tension in a thriller that is comfortably shy of far-fetched and increasingly thrilling as the pages fly by' – *The Times*

When ballsy, bourbon-slugging Marla gets called to help out her friend Elly in New York, she finds herself ensnared in the dangerous twilight world of drug smuggling. Obsession, betrayal and revenge twist into an ever-tightening knot in this breathtaking psychological thriller.

MY SWEET UNTRACEABLE YOU

Sandra Scoppettone

'P.I. Lauren Laurano is one of the best detective characters in some of the best detective novels I've ever read' – *Val McDermid*

Lauren Laurano's intriguing new case breaks records of perplexity. When Boston Blackie hires Lauren to dig out the truth behind his mother's death forty years ago, a cold trail turns into a complex exploration of dark family secrets. Questions without answers plague her – and then a new string of murders kick-start her into pulse-quickening action.

A murder mystery that delightfully spoofs a genre, *My Sweet Untraceable You* has the humour and heart that Sandra Scoppettone's readers have come to love.

☐ The Left Hand of Darkness	Ursula LeGuin	£6.99
☐ Snow Storms in a Hot Climate	Sarah Dunant	£5.99
☐ Transgressions	Sarah Dunant	£15.99
☐ My Sweet Untraceable You	Sandra Scoppettone	£5.99

Virago now offers an exciting range of quality titles by both established and new authors. All of the books in this series are available from:

Little, Brown and Company (UK),
P.O. Box 11,
Falmouth,
Cornwall TR10 9EN.
Telephone No: 01326 372400
Fax No: 01326 317444
E-mail: books@barni.avel.co.uk

Payments can be made as follows: cheque, postal order (payable to Little, Brown and Company) or by credit cards, Visa/Access. Do not send cash or currency. UK customers and B.F.P.O. please allow £1.00 for postage and packing for the first book, plus 50p for the second book, plus 30p for each additional book up to a maximum charge of £3.00 (7 books plus).

Overseas customers including Ireland, please allow £2.00 for the first book plus £1.00 for the second book, plus 50p for each additional book.

NAME (Block Letters) ....

....

ADDRESS ....

....

....

☐ I enclose my remittance for ....

☐ I wish to pay by Access/Visa Card

Number ☐☐☐☐☐☐☐☐☐☐☐☐☐☐☐☐

Card Expiry Date ☐☐☐☐